Available
from Mi

SNOWBOUND WITH THE BODYGUARD

He wanted to kill for her. He wanted to weep for her. Her strength awed him…humbled him.

"Dalton?" Her soft voice penetrated the red haze that had fallen over him as he heard what she'd gone through. "Are you all right?"

He let go of her hand and instead pulled her into an embrace. She laid her head on his shoulder and he stroked the silk of her hair. "I'm just sorry. So damned sorry."

"It's OK. I'm OK." She looked up at him and he saw that there were no shadows in her eyes. They sparkled with hope, with a new peace.

As he held her gaze, her mouth opened slightly and she leaned forward. He intended a soft, gentle kiss, but the moment his lips claimed hers, the kiss became something much different. He knew they were going to make love.

He told himself he didn't want to, that it would do nothing but complicate his conflicting emotions where she was concerned. She would be out of his life within the next two days. But as she snaked her hand beneath his shirt and caressed his chest, he allowed good sense to be swallowed by desire, even knowing it would only make it more difficult when the time came to tell her goodbye.

LADY KILLER

Being as how Brooke Fallon Grant was his buddy Cory's sister and his buddy Cory being a pretty good-looking guy, he hadn't been expecting a troll.

But the woman standing before him…well, the only word that suited her was *lovely*.

Tony had a photographer's eye, of course, one that saw beyond the fatigue lines, no makeup and hair that was limp and dull and in need of washing. What he saw was dark blue eyes that told you they'd seen more than they wanted to of the world's sadness and suffering. And amazing bones, the kind that made him itch to reach for his camera. Which was too bad, because he was pretty sure the first time he aimed a lens in the lady's direction she'd sic her monster dog on him.

At the very least. He'd forgotten for a moment he might be looking at the face of a cold-blooded killer.

First published in Great Britain 2010
Harlequin Mills & Boon Limited,
Eton House, 18-24 Paradise Road, Richmond, Surrey TW9 1SR

Snowbound with the Bodyguard © Carla Bracale 2008
Lady Killer © Kathleen Creighton-Fuchs 2009

ISBN: 978 0 263 88200 1

46-0210

Harlequin Mills & Boon policy is to use papers that are natural, renewable and recyclable products and made from wood grown in sustainable forests. The logging and manufacturing processes conform to the legal environmental regulations of the country of origin.

Printed and bound in Spain
by Litografia Rosés S.A., Barcelona

SNOWBOUND WITH THE BODYGUARD

BY
CARLA CASSIDY

LADY KILLER

BY
KATHLEEN CREIGHTON

SNOWBOUND WITH
THE BODYGUARD
BY
CARLA CASSIDY

LADY KILLER
BY
KATHLEEN CREIGHTON

MILLS & BOON

SNOWBOUND WITH THE BODYGUARD

BY
CARLA CASSIDY

Carla Cassidy is an award-winning author who has written more than fifty novels. In 1995, she won Best Silhouette Romance from *Romantic Times BOOKreviews*. In 1998, she also won a Career Achievement Award for Best Innovative Series from *Romantic Times BOOKreviews*.

Carla believes the only thing better than curling up with a good book to read is sitting down at the computer with a good story to write. She's looking forward to writing many more books and bringing hours of pleasure to readers.

Prologue

"**O**rder up." Smiley Smith, owner and short-order cook at Smiley's Café, banged the small bell on the counter to punctuate his words.

Janette Black wiped her hands on her cheerful red-and-white apron, then walked over to retrieve the Thursday special.

She grabbed the plate and served it to the man seated at the long counter. "Here you go, Walter." She smiled at the old man who came in every Thursday afternoon regular as clockwork for Smiley's meatloaf.

"Thank you, honey. Can I bother you for another cup of coffee?" Walter offered her a sweet smile.

"For you, Walter, it's no bother." She turned around and went to get the coffeepot, grateful that the lunch rush was over and she only had two more hours in her shift. Then she could go home and snuggle her little boy and visit with Nana until it was time for her to be back here first thing in the morning.

"How's that grandmother of yours?" Walter asked as she poured his coffee.

Janette's heart warmed at thoughts of her grandmother. "She's okay. We have her heart condition under control. She tires easily, but she's doing just fine."

Walter laughed. "She's a corker, that one. It will take more than a couple of strokes to keep her down."

As Janette began to wipe down the countertop, she smiled. Her grandmother wasn't just a corker, she was the woman who had raised Janette from the time she was three and the woman who was now helping Janette raise her little boy. Nana's last stroke had been nearly a year ago, but she had astounded the doctors with her recovery.

Janette was just giving the shiny surface a final swipe when the tinkle of the bell over the front door indicated another diner arriving.

She looked up and her blood froze. There were three of them, all wearing the khaki uniforms of law enforcement. Sheriff Brandon Sinclair led the way, swaggering in followed by two of his trusted deputies.

There were only two cafés in Sandstone, Oklahoma, and she'd chosen to work at Smiley's because the other place, Lacy's, was where Sinclair and his men usually ate their lunch.

Sheriff Sinclair surveyed the café like a king overseeing his domain, his ice-blue eyes narrowing just a touch as his gaze landed on Janette.

Take a table, she mentally begged. If they sat at the table, then Heidi, Janette's coworker, would wait on them. Janette had spent the past year of her life doing everything possible to avoid contact with the sheriff.

As he and his deputies headed toward the counter, her stomach bucked with a touch of nausea and her heart began to beat the rhythm of panic.

She couldn't lose it. Not here. Not now. She refused to let him know how he affected her, knowing that he would relish her fear.

He's just another customer, she told herself as the three seated themselves at the counter. "Can I take your orders?" she asked, surprised to hear her voice cool and collected despite all the emotions that quivered inside her.

"Coffee," Sinclair said. "What kind of pie is good today?"

"Apple," Janette replied tersely, then added, "the apple is always good."

"Then let's make it coffee and pie for all of us," Sinclair said.

Janette nodded and turned to get the coffeepot. She could do this. As long as she didn't look at him too long, as long as she didn't get close enough to smell his cologne. She had a feeling if she got a whiff of that cheap, cloying smell she might vomit.

She filled their cups, trying to ignore the way Sinclair's eyes lingered on her breasts. Her throat tightened and her heart banged harder against her ribs.

"Never guess what I heard through the grapevine," Sinclair said to his deputies.

"What's that, Sheriff?" Deputy Jed Billet asked.

"I heard that Janette has a little baby boy. What is he, about five months old, Janette?" Sinclair gazed at her knowingly.

She turned to get their pie, her hands trembling as she opened the display case that held the desserts. He knew. Dear God, he knew.

"Gonna be tough, being a single parent," Deputy Westin said.

As she placed the pie in front of Sinclair he reared back on the stool. "A boy. There's something special about a boy, don't you think so, Jed? I mean, I love my three little girls, but I always dreamed about how great it would be to have a son. Unfortunately, all my wife could pop was girls. Still, a boy needs a father, don't you agree?"

A roar went off in Janette's head. She had to escape. She had to take her son and leave Sandstone because she knew what evil Sheriff Brandon Sinclair was capable of, and as long as she remained in Sandstone he had the power to do whatever he wanted to do.

If he decided he wanted her baby boy, she knew he'd find a way to get him.

Chapter 1

"I'm sorry, ma'am, but I just got word that the bus isn't coming."

Janette blinked and stared up at the man in charge of the Cotter Creek bus station. She straightened in her chair as she realized she must have dozed off. She wrapped her arms around her still sleeping son and gazed at the man with confusion.

"Excuse me?" she said.

"The bus. It's not coming. It's been held up by weather."

"By weather?" Dulled by sleep, she stared at him as if he were speaking a foreign language.

He nodded. "Ice." He pointed out the window. Janette followed his finger and gasped in surprise as she saw the icy pellets falling from the sky. The ground was already covered with at least an inch.

Where had it come from? When she'd arrived at the

bus station two hours ago the skies had been thick with gray clouds, but there hadn't been a hint of snow. Of course the last thing on her mind when she'd left Sandstone had been the weather forecast.

She looked back at the man and tried to swallow against the sense of panic that had been with her since she'd packed her bags and left Sandstone that afternoon. A friend of her grandmother's had driven her the thirty miles to Cotter Creek, where a bus to Kansas City ran every other day. It was supposed to run today.

"Will it be here tomorrow?" she asked.

"Depends if the weathermen are right or wrong. They say we're in for a blizzard, but they're wrong more often than they're right." He shrugged his skinny shoulders and pulled a stocking cap over his head. "You best get settled in someplace for the night. I've got to close down here. Check back in the morning and I'll know more about the schedule." He was obviously in a hurry, tapping his heel as he looked at her expectantly.

"Of course." She stood, grateful that Sammy still slept in his sling against her chest. She didn't want to show how scared she was, didn't want to do anything that might draw unnecessary attention to herself.

She'd find a pay phone, call the nearest motel and get a room for the night. Hopefully she'd still have time to get as far away from Sandstone as possible before Brandon Sinclair even knew she'd left the small town.

She grabbed the handle of her large suitcase and draped the diaper bag over her shoulder, still groggy from the unexpected catnap.

She was barely out the door before the bus station, little more than a shack, was locked up behind her. The ice that fell had coated the sidewalk and created shiny surfaces on everything else in sight. Under different circumstances she might have found it beautiful.

With Sammy safely snuggled beneath her wool coat, she looked up and down the street. She didn't know Cotter Creek well. Perhaps there was a bed-and-breakfast someplace nearby where she could spend the night.

A new disquiet soared through her as she eyed the deserted streets. It was just after six but it was as if the entire town had packed their bags and left. There wasn't a person or a car on the street.

She should have asked to use the phone in the bus station. She should have asked the man where she could get a room for the night. But the nap had dulled her senses, and he'd hurried her out too fast for her to think clearly.

The sight of a phone booth in the distance rallied her spirits. Cotter Creek was near a major highway, and that meant there had to be a motel somewhere nearby.

Pulling the suitcase behind her, she hurried as fast as the slick concrete would allow toward the phone booth, feeling as if luck was on her side as she spied the small phone book hanging on a hook just inside the door.

She stepped into the booth and closed the door behind her, grateful to be out of the cold wind and stinging ice. With cold fingers she thumbed through the book until she found the page with the motel listings. Make that one listing. The Cotter Creek Motel.

Digging change from her purse, she felt Sammy stir as if the rapid beating of her heart disturbed his sleep. She drew a deep breath to steady her nerves.

She'd wanted to get as far away as possible as quickly as possible from Sandstone and Brandon Sinclair. Okay, so she couldn't get on the bus tonight. She'd cool her heels in a motel room and catch the bus the next day. Although she hated to part with a dime of the money that was neatly folded and tucked into a side pocket in her purse, she really didn't have a choice.

She *had* to get out of town tomorrow. Thirty miles was far too close to the devil and his minions. She wouldn't be satisfied until she was a thousand miles away. Once she got settled in a new town, she'd send for Nana and the three of them would build a new life where Brandon Sinclair couldn't bother them.

She dropped the change into the slot and punched in the number for the Cotter Creek Motel. A man answered on the third ring. "No room at the inn," he said.

"Is this the Cotter Creek Motel?" she asked, her hand tightening on the receiver.

"Yeah, but if you're looking for a room, we're full up. They've shut the highway down up north and I've got a houseful of travelers. I've even rented out my sofa in the lobby." He sounded positively gleeful. "Sorry." He hung up.

Janette held the receiver for a long moment, her heart pumping with panic once again. She hung up and frantically thumbed through the skinny phone book, looking for a listing of a bed-and-breakfast, a rental room, anywhere she could get a warm bed for the night. There was nothing.

She wanted to call her grandmother and ask her what to do. Where to go. But she'd only worry Nana, and that was the last thing she wanted to do.

Besides, Janette was an adult. She had to handle this. She was twenty-four years old and a mother, and the most important thing in her life at the moment was little Sammy. She had to get him someplace safe and warm.

She leaned her head against the cold glass of the booth and watched as the ice began to turn to snow and pick up in intensity. What was she going to do? She and Sammy couldn't spend the night out in the elements.

Desperation filled her and she felt a panic attack coming on. The palms of her hands grew slick with sweat as her throat seemed to constrict. She closed her eyes and drew in deep breaths, forcing the attack away. She didn't have time to be weak now. Sammy needed her, and she needed to get him someplace safe for the night.

She opened her eyes once again. The clouds and ice were creating an early twilight. She straightened as she saw a light shining from a window of one of the store-fronts in the next block.

Where there was light there might be somebody who could direct her to a place for the night. She checked to make sure her coat was securely fastened to keep Sammy as warm as possible, pulled up her hood and tied it beneath her chin, then stepped out of the phone booth and into the wind that had begun to howl with fierce intensity.

She kept her gaze focused on the light, a beacon of hope. It didn't take long for her gloveless fingers to turn numb and her cheeks to burn with the cold. Ice pellets pinged on the sidewalk and her bare skin.

She walked slowly, carefully, not wanting to fall on the slick walkways. Before she reached the radiating light, she saw the shingle that hung above the doorway. West Protective Services.

She knew that name. She frowned thoughtfully, then remembered. There had been an article in the paper not too long ago, a human interest story about the family who owned and operated a bodyguard business. The article had described the family as honorable, trustworthy people who put their lives on the line for their clients.

If she remembered the article correctly, they had been instrumental in cleaning up Cotter Creek when a development company had tried to take ranch land and had hired people to kill the ranchers.

You have to trust somebody, a little voice whispered in her head. She had no other choice. Once again she felt her throat closing up, a quickening of her heart and a sense of doom that portended one of her panic attacks.

Not giving herself a chance to second-guess her decision, she started for the door. She reached for the door handle just as a man barreled out and into her.

He bumped her with just enough force to cause her to lose her footing on the slippery sidewalk. She felt herself careening backward, but before she could fall, two big strong hands grabbed hold of her shoulders and steadied her.

"Sorry. Are you all right?" His deep voice was nearly carried away by the wind.

She looked up into the greenest eyes she'd ever seen. In an instant she assessed him. Shockingly good-looking, bold features, tall, with broad shoulders beneath a thigh-length black coat. He looked at her as if she were an apparition blown from the North Pole.

She had no idea if she could trust this man or not. Under any other circumstances she would never ask a stranger, particularly a man, for help. But she was out of options. "Please…I need help."

* * *

All Dalton West wanted was to get home and out of the snow. He'd been absorbed in paperwork and hadn't noticed the weather until he'd gotten up to stretch and had realized the forecasted storm was upon them. He'd hurriedly shut down the computer and turned off the coffeepot, his only goal to get to his nearby apartment. The last thing he wanted was to be snowed in at the office.

But with this woman looking at him with eyes the color of a summer Oklahoma sky, eyes that were filled with both desperation and wariness, he reopened the office door and ushered her inside. She swept past him, pulling a large suitcase behind her as she entered.

As he stepped back inside she turned to face him. "I…you protect people, right?"

He nodded, wondering what she was doing out in the snow. "That's my job."

"I want to hire you for the night…to protect me."

"Protect you from who?" he asked.

She gave a nervous laugh. "Not who…what. I need you to protect me from the weather. I arrived here in Cotter Creek a couple of hours ago to catch the bus, but it seems the bus isn't coming this evening. I need a place to stay for the night, but the motel is all booked up." At that moment the sound of a crying baby came from beneath her coat.

She unfastened the buttons to reveal a tiny boy in a blue coat. Dalton didn't know much about babies, but the little guy looked to be only a couple of months old. As his blue eyes landed on Dalton, he grinned and bounced in his sling.

"This is my son, Sammy, and I'm uh…Jane Craig. I

was hoping you could find us a room or something for the night," she said. "I can pay you for your trouble."

There had been just enough hesitation before she spoke her name that Dalton sensed she was lying. She had a pretty face, heart-shaped with those big blue eyes and pale eyebrows that arched perfectly above them. Her trembling full lips were a faint shade of blue, indicating to him that she had already been outside too long.

Why would she lie about her name? Or had he just imagined that moment of hesitation? Business had been slow enough lately that maybe he was looking for mystery where there was none.

"I'm Dalton West," he replied, then frowned and looked out the window where the blowing snow was creating almost whiteout conditions. He could think of several places he might be able to get her a bed for the night, but none of them were within walking distance, and nobody in their right mind was going to get in a car to come and pick her up.

There was really only one alternative, and it wasn't one that made him a happy man. "Look, I have an apartment two blocks from here. You can stay there for the night and I'll bunk downstairs with my landlord."

It was obvious from the expression on her face that she didn't like the idea. Dalton raked a hand through his hair and tamped down an edge of impatience. He certainly could understand her reticence. She was a young woman alone with a baby and he was a virtual stranger. In her circumstances he wouldn't be thrilled by his suggestion.

"Oh, no…I couldn't," she began.

"Look, Jane. I'm a bodyguard by profession. I make a living protecting people. You'll be safe for the night.

Besides, I don't know what else to tell you. We're out of options." His glance went back out the window, then he looked back at her. "And we need to get going before we can't get out of here."

She hesitated another minute. "I'll hire you for the night to protect me. We'll keep it a business deal."

"Fine. You can write me a check when we get to my place." It was obvious to Dalton that she couldn't afford their usual fee. Her coat was worn and her shoes looked old. This was not a woman rolling in dough.

As she rebuttoned her coat to protect her son from the elements, he grabbed hold of her suitcase.

They stepped back out into the howling wind and stinging snow, and Dalton fought the impulse to take her by the elbow to help her keep her balance on the slick sidewalk. There was something about her posture, something about the look in her eyes that warned him she would not appreciate it.

The howling wind made conversation next to impossible so they trudged side by side in silence, heads bent against the mix of ice and snow falling from the sky.

It was difficult to pull the suitcase on its wheels through the thick snow that blanketed the ground. Instead Dalton picked it up by the handle to increase their pace.

The two-block walk seemed to take an eternity. He breathed a sigh of relief as they turned off Main onto Maple Street. He could barely see just ahead the white two-story house with the wraparound porch he called home.

Normally, Dalton didn't mind being snowed in for a day or two. He was a solitary man who enjoyed being

alone, but it looked as if at least for the short-term he'd
be spending his snow time with his landlord, George.

When they reached the house he motioned toward the
staircase that led up the outside. His apartment was the
top floor. She went up the stairs before him as he hefted
the heavy suitcase up stair by stair.

At the top he unlocked the door, then opened it and
gestured her inside. He followed just after her, flipping
on the interior light and welcoming the warmth the
place offered.

He turned to look at her. Her lips were now completely blue and she trembled almost uncontrollably.
"Let's get out of these wet coats and shoes," he said.

The whole scene felt a little surreal. The snow
outside, a mysterious woman and baby…it was like the
setup of some ridiculous movie.

He unbuttoned his coat and watched her do the same.
Her gaze didn't meet his but rather swept around the
room like a rabbit hunting for a safe burrow.

He followed her gaze, taking in the place he'd called
home for the past two years. When George's wife had
died five years ago, the old man had renovated the house
with this apartment upstairs. It was a way for him to
keep his house and not feel so alone.

The apartment was roomy, with a nice-sized living
room, a small but fully functioning kitchen, a half bath
off the laundry room and a large bedroom with a full
bathroom. Dalton had furnished it in a minimalist, functional style. But as he saw it through another's eyes he
realized it was a cold space, with little personality.

He frowned and took her coat from her to hang in the
small utility room off the kitchen. "Make yourself com-

fortable," he said and gestured to the sofa. "I'm just going to put these wet things in the other room."

He left her there, hung the wet coats on hangers to dry, then returned to find her still standing in the center of the room, rubbing the baby's back as he once again slept.

"Where were you headed?" he asked.

She jumped at the sound of his voice, as if she'd momentarily forgotten he was there. "Uh, Kansas City. I was going to visit my sister."

Again he had a gut feeling she wasn't telling him the truth. She refused to hold his gaze and even though the room was warm, her lips trembled slightly. And he realized she wasn't cold. She was afraid.

"Look, why don't we just get you settled in. The kitchen is there." He pointed to the doorway. "If you want anything to eat feel free to help yourself. I'll just go change the sheets on the bed then I'll be out of your hair." He started toward the bedroom but stopped as she called his name.

"If you just tell me where the sheets are, I'll change the bed. And I need to pay you."

"The sheets are on the bottom shelf in the bathroom, and it really isn't necessary for you to give me any money."

"Yes, it is," she countered, and her chin rose with a show of stubbornness. "It's important we keep this a business transaction."

"Fine," he replied. He named a nominal fee and watched as she opened her purse and carefully withdrew the amount in cash. "I'll just get a few things together then I'll head downstairs," he said as he took the money from her. He shoved the bills into his pocket, then grabbed her suitcase and wheeled it into his bedroom.

He gathered a small overnight bag, then returned to the living room where she still stood in the center of the room, as if frozen in place.

"You should find everything you need for the night, but if you need anything you can't find, I'll write down my cell phone number and leave it on the kitchen table."

She gave an imperceptible nod of her head. "I... Thank you for this. I wasn't sure what I was going to do."

"You'll be fine here for the night and we'll sort things out in the morning."

"Thank you again," she said, then disappeared into the bedroom and closed the door behind her. He heard the click of the lock being turned.

Dalton stared at the closed door for a long moment. His family would probably tell him he was crazy for allowing a stranger to take up residence in his place even for one night. But they hadn't seen the vulnerability, the sheer desperation that clung to her closer than her coat.

Besides, what was she going to do? Tuck his television under one arm, her son under the other and run out into a blizzard? There was nothing here for her to steal that wasn't insured. He didn't know if he believed that she'd told him her real name or her destination, but he knew for sure that she'd needed someplace warm and safe and she'd found it here.

He went into the kitchen and wrote his cell phone number on a sheet of paper and left it on the small oak table. Then he wrote his own home phone number down and returned to the bedroom door and knocked. She opened the door, her eyes wide and wary.

"I just wanted to let you know there's leftover roast beef in the refrigerator if you get hungry and there's extra blankets on the shelf in the closet if you need them. If you need to call your sister to let her know where you are, here's the phone number." He held out the slip of paper.

"Thank you, I'm sure we'll be fine." One hand snaked out to take the piece of paper from him. "I guess I'll see you in the morning." She closed the door again but not before Dalton saw something flash in her other hand, something silver like a blade.

A knife?

Every instinct he owned shot to high alert. He'd been trained to look for trouble, and he had a horrible feeling he'd just invited trouble into his home.

Well, he couldn't do anything about it now. He headed for the interior staircase that led downstairs to George's living quarters.

He would have to face it—her—in the morning.

Chapter 2

She saw the red lights flashing in her rearview mirror and glanced down at her speedometer. Damn. It looked like she was going to get a speeding ticket.

She supposed she was lucky that she hadn't gotten one before now. Two nights a week she'd been making the twenty-five mile drive from Sandstone to a local community college, taking classes to eventually take the GED test. She always drove too fast on this particular stretch of deserted highway.

Pulling over to the side of the road, she wondered how many extra hours she'd have to work to pay for this particular mistake. As if money wasn't already tight enough.

Glancing in her rearview mirror once again she saw the patrol car pull to a stop just behind her. The flashing red light went off, as did the headlights. As the driver's door opened she recognized Sheriff Brandon Sinclair getting out of the car.

She fumbled in her schoolbag for her license as he approached the side of her car. She rolled down her window and offered him a small smile. "Sheriff Sinclair," she said.

"Turn off your lights and get out of the car," he told her.

She frowned, but didn't think about not doing as he asked. As she got out of the car Sheriff Sinclair smiled. "Well, well, don't we look all sexy in that little skirt," he said, and there was something in his eyes that made her suddenly afraid.

Janette awoke with a gasp, heart pounding as she sat up and stared wildly around the unfamiliar room. The large mahogany dresser and the navy overstuffed chair weren't hers. She wasn't in her room. Where was she?

Then she remembered. She was in Cotter Creek, in Dalton West's bedroom. Sammy slept peacefully next to her on the king-sized bed. She lay back down and shoved the last memories of her nightmare away.

The large bed had been a luxury after years of sleeping on a twin in her tiny bedroom in the trailer where she lived with Nana. Despite the luxury, sleep had been a long time coming. She'd jumped and tensed at each moan and groan of the unfamiliar house. Even when she had finally fallen asleep, it had been a night of unrelenting nightmares.

Surely by noon or so the streets would be cleared of whatever snow had fallen overnight and the bus would finally arrive. It had to come today. She needed to get as far away from here as possible.

When the streets are cleared, he'll come looking for you, the little voice whispered in her head. She felt like a fish in the bottom of a barrel, far too close, far too easily caught.

She'd left the bedroom only once during the night, to make a bottle for Sammy. Knowing that he would probably sleep for another hour or so, she got out of bed and headed for the adjoining bathroom. She wanted to be dressed and ready to leave as soon as possible.

It wasn't until she stood beneath a hot spray of water that she thought of the man who had allowed her into his home. In another lifetime, under different circumstances, she might find herself attracted to him. He was certainly easy to look at, with that thick dark hair and those gorgeous green eyes.

He reminded her of another man—a man who had not been quite as handsome but had devastated her, bitterly disappointed her at the time she'd needed him most.

She didn't need a man in her life. She and Sammy and Nana would be fine. All she had to do was get out of this town and decide where they would all begin a new life, far away from the reaches of Sheriff Brandon Sinclair.

After showering she wrapped herself in one of the large fluffy towels and walked over to the window for her first look outside.

She gasped as she saw that the storm hadn't passed by but instead seemed to be sitting right on top of the little town of Cotter Creek. It was impossible to discern street from sidewalk. Snow had transformed the earth into an alien landscape where nothing looked as it was supposed to.

There weren't just a couple of inches on the ground,

there was at least a foot and a half and it was still falling from the gray, heavy sky.

Janette knew someplace in the back of her mind that it was beautiful, that the world looked like a winter wonderland, but all she could think was that the snow was a disaster, big fat fluffy flakes of doom falling from the sky.

Trapped. She was trapped there, and the only faint comfort was that if she were trapped by the weather, then so was Sheriff Brandon Sinclair.

She turned away from the window and crouched on the plush rug to open her big suitcase. The first thing she saw inside was the bright-red book bag she'd thrown in at the last minute. Inside were the books she'd bought to study for her GED and the tape recorder she'd used in class.

It had been more than a year since she'd opened the bag that now represented not only the dream she'd once had for herself of getting more education, but also the worst night of her life.

She hadn't opened the bag since the night she'd been pulled over for a speeding ticket, and she didn't open it now. She set it on the floor and dug out a pair of jeans and her favorite blue sweater. She didn't have a lot of choices as she'd packed only a minimum of clothes for herself. Most of the suitcase contents were cans of powdered formula, cereal and diapers and clothing for Sammy.

Once she was dressed and had brushed out her long, wet hair, she eyed the phone on the nightstand. She should call Nana and let her know what was going on. The old woman would worry if she didn't hear from Janette. Thank goodness the call wasn't long distance, Janette thought as she punched in her grandmother's number.

Nana answered on the second ring and Janette

pressed the phone to her ear as if to get closer to her grandmother. "Nana, it's me."

"Janette, honey, where are you?" Nana asked. "Did you get off before this storm?"

"No, I'm still in Cotter Creek."

"At the motel?" Nana asked.

"The motel was already full by the time I found out the bus wasn't coming. The snow was coming down and I didn't know what to do, but then I saw a light on in the West Protective Services office." Janette twisted the phone cord around her little finger. "I hired Dalton West to be my bodyguard and he brought me to his apartment for the night."

"Are you safe there?" Nana asked, her voice filled with concern.

Janette considered the question. "Yes, I think I'm safe," she finally replied. It was odd, but having survived the night she did feel safe.

"I've heard about those Wests," Nana said. "Supposed to be good solid men. I'm just grateful that you and that precious little boy are away from here and not out in this storm someplace."

Janette glanced toward the window and frowned. "It looks like I'm going to be stuck here for a while." She twisted the phone cord more tightly around her finger. "Has anyone been by to ask about me?"

"Nobody, honey. The storm moved in and nobody is going anywhere at the moment. Don't you worry none. He'll never know from me where you went and by the time he makes his way here to ask questions you'll be far out of his reach."

"Let me give you the phone number here, just in

case you need to reach me." Janette read the number off the piece of paper Dalton had given her the night before. "I'll call you when I'm about to board the bus. Maybe they'll get the streets cleared by tomorrow."

"You just take care of yourself and Sammy. Don't worry about things here. I got my friends at the trailer park to take care of me and I'll be fine as long as I know you're fine."

Janette unraveled the cord from her finger. How she wished she could crawl through the phone line and feel her grandmother's loving arms around her, to go back to a time when she didn't know about fear, about evil.

Afraid that she might cry if she remained on the phone much longer, she quickly said goodbye then hung up. Checking to make sure that Sammy was still sleeping soundly, she arranged the bed pillows on either side of him then walked to the bedroom door.

She hesitated before turning the knob to step out of the room. She'd told Nana she was safe, and at the moment she *felt* fairly safe, but she'd also been unaware of any danger on the night Sheriff Sinclair had pulled her over on the side of the road.

As much as she'd love to stay holed up in the bedroom until the bus pulled in, that was impossible. She hadn't eaten since lunch the day before and her stomach was protesting its neglect in loud angry growls.

The scent of freshly brewed coffee greeted her as she opened the bedroom door, letting her know she was no longer alone in the apartment.

Energy surged through her as all her senses went on high alert. Her feet whispered against the living-room rug as she moved toward the kitchen.

She hesitated in the doorway. Dalton stood at the stove with his back to her. A white, long-sleeved jersey clung across his broad shoulders and worn jeans hugged the length of his legs. He was barefoot and his hair was rumpled like he'd just crawled out of bed.

A sizzling noise was quickly followed by a whiff of bacon and Janette felt the nerves in her stomach calm. It was hard to be frightened of a barefoot man frying bacon.

She must have made some sort of sound for he whirled around to look at her. "Good morning," he said. "There's coffee in the pot if you're interested."

"I'm interested," she replied.

He gestured to the coffeemaker on the counter. "Cups are in the cabinet above."

She walked over to the cabinet, retrieved a cup, then poured herself some coffee. She carried it to the table and sat, unsure what else to do.

Dalton turned back around to flip the bacon. Janette was aware of a tension in the air, the tension of two strangers sharing space.

"It looks like you're going to be stuck here for at least another day or two," he said.

"Maybe I could find another place to go to," she offered.

Once again he turned around to face her. "It would take me half the day to shovel enough snow just to open the outside door. Trust me, nobody is going anywhere today." A muscle in his jaw tensed, letting her know that he wasn't particularly happy about the unforeseen circumstances.

"I'm sorry about all this," she said. He'd never know just how sorry she was that she was stuck here in Cotter Creek.

"We'll just have to deal with it," he replied, then turned his back on her once again.

Taking a sip of her coffee, she had a vision of Brandon Sinclair tunneling his way through the snow to find her. She mentally shook the thought out of her head.

Once again she stared at Dalton's back. He was a fine-looking man and so far he'd been nothing but honorable. He made a living protecting people. Maybe she could tell him. Maybe she could tell him the truth. The thought of telling somebody and having them believe her was wonderful.

"How about an omelet?" he asked. "I'm making myself one and can split it with you."

She felt bad, that this man was not only having to share his personal space but also his food. Still, she was starving and it seemed silly to refuse. "That sounds good," she agreed.

Once again she sipped her coffee, watching as he prepared the ingredients for the omelet. "Is there anything I can do to help?" she asked.

"No thanks, I'm used to doing things my way," he replied.

"Tell me about this business of yours. I read an article not too long ago about West Protective Services. If I remember correctly it's a family business, right?"

He nodded. His tousled hair made him appear less daunting than he had the night before. "It was started by my father, Red West. Eventually all of us started working for the business."

"All of you?"

"I've got four brothers and a sister. Joshua is the

youngest and he just got married to Savannah, who owns the local newspaper. Then there's Clay, who met his wife when he was on assignment in California. They have a little girl, Gracie. There's Tanner, the oldest. He and his wife, Anna, just had a baby."

Janette felt herself relaxing as he talked. Not only did he have a nice, deep voice that was soothing, but it was obvious from the affection in his voice as he spoke that the West family was a close one. It was easier to trust a man who loved his family.

"Then there's Meredith. She recently moved to Kansas City with her fiancé, Chase. She and Chase are planning on coming back here in March to get married. Finally there's Zack. He doesn't work for the family business anymore. He married Katie, the woman who lived next door to our family, and he's the sheriff of Cotter Creek."

Any hope she might have entertained of being truthful with Dalton West crashed and burned. *He's the sheriff of Cotter Creek.* The words echoed inside her head.

There were only thirty miles between Cotter Creek and Sandstone. There was no reason for her not to believe that Brandon Sinclair and Zack West were not only acquaintances but also perhaps friends. She had no idea how far-reaching the good-old-boy network was in the state of Oklahoma.

One thing was clear. For as long as she was stuck in this apartment, she couldn't tell Dalton the truth. Her very life and the life of her son might depend on her keeping her secrets.

At that moment, as if he'd awakened and sensed his mother's despair, Sammy began to cry from the bedroom.

* * *

Dalton drew a deep breath as "Jane" hurriedly left the kitchen to get her son. He was exhausted, having spent the night on George's tiny sofa after hours of listening to George talk. And the old man could definitely talk.

He'd already been feeling a little irritable when he'd climbed the inside staircase back to his apartment. As if spending an evening with George hadn't been enough, he was now stuck in his apartment with a stranger, a woman whom, he had to admit, stirred something inside him just by being there. A woman who'd had a knife in her hand the night before.

Could he really blame her for wielding a knife? After all, as much as she was a stranger to him, he was a stranger to her. She'd had no idea what kind of a man he was, what she'd been walking into when she'd entered his apartment.

He cut the omelet in half and placed it on two plates, then added the bacon and put the plates on the table.

She couldn't know that he was a solitary man who didn't particularly enjoy sharing his space, his world, with anyone. Even though he found her amazingly attractive, all he wanted was for her and her son to move on.

She returned to the kitchen, her son and a bottle in one arm and a box of powdered cereal in the other. "I need to make some cereal for Sammy. Do you have a small bowl I can use?"

Dalton got out the bowl, then watched as she tried to maneuver with the wiggly baby in her arms. "You want me to hold him while you get that ready?" he asked reluctantly. He didn't particularly like kids, had only thought about having a couple once, a long time ago, but it had been nothing more than a foolish dream.

"Thanks." She smiled at him for the first time, a real, open genuine smile that unexpectedly shot a flash of heat through his stomach.

As she offered the baby to him, Sammy seemed to vibrate with excitement and offered Dalton a wide, drooling grin. As soon as Dalton had him in his arms, Sammy reached up and grabbed hold of his nose, then laughed as if finding the West nose vastly amusing.

"He likes you," Jane observed as she measured out the rice cereal and added warm formula.

"You sound surprised," Dalton replied.

"I am. He's usually not good with strangers, especially men."

"What about his father?" Dalton asked as she stirred the cereal, then set the bowl on the table.

Her eyes darkened. "His father isn't in our life." To his relief she took the baby back and sat at the table.

For the next few minutes they sat in silence. She alternately fed Sammy and herself while Dalton ate his breakfast.

Sammy laughed and smiled at Dalton every time Dalton looked at him. He had to admit, the kid was cute with his tuft of dark hair and blue eyes. Dalton finished eating before Jane, or whatever her real name was. "Do you need to call your sister in St. Louis to tell her you've been delayed?"

"I already did," she replied.

Dalton stared at her. She'd told him the night before that she was on her way to visit her sister in Kansas City.

Women interested him, but a woman with secrets definitely intrigued him.

He didn't call her on her slip, but instead leaned back in his chair and watched as she finished feeding Sammy. He didn't want to be intrigued by her. He wanted the snow to melt quickly and her and her cute baby to move along on their way to wherever. However, the weather report that morning hadn't been exactly favorable for her to make a quick escape out of his house.

Taking a sip of his coffee, he gazed out the window where the snow still fell in buckets. At least she didn't seem to be a chatterer. She didn't expect him to entertain her with lively conversation.

Silence had always been Dalton's friend. Growing up in a household with a rambunctious bunch of siblings had made him appreciate his solitary life now. Odd that he suddenly found the silence strangely stifling.

"We're lucky we still have power," he finally said to break that uncomfortable silence. "The news report this morning said that half the town is without power and phone service."

"That's terrible," she exclaimed.

"Most folks around this area are prepared for situations like this. They have wood-burning fireplaces or generators that will be cranked up. We Oklahoma people are solid stock and know how to deal with an emergency."

She frowned. "I certainly wasn't prepared for this particular emergency."

"According to the weather report I heard the snow is supposed to end by nightfall. If that happens, then first thing in the morning the locals will get out and clear the streets."

"It can't happen fast enough for me," she replied. She looked up from Sammy, her blue eyes dark and troubled. "I'm sorry I can't get out of your hair right now. I know when you offered me a place to stay last night you had no idea that I'd still be here today."

Dalton shrugged. "We'll just have to make the best of it."

"I just hope if they get the streets cleared in the morning then the bus comes tomorrow afternoon." There was a thrum of desperation in her voice.

"Surely your sister will understand the delay."

"Of course." She averted her gaze from his and focused on her son in her arms. "I'm just anxious to get gone."

"Is this a vacation trip?"

She kept her gaze firmly on her son. "Yes. It's been a long time since I've seen my sister and she hasn't met Sammy, so I thought it would be nice to take a trip to visit her. I suppose it was foolish to plan a trip in late January. But babies are only babies a short time."

She was rambling, and it was Dalton's experience that people who rambled were usually hiding something. She seemed to realize what she was doing for she suddenly clamped her lips closed and frowned.

Getting up from the table she started to grab for her plate. "I'll take care of that," he said.

She gave him a grateful nod, then once again disappeared from the kitchen. Dalton remained seated at the table. He sipped his coffee and looked out the window. Although he stared at the snow, his mind was filled with those blue eyes of hers.

At thirty-three years old, Dalton had worked the family business for twelve years. He'd spent that time studying people, and the assessments he made of those people sometimes made the difference between life and death.

Jane Craig was lying. He'd seen it in those impossibly blue eyes of hers. Secrets and lies. There had been something in her eyes that had looked not only like quiet desperation, but also screaming fear.

His mind whirled with all kinds of possibilities. Who in their right mind planned a bus trip in the Midwest in January? Especially with an infant? He could write off the appearance of the knife the night before as a wary woman in the home of a stranger. But what was she doing with a wicked-looking knife like that in the first place?

Secrets and lies. What he was suddenly eager to find out was whether her secrets and lies could be the difference between life and death, and whether the snowy conditions had suddenly made him a player in a drama he wasn't prepared to face.

Sheriff Brandon Sinclair stared out the window and silently cursed the snow. He'd been in a foul mood since the day before, when he'd gone back to the diner to have a little chat with Janette and discovered she'd up and quit her job, just like that.

He'd been on his way to the little rattrap trailer where she lived with her grandmother when a six-car accident just outside of town had required his immediate attention. By the time he'd finished up, the ice had begun to fall in earnest.

He tried to ignore the sound of his three daughters playing in the middle of their living-room floor. He hadn't thought about Janette Black since the night they'd had sex over a year ago.

Then yesterday morning he'd heard the rumor that she had a little baby boy, a rumor that had been confirmed when he'd spoken with her at lunch.

Since that moment, he couldn't get her—or more precisely the boy—out of his mind. *His son.* He knew in his gut that the kid was his.

"Brandon, honey, your breakfast is waiting," Brandon's wife, Sherrilyn, spoke from someplace behind him.

He grunted but didn't turn around. Sherrilyn was a good woman. She'd come into the marriage not only crazy about him, but with the kind of respectability and a trust fund that Brandon had desired. She kept the large house neat and tidy, tried to anticipate his needs before he knew them and was an adequate if boring bedmate.

She loved being the sheriff's wife, and while Brandon was feared and respected by the community, Sherrilyn was loved for her charity work and big heart.

But, when it came to giving Brandon what he'd wanted most in life, she'd failed miserably, pumping out three girl babies instead of the boy he desperately wanted.

"Mommy, Susan won't share," Elena, his youngest, whined from the living room. She was always whining about something. Girls whined. Girls cried, and he had three of the whiniest, weepiest girls in the county.

He narrowed his gaze as he turned away from the window and headed for the kitchen. As soon as the snow stopped, he'd get that boy. He didn't much care what he had to do, but eventually that little boy would be living with him, being raised by him. Boys needed their daddies, and if the only way to get that kid was over Janette Black's dead body, well then that could be arranged, too.

Chapter 3

Janette stayed in the bedroom with Sammy for most of the morning. She played peekaboo with him, laughing as he grinned and squealed at her antics. When he started to get sleepy, she picked him up in her arms and sat in the chair near the window, rocking and singing softly to him until he fell asleep.

She placed her lips against Sammy's downy hair, drawing in the sweet baby scent of him. He was her heart, this little boy. Before his birth she had loved him, but nothing had prepared her for the depth of her love for him now.

Her heart squeezed as she thought of the threat that felt ominously close, a threat to this baby and their future together. She would do whatever it took to keep him safe and away from the man who was his biological father. She shoved aside thoughts of Sinclair, unwilling to allow the chill that thoughts of him always produced to consume her.

She was conscious of the sounds of Dalton in the next room. It was a good thing he'd told her about his family before she'd confessed what was really going on.

She should have known it wouldn't be safe to tell him the truth. Bodyguards probably had to work closely with law enforcement officials. For all she knew, Brandon Sinclair could be a drinking buddy of the entire West clan.

When Sammy was sleeping soundly, she gently laid him in the middle of the big bed and tucked the pillows around him to stop him from rolling anywhere. She stood for a long moment staring down at the baby who owned all of her heart.

She would do whatever it took to keep Brandon Sinclair away from Sammy. She would run to the ends of the earth, hide for the rest of her life if that's what it took.

You're nothing but trailer trash, Janette. Nobody is going to believe you if you ever tell. Those were the last words she'd heard from Sinclair that night on the highway. He hadn't spoken to her again or even looked at her until yesterday in the café when he'd told her he knew she had a son.

She'd tried to be so careful during her pregnancy. Thankfully she'd gained little weight and had been able to hide her condition until her eighth month. It was only then that she'd told the people who'd noticed that she was pregnant that she'd had a fling with a man passing through town. Because she believed Sinclair—nobody would ever believe her if she told the truth.

Tired of being cooped up, she finally left the bedroom and entered the living room, where Dalton sat in a chair reading a book as a saxophone wailed the blues from the stereo. She wasn't concerned about the noise waking Sammy. From the time he'd been born he had slept like the dead, undisturbed by loud noises.

Dalton looked up and nodded at her. "Are you ready for lunch?" he asked and closed his book.

"No, thanks. I'm fine." She gestured to the book on his lap. "Please, don't let me interrupt you."

"You aren't. It isn't a very good book, anyway."

She glanced to the overflowing bookcase against one wall. "You must read a lot."

"I enjoy reading," he agreed. His piercing green eyes seemed to peer directly inside her. "What about you? Are you a reader?"

She sat on the edge of the sofa. "I'd like to be, but there never seems to be enough time. Between taking care of Sammy and my job there aren't many hours left in the day."

"What kind of job do you have?"

"Right now I'm a waitress, but that's not what I want to do for the rest of my life." She hesitated a moment, then continued, "I had to drop out of high school my junior year because my nana...my grandma got sick, so the first thing I need to do is get my GED."

She wasn't sure why she told him this. It was more information than he'd asked for and she was certain he didn't care what her future plans might be.

Those direct green eyes of his held her gaze. "Your grandmother is important in your life?"

"Definitely. She raised me. It was just me and her, and of course my sister," she hurriedly added. She'd never been a liar, and the lies she now found herself spouting bothered her more than a little bit.

"What about your parents? Where are they?"

"Who knows? I never knew my father and when I was three my mother dropped me off at Nana's house and we never heard from her again. Nana told me she was a troubled woman with drug problems. I think she's probably dead by now."

Janette had long ago made peace with the fact that her mother had been unable to parent her. At least she'd been unselfish enough to put her in Nana's care, where she'd been loved and looked after.

"I'm sorry to hear that," he said, and she was surprised by the touch of empathy she heard in his deep voice. "My mother was murdered when I was just a boy."

"That's horrible," she exclaimed.

He shrugged. "You deal with the bumps life throws you." He stood suddenly, as if to end the conversation of that particular topic. "Are you sure you aren't ready for some lunch? I'm going to make a sandwich."

"I guess I could eat a sandwich," she agreed and got up to follow him into the kitchen. Once again she found herself sitting at the table while he fixed the meal. "I need to give you more money," she said. "You're feeding me and everything. I feel terrible about all this."

He smiled then, and the power of his smile shot a wave of heat through her. It was the heat of a woman intensely aware of an attractive man. It shocked her, but she embraced it, for it was something she hadn't felt for a very long time, something she'd thought Brandon Sinclair had killed.

"I think I can manage to feed one slender woman for a couple of days without declaring bankruptcy," he said.

She returned his smile. "I just want you to know that I appreciate it." She glanced toward the window where the snow appeared to be slowing down. Surely by tomorrow she could leave.

She gazed back at Dalton. "So, I guess your dad raised you, then? It must have been quite a challenge, considering how many of you there were."

Once again he grinned, transfusing his rather stern features with an unexpected warmth. "Ah, Dad had a secret weapon. He hired a cantankerous old cowhand as a housekeeper. Smokey Johnson not only threatened to beat our butts if we got out of line, he followed through on his threats often enough to make us take him seriously."

Despite his words it was obvious he held a lot of affection for the cowhand turned parental figure in his life. For the first time since she'd stepped out of the bus station yesterday evening, some of the tension that had coiled inside her eased.

"Ham and cheese okay?" he asked.

"Perfect. Is there anything I can do to help?"

"Nah, sit tight. I can handle it. Besides, if you work as a waitress I doubt you get too many people offering to wait on you."

She laughed. "That's the truth." He smelled nice, like minty soap and a touch of sandalwood, and she felt herself relax just a little bit more.

"Is your sister older or younger than you?"

The question came out of left field but reminded her that she couldn't let her guard down for a minute. "Older," she said. "Why?"

"Just curious." He walked over to the table with their

lunch plates. "What would you like to drink? I can offer you milk, water or a soda."

"Milk would be nice."

He rejoined her at the table a moment later with two tall glasses of milk. For the next few minutes they ate in silence. "From what you told me earlier it sounds like all of your brothers and your sister are married and having kids. Why aren't you married?" she asked to break the uncomfortable quiet.

A flash of darkness momentarily chased across his green eyes. "I guess after growing up with a houseful of people I've discovered in my adult years that I enjoy my solitude," he replied. "I like living alone and not having to answer to anyone and have no plans to ever get married."

He took a drink of his milk, then continued, "What about you? I'm assuming things didn't work out with you and the baby's father?"

She looked down at her sandwich and pulled off part of the crust. "No, we tried to make it work. He's a great guy and everything, but we just weren't good together." She looked at Dalton once again and forced a small smile to her lips. "But thankfully we have managed to remain good friends."

How she wished this were true. How she wished that Sammy's father was a good man who could help her instill the right qualities in their son instead of a monster who would taint the innocence of the little boy.

Dalton leaned back in his chair and studied her. "You're a pretty woman. I'm sure you won't have any problems finding some special guy to share your life."

There was nothing in his voice to indicate he was

flirting with her in any way, but she touched a strand of her hair self-consciously. She hadn't felt pretty in a very long time and she was surprised to discover that his comment soothed a wound she hadn't realized she possessed.

"I'm in no hurry at the moment to make any commitment to anyone," she replied. "I just want to be able to take care of my son and myself."

At that moment the phone rang, jolting every nerve in Janette's body. What if it was Dalton's brother, the sheriff? What if Dalton mentioned that he had a young woman and a baby staying with him?

What if Sinclair had already begun the search for her and had contacted Dalton's brother? Horrible scenarios went off in her head, mini-movies of doom.

As Dalton started to rise to answer, she grabbed him by the forearm and held tight. Her heart beat so hard, so fast she wondered if he could hear it. "Please, please don't tell anyone I'm here."

His eyes pierced her with a sharpness that was almost painful. He didn't answer but instead pulled his arm out of her grasp and walked over to the phone.

"Hello?" he said, his gaze never leaving Janette. "Yeah, hi, Dad. I was just eating lunch."

As Dalton continued his conversation, he never broke eye contact with Janette. The tension that had dissipated earlier crashed back through her, twisting in her gut like a deadly Oklahoma tornado.

His voice remained pleasant as he carried on his conversation with his father. When he finally hung up he returned to the table and reached out to grab her forearm as she had done his.

"Now, Jane," he said, his voice deceptively calm. "You want to tell me just what the hell is going on?"

Dalton stared at the woman and tried to ignore how fragile, how warm, her slender arm felt beneath his grasp. Her stunning blue eyes were wide and darted around the room as if seeking somewhere to run, to escape. She tried to pull her arm free from his grip but he held tight, just as she had a moment earlier.

"Talk to me," he said. "Tell me why you don't want me to mention to anyone that you're here."

This close he could smell the scent of her, clean with a touch of honeysuckle fragrance. She closed her eyes and he couldn't help but notice the length of her eyelashes. She tried to pull away from him again and this time he let her go.

She wrapped her arms around herself as if she were cold and looked at him. "I'm sorry. I lied to you before." She looked down at the table.

He frowned. "Lied about what?"

She got up as if she wanted as much distance from him as possible, but he had a feeling that what she was really doing was giving herself time to think. He wasn't at all sure he was going to believe anything that fell out of her mouth at this point.

Moving to stand next to the window, she turned to face him. "I lied about Sammy's father. He isn't a nice man. He…he used to beat me. He was abusive and I needed to get away."

There was a tremble in her voice, a timbre of fear that made him want to believe her. "You think he's looking for you?"

Again she wrapped her arms around her middle. "You can bet on it. And if he finds me he'll hurt me. He might hurt Sammy."

"That's not going to happen here," Dalton said firmly. He offered her a smile. "After all, you've hired me as your personal bodyguard and I promise you I'm damned good at what I do."

She didn't return his smile and that, along with the darkness in her eyes, made him believe her. "Is that why you carry a knife?" he asked.

She raised a pale eyebrow. "How do you know about that?"

"I saw it last night when you opened the bedroom door."

She returned to the table and sat, her gaze going out the window. "I won't let him hurt me again." She looked back at Dalton and there was a hard glint in her eyes. "I just want to get out of here. Once I get to my sister's I'll be just fine."

"What's this guy's name?" Dalton asked.

"What difference does it make?"

He shrugged. "Just curious. I know most of the families in this area. Just thought I might know him."

She blinked once…twice. "His name is Billy Johnson. I doubt if you know him. He's not from around here. His family is from someplace back east."

Once again he had the feeling she wasn't being completely honest with him. Did he care? If he were smart he would stop asking questions now. In the next day or two she wouldn't be his problem.

"I'd better go check on Sammy," she said and rose from the table.

He watched her hurry away, unable to stop himself from noticing how the worn jeans fit snugly across her shapely butt. He was acutely aware of the fact that physically he was attracted to her, but that didn't mean he wanted to be pulled into her life drama.

He got up from the table, carried their lunch dishes to the sink and began to rinse them. As he worked, his thoughts drifted to his last assignment.

It had been over a year since Dalton had worked a case as a bodyguard. Her name had been Mary Mason, she'd lived in Tulsa and she, too, had been the victim of domestic violence. He'd worked for her for almost four months, guarding her between the time she'd filed for divorce and the divorce proceeding itself, which had been expedited by a judge sympathetic to her situation.

Mary had known the statistics, that in these kinds of cases the most dangerous time for an abused wife was in the weeks prior to the divorce.

In those four months, he'd fallen head over heels in love with her and she had appeared to feel the same way about him. They had forged a bond that he thought would last the rest of their lives. They'd made plans for a wedding after her divorce, laughing as they created a fantasy event fit for a king and a queen.

It wasn't until the day after the divorce proceedings that the fantasy exploded. Mary told him she needed some time to regroup, that he should return to his home in Cotter Creek and give her a little time alone.

He'd understood the request, had encouraged it, so certain was he that they would be together. He'd called her often, they'd e-mailed, but after only a month he'd received a Dear John letter. She'd fallen in love with another man. They were getting married. Dalton had made a wonderful temporary hero, but that's all he had been.

He scowled as he put the dishes in the dishwasher. The whole thing had left a bad taste in his mouth, a heartache that had been long in healing. Since that time he'd worked the office, answering the phones and keeping the books. He preferred dealing with paperwork instead of people.

Footsteps sounded on the inside staircase that led from George's place upstairs to Dalton's. A moment later, a knock sounded on the back kitchen door.

Jane might not want anyone to know she was here, but it was already too late to keep that piece of information from his landlord.

George would have thought it damned odd that Dalton wanted to sleep on his sofa if Dalton hadn't told the old man that he'd given harbor from the storm to a young woman and her baby.

He opened the door to see George wearing hot pads on his hands and carrying a fresh pie. "Had some canned apples and thought it was a good day for some pie and coffee." He swept past Dalton and into the kitchen, where he deposited the pie on the table. "So, how about making us some coffee to go with this work of art." He pulled out a chair and sat.

Dalton grinned. "Feeling a little cabin fever, George?" He got a pot of coffee ready to brew.

"I hate being cooped up. You know me, Dalton, I'm a social kind of man. Sitting and listening to my own thoughts bores me to death. Where's your houseguest?"

At that moment Jane appeared in the doorway with Sammy in her arms. She froze at the sight of George. "Jane, this is my landlord, George, from downstairs," Dalton said.

George popped up from the chair and walked over to where she stood. "Jane, nice to meet you. And who is this little fellow?"

Sammy took one look at George's big, silly grin and screwed up his face. He wailed as if George were the devil himself and burrowed closer to Jane's chest.

"Oh my." George quickly stepped back.

"I'm sorry," Jane said. "He's hungry. I was just going to fix him a bottle."

Dalton realized she not only held the boy in her arms, but also juggled a bottle and a can of powdered formula mix, as well. Short of putting Sammy on the floor, it was going to be next to impossible for her to hold him and make the bottle.

"Want me to take him?" he asked and gestured to the crying child.

She shot him a grateful look. "If you don't mind. It will just take me a minute to get this ready."

He nodded and took Sammy from her. Almost immediately Sammy not only stopped crying but grinned at Dalton as if the two were best buds.

"Would you look at that?" George exclaimed. "That boy is plum crazy about you."

"He'll be a lot crazier about that bottle," Dalton replied, grateful a moment later when Jane took her son back. She sat at the table, Sammy in her arms sucking on his bottle with obvious contentment.

"George brought up a freshly baked apple pie," Dalton said as he got out coffee mugs from the cabinet.

"Hmm, that sounds good. Apple is my favorite." She offered George a tentative smile.

"My missus, God rest her soul, loved my apple pies.

Always told me if God served pie in heaven, then he'd be serving mine," George replied. "Guess this snowstorm took you by surprise."

"Definitely," she agreed.

George could talk, and that's what he did for the next hour. Sammy finished his bottle and fell asleep. Dalton sat and sipped his coffee as George entertained Jane with colorful descriptions of people in town, humorous stories of his misspent youth and his fifty-year marriage to the woman who had owned his heart since he was sixteen.

Dalton had heard the stories before. What he found far more interesting than George's conversation was watching Jane interact with the old man.

As she listened to George, she looked relaxed. Her long blond hair was so soft-looking, so shiny, it made a man want to reach out and touch it, coil it around his fingers, feel it dance across his chest. The first time she laughed aloud, Dalton was shocked by the pleasure that swept through him. She had a great laugh, one that would easily evoke smiles in others.

Although she visited with George in general terms, he noticed that she gave nothing of herself. She didn't mention family or friends, didn't speak of her hometown or her job.

Irritated with these kinds of thoughts, he got up to pour himself another cup of coffee, then returned to the table. He didn't want to think about how sweet she smelled or how her lips were just full enough to tempt a man.

She'd given no indication that she might be up for a short, reckless affair to pass the time until she got on the bus out of town. And the last thing he wanted was any kind of an emotional entanglement with any woman. She'd be gone soon, and that was that.

It was just after three when George finally got up from the table. "It's been a real pleasure," he said and smiled at Jane. "There's nothing nicer than spending a snowy afternoon in the company of a beautiful woman. Unfortunately, at my age, a good nap is also a pleasant way to spend the afternoon, and I'm past due mine."

She offered him a sunny smile. "Thank you for the pie, George. Your wife was right. It was the best I've ever eaten," she replied.

George beamed as if kissed by an angel.

"George, have you mentioned to anyone that I'm here?" Jane asked.

"Can't say I have." George scratched the top of his head. "Haven't talked to anyone except Dalton since this storm moved in."

"I would appreciate it if you wouldn't mention it to anyone." She flashed him a bright smile. "I'm kind of hiding out from somebody."

George's eyes lit up. "Ah, a woman of mystery. Your secret is safe with me." He started to turn to head out the way he had come, but paused and pointed to the window. "Would you look at that?"

Both Dalton and Jane looked through the window where the snow had finally stopped and the sun peeked out from behind the last lingering gray clouds.

Chapter 4

"You think the bus will run tomorrow?" Janette asked Dalton. The three of them were in the living room, having just eaten supper. He was seated in the chair and she was on the sofa. Sammy was gurgling happily from a blanket on the floor.

"Doubtful," he replied.

For the past hour they'd heard the sounds of plows starting the storm cleanup and each grind of gears had been like music to her ears. She just hoped and prayed she got out of there before Sheriff Brandon Sinclair somehow discovered where she was.

"Although most of the locals who have plows will be out and have our streets cleaned, it will probably be at least another day or so before the highways are completely cleared and the bus can show up." He gazed at her curiously. "Surely you can't be afraid that your boyfriend will find you here. You didn't know you were going to be here, so how could he know?"

"Logically, I know that, but emotionally, I just have this terrible need to get out of town, to get as far away as possible," she replied. "I just want to stay safe."

"I told you that you'd be safe here," he said. "When that bus comes, I'll personally see you safely aboard and in the meantime nobody is going to harm you while you're in my home."

A new burst of gratitude filled her. She'd taken a terrible chance coming into the home of a stranger, but Dalton had proven himself to be nothing other than a good, honorable man. She leaned back on the sofa. "So, what do you do when you aren't bodyguarding?" she asked. She'd been in his home for twenty-four hours but didn't really know anything about him.

"I mentioned before I like to read, and when the weather's nice I do a little work at the family ranch."

"Family ranch?" She could easily imagine him, long legs astride a powerful horse, a cowboy hat pulled down low over his brow.

"My dad has a huge ranch north of town. It's become something of a family compound. My brother Tanner has a house on the property, and Clay and his wife, Libby, have been talking about building there."

"Hmm, that sounds nice. It must be wonderful to have such a close, loving family unit. I used to wonder what it would be like to have a whole mess of siblings."

He laughed, a deep low sound that warmed her. "Believe me, it's not as wonderful as it sounds. You wait in line for the bathroom, you wait to be served at the table, you share everything you're given and there's incessant noise."

She searched his features. "But there must have been something wonderful in it."

He frowned, the gesture doing nothing to detract from his handsomeness. His gaze drifted to the window and he stared out for a long moment before answering. When he looked back at her the deep lines in his face had softened.

"I suppose there was something wonderful about it," he said as if conceding a huge point. "I definitely never felt lonely and I knew my family always had my back when I got into trouble."

"And did you do that often?" she asked. "Get into trouble?"

His eyes gleamed with a hint of mischief. "Probably more than my share, although nothing serious. What about you? Were you a wild child or one of those Goody Two-shoes who always played by the rules?"

It was the first conversation they'd had where she didn't feel on edge, wasn't afraid of screwing up the lies she'd already told with new lies. Maybe she was feeling more relaxed because the snowplows sounded like imminent escape.

"I was in-between," she said. "I'm sure my grandmother would tell you that I had some wild moments and like your Smokey, she didn't hesitate to burn my butt if I needed it. But I never broke any laws or anything like that."

"That's a relief. I wouldn't want to be harboring a criminal in my house," he said, his green eyes teasing.

She returned his smile. In different circumstances she had a feeling it would have been easy to like Dalton… really like him. Although he seemed reserved, when he smiled at her she wanted to break through that reserve and get to the heart of the man.

But she couldn't afford to be attracted to him. As soon as the streets were cleared she'd be out of his apartment and as far away from Cotter Creek as she could get.

This was nothing more than a temporary respite from the drama that her life had become on the afternoon that Sheriff Brandon Sinclair had walked into the café.

"I'll bet you spend a lot of time with your family," she said.

"Not really. Oh, we get together for the usual holidays, but most of the time I'm perfectly satisfied alone."

"Still, I imagine it's a good feeling to know that they're there if you need them," she replied.

Sammy cooed like a dove as he found his own fingers, his legs kicking with happiness. She watched Dalton as his gaze went to her son. Dalton looked back at her. "You've got a tough road ahead of you."

"What do you mean?"

"A single mother, no father in the picture and you mentioned that you don't have your GED yet. You've got an uphill battle ahead of you."

"I know," she agreed, suddenly sober as she gazed down at Sammy. "I might have grown up poor in a trailer park, but I'm going to make something of myself so that Sammy has everything he needs." She heard the angry resolve in her own voice, a resolve that had strengthened when Sinclair had told her that she was nothing but trailer trash and nobody would believe her if she told what he'd done.

"There's nothing wrong with being poor, or growing up in a trailer park," Dalton said softly.

She smiled. "Spoken like a man who has never known what it's like to be poor."

"You're right," he conceded. "I was lucky never to have to worry about finances. The bodyguard business pays well and we all share in the profits of both the business and the ranch."

"Did you always want to be a bodyguard?"

"When I was ten I wanted to be a rodeo clown," he said. "When I was twelve I wanted to be an astronaut, then a treasure hunter and a gold miner."

She laughed. "For me it was a movie star, a ballerina then a princess." She sobered. "It never entered my mind that in reality I'd be an abused woman on the run with a small baby."

"Your sister will take you in?"

"Of course," she replied around the lump of fear that swelled in her throat. She had no idea where she was going, no idea what she'd find when she arrived. Her only support system was a sixty-eight-year-old woman with a bad heart.

Dalton ran a hand through his thick dark hair, not breaking eye contact with her. "Why do I get the feeling that you aren't telling me everything?"

"I don't know what you're talking about," she said and looked down at Sammy, who had begun to fuss. "I'd better get him a bottle," she said as she got up from the sofa.

It was a relief to escape those piercing, intelligent eyes of his. She didn't know what he saw that made him think she was keeping secrets, but there was no way she could tell him the truth. And in any case, it didn't matter. She would be gone soon enough.

She fixed Sammy his bottle, then picked him up off

the floor. "I think I'm going to go ahead and call it a night," she said.

He nodded. "Unless it will freak you out entirely, I'm planning on sleeping here on the sofa tonight. I like George a lot, but his sofa is small and last night he kept me up until long after midnight telling me stories I'd heard a dozen times before."

She was surprised to realize the idea didn't freak her out. She trusted him to remain the perfect gentleman he'd already been. "Would you rather stay in your own bed? Sammy and I could bunk in here," she offered.

"No, I'll be just fine. Good night, Jane," he said.

She wished she could hear her real name on his lips, but fear still ruled her decisions, including the decision to tell him little white lies, as much as she hated it. "Good night, Dalton."

Even though it was relatively early, Janette breathed a sigh of exhaustion as she got ready for bed. It was hard work watching every word that fell from her mouth and being careful not to say too much or too little.

When she was in her nightgown she moved to the window and stared outside. The street in front of Dalton's had been plowed, leaving piles of snow on either side that glistened in the streetlights.

The sooner she got on the bus the better she'd feel, but escaping this part of the country certainly didn't ease the fear that was a constant inside her.

She might escape Sinclair but then she'd have to face settling into a new place, finding work and taking care of Sammy *and* earning enough money to send for Nana. Dalton was right. She had a tough road ahead of her.

Sammy finished his bottle, and she sang softly to

him until he fell asleep. It took her longer to sleep and when she finally succumbed, the dream began almost immediately.

"Well, well, don't we look all sexy in that little skirt," Sinclair said, and there was something in his eyes that made her suddenly afraid.

Janette held out her driver's license, but he didn't take it from her. Instead those cold, blue eyes of his swept leisurely down her body. "You were going awfully fast. You doing drugs?"

"I don't do drugs, Sheriff," she exclaimed.

"I'm going to have to frisk you to make sure you have nothing illegal on you." He stepped closer to her and she smelled the scent of him, a stale sweat odor mingling with an overly sweet cologne.

Unconsciously she took a step backward, heart pounding painfully hard. He narrowed his eyes. "Don't you fight me, girl. I'll have you in handcuffs so fast your pretty little head will spin." He grinned. "Or maybe I'll just have to shoot you for resisting." And then he put his hands on her.

Hands. Everywhere on her. And hot breath on her face. And in her dream she did something she hadn't been able to do that night.

She screamed.

The scream pulled Dalton from a dream of a naked Jane in his bed. He shot upright on the sofa, for a moment not knowing what it was that had awakened him. Then it came again, a scream of such terror it raised the hairs on his arms, on the nape of his neck.

Jane!

He stumbled from the sofa and into the bedroom, adrenaline surging and heart pounding. He flipped on the overhead light and instantly realized Jane was in the middle of a nightmare. She thrashed on the bed, flailing her arms and legs as if fighting for her life.

Sammy cried out, too, and his eyes fluttered open, but he settled back to sleep, as if accustomed to his mother having bad dreams. "Jane," Dalton called softly.

She moaned, whipping her head from side to side, but she didn't open her eyes. He approached her, trying not to notice that the sheets had slipped down to her waist and the pale-blue silk nightgown she wore did little to hide her full breasts.

The fight or flight adrenaline that had filled him at the sound of her scream now transformed to another kind of energy as a surge of desire struck him midsection.

"Jane," he said again as he moved closer to the edge of the bed. Still she didn't respond. He was going to have to touch that soft-looking pale skin and he knew he was going to find it far too pleasant.

"Jane, wake up. You're having a nightmare." He leaned over and took her by the shoulders.

Her eyelids snapped open and she looked at him, wildness in the depths of her eyes. She stared at him and the wildness left as recognition struck. She released a little gasp and to his surprise launched herself out of the bed and into his embrace.

She trembled in his arms and sobbed silently into the crook of his neck. He tentatively slid a hand down the cool material that covered her back. "Shh, it was just a dream," he said softly.

It would be easier to comfort her if he wasn't bare-chested, if he wasn't so intensely aware of every point where her bare skin made contact with his.

She raised her face to look at him. Her eyes were misty with tears but her full lips parted as if in invitation or some kind of strange desperation.

He didn't think about kissing her ahead of time. He didn't consciously plan to. It just happened. One minute he was gazing at her face and the next minute his mouth covered hers. He didn't just kiss her, she kissed him back, her mouth opening against his as he pulled her closer to him.

The kiss lasted only a second or two, then she pulled away from him, a horrified look on her face. "I'm sorry," she said, her cheeks blossoming with high color.

"No...I'm sorry," he replied stiffly. "You were screaming and obviously having a nightmare and I...I just meant to wake you."

She released a breathless, embarrassed laugh. "I'm definitely awake."

"Then I'll just...uh...let you go back to sleep." Dalton backed out of the room, afraid that if he remained another minute longer he'd want to kiss her again.

What was he doing? he wondered as he threw himself back on the sofa. Every nerve in his body was electrified, every muscle tense. His response to that kiss stunned him. He knew virtually nothing about Jane Craig except that her skin had been soft as silk and her lips had been hot and willing.

It was possible by tomorrow she'd be gone. It was even more certain that he didn't want to be involved with her. He didn't want to know what she dreamed about, he didn't want to share his life with her in any way, shape or form. It had been wrong to kiss her, because all he could think about now was how much he wanted to kiss her again.

He fell asleep dreaming of the sweet heat of her mouth and awakened the next morning stiff and sore from the night on the sofa. He got up, nearly tripping over Sammy's diaper bag on the floor. He swallowed a curse.

By the time he'd made coffee, some of the stiffness of his muscles had begun to ease, as had his foul mood. He sat at the table, his hands wrapped around a mug of fresh brew. Even though it wasn't quite seven o'clock he could hear the sounds of plows already at work.

Maybe the bus would come this afternoon, he thought. That would be a good thing. He could see Jane and Sammy to the bus stop, wish them well on their way, then return to his solitary life without temptation. And Jane Craig had become a definite temptation.

He still sat at the table with thoughts of Jane when a knock sounded on his door. He jumped up from the table and hurried to answer. He pulled open the door to see his brother Zack standing on his landing, his gloved hands holding a shovel.

"Hey, bro, just thought I'd check in to see if you survived the storm. I just finished clearing off the driveway and your car and thought you might have a hot cup of coffee for me."

Dalton held the door tightly. *Please, please don't tell anyone I'm here.* Jane's words pounded in his head as he stared at his brother. "You didn't have to do that," he said. "And you don't want to come in here, Zack," he finally said. "I've got the flu, been throwing up off and on all night."

Zack frowned and took a step backward as if to avoid any germs floating in the air between them. "You need anything? We've about got all the major roads cleared in town and some of the stores are opening this morning."

"Nah, I'm fine. I just think I might be contagious so it wouldn't be a good idea for you to come inside, but I really appreciate you cleaning off the driveway. I'm sure George appreciates it, too. I'd love for you to come in, but I'm really not feeling well." Dalton couldn't tell if Zack believed him or not but he breathed a sigh of relief as Zack backed down the stairs, promising to check in on him later.

Dalton closed the door, hating the fact that he'd lied to his brother for reasons he didn't quite understand. If Jane's abusive ex-boyfriend had somehow tracked her to Cotter Creek, then why on earth would it matter if the local sheriff knew about it?

He turned to see Jane standing in the bedroom doorway, Sammy in her arms. "Thank you," she said.

"Don't thank me. I'm not happy about lying to my family." He walked back into the kitchen, aware of her following just behind him.

When he saw that she was about to prepare a bottle for Sammy, he held out his hands to take the kid from her arms. As always, Sammy looked delighted to see him. He launched himself into Dalton's arms with a big grin that lit up his entire little face.

"Is this kid ever in a bad mood?" Dalton asked as he sat in a chair. Sammy smelled like baby powder and lotion, a pleasant scent that reminded Dalton of dreams half-forgotten and abandoned.

"Rarely," she replied, moving to the sink. As she stood with her back to him he couldn't help but notice again the tight fit of her worn jeans across her butt. She had a great butt. Besides the jeans she wore a pink sweater that hugged her slender curves and complemented her blond coloring.

She fixed the bottle, then took Sammy from his arms and sat in the chair next to his, her hair falling softly around her shoulders. "If the streets are clear enough maybe it would be best if I found someplace else to go until the bus runs again."

She looked so small, so utterly vulnerable, and at that moment Sammy smiled at him around his bottle's nipple, the gesture sending a stream of formula down the side of his mouth.

"That isn't necessary," he replied. "Zack just told me the streets are practically clear, so I imagine that the bus will run tomorrow."

"Good." She held his gaze. "About last night…"

"You had a nightmare. I comforted you. That's all there was to it." He got up to pour himself another cup of coffee. "You want some breakfast? I was thinking maybe I'd make a stack of pancakes."

"You don't have to go to all that trouble for me," she protested.

He grinned at her. "I'm more than willing to go to that kind of trouble for me."

She returned his smile. "Well, in that case pancakes sound wonderful."

Breakfast was pleasant. Sammy entertained with coos and grins as his mother and Dalton ate pancakes and talked. The conversation was marked with a new easiness that he suspected came from the fact that they both saw the end of their confinement together.

She made him laugh as she shared with him funny stories about her grandmother. He noticed that in none of the stories did she mention the older sister she was supposedly on her way to visit, but he didn't call her on it. Instead he simply enjoyed the way her eyes sparkled as she spoke of the old woman who had raised her.

She might not have graduated high school, but she was smart as a whip. She argued politics with him and spoke easily of current affairs. He had a feeling she would do well no matter what path she chose in life.

The rest of the day passed pleasantly. As Sammy took a late-afternoon nap, Dalton and Jane sat at the table and played poker with toothpicks as chips.

"You're one heck of a bluffer," he said after she'd won her third pot.

She laughed. "If you think I'm good, you should play with Nana. She's the ultimate poker player in the family. In fact, she gets together once a week with some of the other ladies in the trailer park and they tell everyone they're playing bridge, but they really play poker."

He laughed, but his laughter was cut short by a knock on his door. "Sit tight. I'll get rid of whoever it is." She cast him a grateful look as he got up from the table.

It was probably one of his other brothers coming to check in on him. He'd have to play the sick card again. Hopefully he could bluff as well as Jane when it came to fooling his family members.

He pulled open the door to see a burly, dark-haired man he'd never seen before standing there. He wore the khaki pants and coat of law enforcement. "Yes?"

"Dalton West?"

"Yeah, I'm Dalton."

"I'm Sheriff Brandon Sinclair from over in Sandstone. I hate to bother you, but I'm looking for a woman named Janette Black. She's traveling with a baby and I have reason to believe she might have come here." His gaze went over Dalton's shoulder, as if trying to see inside the apartment.

Dalton tensed but offered the man a frown of confusion. "There's no woman or baby here," he said. "What makes you think she'd come to me? I've never heard of this Janette Black before." That part, at least, was true. But it didn't take a rocket scientist to know that Jane was really Janette.

"She stole money from the café where she worked and when we went to find her just before the storm hit we discovered more serious crimes. Her grandmother has been murdered and Janette is a person of interest. Your name and phone number were on a piece of paper next to the old woman's bed, so we thought maybe she'd come here."

"Sorry, I'm afraid I can't help you." Dalton's head whirled with the information Sheriff Sinclair had just given him. What in the hell was going on?

Sinclair studied him for a long moment, then held out a card. "If you see her, or if she tries to make contact with you, give me a call. She's dangerous, Mr. West. She needs to be behind bars."

"I'll keep that in mind," Dalton said. He murmured a goodbye, then closed his door. He waited until he heard the sound of the sheriff's boots going back down the stairs, then he went into the kitchen.

Janette sat at the table, her face devoid of all color. As she stared at him a deep, wrenching sob ripped from the back of her throat. "He killed Nana. First he raped me, and now he's killed Nana," she cried.

She jumped up from the chair. "I'm—I'm going to be sick." She ran for the bathroom as Sammy began to cry.

Chapter 5

Janette stood in the bathroom fighting not only an all-encompassing grief, but wave after wave of nausea, as well. Just hearing his deep voice had made her ill. Knowing he'd been on the other side of the door had sickened her.

He'd found her.

He'd said he found a notepad with Dalton's name and number next to Nana's bed. There was no way Nana would have willingly given him that information. Oh God, she must have died trying to protect Janette and Sammy.

Blinded by her tears, she leaned weakly against the wall and wondered if it were possible to die of grief. She felt as if she were dying. Her heart felt as if it might explode at any moment.

Nana was dead.

Nana was dead.

Never again would Janette feel Nana's arms around her, never again would she see the old woman's eyes shining with love, her wrinkled face wreathed with laughter.

And Janette was wanted for her murder. That's how he would get Sammy. He'd see her tried for a murder she hadn't committed. She'd spend the rest of her life in prison, and Brandon Sinclair would have her precious boy. And her nana, the woman who had meant the world to her, was dead.

"Janette?" Dalton knocked on the door.

She sucked in air, trying to staunch the deep sobs that ripped through her. She didn't want to face him, was afraid that he might believe all the horrible things that Sinclair had said. And if he did believe Sinclair, there was nothing to stop him from contacting the lawman and letting him know she was here.

"Janette, come on out. We need to talk." His voice held a quiet command.

She grabbed a handful of tissues and wiped at her eyes, at her nose, then tossed the tissues into the trash. But she was reluctant to open the door, afraid to face him. What if she told him the truth and he didn't believe her? She didn't think she could handle it.

"Janette, you can't stay in there all night."

He was right. She couldn't stay in the bathroom. She opened the door. He no longer held Sammy, but as she stepped out of the bathroom Dalton opened his arms to her. She walked into them as tears of rich, raw grief began to flow again.

His strong arms surrounded her, and they felt like shelter from a world that had been terrifying for a very long time. She cried into the front of his shirt, wondering how she was going to survive without Nana's loving support.

After several minutes, Dalton released her and led her to the sofa. Sammy was once again on his blanket on the floor, staring up at the ceiling as if fascinated by the patterns the late-afternoon sunshine made as it drifted through the window.

Dalton sat next to her, his features inscrutable. "The truth, Janette. I need to know the whole truth," he said softly. "You said *he* raped you. Were you talking about your old boyfriend?"

She had two choices. Continue with the lies she'd told him, or tell the truth about everything. Her heart banged against her ribs. "No." The word whispered out of her on a wave of despair. She knew it was time to tell the truth. She had nothing to lose now and she wanted—needed—Dalton to know.

She grabbed a strand of her hair and twisted it around her finger. "There is no ex-boyfriend. The man who raped me, the man who killed my grandmother, is Sheriff Brandon Sinclair."

Dalton's eyes narrowed and he drew in a quick breath of surprise. "I think maybe you need to start at the beginning and tell me everything."

She leaned back against the plump sofa cushion and closed her eyes, fighting the overwhelming grief that still reached out to smother her in its clutches. She opened her eyes and gazed down at Sammy, who in the midst of her heartbreak had fallen asleep.

Looking at Dalton, she fought against the tears and drew a deep, steadying breath. The beginning. "It happened one night when I was driving home from the classes I was taking to study for my GED. They took place at a community college about twenty-five miles from where I lived in Sandstone."

She rose from the sofa, unable to sit as she fought against the panic that remembering that night always brought. It was a panic that constricted her lungs, closed up the back of her throat and quickened her heartbeat. It was the fear of having to remember and the additional stress of wondering if Dalton would believe her.

"Janette." He reached out and took her hand. Holding it firmly he drew her back on the sofa next to him. "It's okay, you're safe for now." He didn't let go of her hand. It was as if he knew she needed support, something to cling to as she went back to that horrible night.

She nodded and swallowed hard. "The highway between the community college and Sandstone is pretty deserted after dark. I was about halfway between the college and home when I saw the lights of a patrol car in my rearview mirror. I knew I was speeding so I pulled over to the side of the road, figuring I was about to get a ticket."

She paused and drew another deep breath, trying to still the frantic beat of her heart. Dalton squeezed her hand, as if to give her strength and she desperately needed it. She needed all the strength he could give her to get through the rest of it.

"I thought something was odd when he told me to turn off my headlights and get out of the car. He told me I had been speeding and asked if I was doing drugs. I've never touched drugs in my life," she stated emphatically.

Dalton nodded, his expression giving nothing away of his inner thoughts. "Had you had run-ins with him before that night?"

"Never," she replied. "I'd seen him around town, on the streets, but he'd never spoken to me before, never even noticed me that I knew of."

"What happened next?" he asked.

A trembling began deep inside her. It was as if all the warmth of the room had been sucked out and an arctic chill had taken over the world. Tears blurred her vision once again and she blinked them away, angry that after all this time the memory of what happened still had the power to make her cry.

"He told me he needed to frisk me and he warned me that he'd hate to have to shoot me for resisting." She looked down at Dalton's hand around hers, unable to look him in the eyes.

"He raped me there on the side of the road." The words didn't begin to describe the horror, the violation of that night.

Her nose filled with the sweaty, ugly scent of Sinclair. Her skin wanted to crawl off her body as she thought of the way he'd touched her, the sounds he'd made as he pushed himself against her. "I won't bore you with all the ugly details."

She pulled her hand from Dalton's, afraid he could feel the ugliness inside her. She couldn't look at him, was afraid to see disbelief in his eyes. She'd fall completely to pieces if she saw doubt or condemnation there.

"What happened after?" His voice was soft, as if he understood the emotions blackening her soul. Thank God he didn't press her for any of the details of the rape itself, for she'd shoved those particular memories deep inside her in a place where she wouldn't easily retrieve them.

She looked up into those warm green eyes of his.

"Nothing," she said simply. She forced a smile of dark humor. "I guess I should be grateful that at least I didn't get a speeding ticket." The smile faltered and fell away as tears once again burned at her eyes.

He raised a dark eyebrow. "You didn't tell anyone?"

She leaned back and stared at a point just over his shoulder. "Who was I going to tell? I couldn't exactly report the crime to the sheriff." There was more than a touch of bitterness in her voice.

She shook her head. "I didn't tell anyone. I didn't want to tell Nana because I thought it might destroy her. It wasn't until I realized I was pregnant that I finally told Nana and the man I'd been seeing at the time." A shaft of pain stabbed through her. "He asked me what I'd been wearing that night, implying that it was somehow my fault. Needless to say that was the end of that relationship."

"And you're sure Sheriff Sinclair is Sammy's biological father?" There was a faint note of apology in his voice.

She wanted to be offended by the question, but realized Dalton really didn't know anything about her. It was a fair question, she supposed.

"I'm positive. The guy I was seeing at the time...we hadn't...you know, been intimate." Her cheeks burned and she kept her gaze averted from his.

"So, you realized you were pregnant. What happened then?"

She looked at him once again. It was impossible to read him. She had no idea if he believed her or not, couldn't get a sense of anything that might be flowing through his head.

"The last thing I wanted was for Brandon Sinclair to know that I was pregnant. I managed to hide my condition from everyone until late in the pregnancy, then I told people who noticed that I'd had a fling with a salesman passing through town." She gazed down at Sammy. "As far as I was concerned Brandon Sinclair had no right to know about my condition. From the very beginning Sammy was my baby and nobody else's."

"So, he didn't know anything about Sammy."

"I didn't think he knew until three days ago when he walked into the café where I worked." She told him about Sinclair and his deputies coming in and the sheriff asking her about her son.

"There was something in his eyes, something in the things he was saying that let me know I had to take Sammy and run and so that's what I did. I didn't steal anything from the café, but the moment the sheriff left, I told Smiley, the owner, that I didn't feel well. I also told him I wasn't happy working there and I was quitting, then I went home."

She paused a moment to draw a deep breath then continued, "Nana agreed that I needed to take Sammy and leave town, get as far away as possible from Sheriff Sinclair. One of Nana's friends drove me here to catch the bus. Our plan was that I'd get settled someplace far away from Oklahoma, then I'd send for Nana and we'd start building a new life together." Grief once again rocked through her and new tears burned at her eyes as she thought of her grandmother.

Dalton studied her, a tiny frown furrowing the area in the center of his forehead. "After that night of the rape, did he continue to bother you? To threaten you in any way?"

She shook her head. "No. Of course, I went out of

my way to avoid him. I kept my pregnancy pretty well hidden, too. The few times we did run into each other, it was as if nothing had ever happened. He'd look right through me, as if he had no memory of what he'd done."

She wrapped her arms around herself, fighting a new chill. A bitter laugh escaped her. "Who was I going to report it to?" she said more to herself than to him. "Who was I going to tell about the rape? The sheriff? His deputies? Brandon Sinclair owns Sandstone."

Leaning forward she stared at the wall just over Dalton's shoulder. "Everyone is afraid of him. He'll get Smiley, my boss at the café, to agree that I stole money. He'll get anyone in town to say anything whether it's true or not, because nobody wants to get on his bad side. Besides, when he was done with me he reminded me that I was nothing but trailer trash and nobody would ever believe my word over his."

"I believe you."

Those three words, so simply spoken, wove a strand of warmth around her heart. She hadn't realized how badly she'd wanted to hear somebody other than her nana say them. She began to cry again.

Dalton pulled her against his broad chest as her tears flowed once again. He believed her. Dalton, better than anyone, knew that a gold badge of law enforcement could hide a sick, twisted soul.

There was no way she could fake the grief she felt for her grandmother and there was no way she could have manufactured the trauma she'd exhibited as she'd told him about the rape.

He tightened his arms around her. There was a special

place in hell for men who raped women, and a place beyond hell for men in authority who abused women.

Janette's tears finally ebbed and she raised her head and looked at him, the blue of her eyes dark with tortured sorrow. "I just can't believe she's gone," she said, her voice hoarse with emotion. "I just talked to her yesterday morning."

"Yesterday morning?" Dalton frowned, the sheriff's words replaying in his mind. "You spoke to your grandmother yesterday morning?"

She nodded and moved out of his embrace. She wiped at her cheeks and tucked a strand of her shiny hair behind her ear. "I called her from here to let her know that I was stuck here because of the storm."

"But according to what Sheriff Sinclair told me, he found her dead before the storm moved in."

Janette blinked in confusion. "But that's impossible." Her tears disappeared as a tenuous hope shone from her eyes. "He lied. And if she wasn't dead when he said she was, maybe she isn't dead at all. Maybe he just said that to get you to turn me over to him." She jumped up from the sofa and headed to the cordless phone on the end table.

Dalton leaned forward and watched her. As she punched in numbers she looked small and fragile, and the thought of a man touching her, taking her with force filled him with a simmering rage.

He watched her face as she gripped the phone receiver tightly against her ear. The hope that had momentarily lit her eyes faded.

"Nobody answered," she said as she hung up. "Even the answering machine didn't pick up." Her eyes grew shiny with tears once again.

"Is there anyone else you can call to see what's going on?"

"Nana's friend, Nancy." She quickly punched in the number. "She lives next door to Nana at the trailer park. She'll know what's going on. Nancy," she said into the phone. "It's me."

Myriad expressions played across her face as she listened to the voice on the other end of the line. "Oh, God, is she…" Tears once again fell from Janette's eyes but she offered him a tremulous smile.

"Nana, are you all right?"

As she said these words a knot of tension eased in his chest. Either she was a better actress than Meryl Streep or she was now talking to the grandmother she'd thought murdered.

"Does he know where you are now?" Janette asked. "Are you sure you'll be okay?" She paused and listened for several minutes, then continued, "We're fine and hopefully tomorrow we'll be on the bus. Don't worry, Nana, everything is going to be okay. I love you, too. I'll stay in touch."

Janette hung up the phone and stared at Dalton, her eyes once again haunted with fear. "She's alive, thank God." She returned to the sofa. He saw the tremor that went through her body, but when she gazed at him he realized it was anger shining from her eyes, not fear.

"What's happened?" he asked.

"Yesterday morning Nana braved the snow to go to Nancy's and have coffee. She was there for about two hours. When she got home she had the feeling somebody had been in her trailer. She didn't find anything out of place or missing so she chalked it up to her imagination. Then last night she was feeling lonely and unsettled, so she went back to Nancy's to play some cards and spend the night. During the night her trailer was set on fire."

Shock filled Dalton at her words.

"Thank God she wasn't home. He meant to kill her, Dalton." Janette's hands clenched into fists at her sides. "He meant to kill her and blame me so he can see me in prison. Then he'll be free to claim Sammy."

They both looked at the sleeping child on the floor. A weary resignation filled him. He'd offered her safe harbor from a snowstorm but now it appeared that the storm in her life had nothing to do with the weather outside. And he had a feeling whether he wanted it or not, her storm had become his.

"Why don't we get something to eat? It's past dinnertime and I think we both could use something warm in our bellies." He got up from the sofa and she followed him into the kitchen. "Grilled cheese and soup?" he asked and pointed her to the table.

She shrugged, as if it didn't matter what he offered her. He opened a can of tomato soup and poured it into a saucepan, then when he had it warming up he prepared the grilled cheese for the awaiting skillet. As he worked, she stared out the window where darkness had begun to fall.

He had to admit that there was something about her that touched him, that called on protective instincts he'd thought had been lost when he'd lost Mary.

"It must have been a tough decision to have the baby under the circumstances," he said. "A lot of women would have chosen a different option."

"I thought about an abortion," she replied. "But, to

be honest it was just a passing thought. It might be an option for a lot of women, but it wasn't for me. I was easily able to separate the innocent baby from the monster who had raped me."

She smiled then, the first smile he'd seen from her since the appearance of Brandon Sinclair on his doorstep. It was like sunshine breaking through chill wintry clouds. "Sammy is the best of me and there hasn't been a single minute that I've regretted my decision to give him life."

That's mother love, he thought. That fierce, shining emotion he saw in Janette's eyes, that was what he'd lost when his mother had been murdered. Dalton rarely thought about the mother he couldn't remember, but a shaft of unexpected grief stabbed him now.

"It was a sheriff who murdered my mother twenty-five years ago," he said. Her eyes widened as she stared at him. "The sheriff of Cotter Creek, Jim Ramsey. He was arrested a couple of months ago when he stalked my sister."

"Why? Why did he kill your mother?"

Dalton stirred the soup, then placed the first two sandwiches into the skillet. "He said he loved her, but it wasn't love, it was a sick, twisted obsession. He approached her one night on the highway and told her he loved her, that he wanted her to leave my dad, and when she refused he lost it and strangled her."

He didn't miss the parallel in what had happened to his mother and what had happened to Janette. Men they should have been able to trust had accosted both on a lonely stretch of highway. The only difference was, Janette had survived and his mother had not.

"Oh, Dalton, I'm so sorry."

He nodded and swallowed around the unexpected lump of emotion that rose up in his throat. "It was a long time ago. She was a wonderful, loving person."

"And your father never remarried?"

Dalton flipped the sandwiches. "No, never even looked at another woman. He and my mom were true soul mates and when she was gone he never showed any interest in pursuing a relationship with anyone else."

"From what my grandmother told me, my mother wasn't even sure who my father was." Her gaze went back to the window again and when she looked back at Dalton a tiny frown furrowed her forehead. "Why would he tell you that I'd killed Nana?"

Dalton took up the grilled cheese sandwiches and placed them on two separate plates. "If he burned down her trailer last night it's possible he doesn't know she isn't dead. If he puts out the word that you're wanted for questioning in a murder case, then you're going to have trouble hiding out. He can get law enforcement officials in every county keeping an eye out for you."

He set the plates on the table then went back to grab the two bowls of soup. "If you're trying to cheer me up, it isn't working," she said dryly.

She placed her spoon in her bowl, but didn't begin to eat. Instead, she looked back out the window, where night had completely fallen. "Do you think he believed you when you told him you didn't know me, that I wasn't here?"

Dalton followed her gaze to the window and a tight knot of tension formed in his chest. "I have a feeling we'll know before the bus shows up in town."

* * *

Brandon raised his collar against the stiff wind that blew from the north. He stood across the street from Dalton West's place, eyes trained on the upper windows. She was in there. He smelled her, the trailer trash tramp who was trying to keep his son from him.

He'd known that she'd blown town, had taken his son and left Sandstone. A visit to her grandmother's house yesterday had given him his clue. The old lady wasn't home but he'd gotten inside and taken a look around. The minute he'd seen the name and phone number on the nightstand, he knew in his gut that he was on her trail.

It was obvious from the condition of the small bedroom in the trailer that Janette had packed up and left. Clothes were thrown helter-skelter and there wasn't a baby article to be found except for the crib, which was stripped of bedding.

He'd been enraged. He'd gone back to his office, re-searched to find out what he could about Dalton West, then late last night had returned to the trailer and set it on fire. He considered the death of Janette's grandmother collateral damage. He hadn't yet gotten the official report of the fire from their fire chief, but he knew the man would write up whatever Brandon told him to.

With the old woman dead and Janette wanted as a suspect in an arson-murder case, she'd find it difficult to get out of Cotter Creek. She was a wanted woman, and if he put a reward on her head, she wouldn't be able to show her face anywhere.

He'd known he'd find Janette, and he had. He narrowed his eyes as he watched the windows. Even though Dalton West had told him he'd never heard of

Janette Black, that there was no woman with a baby inside his place, Brandon knew he'd lied.

The sheriff had done his homework. He knew Dalton West was a bachelor who lived alone. But he'd watched the silhouettes move back and forth in front of those windows and knew the professional bodyguard wasn't alone. And if that wasn't enough, when Dalton had opened the door and Brandon had gotten a glimpse inside, he'd seen a diaper bag on the living-room floor, a diaper bag with the same blue teddy bear print that had decorated one area of one of the small bedrooms in the trailer.

She was in there, and there was no way she was going to escape him. One Oklahoma bodyguard wasn't going to stand in the way of Brandon Sinclair getting exactly what he wanted.

Chapter 6

The cough woke Dalton. An irritating cough that pulled him groggily from his sleep. His eyes burned as he sat up on the sofa and realized the air was filled with the acrid scent of smoke.

Fear shoved aside the last of his sleepiness as he grabbed his gun off the coffee table where he'd placed it before going to sleep the night before.

He turned on the lamp next to the sofa and gasped as he saw the dark smoke that swirled in the room. Fire! They had to get out.

Maybe George had forgotten to turn off a stove burner and something had caught flame. Dalton didn't give much thought to what caused the smoke, he just knew he needed to get Janette and Sammy out, for the smoke appeared to be thickening by the second. Fire could be dangerous, but smoke was just as deadly.

He pulled on his boots, then grabbed a coat, his cell phone and car keys and hurried into the bedroom where Sammy and Janette were asleep. He turned on the overhead light and Janette stirred, but didn't awaken.

"Janette." He walked over to the bed and shook her shoulder with a sense of urgency. A spasm of coughing overtook him as she opened her eyes. "We need to get out of here," he finally managed to gasp.

She didn't ask questions, obviously aware of the imminent danger that whirled and darkened the room despite the overhead light. "I'll get your coat," he said. "Just grab what you need."

As Dalton raced back through the kitchen into the small utility room where he'd hung her coat the night she'd arrived, he felt no heat beneath his feet, heard no ominous crackle of flames. But that didn't mean they weren't in danger.

She met him at the bedroom door, pulling her suitcase behind her and Sammy in her arms with a blanket over his head. He thought about telling her to forget the suitcase, but realized the case contained all the possessions she and Sammy had left in the world.

He grabbed the suitcase from her and motioned her toward the door that led to the interior staircase. He needed to make sure George got out as well.

Before he opened the stairwell door he felt the wood, wanting to make sure it wasn't hot, that deadly flames weren't already attempting to burn through. The door radiated no heat so he opened it and motioned for her to precede him down the stairs.

The smoke wasn't as intense in the staircase, and still

he could feel no heat radiating from any of the walls. But where there was smoke, there had to be a fire.

They hit the landing to the first floor and Dalton entered George's area of the house. "Wait here," he said to Janette as he raced through George's living room and down the hallway to the bedroom where the old man slept.

It took him only minutes to rouse George from sleep and get his coat and shoes on him, then together they all made their way to the front door.

It wasn't until they opened the front door to get out that Dalton's brain fully kicked into high gear. "Wait," he said urgently before Janette ran outside.

His mind whirled with suppositions. Brandon Sinclair had burned down Janette's grandmother's place. This evening he'd come to ask if Janette was here. Was it possible Sinclair hadn't believed Dalton when he'd said he didn't know Janette? Was it out of the question that he'd set a fire to try to smoke her out?

"Janette, my truck is in the driveway. I'm going out first and when I get outside you run for the truck. George, you come out after Janette." He released the lock on his gun, knowing he might have to provide cover for her if Sinclair was outside.

He knew by the look in Janette's eyes that she perceived his thoughts, realized the potential for danger. She gripped Sammy more tightly against her as George took the suitcase from her hand.

"Problems?" George asked.

"Possibly," Dalton replied. George nodded and straightened his thin, sloped shoulders.

Dalton went out the door, gun drawn, and with every sense he possessed on high alert. The night held the eerie silence that snow-cover produced, a preternatural calm that could be deceptive.

Snow crunched beneath his boots as he stepped onto the front porch. The cold air stabbed his lungs as he drew deep, even breaths. He looked both directions, seeing nothing amiss but unwilling to trust that the night shadows held nothing dangerous.

He took several more steps, then turned back to the house, noting dark smoke rolling out of a partially opened basement window. Had George left it open? The old man had a workshop downstairs where he did some woodworking. Had he left his wood-burning tool on, and somehow it had caught fire?

His heart pounded as adrenaline continued to pump through him. He had no idea how big a fire might be burning there, but it was apparent he needed to get the others out of the house as soon as possible.

Looking around once again he saw nothing that indicated any danger. He walked back up to the door and motioned for Janette to follow him as he tried to watch every direction around them.

The gunshot came from the left, the bullet whizzing by Janette's head as she screamed in terror. Dalton's body slammed her to the ground, and he hoped that in the process Sammy wasn't hurt.

"Get down, George," he yelled at the old man, who had just stepped off the porch. George dove into a snowbank with the agility of a man one-fourth his age.

Another gunshot exploded in the quiet of the night and the snow next to where Dalton and Janette lay kicked up. The shots had come from the direction of a large oak tree in the distance. Janette screamed again and Sammy's cries added to the melee.

Dalton's heart crashed against his ribs and he thought he could feel Janette's heartbeat through their coats. "I'm going to roll off you and start firing. When I do, run like hell to the truck and get inside. Stay down." He fumbled in his pocket for his keys and gave them to her. "And if anything happens to me, drive away and don't look back."

He didn't give her time to protest or accept, he rolled off her and began firing at the tree. At the same time he heard the sound of a siren in the distance and knew that somebody had heard the shots and called for help.

When he saw that Janette was safely in the truck, he stopped firing and waited to see if there would be an answering volley.

Nothing.

For a long moment he remained where he was, not moving, but listening…waiting…wondering if the threat still existed or not.

He got up into a crouch as the siren grew louder. Still no answering shots. He had a feeling the shooter had run at the first sound of the siren. He hurried to the driver's side of the truck and was surprised to see George come burrowing up from the snowdrift and running to throw the suitcase in the back of the truck bed.

Dalton had just backed out of the driveway when Zack's patrol car came screaming to a halt. "Get down," he ordered Janette. She bent so she wasn't visible and Dalton was grateful that at the moment Sammy wasn't wailing. He rolled down his window as Zack rolled down his.

"Call the fire department, and see to George," Dalton said. "I'll be in touch." As Zack yelled a protest, Dalton pulled out onto the street and sped away from his brother, the house and the quiet, solitary life he'd led.

Thankfully, Janette remained silent as he headed out of town and kept a watchful eye on the street behind him for anyone that might be following.

He needed to think.

Zack was a newly elected sheriff and aware of everyone's eyes on him. After the disgrace of Jim Ramsey, the last sheriff of Cotter Creek, Zack was proving himself to be a strictly by-the-book kind of lawman.

Dalton believed in rules, but sometimes rules had to be bent, even broken, and he wasn't convinced that Zack would see things his way.

If Brandon Sinclair had an arrest warrant for Janette, then Dalton feared his brother would feel it necessary to turn her over to him. He wouldn't want to put himself in the middle of a problem that wasn't his, especially in bucking the authority of a fellow sheriff.

"Where are we going?" Janette asked, finally breaking the tense silence in the truck as they left the town of Cotter Creek behind.

"A place where you'll be safe until we can figure things out," he replied.

Besides, if he did decide to confide in Zack, what could he tell him? That a strange woman had shown up on his doorstep and had initially lied about everything, but finally had told him a story that he believed?

Zack would ask for cold hard facts and Dalton had none. He couldn't prove that Brandon Sinclair had set the fire tonight or fired the shots. No doubt Sinclair hadn't used his service weapon; ballistics would probably lead to a dead end. He couldn't prove that

Janette hadn't stolen money from her employer, although he could attest to the fact that she hadn't been anywhere near that trailer when it had gone up in flames. Unless Sinclair screwed around with the reported date of the fire.

He didn't want to put his brother in the untenable position of having to choose between doing his job or supporting Dalton's decision to break the law by hiding Janette.

He'd talk to Zack, tell him who he thought was responsible for both the fire tonight and the gunfire, but he wouldn't tell Zack where Janette was hidden away. He wouldn't give her over to Zack, who might find himself with no alternative than to turn her over to Sinclair.

He cast a quick glance at the woman in the passenger seat. She bounced Sammy in her arms and asked no more questions about where they were going or what they were going to do.

She trusted him.

After two snowbound days together, she trusted that he was taking her someplace where she'd be safe. It shocked him, awed him, and if he were to admit the truth to himself, it scared him more than just a little bit. She was placing not only her life, but also the life of her little boy directly in his hands.

He clenched the steering wheel tightly. He hadn't signed on for this, had simply offered a woman and her baby shelter from the storm. A tiny spark of anger filled him. He didn't want this responsibility. Since the debacle with Mary he'd consciously backed away from being involved with anyone, even his family. He didn't want anyone depending on him, needing him.

He didn't want the responsibility, but now that he had it, he couldn't turn his back. Janette had been trapped by the storm, and now he was trapped by her circumstances.

Janette thought she might be in a mild state of shock. She couldn't process the fire, the gunshots and now a drive down narrow, slick roads with darkness all around.

She should be terrified, but she wasn't. She was beyond terror and instead felt only a weary resignation, a stunning knowledge that she was no longer in control of her own life.

She glanced at Dalton. In the faint illumination from the dashboard his handsome features looked grim and more than a little bit dangerous. She could only imagine what was going through his mind right now.

Because of his kindness to a stranger, his home had been set on fire, he'd been shot at and he was now making a dash over the snow-slick roads to a safe place.

"I'm so sorry I got you involved in all this," she said. "All I wanted to do was leave town."

His knuckles turned white on the steering wheel as she felt the back end of the truck slide out. She caught her breath, then relaxed as he skillfully steered into the skid and straightened out the truck.

"I know," he replied. "We'll talk when we get where we're going."

That comment effectively staunched any other conversation she might have wanted to have. She cuddled Sammy closer against her and stared out the passenger window, where no lights from houses broke the darkness of the night.

He seemed to have a plan and she was grateful, because she had none. She couldn't return to his apartment because it was obvious Sinclair knew she was there. She felt terrible that she'd now placed Dalton in a horrible position. If he didn't turn her over to the sheriff, then he was breaking the law and could face even uglier repercussions of his own.

She'd like to be able to tell him just to drop her off somewhere, that she'd figure things out on her own. But that wasn't an option either. She couldn't go back to Sandstone and she couldn't get out of Cotter Creek. She was in a horrible state of limbo, with Brandon Sinclair like a hound dog sniffing her scent.

She sat straighter in the seat as Dalton turned off the main road and through an iron gate. He doused his headlights as they approached a large ranch-style home.

"That's my dad's place," he said as they drove past the sprawling one-story house. "It would be better if nobody knows you're here on the property."

That explained him dousing the truck lights. They entered a pasture area and he threw the gears into four-wheel drive as they hit the thicker snow where no plows had been.

They passed another house where lights shone from several windows. "That's my brother Tanner and his wife's place," Dalton said.

Still they didn't stop. Once they'd passed the second house Dalton turned the truck headlights back on. There were other tracks in the snow. In one area it looked as if several trucks or cars had made figure eights.

An area of thick woods was on their right, mostly evergreen trees, which she assumed provided windbreaks. Eventually Dalton turned through a small break in the trees and pulled to a halt in front of a small cabin. Trees completely surrounded it, tall evergreens that made it impossible to see the place unless you were right on top of it.

"Who lives here?" she asked, nerves jumping in her stomach.

"For now, you do," he said as he shut off the engine. "At one time or another, I think all of my brothers have lived here for short periods, but for the last couple of months it's been empty. You should be safe here."

She *should* have been safe on the road between her home and the community college. She *should* have been safe in Dalton's apartment. She couldn't afford to take her safety for granted anymore.

"Come on, let's get you inside and settled," he said as he opened his truck door.

Janette got out of the truck and stared at the cabin. There was nothing welcoming about it. Illuminated only by the faint cast of the moon filtering through the trees, it looked dark and cold and forbidding.

She tightened her grip on Sammy as she followed Dalton up the stairs to the front door. He used a key to unlock it, then pushed it open, flipped on a switch that lit a small table lamp and ushered her inside.

The sense of welcome that had been absent from the exterior was present inside. Plump throw pillows covered a dark-green sofa, and a rocking chair sat next to the fireplace. The wood floor gleamed with richness except where it was covered by braided rugs.

"It's nothing fancy," Dalton said as he wheeled the dial of the thermostat on the wall. "There's a bedroom and bath and a small kitchen." He turned to face her. "We're deep enough in the woods that no one should see the lights, but I won't light a fire. I don't want smoke from the chimney to draw any curious people."

He motioned her to follow him into the small kitchen, where he opened cabinets to show her a stockpile of canned goods. "There's enough here to hold you for a night or two."

"You're not staying?" She tried to keep the fear out of her voice but didn't quite succeed.

"I've got to get back to town and check on George and talk to my brother."

"What are you going to tell him?" She studied his features, wondering if he'd decide to give her up, that this was all trouble he hadn't bargained to take on and he was finished with her and her mess.

He swiped a hand through his thick dark hair and leaned against the wall, his expression unreadable. "I don't know for sure. I'm still sorting out things in my head. But I promise you I won't tell him you're here."

He shoved off from the wall. "Things are pretty dusty in here, but there's fresh bedding in one of the dresser drawers in the bedroom, and it won't take long for the furnace to warm things up."

"I'm sure we'll be fine," she replied, although she wasn't sure of anything. She wanted to tell him not to leave her, that she needed him to hold her, to wrap her in his strong arms and make her feel safe.

She couldn't remember the last time she'd truly felt safe. On second thought, yes, she did remember. It had been the night of her bad dream when he had held her and soothed away her fear.

He walked over to the doorway that led off the kitchen and flipped on the light to illuminate a small bedroom with a double bed and a long dresser. "It's late. You should try to get some sleep. There's a phone in the living room. I'm assuming you don't have a cell phone."

"Where I come from cell phones are a luxury, not a necessity."

He nodded and headed for the front door. "You've got my cell phone number. If you need anything don't hesitate to call."

She followed him to the front door, nerves jangling inside as she watched him go out to the truck then return with her suitcase, which George had thrown into the back at the last minute.

"Will you be back later tonight?" she asked.

His green eyes narrowed intently. "I don't know. I can't make any promises. For sure I'll try to be back here sometime tomorrow. Is there anything you need for Sammy?"

"It depends on how long we're here. If it's for too much longer I'm going to need some more diapers." A sense of urgency swept through her. "Surely the bus will run tomorrow and I can get on it and away from here."

He stared at her for a long moment, and she had a feeling he wanted to say something to her, something she might not want to hear. Instead he turned toward the door. "I'll see you sometime tomorrow."

And with that he was gone.

Sammy slept soundly as she laid him on the sofa with pillows surrounding him while she went into the bedroom to make up the bed.

The last thing on her mind was sleep. Restless energy

filled her, coupled with a simmering sense of terror that was unrelenting.

Was Sinclair still in Cotter Creek? Those gunshots tonight were intended to kill her. Had his intention been to kill them all, then pluck Sammy from her dead arms?

She now recognized that Sinclair would do anything to get Sammy. The man was insane. Was it truly about him wanting a son, or was it more than that?

Maybe he was angry that she'd left town and was afraid that once she was out of Sandstone, she'd feel safe enough to talk about what he'd done to her. It was impossible to know the man's mind. A chill washed over her, and it had nothing to do with the coolness of the room.

Once the bed was made she placed Sammy in the middle, then walked back into the living room, knowing that sleep would be a long time coming.

She stood at the living-room window and stared out into the darkness of night, her thoughts going to the man who had just left.

Smelling the scent of his pleasant cologne, which lingered in the air, she wrapped her arms around her middle and tried not to allow herself to wish for a life different than the one she'd been handed.

The memory of that single kiss she'd shared with Dalton warmed the chilled places inside her. What would it be like to kiss him longer, harder? What would it be like to lie naked in his arms, to make love with him?

She hadn't been with any man since the night of her rape, but she knew how good lovemaking could be if it was between two people who cared about each other. When she was twenty-one she'd had a relationship with a man that had lasted almost a year. They had enjoyed a healthy sex life for the last three months of their time together.

Although that relationship had ended, she was grateful now that she'd had it. It would have been terrible to know nothing about sex except those horrid minutes on the side of the road with Sinclair.

She could care for a man like Dalton West, a man who not only stole a bit of her breath away whenever she looked at him, but also radiated the strength and assurance of a good man.

Turning away from the window she released a deep sigh. The last thing she needed to be thinking of was indulging in an affair with Dalton. She was an uneducated woman with a son who was the product of rape. What made her think a man like Dalton West would ever want anything to do with her?

What she'd better figure out instead was how she was going to stay one step ahead of a demented man who wanted to take the only thing she cared about, a man who would stop at nothing to get what he wanted.

Chapter 7

Zack's patrol car was still in front of George's place when Dalton pulled into the driveway. He'd spent the entire drive back from the cabin trying to figure out exactly what he intended to tell his brother.

His first priority was to protect Janette, but equally as important was his desire to protect his brother. He refused to put Zack in a position where he had to choose between doing the right thing and handing Janette over to Brandon Sinclair, or doing the wrong thing and jeopardizing the job he loved.

He got out of his car, aware that he was about to walk a very fine line. George's front door was open, and when Dalton walked in Zack greeted him with a deep frown of frustration.

"It's about time you showed up. You want to tell me what's going on?" Zack asked. "A fire of suspicious origins and gunshots, and I can't get George here to tell me anything."

George sat on his sofa, his arms folded across his chest and a stubborn glint in his brown eyes. "I can't tell you what I don't know," he exclaimed fervently. "I don't know how those rags started on fire in my basement and I sure as hell don't have a clue who shot at us when we ran out of the house."

"How much damage did the fire do?" Dalton asked, stalling for time.

"Thank God it was more smoke than flame," George replied. "Burned up a couple of boxes I had stored down there, but nothing too serious."

"Good." Dalton turned to his brother. "Why don't you and I go up to my place and let George get some sleep? He's not used to this much excitement in the middle of the night."

"You got that right," George exclaimed.

Zack nodded, his jaw muscle knotted with obvious frustration. Dalton told George good-night, then together he and Zack went upstairs.

Once in Dalton's living room Zack sat on the edge of the sofa and stared at his brother. "Now talk," he demanded. "I need some answers from somebody and as far as I can tell you're the only one around here who might have them."

Dalton remained standing. "Earlier this evening Sheriff Brandon Sinclair from Sandstone knocked on my door and told me he was looking for a woman wanted for theft and questioning in a murder case and had reason to believe she had come to me. I told him I didn't know the woman, but I don't think he believed me."

Zack frowned. "Why would he think this woman would come to you?"

"I don't know. He said something about finding my name and number in the trailer where this woman lives."

Zack watched him intently. "And you don't know this woman. What's her name?"

"According to Sinclair, her name is Janette Black, and, no, I don't know her. I can't imagine why she would have had my name and phone number."

"So, what? What does Sinclair have to do with the fire and the gunplay that took place here tonight?"

Dalton shrugged. "All I can tell you is that he was here asking about a woman named Janette Black. I told him I'd never heard of her and she certainly wasn't here, then he left. Hours later I woke up to smoke filling the house and I ran downstairs and woke up George. We ran out the front door and somebody started shooting at us."

Zack's frown deepened. "Why would Sinclair do something like that?"

"I don't know. All I can tell you is what happened," Dalton replied. The most difficult thing he'd ever done was hold his brother's gaze while he knew he wasn't telling the whole truth.

"Was the shooter targeting both you and George?"

"No, just me," Dalton answered. "I returned fire, jumped into my truck and that's when you got here."

"Handy that you just happened to have your gun with you when you ran out of the house."

"Dad always taught us to be prepared for anything," Dalton replied easily. "And to be honest, something about Sinclair didn't sit quite right with me. Call it instinct."

"Where have you been for the last hour?" Zack asked, watching Dalton intently.

"Driving...making sure nobody was following me." Although the lie fell effortlessly from his lips, he hated the way it felt inside. "I wanted to draw any danger there might be away from this house and George, but I didn't see anyone following me."

Zack frowned again. "This just doesn't make any sense. Why would Brandon Sinclair do something like this? I know Brandon. We've met for beers a couple of times. He's always seemed like a stand-up guy to me."

"If you're investigating the shooting and the fire, I recommend you start the investigation by checking Mr. Stand-up Guy's alibi," Dalton countered lightly.

"Is there some history here that I don't know anything about? Have you and Brandon had run-ins before?"

"Definitely not. I'd never met the man before he showed up on my doorstep earlier this evening."

"You having problems with anyone else? Are you working on something that I don't know about? Something to do with West Protective Services?"

"Nothing."

Zack stood, obviously as frustrated as he had been when Dalton had arrived. "I don't know, bro. I get the feeling you're not telling me everything."

"Believe me, when I figure out what's going on you'll be one of the first to know," Dalton promised.

Zack headed for the door. "You want me to put one of my deputies on the house? Keep an eye on things for the rest of the night?"

Dalton shook his head. "I have a feeling the excitement is over for the night." With Janette out of the apartment there was no reason for Brandon Sinclair to come calling again. And if he did, Dalton would be ready.

"You'll let me know if you think of anything else?"

"Of course," Dalton said. He watched as his brother opened the door and started to step outside, then paused and turned back to look at Dalton.

"Must have been a fast moving bug," he said.

"Excuse me?" Dalton frowned in confusion.

"The flu. You seem to be feeling much better now." Zack had a knowing glint in his eyes.

"I am. Must have been a twenty-four-hour bug that ran its course." Dalton hoped his cheeks weren't dark with the color of the lie.

Zack held his gaze for a long moment. "Dalton, you'd tell me if you were in trouble, right?" This time there was no frustration on Zack's features, only the deep concern of a brother.

Dalton wanted to tell him everything, but before he could do that he needed to talk to Janette. "I'm fine, really," he said, but he could tell his words did nothing to assure his brother.

Zack disappeared out the door. Dalton breathed a huge sigh of relief and sat on the edge of the sofa where Zack had been only seconds before.

It was obvious that George had stayed true to his word and hadn't breathed a word to Zack about Janette and Sammy being there.

A glance at the clock let Dalton know it was almost four. The last thing on his mind was sleep. He dropped his head into his hands and tried to make sense of everything that had gone down, everything he hadn't told his brother.

If he were smart, he would have told Zack everything. Zack would have probably honored whatever arrest warrant Sinclair had and turned Janette over. Then she would have been out of Dalton's life. He wouldn't feel responsible for her.

Zack would tell him that he was making decisions based on something other than his brain. Was that what he was doing? Was he allowing Janette's beautiful blue eyes and the memory of the hot kiss they'd shared to twist his logic?

Was it possible she and Sinclair had indulged in an affair, one that had gone bad? Was she the kind of woman to take money from her workplace? Make up a story about rape?

No. Even though he'd only known her for a brief time, he knew she wasn't that kind of a woman. Granted, he couldn't deny that he felt a strong sense of physical attraction to her, but that didn't mean he didn't believe what she'd told him. That couldn't take away the likelihood that tonight Brandon Sinclair had set a fire, then had tried to kill them both. Those weren't the actions of a man who had nothing to hide.

Dalton had no doubt that the sheriff was behind what had happened. But knowing and proving were two different things and until he had proof, he wasn't going to tell his brother anything. He stretched out on the sofa and listened to the quiet.

He should be thrilled. He finally had his place to himself again. He was blessedly alone, just the way he liked it. No fuzzy baby, no soft female voice singing lullabies. So why did it suddenly seem far too quiet?

* * *

She thought she might scream. It was too quiet. Janette sat at the kitchen table in the little cabin sipping a cup of hot tea. It was just after eight, but there was no morning sun shining through the windows. The skies were as gray as her mood.

Sinclair knew she was in Cotter Creek. He'd be looking for her. He also knew she'd been with Dalton, so he'd be watching Dalton's every move, waiting to see if Dalton eventually led him to her. How long would it take before he'd think that she might be holed up on the West property?

She wrapped her hands around the mug, seeking the warmth to banish the chill inside her. The short night had seemed to last forever. Sleep had been impossible even though she'd eventually gotten into bed and tried to rest.

Her mind had whirled, trying to process the events that had brought her to the small cabin, and each thought was tinged with an underlying fear. Would *he* find her there? Would *he* somehow be able to ferret out where Dalton had stashed her? She was all alone, without a weapon except the knife she carried.

She'd finally gotten up and retrieved her knife from her purse, then had slid it beneath her pillow where it would be in easy reach should she need it. The night had held sounds that made her jump and had kept sleep at bay.

Releasing a deep weary sigh, she gazed out the window and took another sip of her tea. Would Sinclair be watching the bus stop, ready to pounce if she so much as showed her face?

How was she ever going to get out of town? Out of Dalton's life? Certainly he'd made it clear on more than one occasion that he didn't want to be responsible for anyone, that he preferred a life lived alone.

He probably couldn't wait to get her on her way. How long before he tired of this…of her? And when he got tired of the hassle, of the drama, it was possible he'd turn her in to Sinclair.

He wouldn't do that, the little voice inside her head protested. If he intended to do that he would have done so when the sheriff showed up on his doorstep.

The morning passed with her feeding and playing with Sammy and her thoughts alternating between worst and best case scenarios. After lunch when she put Sammy down for his nap and stretched out on the bed next to him, she wondered when Dalton would show up.

What if he never showed up? What if Sinclair murdered him? Her heart began to pound at the very idea. A new grief tore through her as she thought of the possibility.

Stop it, she commanded herself. Dalton had proven the night before that he was more than capable of taking care of himself. He was far too strong, too smart to get taken by surprise.

She must have fallen asleep, for the banging on the front door shot her up to a sitting position as her heart crashed against her ribs.

Who was at the door? It couldn't be Dalton. He had a key. Had Sinclair found her? Was he out there now waiting for her to come to the door? She pulled her knife from beneath her pillow and gripped it tightly in her hand.

She slid out of bed and crept to the doorway, unable to see the front door from her vantage point. Her throat narrowed as her breathing came in half-panicked gasps.

There was a phone in the living room, but she couldn't get to it without the person at the front door seeing her.

Once again the sounds of a fist against the door filled the cabin. "Janette, open the door. Dalton sent me." It was a female voice and some of Janette's panic dissipated.

Still clutching the knife, afraid of a trick, she walked cautiously to the door. Peering out she saw a woman with shoulder-length riotous red hair standing on the porch, a grocery bag in her arms.

Janette unlocked the front door and pulled it open only an inch, just enough to see the friendly brown eyes of the woman. "Who are you?" she asked.

"I'm Savannah—Savannah West—and I have some groceries for you."

Janette opened the door and Savannah flew past her on a burst of cold air and with enough energy to light up the entire cabin. Janette relocked the front door then hurriedly followed Savannah into the kitchen.

"I hope you're planning on peeling an apple," Savannah said dryly and looked pointedly at the knife still clutched in Janette's hand.

A blush warmed Janette's cheeks as she set the knife down on the counter. "So, you're Dalton's sister? I'm sorry, but I can't remember the names of everyone even though he mentioned them."

"Sister-in-law," Savannah said as she began to take items out of the bag. "I'm married to Joshua, the youngest of the bunch."

"Is Dalton not coming?"

"Maybe later. He was worried about being followed so he called me." Savannah's brown eyes radiated sympathy. "He told me what's going on and asked for my help. Don't worry, I won't tell anybody you're here." She pulled a package of disposable diapers from the bag. "Is your baby sleeping?"

Janette nodded. "So what exactly did Dalton tell you?"

"That you were in trouble, that he was keeping you hidden here until you both can figure out the next step. You want to put these in the freezer or refrigerator or wherever you want them?" She pulled out two small packages of hamburger and a wrapper of deli meat.

"How about you make a pot of coffee while I finish unloading these things," Savannah suggested. "Then we can have a nice chat."

Janette readily complied, grateful to have somebody to talk to, somebody to break up the silence that had plagued her since Dalton had left.

Within minutes the groceries were put away and the two women sat at the table with fresh coffee. "I'm so grateful to have somebody to talk to," Janette said. "The silence was really starting to get to me."

Savannah smiled. "Joshua would tell you that silence never bothers me. If I don't have anyone to talk to then I'm perfectly satisfied to talk to myself."

Janette returned her smile, deciding at that moment that she liked Savannah West. "How long have you been married?"

"Only three months. We're practically newlyweds, but at the moment he's off in New York. He flew up last week to do a job for a friend and should be coming home sometime later this week. I can't wait for him to get back to me."

For the next few minutes Savannah told her about

leaving Arizona and settling in Cotter Creek. She'd met her husband-to-be when a mutual friend of theirs had been murdered and the two had put their heads together to investigate a land scandal taking place in the small town.

"Are the West men all so…so…"

"Handsome? Strong? Stubborn?" Savannah laughed. "All of the above. They're good people, the whole West clan." She sobered. "You can trust Dalton. He's quiet and reserved, but he's a good man."

Janette nodded. "Are you a stay-at-home wife?"

"Heavens, no. I bought the local newspaper not long ago and most days I'm either writing news stories or editing to get out the daily newspaper."

"I appreciate you taking time off to come here."

"I'd do anything for Dalton, for any of the Wests, but I have to admit I was also curious when he explained everything to me. Consider it my reporter nose for news."

Janette shot up straighter in her chair, heartbeat quickening. "But you can't print anything. I don't want any of this to get out. If you even breathe a word of this to anyone you could put my life, my son's life, in danger."

"Relax," Savannah said. "I'm one of those rare birds, a reporter with ethics. I would never do anything to put you and your son at risk. But, I do have a few questions to ask you."

Tension twisted Janette's stomach. "Questions about what?"

"About Brandon Sinclair."

Janette got up from the table to pour herself another cup of coffee. "Why would you want to know anything about him?" She remained standing by the counter, certain that she didn't want to have this conversation.

"Because I intend to do a little investigative reporting on my own and see what I can find out about this creep," Savannah said.

Janette returned to sit at the table. She set her cup to the side and grabbed one of Savannah's hands. "Please, please don't do that. If he finds out you're asking questions about him, he'll hurt you."

Savannah squeezed Janette's hand and offered her a reassuring smile. "Believe me, the last thing I want is for Brandon Sinclair to have me in his sights." She released Janette's hand. "I'm very good at what I do and he'll never know I'm gathering facts about him."

"Why would you even want to get involved in all this?" Janette asked.

Savannah leaned back in her chair, her brown eyes contemplative. "From everything I've ever heard about sexual predators, they don't just indulge their ugly impulses once then never do it again. My guess is that you probably weren't the first victim of Brandon Sinclair and you won't be the last."

"I'm sure you're right," Janette said softly.

Savannah leaned forward. "You know something about another victim? Have you heard rumors? Sandstone is a very small town, surely somebody whispered something about the good sheriff."

Janette shook her head. "I never heard anything specific, but I suspected that one of the waitresses I worked with at the café might have had a run-in with Sheriff Sinclair."

"What made you suspect that?"

Janette reached back in her memory to the painful days just after her rape. She'd spent the days trying to act normal, trying to pretend that the terrible violation hadn't taken place. But she'd been desperate to talk to somebody, to anybody.

"Right after it happened to me, I asked Alicia if she'd ever been pulled over for a speeding ticket by Sheriff Sinclair. She said no, but there was an expression in her eyes that made me think she was lying. When I pressed her about it she told me to back off and the next day she quit the job."

"You said her name was Alicia. Alicia what?"

"Alicia Patterson, but she won't tell you anything. Everyone in Sandstone is afraid of him," Janette exclaimed and her throat tightened up a bit. She felt as if things were spinning out of control.

Savannah offered her a reassuring smile. "Too bad for him I'm not from Sandstone."

"Please, don't do this for me."

"I'm not," she replied easily. "I'm doing it for every young woman who lives in Sandstone and the surrounding areas." She finished her coffee and stood. "Don't worry, I know how to be invisible when I need to be and somebody needs to step up. I want to get the goods on this guy and put him away."

"I just want to *get* away," Janette said, more to herself than to Savannah.

She walked Savannah to the front door and on impulse gave her a hug. "Thank you for the groceries and for the talk."

Savannah pulled her hood up and opened the door. "I'm sure we'll see each other again."

Janette watched from the doorway as Savannah got into her car and pulled away. She closed and locked the door and leaned her head against the wood.

Somebody needs to step up.

Sammy began to cry from the bedroom, having awakened from his nap. She hurried into the room and his tears instantly transformed into a watery grin. She picked him up and cuddled him close.

Somebody needs to step up.

"Not me," she whispered. With the weight of her son in her arms, she fought back tears. "Not me," she said more forcefully.

Chapter 8

It was dusk when Dalton pulled up to the cabin. It had been a long tense day. He'd spent most of the day in his apartment, staring out the window, watching for Sinclair and thinking.

He'd set in motion a quiet investigation into Sinclair, enlisting both Savannah and his brother Tanner's aid. As the eldest of the brood, Tanner was not only the most levelheaded of the bunch, but also a whiz with computers.

By morning Tanner would know everything there was to know about Brandon Sinclair. He'd know where he shopped, where he ate, how much he had in his bank account and if there had ever been a complaint filed against the man.

He hadn't told Tanner anything about Janette and Sammy. He'd only said that he was doing a favor for a friend and needed to keep it quiet, especially from Zack.

What had surprised him more than anything during the day was how he'd noticed Janette and Sammy's absence. The quiet of his apartment had never bothered him before, rather he'd relished it. But, today, the quiet hadn't felt good. It had felt lonely. And that had irritated him.

As he shut off his truck engine, the front door opened and she stepped just outside and greeted him with a beautiful smile. Tension instantly built inside him. She looked gorgeous in a pair of jeans and a lavender sweatshirt, and her bright smile only added to her beauty.

He got out and walked to the back of the truck, picked up an oversized wooden cradle, then carried it toward where she stood.

"I thought Sammy might be able to use this while you're here," he said as she held open the door to allow him inside. He set the cradle on the living-room floor. "I know the bed in the bedroom is pretty small, especially by the time you surround Sammy with pillows. I figured this would be more comfortable for both of you."

She knelt down next to the cradle and looked up at him, those Oklahoma sky-blue eyes of hers shining brightly as she ran her hand over the rich wood. "It's beautiful. Where did you get it?"

"It was packed in a shed. It hasn't been used since Joshua was a baby."

"So it's a family heirloom."

"Yeah, I guess." The cabin smelled of lemon furniture polish and that evocative scent of honeysuckle. "You've been cleaning," he observed, noting that all the furniture gleamed with a new sheen.

She stood. "I got bored and found some furniture polish under the kitchen sink."

"Sammy sleeping?"

"I just put him down." She ran a loving hand over the cradle once again. "I think I'll clean this up and move him into it."

As she disappeared into the kitchen, Dalton sat on the sofa. She was in a good mood now, but he had a feeling she wouldn't be in such a good mood when he told her what was on his mind.

She returned with the bottle of furniture polish and a rag and sat on the floor to begin the cleanup on the cradle. "I like your sister-in-law," she said as she worked.

"I know you didn't want me to tell anyone, but I knew I might need some help since Sinclair might be watching my place."

She looked at him worriedly. "Do you think he was watching when you left tonight?"

Dalton shook his head. "He's back in Sandstone."

"How do you know that?"

"I called his office and he answered the phone." Dalton leaned back against the sofa cushions. "He can't stay in Cotter Creek all day and night. He has a job and a family in Sandstone. He can't spend every waking hour hunting you down."

"Thank God for small favors, right?"

It took her only minutes to finish cleaning off the cradle. She folded several thick bath towels into the bottom of it, making a nice soft mattress for Sammy.

She left to get Sammy and Dalton drew a deep breath. Her scent eddied in the air and evoked memories of that single kiss they had shared, a kiss he wouldn't mind repeating even though he knew he was all kinds of a fool to even think about it.

Sammy didn't stir from his sleep as she gently laid him in the cradle and covered him with another towel. She stood and smiled down at him, her smile so soft, so loving, Dalton felt it in the center of his chest.

"You want some coffee or something?" she asked.

"No, I'm fine. But I would like to talk to you." He sat on the sofa and patted the space next to him.

She eyed him warily but sat, close enough that he could smell her fragrance, but not close enough to touch in any way. "Talk about what?" Her eyes were darker blue than they had been moments before.

"About bringing Brandon Sinclair to justice." He leaned back against the cushion. "I know the special prosecutor in Oklahoma City. His name is Trent Cummings and it's his job to prosecute elected officials, like sheriffs, who break the law. I intend to contact him about Sinclair."

She nodded slowly, her expression guarded. "Good. Somebody needs to stop him before he hurts more women."

"What we need if we're going to stop him is cold hard evidence and that's where you come in."

Her eyes narrowed slightly. "I don't have any evidence," she protested. Her entire body tensed and she appeared to shrink back from him, becoming smaller and looking more vulnerable.

"You are the evidence," he said, trying not to be affected by her obvious discomfort. "You and Sammy, especially Sammy. His DNA confirms that Sinclair is his father."

Her eyes flashed darkly. "But that doesn't prove he raped me. That just proves we had sex." Her voice was an octave higher than usual and she jumped up from the sofa as if unable to stand sitting next to him another minute longer. "Don't you see? He'll just tell everyone we had an affair. Nobody will ever take my word over his. He's the 'good and noble' sheriff and I'm 'uneducated trailer trash'. Nobody will believe me."

Her chest heaved and her hands clenched into fists at her sides. "Stop saying you're uneducated trailer trash," he said with more than a touch of irritation. "That might be Brandon Sinclair's definition of you, but it sure isn't mine."

"Have you forgotten that he probably has an arrest warrant for me?"

"No, I haven't forgotten," he said. "But he can't make a murder charge stick without a dead body, and we both know your nana is alive and well."

"He can still arrest me on theft charges, or maybe arson, or whatever he decides to conjure up."

"And he tried to kill us last night. He needs to be stopped."

Her eyes flashed once again. "And we can't prove that it was him who set the fire or shot at us last night. And you can bet he's already got a solid alibi set up for the time of the shooting."

She drew a deep breath and her hands slowly unclenched. "Look, I appreciate what you're trying to do, but I just want to get out of here. I intend to be on the next bus out of town, with or without your help."

"And you intend to spend the rest of your life looking over your shoulder? Wondering if and when he's going to find you? Wouldn't you rather stand and fight and stop him from raping other women?"

Her eyes filled with the sheen of tears. "Please, don't ask me to stay."

"But that's exactly what I'm asking of you," he said softly. "Stay and fight. Help us put him away." He stood to face her.

"It's so easy for you to ask that of me." For the first time a hint of anger deepened her voice and hardened her eyes. "You've probably never had to face anything alone. You have this great big wonderful family to support you in whatever decisions you make. You've never been poor and powerless and all alone."

Her anger rose with each word that left her mouth. "It's easy for you because if things go badly you lose nothing. You go back to your quiet, solitary life and never think about me or Sammy again."

"That's not true," he protested. He had a feeling no matter what happened here and now, it was going to be a very long time before he could forget Janette and her little boy.

He took two steps toward her. "Janette, you won't be alone in this. I'll be right by your side. I've got my brother Tanner checking into Sinclair's background. Savannah is going to try to touch base with the waitress you said might have been another victim."

She backed away from him, tears once again shining in her eyes, but he pressed on. "Don't you want to stand up and put this man behind bars where he belongs? Wouldn't you sleep better at night if you knew he wasn't someplace out on the streets? Maybe hunting you down?"

"You and your sister-in-law and brother can do whatever you think is right, but I intend to be on the first bus out of here." She flew into the bedroom and closed the door after her.

Dalton released a sigh of frustration. He understood

her fear, sympathized with it, but he knew she was their best chance in taking down Brandon Sinclair. And he was determined to do just that.

Janette sat on the edge of the bed, her entire body trembling with emotion. Fear, regret and a burning shame all coursed through her.

Somebody needs to step up.

The words haunted her, playing and replaying in her mind like the refrain from an irritating melody that refused to be forgotten.

Somebody needs to step up.

She closed her eyes as a vision of Alicia Patterson filled her head. She remembered vividly the whisper of horror that had filled her eyes when Janette had asked her if she'd ever been pulled over by Sheriff Sinclair. She'd recognized that horror because she'd lived it and it had become an unwanted part of her.

Rubbing her temple where a headache had begun to pound, she tried to banish the vision of Alicia from her mind but it refused to completely go away. How many others had there been? How many more would there be?

He needed to be stopped.

Somebody needs to step up.

None of the women who had been abused by Sinclair were likely to look for a way to bring him to justice. They would feel the same hopeless helplessness that she'd felt. Stuck in a town where the sheriff was king, it was impossible for a mere vulnerable isolated woman to stand up against him.

But she was no longer in Sandstone. She was one step ahead of those women, for she'd already escaped the evil king's kingdom. And she wasn't all alone. She had Dalton standing beside her.

Do the right thing, that little voice whispered in her head. She'd tried to live her life always choosing to do the right thing. When Nana had gotten sick, the right thing for Janette to do had been to quit school to take care of her. When she'd discovered she was pregnant, for her, making the choice to give Sammy life had been the right thing to do.

And stopping Sheriff Brandon Sinclair from preying on any other women was the right thing to do. She got up from the bed, a bone-weariness weighing down her feet as she walked back to the door.

The idea of what she was about to agree to terrified her, but for the first time since that horrible night on the deserted highway, a rage began to build inside her.

Brandon Sinclair had not only raped her. He'd also tried to kill Nana, and last night had tried to shoot an innocent man. It hadn't been safe before this moment to get angry, because while she'd been a resident in Sandstone, anger had been an emotion she couldn't afford.

As she swung open the door and walked back into the living room, the anger flowed, rich and thick and righteous through her veins. Dalton sat on the sofa, but he stood when she came back into the room.

"All right," she said, her voice trembling with the raw emotion. "I'll stick around. I'll talk to your special prosecutor. I'll do whatever it takes to destroy Sinclair, but I have a few requests of my own."

"Like what?" Dalton sat back down and she joined him on the sofa.

"I want Nana out of Sandstone. Sooner or later he is

going to find out that she didn't burn up in that trailer. He'll find her, and we can't let that happen."

Dalton nodded. "We can pick her up and bring her here."

She would have loved to have her nana here in this little cabin with her, but she shook her head. "No, I don't want her here. I want her someplace where she'll be safe if this goes bad."

Dalton frowned thoughtfully. "West Protective Services owns a safe house in Kansas City. We could set her up there for the time being," Dalton said. "I can make arrangements with my sister, Meredith, to meet her plane and get her settled in."

"I have one other thing to ask of you." The pounding in her head intensified and she raised a hand to press her cold fingers against her temple. The anger that had filled her dissipated, usurped by a new well of grief.

"What?" he asked, his voice a soft caress. "What else do you need?"

She closed her eyes for a moment and a picture of Sammy's little face filled her head, his downy dark hair above laughing blue eyes and that grin of his that had the capacity to melt her heart.

She opened her eyes and stared at Dalton with intensity. "If something happens to me, if I end up in jail or worse, you have to promise me that you'll take Sammy. You'll hide him where Sinclair will never get hold of him." She reached out and grabbed hold of Dalton's forearm. "You have to promise me that you'll keep him safe, that you'll never allow that man to get custody of him."

Dalton took her hand between his, surrounding her cold fingers with warmth. "Nothing is going to happen to you. You're going to be fine, and you and Sammy are going to have a wonderful life with your nana."

"But you can't promise that."

His eyes darkened slightly. "No, I can't promise that," he admitted. "We'll do everything we can to make sure that all of you are safe. I know how difficult this decision is for you, and I know it probably doesn't matter to you, but I'm proud of you and admire your courage."

She realized it did matter to her, that she cared about what he thought of her. She cared more than she thought possible, but she wasn't satisfied yet. "You have to promise me that you'll take care of Sammy if something happens to me. That's the only way I can go forward with this."

The gravity of his expression let her know he wouldn't take this vow lightly. "Okay, I promise," he replied.

She was surprised by the depth of relief that flooded through her. At least she wouldn't have to worry about Sammy ending up with Sinclair.

"So, what happens now?" she asked. His hands no longer warmed the chill that resided deep inside her.

"First thing in the morning I'll call Trent and we'll set up a meeting with him, then I'll make arrangements to get your nana out of Sandstone. We'll see what Savannah and Tanner found out about Sinclair and hope that they can get us something to help make a case."

"Are you going to tell Zack about all this?" she asked.

He frowned. "Not until we have some solid evidence to present to him."

"I know how much you don't like keeping secrets from him."

He nodded. "That's true, but in this particular case I think it's necessary."

A new cold wind blew through her. "He'll know. Somehow Sinclair will find out that we're plotting against him. That's going to make him more dangerous than ever."

"Then we'll just have to be careful." He reached up and tucked a strand of her hair behind her ear.

At the moment she felt his gentle touch, she knew that she wanted to make love with him. She wanted...*needed* to make love with him in order to banish the memory of Sinclair's hands on her, his breath hot and sour on her face.

She knew it was crazy, that Dalton West was only a temporary man in her life. Eventually this would all be over and he'd get back to his uncomplicated private life and hopefully she'd get on with her life.

She wasn't fool enough to think that there might be a future with him. Nature had blown her into his life and danger kept her bound to him. But once the snow was gone and the danger had passed, it would be over.

But there was tonight and she felt the need for his warmth, for his gentleness. She felt the need for him. Even as her desire swelled inside her, she was suffused with doubt.

Would he even want her? Certainly she'd tasted hot desire in the single kiss they'd shared. Had that been a momentary flare of madness, or was it reflective of the fact that he might be attracted to her?

"You've gotten quiet. What are you thinking?" he asked.

She breathed in deeply and looked into his beautiful green eyes. Her mouth suddenly felt dry and a trembling began deep within her. "I think maybe I'd like some coffee after all," she said and jumped up off the sofa.

Don't be a fool, a voice whispered inside her head as she went into the kitchen. Making love with Dalton wouldn't make things better. It would only make things worse when she had to tell him goodbye.

As she fixed the coffee, he came into the kitchen and sat at the table. She was acutely aware of his presence, as if the very thought of making love with him had fine-tuned every one of her senses.

Once the coffee was dripping into the carafe, she joined him at the table. "I don't want to talk about Brandon Sinclair anymore," she said. "I don't even want to think about him. Tell me more about your family. Fill my head with something good and positive."

And he did. As they drank coffee he talked to her about his brothers and sister, sharing childhood memories that made her laugh, sharing moments that made her more than a little bit envious of the close-knit West clan.

Darkness fell, and as he finished his coffee he stood. Dread swooped through her. She knew he was preparing to leave.

"I should get back to town," he said.

She got up from the table, as well. "You could stay here for the night." She swallowed, her mouth once again too dry. "With Sammy in his new cradle, the bed is big enough for both of us." She held her breath.

His eyes flared wider and filled with a heat that swept over her, through her. "I'm not sure that's a good idea."

Emboldened by the look in his eyes, she stepped closer to him. "Why not?" Her heartbeat raced in her chest, this time not with fear, but with something even more primal.

"Because I don't think I can sleep in the same bed as you." His voice was deeper than usual.

"I don't kick and I don't think I snore." She took another step toward him.

"That wouldn't be the problem," he replied.

"Then what is the problem?" She stood so close to him she could feel his body heat radiate toward her, could see the gold flecks that gave depth to his green eyes.

"The problem is that it's been a long time since I've been with a woman and I find you incredibly attractive."

His words gave her permission to take a final step toward him. She now touched him, her breasts against the hard width of his chest. "And I find you incredibly attractive." She raised her hands to his shoulders and leaned into him, her face raised.

She saw the kiss in his eyes before he lowered his head to deliver it. When his lips took hers a fiery heat flooded through her veins and she welcomed it, welcomed him with open mouth.

He wrapped his arms around her and pulled her close...closer still. His arms felt like safety, like security, and she reveled in the sensations that coursed through her.

His tongue swirled with hers, creating a fire of want inside her. She knew exactly what to expect, a night of passion satisfied and nothing more. At this moment it was enough.

When he broke the kiss she took his hand and led him into the bedroom. Although she didn't think it possible, her heartbeat raced even faster. She wanted this. She wanted him. But, she couldn't ignore a tiny sliver of disquiet that raised its ugly head.

The last time she'd had sex it had been a violent,

terror-filled event, and she wanted none of that experience to bleed over into this time with Dalton.

When they reached the bedroom he once again took her into his arms and kissed her. The kiss was long and deep, and as he kissed her his hands caressed her back.

She loved the feel of his hard chest, his firm thighs and his obvious arousal against her. He held her tight, but not so tight that she felt captive...helpless.

This time when the kiss ended, her fingers trembled as she unbuttoned his shirt. He stood motionless, as if holding his breath as she pulled the shirt from his chest.

Only then did he move away from her. He walked to the side of the bed and placed his gun, his cell phone and his wallet on the nightstand, then turned to face her. "Are you sure about this?" His voice vibrated with tension.

Instead of answering him with words, she pulled her sweatshirt off over her head and dropped it to the floor beside her.

His eyes glowed in the semidarkness of the room and her breath caught in her throat as his hands moved to the waist of his jeans and he unfastened the button fly.

As he took off his jeans she did the same. Then, with only the aid of the moonlight filtering through the window, they got into the bed.

Instantly he pulled her back into his arms as his lips found hers once again. His delicious skin warmed hers as his mouth took possession of her lips.

It felt right. It felt good, and it didn't matter what tomorrow would bring. Whatever happened, wherever she ended up building her life, she'd have the memory of this kind and good man to carry with her.

They lay side by side facing each other and his lips left hers and rained nipping kisses down her neck to the hollow of her throat. She tangled her fingers in his thick hair as his hands caressed her breasts through the thin material of her bra.

It didn't take long before she wanted to feel the palm of his hands against her naked breasts. She reached behind her and unfastened her bra, loving the deep moan that escaped him as she tossed it to the floor. Within minutes the last of their clothing was gone and their touches grew more intimate.

It wasn't until he moved on top of her that the first stir of panic closed her throat.

His breath was warm against her neck, his body not surrounding her so much as imprisoning her. Just like before.

Hot breath.

Hard body.

Trapped.

She squeezed her eyes tightly closed, fighting the overwhelming sense of dread, trying to catch her breath as the panic fired higher inside her. This wasn't Sinclair, and they weren't on the side of the road. There was no gun pressed to her throat, no reason for her heart to pound so painfully hard.

Dalton seemed unaware of the torment that had unexpectedly stolen passion and exchanged it for dark flashbacks to the worst night of her life. As he kissed her neck, she fought the scream that worked up from the depths of her.

He was suffocating her, his weight oppressive and scary. She couldn't move, had lost control. She couldn't breathe. Unable to stand it another minute she shoved against his chest. "I'm sorry. I can't do this. Please, get off me. Get off me!"

He instantly rolled to the side of her as she burst into tears.

Chapter 9

"I'm sorry. I'm so sorry," Janette cried into the pillow next to Dalton.

"It's okay," he said even as he fought to get control of himself. "It's all right, Janette. We don't have to do anything you don't want to do." Tentatively he reached out and touched her back, trying to comfort but afraid of frightening her.

It was obvious what had just happened, and his heart clenched with her pain. Brandon Sinclair should be stood before a firing squad for what he'd done to her, for the scars he'd left behind.

She didn't move away from his touch so he continued to rub her back and tell her it was okay. He tried not to notice the sexy curve of her back or the sweet scent that emanated from her warm skin.

Slowly her tears dried, but she still kept her face

buried in the pillow, as if afraid to turn over and look at him.

"Janette, I'm not mad. Come on, turn over and look at me."

"How can you not be mad? Women who do what I just did to you are called a terrible name."

"There's a difference between women who get off on the power of playing a man and a woman who is suffering post-traumatic stress. I promise you I'm not mad."

She finally rolled over, the sheet clutched to her chest as she faced him. He leaned up on one elbow and smiled down at her. "It's okay, really."

She reached a hand up and touched the underside of his jaw. "How did you get to be such a nice man, Dalton West?"

"Trust me, at the moment I'm not feeling like such a nice guy. I'd like to find Brandon Sinclair and torture him slowly for a very long time." He started to roll out of the bed but she caught him by the arm.

"Don't go," she said softly. "Can't we just lay here and talk for a little while?"

She had no idea what she was asking of him. Blood still surged thick and hot through his veins. He was a man, not a saint, but maybe if he didn't touch her again he could stand remaining next to her.

He rolled over just long enough to turn on the lamp on the nightstand, then turned back to face her.

"Would it help to talk about that night?" he asked gently.

"No. I was doing fine until you got on top of me." Her cheeks turned pink and she averted her gaze from his. "It wasn't until then that I had a flashback. With you on top of me I felt trapped…like I was suffocating…like I did that night with Sinclair."

"That will teach me to try to be in control," he said with a forced lightness.

She looked at him. "Maybe if I stay in control it will be okay. I mean, my head and my heart want to make love with you, it was just in that last minute that everything went wrong."

"Maybe we should both just try to get some sleep," he countered. He wasn't sure he could go through the same thing again and not get relief. His body still ached with the need she'd wrought inside him.

He tensed as she reached over and stroked a hand across his chest. Instantly desire fired through him. Her fingers curled in his chest hair, then uncurled and moved down lower.

As she wrapped her fingers around him more intimately he hissed in a breath. She was trying to kill him with pleasure. "Janette," he said, the word more a plea than a protest as he'd intended.

"Just…just let me," she replied, her voice husky and deep.

Dalton had always been an active participant when he made love to a woman, but as she stroked him he remained on his back, not moving to touch her in any way.

She leaned forward and pressed her lips against his chest, and that coupled with her warm hand surrounding him nearly undid him. He hung on to control by a thread.

She moved her lips up his chest to capture his in a fiery kiss. Her breathing increased, and when she raised her head to look at him he saw the glaze of want in her eyes.

The most difficult thing he'd ever done was to remain

passive. He wanted to reach up for her, take her into his arms. He wanted to taste her skin, feel the soft weight of her breasts, but he remained unmoving, allowing her to stay in total control.

Her naked body gleamed in the lamplight and her blond hair glistened as it fell forward, the tips trailing across his chest in added torment.

Her nipples were out and he fought the impulse to lean up and capture one in his mouth. Although he wanted to touch her, there was something unbelievably erotic in allowing her to make love to him on her own terms.

It wasn't until she moved to get on top of him that he finally spoke. "There's a condom in my wallet," he managed to gasp.

She left him just long enough to open his wallet and retrieve the foil packet inside. She opened the packet and rolled the protection into place. He moaned with pleasure as she eased onto him, her sleek legs on either side.

He closed his eyes, knowing that if he continued to look at her he'd lose control too quickly. Her warmth gripped him tight as she rocked against him.

Her breaths came in quick pants and when he looked at her again her eyes were tightly closed and an expression of intense bliss shone on her features.

She moved faster and then she gasped and cried out his name. That was all it took. Dalton's release came in an explosion that rocked him to his very core. It was only then that he touched her. He cupped her face with his hands and drew her down for a kiss.

She melted against him, her body warm against his, her lips sweet and yielding. When they finished kissing she rolled off him and to her back.

"Thank you," she said softly.

A small burst of laughter escaped him. "Don't thank me. That was absolutely amazing." He rolled off the bed. "Don't move, I'll be right back."

He padded into the bathroom to clean up. Once alone, he thought about what had just happened and the fact that it shouldn't have.

She was getting to him. Oh, but she was getting into places inside him that he hadn't allowed anyone in for a very long time. And that scared him. That scared the hell out of him.

This situation...*she* was temporary. He'd sworn to himself that he would never again put himself in the position to help heal a woman so she could move on and fall in love with another man.

He'd sworn to himself he'd never again be a temporary hero for any woman, and yet wasn't that exactly his role in this case? If he were smart he'd go back into the bedroom, get dressed and get the hell away from her.

But the moment he reentered the bedroom, all thoughts of leaving fled his head. She gave him that smile of hers, the one bright enough to light up the room, and patted the empty side of the bed.

"I hope you aren't one of those men who fall immediately to sleep after sex," she said.

No, he was the type of man who felt the need to run for the door and escape. Not exactly the actions of a gentleman. He slid back beneath the sheets.

"Are you accustomed to men who fall asleep after sex?" he asked teasingly.

She plumped the pillows behind her head and sat up,

the sheet clutched modestly at her neck. "I've only had one real long-term relationship and, yes, he used to fall asleep."

He rolled over on his side to face her and propped himself up on his elbow. "Is that why you aren't with him anymore?"

She grinned, looking incredibly sexy with her hair tousled and her full lips still slightly swollen from his kisses. "No. He worked as a rehab nurse and I met him when Nana needed rehabilitation after her stroke. We dated for almost a year." She pulled her knees up to her chest and wrapped her arms around them, her features contemplative. "He got a job offer from a hospital in Indianapolis and moved there."

"He didn't ask you to go with him?"

"No. I think he knew I wouldn't go, that I couldn't leave Nana. It wasn't a great love affair. It was pleasant and nice while it lasted, but after he was gone I realized I wasn't deeply, madly in love with him."

"And that's important to you? To be deeply, madly in love?" he asked.

She flashed him that brilliant smile of hers. "Of course. I think it's what every woman wants, among other things."

"And what other things do you want?" He tried to tell himself that he really didn't care, that he was just trying to hold up his end of the conversation. But deep inside he knew that wasn't true. He wanted to know her desires, her wants, the very dreams that drove her.

"A home, security. I want a job that I love and to be able to provide Sammy with things and opportunities I didn't have. I want to be able to afford to order pizza whenever I want it. Oh, yeah, and world peace."

He laughed and she unclasped her hands from around her knees and stretched out on her side facing him. "Now tell me about the women in your past."

"There's nothing to tell. I've had a few relationships, but nothing too serious. I've told you before, I like living alone, being alone." He needed to remind himself as much as her of this fact.

At that moment Sammy began to cry from the living room. He watched as she slid from the bed, grabbed a robe from the nearby chair and pulled it on. "I'll be right back. Don't go away."

As she left the room Dalton rolled on his back and stared up at the ceiling. The feeling returned—the need to run, to escape. Not just from Janette, but from the whole situation. He'd talked her into agreeing to stick around, to help them bring Brandon Sinclair to justice.

The man was dangerous and until they could get the evidence they needed to put him behind bars, he was a threat to Janette's very life.

He felt fairly confident having her here at the cabin. Deep on West property, the cabin was known only by a few. The ranch hands would certainly notice a stranger wandering the property and would demand an explanation of his presence.

Still, if anything happened to her or to Sammy, Dalton would feel responsible for the rest of his life. He hoped he hadn't made a mistake in talking her into staying and fighting, because it could be a mistake with deadly consequences.

Janette stopped in the kitchen to fix Sammy a bottle and carried it into the living room. The minute he saw her he stopped fussing. He'd drink this bottle then would sleep through the night.

She changed his diaper, then carried him back into the bedroom and sat on the edge of the bed to give him the bottle. She was conscious of Dalton's gaze on her as she looked down at her son. "He makes me want to be better than I am," she said. She looked at Dalton. "That's what kids do for you." Sammy grinned at Dalton around the bottle nipple, as if punctuating her sentence.

For a few minutes they were silent, the only sound Sammy greedily drinking his formula. Janette's head was filled with myriad emotions. Love for her son tangled with an underlying fear of what lay ahead and, as she cast a surreptitious glance to Dalton, other less easily defined emotions rose up inside her.

Certainly gratitude filled her heart, not just for what he'd done in taking her in and keeping her safe, but also for allowing her to reclaim a piece of herself, a piece she'd thought forever broken.

"You gave me back my life tonight," she said to Dalton.

He raised a dark eyebrow. "Don't you think that's a little dramatic?"

"No, I don't," she countered. "I didn't think I'd ever be able to experience joy in lovemaking again. I thought my experience with Sinclair had destroyed that part of me. You showed me tonight that he didn't."

She frowned thoughtfully, remembering those moments of sudden panic when Dalton had moved on top of her. "I know it's going to take time before all the trauma of Sinclair is gone, but tonight definitely went a long way in my healing process."

"You'll be fine," he assured her. "Someday you'll find the man who can give you all the things you want from life."

She smiled. "I don't need a man to give me all the things I want. I intend to go out and get them. But, it would be nice to have somebody to share it all with."

She looked back down at Sammy. She had the feeling Dalton had said what he had to remind her that he wasn't the man for her. He didn't have to bother.

Even though she realized her heart was getting hopelessly involved with him, she knew better than to expect a happy ending. He'd made his position perfectly clear and she didn't expect that to change.

"Once Sinclair is in jail, do you intend to return to Sandstone?" he asked.

"To be honest, I haven't had enough time to think about it." She glanced back down at Sammy. The trailer they'd called home was gone. "There's really nothing left for us there except bad memories. If you're putting Nana in a safe place in Kansas City, then maybe that's the place where we should start over."

Sammy had fallen back to sleep, his bottle empty and his belly full. "You want me to bring the cradle in here?" Dalton asked.

"Do you mind?"

He got up and pulled on his briefs, then left the room. As he exited, she couldn't help the flutter of heat that swept through her at the sight of his near-nakedness. He had a physique that most men would envy and most women would want. And she wanted him again.

It surprised her, the healthy burst of lust that filled her. She hadn't thought about sex in over a year, but one time with Dalton and suddenly her head was filled with lustful thoughts.

And there was nothing more sexy than a man in briefs carrying a cradle, she thought as he returned to the room. He set the cradle on the floor on her side of the bed, then got back beneath the sheets.

She got up and put Sammy back into the cradle, then got back into bed next to Dalton. He turned off the lamp and the room was plunged into darkness with just a faint cast of moonlight dancing shadows on the walls.

Closing her eyes, she tried not to think about what she'd agreed to do by staying here. Even if the bus pulled up in Cotter Creek tomorrow, she wouldn't get on it.

A sliver of fear iced through her, chilling her to her bones. What if the special prosecutor didn't believe her story? Right now Sinclair could be manufacturing all kinds of evidence against her. He could bully anyone in town to say anything he wanted about her.

She fought the impulse to lean over and take Sammy from the cradle and hold him in her arms. She wanted to hold him tight, kiss his cheeks and smell his baby sweetness, because she had no idea if a time would come in the future when he'd be lost to her forever.

Dalton awoke first and found his arms filled with a warm, sleeping Janette. They were spoon fashion, him curled around her slender back. He drew in the scent of her, that floral perfume that enticed him.

It was only now, in this moment with her body warm against his and his defenses not erected that he could admit to himself that he'd grown to care about her more than he'd ever thought he'd care about a woman again in his life.

It was late. He could tell by the cast of the sun shining through the window that he'd slept longer than he'd intended. Of course, he hadn't drifted off to sleep until the wee hours of the morning.

He'd spent much of the night listening to Janette breathing peacefully in sleep and worrying about the decision he'd encouraged her to make. He now contemplated what he needed to accomplish that day because it was easier to focus on that rather than the feelings he had for Janette.

He needed to call Trent Cummings, the special prosecutor, and see when he could get the man out here to meet with Janette. He also needed to make arrangements to get Nana out of Sandstone and to the safe house in Kansas City.

Hopefully they could connect with Trent in the next day or so and get things rolling. He closed his eyes and breathed in Janette's scent.

In many ways she amazed him. He'd expected her to fight him about staying and seeking justice, he'd expected her to demand he put her on the next bus out of town. The fact that she'd agreed to stand and fight against Brandon Sinclair instead of running showed him the immense inner strength she possessed.

He knew he wasn't only getting too close to her, but she was getting too close to him, as well. Their relationship, such as it was, was built on forced proximity and circumstances beyond their control.

It had nothing to do with reality. He was a temporary measure of safety in her life, just as he'd been in Mary's. He rolled away from Janette and off the bed, glad that he didn't awaken her in the process.

He grabbed his clothes from the floor and padded into the bathroom. Minutes later, standing beneath a hot shower, he tried not to think about how her long legs had felt when she'd straddled him, how hot her mouth had been against his skin.

Brandon Sinclair had left scars inside her that would take time to heal, but Dalton felt certain that eventually Janette would be able to have a loving, passionate relationship with a special man.

He frowned, irritated by the fact that he didn't like the idea of Janette making love with another man.

By the time he was out of the shower and dressed, Janette was up and making coffee in the kitchen. Clad in her pink robe, she looked soft and utterly feminine and a renewed burst of desire hit Dalton hard in the stomach.

"I've got to get back to town," he said gruffly.

"Surely you can stay long enough to have coffee and some breakfast," she replied. "I was just going to make some scrambled eggs and toast."

"Okay," he conceded. "I've got a lot to do today. And you need to call your nana and tell her what's going on." He sat at the table. "I'll call you later with details and we can set up getting her moved as soon as possible."

"Good, that will make me feel better." She poured him a cup of coffee, set it in front of him then returned to the counter where she put two slices of bread into the toaster, then began to crack eggs into an awaiting bowl. Sammy began to fuss from the bedroom.

"Want me to get him?" Dalton asked, figuring he needed to go back in the bedroom to get his wallet and gun, anyway.

"Thanks, I'd appreciate it."

The minute Dalton entered the room, Sammy stopped his fussing and began to coo, as if attempting to tell Dalton something very important.

Dalton grabbed his wallet and shoved it into his back pocket, then tucked the gun into the back of his waistband and picked up the little boy.

Sammy wiggled in his arms and flung out a hand that promptly latched on Dalton's nose. "Hey, little buddy," Dalton whispered. "That's my nose." Sammy smiled in delight and Dalton's heart moved. This little boy had no idea that he was in the center of a storm, a storm that had the potential to see his mother either in jail or dead.

I can't let that happen, Dalton told himself. He had to summon every skill he possessed as a bodyguard in order to keep Janette safe until this was all over and she could begin a new life in whatever city she chose.

He carried Sammy back into the kitchen where Janette had already fixed a bottle for the little guy. As Dalton sat once again at the table with Sammy in his lap, she held the bottle out to him. "Do you mind?"

Dalton took the bottle and gave it to Sammy, who sucked greedily on the nipple. His innocent little blue eyes stared up at Dalton with intense concentration.

Dalton was shocked to realize if he wasn't careful Sammy would steal his heart completely and make him remember all the old dreams that he'd once possessed.

He refused to entertain those dreams again, especially with Janette and her son in a starring role. That would only lead to a new heartache and he wasn't interested.

By the time they finished breakfast it was after nine o'clock. With Sammy on a blanket in the living room,

Dalton picked up the phone and dialed the number for the special prosecutor's office in Oklahoma City.

It took him nearly fifteen minutes, but he was finally connected to his old friend Trent. He quickly explained the situation and was disappointed in Trent's reply.

"I definitely want to pursue this and talk to your friend, but there's no way I can get to Cotter Creek for at least a week. I'm in the middle of something here that I'm hoping to tie up in the next week to ten days."

Dalton frowned. He'd hoped to get Trent here a lot sooner…like the next day at the latest. "You'll call me if you get free sooner?"

"Definitely." The two men spoke for a few more minutes, then Dalton hung up.

"Is he coming?" Janette asked hopefully.

"Not for a week to ten days."

A look of panic swept over her features. "So long? What happens in the meantime?"

A new burst of tension twisted Dalton's guts. "In the meantime we can only hope that Brandon Sinclair doesn't discover where you are. You know how to shoot a gun?"

Her eyes widened. "No. Why?"

He pulled his gun from his waistband. "I'd feel better if I left this here with you."

"I wouldn't," she said flatly. She leaned back against the sofa, a troubled expression on her face. "As much as I hate him, as much as I fear him, I'm not sure I could shoot him." She looked from the gun to Dalton. "I don't know if I could really pull the trigger and kill somebody."

Dalton tucked the gun back into his waistband. He knew that a gun was only as effective as the person who held it. "Maybe I should have Tanner or one of my other brothers keep an eye on you."

"No, please. I feel safe here. There's no way Sinclair can know about this cabin and I'd rather nobody else know I'm here. It's been my experience that the more people keeping a secret, the more difficult the secret is to keep."

Dalton nodded, his head whirling. "When I get back to town I'm going to rent a room at the motel and I'll have one of my brothers sit on it. Maybe we can catch Sinclair breaking the law and put him behind bars before Trent ever gets here. If nothing else the ruse of the empty room might keep Sinclair focused on the idea that you're there."

"I'm all for any plan that keeps him as far away from me as possible," she replied.

"I'd better get moving," he said.

She got up and walked with him to the door and he fought the impulse to lean down and capture her lips before he left. Minutes later, as he headed back toward town, he could only hope that he could keep Brandon Sinclair at bay until Trent arrived in town.

Chapter 10

It snowed again late that afternoon and Dalton called Janette to tell her not only would the weather make it impossible for anyone to get to Nana, but also he wouldn't be coming to the cabin that night.

She was bitterly disappointed with the length of time it would take before she could talk to Trent Cummings, with the damnable winter weather that complicated everything, but more importantly with the fact that she wouldn't have Dalton's company for the evening.

Falling asleep the night before with him lying next to her had been heavenly. The very sound of his even breathing had made her feel safe and warm. Watching him give Sammy his morning bottle had stirred a wistful hope that she knew could only lead to disappointment.

For just a moment, as she'd scrambled eggs and Dalton had held Sammy in his arms, she'd wanted this life with him to last forever. With each moment she spent in Dalton's company it was getting easier and easier to imagine what life with him would be like.

And that was dangerous. Dozens of times he'd said in one way or another that he wasn't interested in a relationship. He had no desire to be a husband or a father. It was a shame, because she thought he would be wonderful at both.

She now stood at the living-room window and watched the snow falling in big fat flakes. She hoped it didn't snow too much. She didn't like the idea of being snowed in here all alone.

Sammy was taking a nap, the cabin was silent and she was restless, filled with an uneasy sense of impending doom. "It's just the snow," she said aloud, hoping the sound of her own voice would soothe her. It didn't.

But she knew what would make her feel better. She walked over to the sofa, curled up in one corner and picked up the telephone. She punched in Nancy's number, and the older woman answered on the second ring. "Nancy, it's me. May I speak to Nana?"

When Nana's voice came across the line Janette fought against a swell of emotion that momentarily clogged her throat. She hadn't spoken to her grandmother since the night Sinclair had shown up on Dalton's doorstep, and she realized now that she had so much to tell her.

"Are you still at Dalton West's apartment?" Nana asked.

"No, I'm in a little cabin on the West property." She explained about the sheriff showing up, about the fire and subsequent shooting.

"Nana, I'm not leaving. I've decided to stand and fight him."

There was a long moment of stunned silence. "You know I've always supported you in every decision you've made," Nana said. "And I'm proud of you for wanting to fight him, to bring him to justice. But, I'd be lying if I told you this is what I want for you. I'm scared for you, for Sammy. Are you sure you're making the right decision?"

Janette wanted to laugh. Was she sure? Definitely not. She was filled with trepidation and doubts. But despite her fear and doubts she was committed to doing what was right.

"Of course I'm nervous and afraid. But Dalton believes me. He believes my story and he knows a special prosecutor who handles cases like this. Nana, I don't want to spend the rest of my life looking over my shoulder, afraid that Sinclair will find me, will find us. I want him to pay for what he did to me."

A swell of anger tightened her chest. "Nana, I'm not sure I'll ever be whole if I don't do this."

"Baby, if this is what you need to do, then do it. You know I'll stand right beside you," Nana replied.

For the next few minutes Janette explained to her grandmother about moving to the safe house in Kansas City. "I'm not doing that," Nana argued with a touch of her legendary stubbornness. "I'm perfectly fine here with Nancy and I'm not going to go anywhere unless you're with me."

"But, Nana, I'd feel so much better if I knew for certain you were safe."

"Don't you worry about me none," she said. "I've got so many friends in this trailer park, that man will never be able to find me."

Janette wasn't surprised by her grandmother's vehemence in remaining where she was. She'd had a feeling she'd never be able to talk her into going to Kansas City.

"Janette, honey. I'll leave Sandstone when this is all over and the three of us can go someplace new, if that's what you want. But, in the meantime I'm staying put right here where I'm at least close enough to you to get to you in a half an hour."

"Somehow I had a feeling you'd say something like that," Janette said dryly.

"Do you trust this man? This Dalton West?"

"With my very life," Janette responded without a second thought. "More important, I trust him with Sammy's life."

"Then that's good enough for me."

"He's a wonderful man, Nana. He's smart and kind. He can make me laugh and he makes me feel smart and pretty."

"Don't you go getting your heart all twisted up in this," Nana warned softly. "Dalton is helping you bring a bad man to justice, but that doesn't mean he's making a place for you in his life."

"I'm aware of that." Hadn't she spent most of the morning reminding herself of that very fact?

The two talked for a few more minutes then finally Janette said goodbye and hung up. *Don't you go getting your heart all twisted up in this.* Nana's words whirled around and around in Janette's head.

It was too late for the warning. She got up from the sofa and walked once again to the window to stare out at the falling snow. Her heart was already twisted up with Dalton.

She wasn't sure how it had happened, that in the space of so few days her heart could get so tangled up. But she knew she was precariously close to falling completely and irrevocably in love with Dalton West.

She drew a deep sigh. This cabin was so isolated. She'd never known such darkness as that which came with nightfall here. Last night there had been the faint illumination of the moon. But tonight, with the clouds, there would be no moonlight, no star shine, just deep, impenetrable darkness. If Sinclair somehow found her here, nobody would even hear her scream.

Releasing another tense sigh, she stepped away from the window and paced the length of the living room. The evening stretched out before her, empty and lonely.

The living room had a television but Janette had never been much of a TV watcher. She thought about waking up Sammy, but decided that was the height of selfishness, to wake up her infant son because she was lonely and bored.

Maybe it was time for her to get out her book bag and do a little studying. She didn't intend to work as a waitress for the rest of her life, and the best way to get ahead was to get that GED.

She went into the bedroom and opened her suitcase. For several long moments she simply stared at the red book bag. She remembered vividly the last time she'd carried it out of the building where she'd been taking the classes.

Proud. She'd been so proud of herself for taking her future in her hands, for making the effort to change her life for the better. Now as she stared at the book bag all she could think about was what had happened on her way home that night.

As she carried the bag to the kitchen table she

realized Sheriff Sinclair hadn't just raped her body that night on the side of the road. He'd also raped her mind. He'd taken all her insecurities and thrown them in her face, telling her she was poor, stupid trailer trash.

Janette refused to allow Brandon Sinclair to define her. She'd been his victim for a brief period of time, but she wasn't a victim anymore.

With a new burst of determination she reached into the book bag and withdrew her notebook, a study guide and her mini-tape recorder.

She punched the rewind button on the tape recorder then opened the study guide to find the page she'd last worked on. She'd loved school and it didn't take her long to become totally absorbed in the work.

It was long after dark when she decided to fix herself a cup of tea. She punched on the tape recorder to hear the last lecture that she'd taped, then got up to heat some water for the tea.

"The United States constitution consists of a preamble, seven articles and twenty-six amendments." A pleasant female voice filled the room. Mrs. Rebecca Winstead had been the woman working to help adults achieve their GED. The last class Janette had attended had been going over the constitution.

"Over the next couple of nights we're going to be talking about the components that make up the document that is the supreme law of the land."

As Janette made her cup of tea, she listened to the tape, trying to absorb everything that might be important when she eventually took her test.

She carried her cup of tea to the table and at that moment Sammy awakened. She hurried into the bedroom. "Hey, little man." She picked up the smiling, wiggling boy and placed him on the bed to change his diaper. "Did you have a nice little nap?" she asked and efficiently took care of the wet diaper, replacing it with a clean one.

"Turn off your lights and get out of the car." The deep male voice boomed and Janette froze.

Sinclair. His familiar voice shot a stabbing panic through her. He was here! He'd found her! Wildly she looked around the room, trying to remember where she'd put her knife.

"Well, well, don't we look all sexy in that little skirt?"

She frowned, picked up Sammy and stepped back into the kitchen. The hated voice came from the small recorder in the center of the table.

She stared at the tiny machine as it continued to play the sounds of that night...the sounds of her rape. Somehow when she had reached into her book bag that night to retrieve her driver's license, she must have hit the record button.

Tears streamed down her cheeks as she hugged Sammy close.

They were tears of sorrow, for the innocent girl she'd been and tears of happiness because the tape was evidence, solid evidence that would put Brandon Sinclair behind bars for a very long time.

She started for the phone to call Dalton, to tell him the news, but halfway to the phone she changed her mind. She'd tell him tomorrow when he was here. It would be her surprise.

"We've got him, Sammy," she whispered, and for the first time since this all began, hope filled her up.

* * *

Dalton sat in the West Protective Services office and stared out the window. The snow that had fallen the day before hadn't been enough to create anything but minor problems and Main Street of Cotter Creek was back in business.

He'd called Janette first thing that morning to tell her he'd try to get to the cabin that evening. He'd come into the office in an attempt to keep his schedule as normal as possible. He didn't want anyone noticing that he was acting out of character until they had Brandon Sinclair in Trent Cummings' custody.

A room at the motel was now rented in his name and his brother Clay was sitting on it, watching for Sinclair to make a move. He'd told his brother only the minimum of information and that if he saw a man resembling the good sheriff trying to get into the room, he was to call Zack and Dalton.

He leaned back in his chair and frowned. He'd rather be at the cabin. He'd rather be with Janette and Sammy than sitting here wondering where Sinclair was now and what he might be doing.

Drumming his fingers against the desktop, he fought against a feeling of impending catastrophe. He had no idea why the disquiet roared so loudly in his head. He had a plan, he'd set it in motion and all they had to do was keep Janette hidden until Trent arrived in town.

Unless Sinclair knew the specific location of the cabin, Dalton couldn't imagine how he would find it, find her. Everything was under control, and yet he couldn't stop the worry that whispered through him. He wished Janette would have agreed to keep his gun. He wished she would have told him she was a sharpshooter in another lifetime.

It was just after noon when the door opened and Zack walked in. Following at his heels was Brandon Sinclair. Dalton narrowed his eyes.

If he'd been a dog his hackles would have risen. As it was, every muscle in his body tensed. He nodded to his brother but didn't get up from behind the desk.

"Dalton, I understand you and Sheriff Sinclair have met," Zack said. Dalton merely nodded.

Sinclair cleared his throat and stepped closer, a flyer in his hand. "I've been passing out these photos of the woman I've been looking for. Maybe you've seen her around town."

Brandon Sinclair had the eyes of a predator, ice-cold, and as he looked at Dalton they were filled with a silent challenge.

Dalton took the flyer from him, gave it a cursory glance then tossed it on the desk in front of him. "Sorry, haven't seen her."

"She's a bad one, Mr. West. I told your brother here, Janette Black is a danger to anyone she gets close to. I want to get her into custody before she harms anyone."

Dalton raised an eyebrow. "I thought you told me the other night that she had already hurt somebody. Didn't you tell me she'd killed her grandmother?"

Red splotches appeared in Brandon's cheeks. "We don't know for certain what's happened to her grandmother. Initially we thought she was in the fire that destroyed the trailer where she and Janette lived, but our investigation turned up no bodies."

"Then what exactly is it she's wanted for?" Dalton held Sinclair's gaze intently.

"She's wanted on a number of charges. Theft and drug trafficking for starters. There's also been a number of home invasions recently and we think she was involved in those."

"She's just a regular one woman crime spree," Dalton replied. Zack shot him a sharp glance. "Look, I told you the other night I hadn't seen her, and nothing has changed, so if you'll excuse me I've got work to do." He pointedly turned his chair to face the computer, effectively dismissing both his brother and Sinclair.

"I've got to get the rest of these flyers handed out," Sinclair said to Zack.

As the two men left the office Dalton picked up the flyer. The photo of Janette looked like a typical school photo. She looked younger and her hair was shorter. She'd said she'd had to quit high school her junior year. If he were to guess, this was probably the last school picture she'd had taken.

He still held the photo when the door opened and Zack came back in. He set the flyer aside. "I figured you'd be back."

Zack sat in the chair opposite the desk and studied his brother. "You want to tell me what's going on?"

"What makes you think anything is going on?" Dalton countered.

Zack's dark eyebrows pulled together in a frown and he leaned forward and thumped a finger in the center of the flyer. "You know something about this, about her. I know you do."

"What makes you think that?"

"Because I'm your brother, Dalton. I know when you're lying. Look, you don't want to put yourself in the middle between a lawman and a criminal. If you know anything about the whereabouts of this woman you need to tell me now."

"I've got nothing to tell you." Dalton leaned back in his chair. He hated lying to Zack, but until they connected with Trent Cummings he wasn't willing to share anything with his brother. As much as he didn't want to be between a lawman and his criminal, he didn't want Zack to be in the middle of a lawman and his own brother.

Zack leaned back in his chair and expelled a deep sigh, his gaze still on Dalton. "What's up with you lately?"

Dalton frowned. "What are you talking about?"

"It seems like for the last six months or more you've withdrawn from all of us, withdrawn from life. You stay holed up either in here or at your apartment. You don't visit anyone, you don't date. You don't share anything of yourself with anyone."

"When did you get to be Dr. Phil?" Dalton asked with more than a touch of irritation.

"If I were Dr. Phil, I'd not only be able to point out the problem, but I'd also have an idea what had caused it."

"There's no problem," Dalton replied emphatically. "I like being alone. Why is that an issue?"

Zack raked a hand through his dark hair. "I guess it's not, if that's the life you choose." He stood and started for the door, but before he reached it he turned back to face Dalton. "Dad said he's seen your truck passing by the house a couple of times in the last couple of days."

"I've been staying off and on at the cabin. George is doing a little remodeling work."

Zack held his gaze for another long minute, then turned and left the office. The moment he was gone Dalton picked up the phone and called Emmett Tread-wall, a local handyman and made arrangements for him to paint Dalton's apartment immediately. He then called George to let him know that the apartment was going to be painted. Covering tracks, covering his lies.

Maybe he should have confided in Zack, but without any real evidence to damn Sinclair, he just wasn't sure what his brother would be forced to do.

In just a matter of days it would all be over. Hope-fully Trent would believe Janette enough to start a full-blown investigation that would lead to Sinclair's arrest. Then Janette and her grandmother and little Sammy would begin a new life someplace where there were no reminders of the horror she'd experienced.

Temporary. All of this was temporary. Another week or so and she'd be gone. Once again he picked up the flyer and stared at her picture.

He'd been irritated the night of the snowstorm, irri-tated that even for a single night he had to share his space, accommodate somebody else's needs. He'd told himself he was living a solitary life, but maybe it was in reality a selfish life.

He tossed the picture aside and frowned, not wanting to chase that thought any further. Just a couple more days, then he could get back to his own life.

What he didn't understand was why that particular thought didn't hold much appeal.

Chapter 11

She was waiting for him at the door when he pulled up in front of the cabin just after seven. Knowing that Sinclair was in town, he'd driven around for an hour before coming here, making sure that he wasn't being followed.

The sight of her with Sammy in her arms warmed his heart despite his need to remain emotionally distant. As he approached, Sammy wiggled with delight, arms flailing as if to reach for him.

There was no way to maintain any kind of distance from an almost six-month-old baby. Dalton took the little boy from her arms as he stepped through the door. "Hey, buddy," he said, then smiled at Janette. "I think you've got a heartbreaker on your hands."

She laughed. She looked brighter, happier than he'd ever seen her and a thrum of tension wound tight in his gut. He wanted her. God help him but he wanted her again. Even knowing that in a matter of days she'd be out of his life, even knowing that he could only be a temporary fixture in her life, he wanted her.

She grabbed him by the arm and pulled him toward the kitchen. "I hope you haven't eaten yet. I made a meatloaf and I've got a wonderful surprise."

"I haven't eaten and what's the surprise?"

"Let's have dinner first, then I'll tell you."

"Sounds good. And I have some news, too," he said.

He stepped into the kitchen and looked around in surprise. The table was set and in the center were two tall candles and a bottle of wine. He shifted Sammy from one arm to the other. "Where did all this come from?" he asked.

"I called Savannah. She did me a favor and picked up some things from the store and brought them out this afternoon." She took Sammy from his arms. "Sit. I'm just going to put him down, then I'll be right back to serve the meal."

As she disappeared into the bedroom Dalton sat at the table. The candles gave off a pleasant glow and their vanilla fragrance mingled with the scent of the meatloaf. And beneath it all he could smell the scent of Janette, the honeysuckle that now reminded him of making love with her.

He could get used to this, coming home from work to her and Sammy. He steeled himself against the very thought, against the sense of homecoming that had filled him the moment he'd seen her and Sammy at the front door waiting for him.

She came back into the room a few minutes later, the glow of happiness still lighting her features. "You look unusually happy tonight," he said.

"I am." She went directly to the oven and pulled out a meatloaf surrounded by potatoes. "First of all, I cooked Smiley's special meatloaf. Even people who profess to hate meatloaf love Smiley's recipe." She set the dish on the table. "Secondly, there's nothing better than candlelight to put a woman in a good mood. And third, I can't wait to tell you about my really big surprise. But first, we eat."

From the refrigerator she pulled out a salad, then joined him at the table. "And how was your day?"

He opened the bottle of wine and filled their glasses, then began to fill his plate. "Boring," he said, "except for the visit I got from Sinclair and Zack." One of her pale eyebrows danced upward. "Sinclair has been passing around flyers in town with your picture on it."

"Where did he get a picture of me?" She passed him the salad bowl.

"Looked like an old school photo. Did anyone else in town see you besides me?"

"The guy at the bus station was the only person I saw, and if Sinclair asks him any questions all he'll be able to say is that he saw me the night of the storm but didn't know where I went."

Dalton nodded. "I do have some good news."

"What's that?"

"I got a call from Trent today. He was able to wind things up sooner than he expected in Oklahoma City so he's planning on coming to Cotter Creek sometime late tomorrow afternoon. As soon as he arrives in town I'll drive him out here to hear your story."

Her blue eyes held his steadily. "So this could all be over by tomorrow night."

"That's right. If everything goes well, Sinclair could be in custody as early as tomorrow night." He looked at her curiously. "Why don't you look pleased with that news?"

"Oh, I am pleased," she quickly said, then frowned, a charming little wrinkle appearing between her brows. "I was just thinking that I need to figure out what happens next."

"When you get your GED, what are your plans then?"

She took a sip of the wine, the set her glass back on the table. "I'd like to get a job that pays well enough that I can help support Nana and Sammy and also pay for college night classes. Eventually I'd like to be a teacher."

"An admirable profession. Is that something you've always wanted to do?"

She grinned at him. "Only after I'd finally given up my desire to be a princess."

He laughed and for the next few minutes they ate and exchanged small talk. Again Dalton was struck not only by her beauty, but by her intelligence and sense of humor, as well. Whenever she finally got settled in someplace she would have no problems dating and would eventually find a man who didn't want to live without her.

After they'd eaten they cleared the table and cleaned up the kitchen. Despite his desire to the contrary, every bump of their shoulders, every brush of their hands as they worked side by side, sent sizzling electricity through him.

"Now are you going to tell me the secret that has you so excited?" he asked.

She poured them each another glass of wine, handed him his then pointed him toward the living room. "Go make yourself comfortable and I'll be right back." She disappeared into the bedroom.

Dalton carried both his wine and hers to the living room and sank down on the sofa, his curiosity piqued. A moment later she came into the living room carrying a red book bag.

"This is the bag I carried back and forth to the GED classes I was taking," she said as she set it on the coffee table. "I hadn't opened it since that night with Sinclair. Yesterday afternoon I decided maybe it was time to pull out the books and start studying again."

She sat next to him on the sofa and took out the books that were inside, then pulled out a small tape recorder. "I used to tape the classes so if I got confused about something or felt I missed something I could listen to the class as many times as I needed to."

He nodded, wondering where she was going with this. He reached out for his wineglass and took a sip, aware of a palpable tension radiating from her. He set his glass down and frowned. "Are you okay?" She was staring at the tape recorder as if it were a coiled rattle-snake getting ready to strike.

She looked up at him and smiled, a beatific smile that shot a new ripple of desire through him. "I'm better than okay. Anyway, that night I had the book bag next to me in the car when Sinclair pulled me over. The best way to explain all this is this." She leaned forward and pushed the play button on the recorder.

"Turn off your lights and get out of the car."

Dalton nearly fell off the sofa as Brandon Sinclair's deep voice boomed from the recorder.

"Well, well, don't we look all sexy in that little skirt."

As the tape played, a sickness welled up inside Dalton as he heard the sheriff bully Janette. It was only when he heard Janette whimper from the tape and say no that he leaned forward and shut off the recorder. He couldn't stand to hear the rest. He didn't want to hear the sounds of her being taken against her will.

For a long moment they were both silent. Dalton stared at the tape recorder with a vague nausea rolling around in his stomach.

"I didn't know I had it until yesterday," Janette said, her voice seeming to come from far away as it penetrated the veil of rage that had descended over him. "I must have accidentally hit the on button when I went into the book bag to get my license."

She reached out and took one of his hands between hers. "The whole thing is on tape. We've got him, Dalton. It's not just my word against his. There's no way he can dispute what's on that tape."

Dalton stared at her. Although intellectually he'd understood that she'd been raped, that whimper he'd heard coming from the tape, the terror-filled protest that she'd released, moved it from intelligent knowledge to emotional sickness.

He wanted to kill for her. He wanted to weep for her. Her strength awed him…humbled him. He squeezed her hand, fighting for words.

"Dalton?" Her soft voice pierced the haze that had fallen over him. "Are you all right?"

He let go of her hand and instead pulled her into an embrace. She laid her head on his shoulder and he stroked the silk of her hair. "I'm just sorry. So damned sorry." Tears burned at his eyes.

"It's okay. I'm okay, especially now that I know he is going to pay for what he did." She looked up at Dalton and he saw that there were no shadows in her eyes, no pain of any kind. Instead her eyes sparkled with hope, with a new kind of peace.

As he held her gaze her mouth opened slightly and she leaned forward. He intended a soft, gentle kiss of healing, but the moment his mouth claimed hers and her tongue swirled with his the kiss became something much different.

Her arms curled around his neck as her kiss grew hot and demanding. He knew they were going to make love again, tasted it in her kiss, felt it in the willing way she filled his arms.

He told himself he didn't want to, that it would do nothing but complicate his conflicting emotions where she was concerned. But as she snaked her hand beneath his shirt and caressed his chest, he was helpless against the onslaught of sensations her touch evoked.

In all probability she would be out of this cabin, out of his life within the next two days. But at the moment she was warm in his arms and he allowed good sense to be swallowed by desire, knowing that it would only make it more difficult when the time came to tell her goodbye.

A quiet desperation simmered inside Janette as she kissed Dalton. It was the desperation of a woman who had fallen in love with the wrong man.

She kissed him with all the heart, all the soul she possessed, needing to take the memory of this last chance to be in his arms with her when she left.

Her fingers danced across the warmth of his broad

chest as their kiss grew more frantic, more needy. She broke the kiss only long enough to pull her sweatshirt over her head, then to draw him down to the floor.

"I want you, Dalton," she said fervently.

"I want you, too." He ripped his shirt over his head and tossed it aside, then stood and took off his jeans. While he was doing that Janette finished undressing, then when they were both naked, she lay back on the rug and beckoned him back into her arms.

He lay beside her, his gaze as hot as his hands as he caressed the length of her. His lips followed the path of his hands, nipping lightly at the base of her throat then kissing the fullness of one breast. A moan escaped her lips as rivulets of pleasure swept over her.

She knew this would be the last time she'd make love with him and she wanted to capture his taste and his touch in her memory. She knew his strength and his belief in her would sustain her through whatever her future held.

When she reached down to wrap her hand around his hardness, he released a low deep moan that only increased her excitement.

She hadn't realized that as a woman she'd been dead until Dalton had brought her back to life. Gratitude mingled with love, intensifying this moment in time with him.

They caressed each other as if they'd been making love together for years, with easy, sure movements that evoked the most intense sensations.

As he touched her intimately the build began, a rising wave of pleasure so intense she thought she'd go mad with it. And when the peak came, she cried out his name, trembling as the release swept her away.

She knew he was waiting for her to take the lead as she had the last time they'd made love. But she didn't want the lead. She parted her legs and motioned for him to get on top.

He hesitated, his eyes glowing and the muscles in his neck strained. "Are you sure?"

"I'm sure."

He moved on top of her and she waited for the panic to strike. The scent of him surrounded her, clean and with that touch of sandalwood she found so attractive.

He didn't take her, but instead held himself above her, as if waiting to see if she'd freak out. She realized at that moment that she wasn't going to freak, that her trust in Dalton was so complete, all she wanted was to be surrounded by him.

She pulled him closer and as he eased into her, there was no thought of anything but him. His mouth sought hers as his hips moved against her. She clung to him, loving the feel of his broad back beneath her fingers, wanting to urge him deeper into her.

He moved faster, faster still, his lips leaving hers as their breaths mingled in quick pants. When he stiffened against her she wanted to cry, because she was free of the specter of Brandon Sinclair, because she loved Dalton West.

He moved his upper body off of hers and stared at her in the waning light. "We didn't use protection."

"Don't worry, I'm on the pill. After…what happened, I wanted to make sure that if I ever got pregnant again, it would be my decision." His statement was a jolt back to reality. He was worried because he didn't want a baby. He didn't want a wife. There was no happy ending here with him.

She scooted out from beneath him. "I'll be right back. I'm going to take a quick shower." She left the living room and went into the bathroom and a moment later stepped beneath a warm spray of water.

Although she'd been with Dalton less than a week, the love she felt for him was deeper and stronger than anything she'd ever felt for any man. And visualizing a future with him was just as silly as visualizing herself a princess or a ballerina.

The door to the shower opened and Dalton peeked in. "Mind some company? I'm great at washing backs."

She smiled at him and stepped aside to allow him entry into the small shower. Even knowing that loving him was a study in futility, there was no way to guard her heart against him.

Twenty minutes later he was dressed and she sat at the kitchen table in her robe. "The next time you see me I'll have Trent with me," he said as he pulled on his coat. "I'll call you tomorrow and let you know what time we'll be here. Meanwhile, I'll fill in Zack and play the tape for him."

She nodded and stood to walk him to the door. She was glad he wasn't spending the night. Sleeping in his arms would only make things more difficult.

When they reached the front door he turned, drew her into his arms and smiled down at her. "Just think, by tomorrow night this will all be over. You can move on with your life and not be afraid of Brandon Sinclair any longer."

"It's truly over, isn't it?"

He nodded, his eyes suddenly dark. "You and your nana and Sammy are going to have a wonderful life." He kissed her on her brow, then released her and walked out.

She stood at the door and watched as he got into his truck. It was over. Tomorrow night she would tell her story to a man who had the power to bring Sheriff Sinclair to justice. With the tape, it was no longer a question of she said, he said. There was enough evidence to put him behind bars.

She should be feeling euphoric, but instead an unexpected chill walked up her spine. Twenty-four hours, she told herself. That's all she had to get through. Another twenty-four hours and it would all be over.

He knew where she was, and it wasn't in the motel room that had been rented by Dalton West. Brandon lay in bed next to his sleeping wife, his mind whirling. He'd thought Janette might have been moved to the West property, then had dismissed the idea as being too obvious.

A headache that afternoon had given him the information he needed. He'd been standing in front of the pain relief medications in the grocery store when he'd heard a woman asking about baby formula in the next aisle.

A glance around the corner had let him know it was Savannah West. He'd done his research on the West clan and knew she didn't have a baby.

He'd paid for his medicine, taken two of the gel-coated tablets, then had gotten into his car and waited for Savannah to emerge from the store.

A few minutes later she'd come out with a basket of groceries, then had gotten into her car and driven off. Thank God, he had driven his personal car that day instead of his official car. It had been easy to follow her as she headed north of town.

When she'd turned onto the West property, he'd

known Janette was there. He'd returned to Sandstone to plot and plan.

Damn the bitch for leaving Sandstone, for thinking she could escape him. And damn Dalton West for sticking his nose where it didn't belong.

He didn't just want that kid, he wanted Janette Black dead, dead so she couldn't talk, dead so she couldn't cause him any more problems.

She'd probably already told Dalton a tale, but he could easily deny that he'd done anything wrong. Okay, he'd had sex with her, but that didn't make him a criminal. He'd tell Dalton that they'd had a brief affair, that the sex had been consensual.

He smiled in the darkness of the room. By this time tomorrow night his life would be back to normal. Janette would be dead and, eventually, after all the red tape was through, that boy would be his.

Chapter 12

It snowed again the next afternoon. Janette stood at the window and stared at the fat flakes falling from the sky. She hoped it didn't snow enough to postpone Trent Cummings' arrival in Cotter Creek.

She was ready to get it over with, needed to get on with her life away from Dalton. He'd crawled too deeply into her heart. He'd made her wish for things that would never come true.

It was time to go, while she still had her dignity. She had a life to build for her, for Sammy and for Nana. She moved from the window and to the kitchen table where a cup of tea was growing cold.

Sammy was napping and she had spent much of the time after lunch trying to decide if they should go back to Sandstone or move to a whole new city.

When Sinclair was arrested the whole story would

come out and Janette wasn't sure she wanted to be known around the small town as the woman the sheriff had raped. Still, Nana had a support system in Sandstone and she would miss her friends desperately if they chose to locate someplace else.

The trailer had been insured, so there would be some money from the insurance company that might be enough to buy another mobile home and place it on the lot where the old one had been.

Once again her gaze shot out the window where the snow seemed to have picked up in intensity. She couldn't wait for spring. She ached for budding flowers and greening grass and a sun of healing warmth.

Where would she be in the spring? At the moment Tucson sounded like a great idea.

She'd called Nana earlier to let her know that by the end of the evening, the nightmare should be over. She'd mentioned to the older woman that, if all went well, she hoped Nana could get a ride to Cotter Creek in the morning and meet Janette at the motel. They'd figure out what to do from there.

She took a sip of the lukewarm tea and frowned thoughtfully. Maybe she should turn on the television and see if they were under any sort of snow watch or warning.

That's just what she needed, another blizzard moving in that put her life on hold for another week or so. What worried her most with each day that passed was the fear that Sinclair would eventually figure out where she was.

Even if he thought she was on the West property, she was comforted by the fact that the cabin was so well hidden. And surely if a stranger were wandering the

West land, somebody would notice, a ranch hand or one of the Wests themselves.

She finished her tea, then went into the living room and sat on the sofa trying to decide if she should call Nana or not. Before she'd made up her mind the phone rang.

It was Dalton, and at the sound of his deep, familiar voice she sank back against the cushions and squeezed the receiver closer to her ear.

"Hi," he said. "How are things there?"

"Okay. I've just been watching it snow. I used to love the snow, but lately it seems like all it does is complicate things. Did you meet with Zack, and have you heard from Trent? Is the snow going to postpone his arrival?"

"I tried to reach Zack, but he got called to an accident and didn't get back last night. I've left a message for him to get in touch ASAP. And I spoke to Trent just a few minutes ago," Dalton said. "He can't get away from Oklahoma City until about three this afternoon. That would put him here after six and he promised me that the weather wouldn't interfere except that it might take him longer to make the trip."

"Thank God, because I'm ready to get this over with," she said.

"Yeah, it's past time we both got on with our normal lives," he said.

She knew he didn't mean the words to hurt, but somehow they did. They reminded her that she was really nothing more than an inconvenience in his life. Oh, he might have enjoyed their lovemaking. After all, he was a man, but just because he'd liked having sex with her didn't mean he felt any kind of emotional attachment to her.

"That's what I've been doing all morning. Trying to figure out where I want to pick up the pieces of my life and start again."

"You aren't going back to Sandstone?" he asked.

She twisted the phone cord around her finger. "I don't know. I'm sure Nana would be pleased if I decided that we were going to stay there, but I'm not sure that's where I want to be. After tonight everyone in town will know that Brandon Sinclair raped me. I'm not sure I want to raise my son someplace where people know that information."

"What are you going to tell Sammy about his father?"

"Eventually the truth, but I want him to hear it from me, not from some kid down the block or some whispers in a store. I'll choose the right time and place to tell him about his father. Maybe by that time there will be a man in my life, a man in Sammy's who will fill any void he might feel."

There was a long moment of silence. "I hope so," he finally said.

"Any sign of Sinclair today?" she asked.

"Haven't seen or heard from him all day. I did hear from my brother Tanner. I'd had him working on a background check of Sinclair and unfortunately it turned up nothing."

"Did you expect it to turn up anything?" she asked.

"I figured it was worth a try, but no, I guess not. Savannah has tried to make contact with that waitress you spoke to her about, but so far she hasn't had any luck."

"None of that matters now," she replied. "We have Sammy and we have the tape and we have me. That's all we need to put him in prison. Do you have the tape in a safe place?" He'd taken the tape player with him the night before when he'd left.

"It's in the safe here in the office," he said.

She twisted the phone cord more tightly around her finger, vaguely wondering in the back of her head why nobody had replaced the phone with a newer cordless model. "What happens after tonight? Once I tell my story to Trent?"

"Hopefully Trent will be able to get a judge to issue an arrest warrant, then we'll have my brother Zack pick him up." He paused a moment, then continued, "Janette, I know you aren't sure what your next move might be, but I want you to know that you're free to stay in the cabin as long as you need to until you figure out where you're going to go."

"Thanks, but I'm planning on having Nana meet me at the motel here in town tomorrow afternoon so if you can just take me there tomorrow, I'll be fine." She couldn't stay here, not in the place where she'd realized her love for him.

"Have you checked with the motel to make sure they have a room?" he asked.

"I intend to do that as soon as we hang up."

"If they don't have any available rooms, I have one rented there in my name. You could stay in it as long as you want or need."

"I'll play it by ear," she said.

They spoke for a few more minutes then hung up. She got up from the sofa and walked back to the window where the snow was still falling in small flakes.

What she really wanted he couldn't give her. Two wishes filled her heart. The first was that Brandon Sinclair would pay for what he'd done to her, and that was going to happen. The second wish was that Dalton

West would love her enough to want to leave behind his solitary life and spend his future with her and Sammy.

She supposed she should be happy with fifty percent of her wishes being fulfilled, but just as Brandon Sinclair had left an indelible mark on her soul, Dalton had left a very different, but equally powerful mark there.

Brandon Sinclair was a lucky man. Dalton shut off the tape player and got up from his desk, fighting a raw aching grief and a rage so great it threatened to consume him. Sinclair was lucky in that he wasn't around for Dalton to put his fist in his face. He wasn't around to be introduced to the explosive rage that Dalton barely managed to contain.

He'd decided to listen to the tape in its entirety before Trent Cummings arrived. He'd known Trent would want to hear it and Dalton hadn't wanted to be blindsided by unexpected emotion in front of the special prosecutor.

And he had been surprised by the depth of his emotion as he'd listened to Janette's rape at the hands of Brandon Sinclair.

She'd never screamed. Although the rape had been brutal and there had been moments when he'd wanted to scream for her, she'd never screamed. But she'd said no. Fourteen times, she'd said the word. Twelve times she'd pled with him to stop.

Dalton slammed his palm against the doorjamb, needing to vent some of the rage that clawed through him. He was sorry he'd heard the tape, but much more sorry that Janette had experienced the ordeal.

How strong she was, how utterly amazing. A survivor, not a victim. A woman who had decided not

to run but rather to face her abuser even when she'd
known the stakes were so high.

He would make certain her bravery counted. He
wouldn't rest until Sinclair was in jail, serving hell time
for his crimes. It was the least he could do for Janette
before he told her goodbye.

He stared out the window where the snow was once
again falling. It had snowed off and on all day. Thank
God Trent had called him a little while ago and told him
he was half an hour outside of Cotter Creek and should
arrive within the next forty-five minutes. It would be
after dark by the time they got to the cabin.

He had fallen in love with her. The thought came out
of nowhere and hit him hard in the gut, taking his
breath half away.

He'd made the same mistake he'd made with Mary.
He'd gotten too close, allowed himself to get too
involved. Only this time it was worse. The depth of his
emotion for Janette was so much greater than anything
he'd ever felt for Mary. He'd opened his heart not just
to Janette, but to Sammy, as well, and when they left
they'd take a huge piece of him with them.

And they would leave and he wouldn't try to stop
them. He knew the drill. He'd been an important part of
her life for a brief time, but he'd never been meant to
have a permanent place there. She was in transition, had
come to him in the middle of a storm, but the storm
would pass and she'd move on.

He moved away from the window and returned to his
desk where the small tape recorder awaited the arrival
of Trent. Again his heart clenched as he thought of what
Janette had endured.

She deserved happiness and he knew without a doubt she'd find it. She'd build a wonderful life for herself, her son and her grandmother. She was strong and beautiful and eventually she'd find a man who wanted to share his life with her.

He knew she'd grown close to him, but that was only because she'd had to be dependent on him for a brief time. Once she got back her independence and was no longer ruled by fear, she'd recognize what she thought was love for him was actually gratitude.

Apparently that was his place in life, to protect and serve, to help heal vulnerable women, then let them go to find happiness elsewhere. He'd thought he was happy alone, believed that his life was exactly the way he wanted it.

He realized he'd been fooling himself. He was a man meant for a family. The days that Janette and Sammy had shared his space had made him recognize that he didn't want to live a solitary life.

He wanted laughter. He wanted love. He wanted somebody to share his life with, somebody to kiss good-night. Maybe eventually he'd find that special somebody. But in the meantime he just had to figure out how to tell Janette goodbye.

Brandon pulled the collar of the white parka closer around his neck and narrowed his gaze. A half an hour ago, when he'd parked his car, he'd cursed the falling snow, but now he welcomed it as he crept closer to the sprawling West house.

It had been a day of frustration. His presence had been required in Sandstone for a meeting with the mayor of the small town. During the meeting, which had seemed to last an eternity, all Brandon could think about was finding Janette and shutting her up for good.

Finally, at five that evening, he'd told his wife he would be gone all night on a stakeout and had left the small town. He'd come prepared. Not only was he wearing white ski pants and the white parka that would allow him to blend in to the surroundings, but he also had another unregistered, throwaway gun and a high beam flashlight.

Now all he had to do was find her, and it was reasonable to assume that she was somewhere on the West property. He'd driven in earlier, holding his breath as he'd coasted past the main house with his lights off. He'd parked behind an old shed and now was headed toward the house where he knew the patriarch, Red West, had raised his family.

Before the night was over, he'd search every structure on the West land, scour every inch of the place in an effort to find her.

He approached the main house, where light danced out the windows. The illumination would make it easy for him to peer inside.

The wind howled like a banshee and sliced at any area of skin that was exposed. Snow crunched underfoot and he cursed beneath his breath, irritated with the weather, but more irritated by the very existence of Janette Black.

His heart beat fast as he eased up to one of the lit windows and looked inside. It was the kitchen of the house and there were two people there, an old man and woman. That would be Smokey Johnson and his new wife, Kathy.

Brandon had done his research. He knew that the old cowhand had married the retired FBI agent a month before and the two shared the house with Red West.

There was no sign of the bitch he sought in the kitchen, so he moved on to the next lighted window. In the living room an older man was in a recliner with a book open on his lap. He was asleep, and Brandon assumed the man was Red West.

So where was Janette?

He wasn't a stupid man. He knew that if the right people listened to her, she had the potential to screw up his life. He couldn't let that happen.

He moved from window to window, fighting a swell of frustration that nearly blinded him. Patience, he told himself. He needed patience. At any minute she might walk into the living room, or go into the kitchen to get something to eat or drink. Once she showed herself to him, it would all be over.

It didn't bother him that she might be in a house filled with others. Three old people were not going to stop him from getting what he wanted.

It took him twenty minutes or so before he decided to move on. He knew that Red's oldest son, Tanner, had a house somewhere on the property. Maybe Dalton had stashed Janette there.

The snow was coming down more heavily now. Already his footprints around the house were disappearing, covered by the new layer of snow. That was fine with him. Hopefully by the time the dead were found the weather would have destroyed any evidence the authorities might try to find.

He'd had chains put on his car tires, so hopefully

when it was time to leave the snow wouldn't impede his escape. He got into the car and pulled forward, seeking the house where Tanner lived.

He continued to drive without headlights, using the pasture fences as guidelines to stay on the road, until he spied the next house. His deadly intent burned inside him, warming him despite the plunging temperatures and the icy wind that blew from the north.

A half an hour later his frustration was a gnawing beast inside him. As far as he could tell there was nobody home in Tanner's two-story house.

He returned to his car. Maybe she was in that motel room that Dalton had rented. Maybe he'd done the expected, thinking that Brandon would think it too obvious. He *had* thought it was too obvious and had made the decision to stay away from there.

Dammit. He'd been so certain she was here. In his mind there was no other logical place for her to be. He drove further into the property and came to a house under construction. Brandon had heard that Clay West was in the process of building a home, and this was probably it. It had been framed, but the walls weren't up. Janette couldn't be hiding there.

He knew he should head back to Sandstone before the snow got so deep that even chains wouldn't allow forward movement. But he kept creeping forward, unwilling to give up the hunt.

He had just decided to head back to Sandstone when he saw it…a faint light glimmering among a grove of evergreen trees.

Where there was light, there was a source of that light. New energy filled him as he parked the car, got out and moved as quickly as a streak of moonlight over the snow.

He saw the cabin nestled among the trees and he knew she was there. He also knew there was no way Janette Black was going to survive this night.

Chapter 13

Janette paced the living-room floor as she waited to tell her story to Trent Cummings. Dalton had called a few minutes before and told her Trent had arrived in Cotter Creek and they would be leaving the West Protective Services office within the hour.

She had a feeling the hour would be spent discussing her case with Trent and listening to the tape that had captured Sinclair's crime against her.

She was glad Dalton was playing it for Trent in his office. She hoped to never hear it again unless it was at Brandon Sinclair's trial.

It was strange. She was at the end of this particular journey in her life, but she didn't feel the expected relief she'd thought tonight would bring. An uneasiness filled her.

She thought it was because tomorrow she'd have to

face the rest of her life—a life without Dalton. On impulse she went over to the sofa and picked up the phone. She punched in the number that would connect her to her grandmother.

Nancy answered on the second ring and immediately put Janette's grandmother on the phone. "Honey, how are you doing?" Nana asked. To Janette's surprise she began to cry. "Janette, what's wrong?" Nana asked urgently.

"Nothing...nothing's wrong," Janette managed to say. She swiped the tears from her cheeks and warbled an uneasy laugh. "I don't even know why I'm crying. Dalton is supposed to be here anytime with the prosecutor, and it looks like things are finally at an end."

"Then maybe those tears are ones of relief and hopefully a little bit of closure," Nana replied.

"Maybe," Janette agreed, but she knew where the tears were formed. They were created in her heart as she thought of never seeing Dalton again.

"Nancy's brother is driving me into town tomorrow afternoon," Nana continued. "I'll be at the motel by three or so."

"Good. I thought we'd stay a day or two and talk about where we go from here," Janette said.

"Janette, I want you to know that I don't want you making decisions with me in mind. I want you to build a life for you and that precious little boy of yours. Nancy has told me I can live here with her. I don't want you thinking you have to provide for me. I'm an old woman at the end of my life and you're a young woman, a new mother with your life ahead of you. Reach for all the happiness you can grab, honey. You deserve it."

They spoke for another few minutes then hung up.

Janette got up from the sofa and walked to the doorway of the bedroom to stare at Sammy sleeping in the beautiful cradle.

Once again she felt the burn of tears in her eyes. Maybe it was just the relief of knowing it was all finally over. She could let go of the fear that had been with her every day since the rape. She'd never again have to look over her shoulder and be afraid that Brandon Sinclair was just behind her, ready to wreak havoc in her life.

She turned away from the doorway and instead paced the kitchen, thinking about her conversation with Nana. Even though Nana had said she could live with Nancy, had insisted that Janette think only of herself and Sammy, Janette knew Nana would miss them desperately if Janette chose to leave her behind.

And to tell the truth, she didn't want to leave her behind. There was no question that Janette's life would be easier with Nana in it. While she worked and went back to school, somebody would have to watch Sammy, and Nana was the one person she trusted to take care of her little boy.

She didn't just need Nana in her life, she wanted the old woman to play a major role there. Wherever she went, she wanted Nana to go with her.

Maybe Kansas City was a good place to start again, she thought as she drifted into the living room. There would be plenty of job opportunities there and community colleges galore. She and Nana could make a decision tomorrow at the motel.

Reach for all the happiness you can grab, Nana had told her. If she were to reach for what she truly wanted, she'd grab Dalton West and never let him go.

She'd build a life with him that others would envy. They'd share their lives during the days and share their passion for each other during the nights. He'd be the one who would teach Sammy how to be a man, and Sammy would grow up to be strong and morally decent and good.

It was a wonderful fantasy, but it had nothing to do with reality. She glanced at the clock on the top of the television. After seven. Where were Dalton and Trent? It had been well over an hour since Dalton had called.

She moved back to the front window and peered out. It was still snowing, more heavily than it had all day. She hoped the weather didn't hold up Dalton and Trent too long. She wanted tonight to be done and tomorrow to begin. She needed to get away from this cabin, away from thoughts of Dalton and what might have been.

She started to turn away from the window when, from the corner of her eye, she saw movement. It was just a flash, a blur of something, but fear spiked through her and she backed away from the window with a small gasp.

Although she hadn't gotten a real look at whatever was moving outside, the impression that burned in her head was that it had been far too big to be an animal. It had been big enough to be a man.

Dalton or Trent wouldn't be walking around outside, and if it was one of the Wests, surely they'd knock on the door to find out who was staying in the cabin.

It could only be one person.

Brandon Sinclair.

Somehow he'd found her. Her heart beat so fast she couldn't catch her breath for a long moment. The back of her throat closed up as panic took over.

He was here!

She couldn't think, couldn't move. It was as if the cold of the night had moved inside and frozen her in place. *Nobody will hear you scream.* The words pounded in her head. She was so isolated that when Sinclair got inside the cabin, as he killed her then stole her son, nobody would hear her cries.

"No." The word of protest broke her inertia. No, she wasn't going to allow that to happen, at least not without a fight.

She raced to the phone and picked it up. No dial tone greeted her. The line was dead. If she needed any further evidence that Sinclair was somewhere outside, the dead phone was it. He'd made certain she couldn't call for help.

As she left the living room and hurried into the bedroom, a fist slammed against the locked front door. "Janette, open the door. We need to talk." His deep voice held the authority and confidence of his position.

Inside the bedroom Janette fumbled beneath her pillow and pulled out the knife she'd carried since the night of her rape. The knock came again, this time harder against the wood of the door.

"Janette, open the door or I'll break it down. We have official business to discuss."

Frantically she looked around the small bedroom, seeking a weapon or an escape route. Her gaze landed on the window. She raced to it and threw it open. Frigid air blew in, chilling the last of any warmth that might have been left in her body. With trembling fingers she removed the screen.

Where were Dalton and Trent? She needed them here now. As she picked up the sleeping Sammy and wrapped him tightly in the towel she'd used as an extra blanket, she heard a crash at the front door and knew Sinclair was breaking it down.

She couldn't stand and fight him, knew that she'd never stand a chance against him. There was only one possible means of escape, and that was out into the snowstorm.

Holding Sammy tight against her, she went out the window, the icy cold and snow stinging every inch of her bare skin. Someplace in the back of her mind she knew it wouldn't take long for her to die of exposure. She wore no coat, no hat and no snow boots. She was clad in only a T-shirt, a pair of jeans and a pair of thin cotton slippers. But that couldn't be helped now.

As she began to run away from the cabin, away from Brandon Sinclair, the snow continued to fall like beautiful white death from the sky.

Behind her she heard the crash and a roar and knew that Sinclair had gotten inside. A sob ripped through her as she ran, knowing that she'd rather die in the snow than at the hands of the man who had raped her.

Dalton hung up the phone and tried to squash the worry that roared through him. "The phone's dead," he told Trent, who stood at the West Protective Services front door.

"Maybe the storm blew down a line," Trent offered.

"Maybe," Dalton said, but wasn't sure he believed it. A thrum of disquiet kicked up inside as he grabbed his truck keys off the desk. He hadn't talked to Zack yet, which didn't help his mood. "Let's get out of here. We need to get to the cabin."

Together the two men left the office and got into Dalton's truck. They had spent the past hour with Dalton filling in his old friend about the particulars of the case. Trent had heard the tape and had also listened to Dalton's suspicions that it had been Sinclair who had set the fire and fired the shots the night Dalton had moved her to the cabin.

Trent's expression had grown more grim with each word that Dalton spoke about Sinclair. Dalton knew there was nothing Trent loved more than putting away bad guys who masqueraded as good guys.

Dalton tried to ignore the uneasiness that coursed through him as he started the truck engine. She'd never not answered the phone before.

He attempted to tamp down the anxiety as he turned on the wipers to swipe at the snow that had gathered on the windshield.

"You're sure she'll testify?" Trent asked as Dalton backed out of his parking space.

"She'll do whatever she needs to do to make sure Sinclair goes to prison."

"The tape is good evidence, but could be easily disputed without her testimony," Trent said thoughtfully.

"She's solid," Dalton said. "She's come too far now to back down. She wants Sinclair behind bars far more than you or I do."

"I'm not sure that's possible," Trent said as he narrowed his eyes. "There's nothing I love more than putting a crooked lawman behind bars. Sinclair is a disgrace to the men and women who put their lives on the line every day for the good of their communities."

"I wish I would have seen him the night of the fire," Dalton said. "Then we could get him for attempted murder."

"We'll get him," Trent replied. "And I'll see to it that he's put away for as long as possible."

The street was slick and Dalton had to keep his speed at a minimum. As he drove he fumbled for his cell phone and punched in the number for the cabin. The phone rang and rang and rang. He clicked off, his apprehension exploding into full-blown fear.

"No answer?" Trent asked, his handsome features lit by the dashboard light.

Dalton shook his head. "I've got to admit, I'm worried." That was the understatement of the day.

He opened the cell phone again and quickly punched in a new number. "My brother Tanner lives close to the cabin where Janette is. He can get there quicker than we can." He sighed in frustration as Tanner's phone went directly to voice mail.

Tossing his cell phone to the seat between them, Dalton tightened his grip on the steering wheel and stepped on the gas.

Janette was in trouble and it was his fault. The knowledge thundered in his head. He should have insisted she keep a gun with her, he should have made other arrangements for her. Jesus, he should have done something different to assure that Sinclair wouldn't find her.

Dammit, what had made him think that she'd be safe in the cabin all alone? He hadn't believed that Sinclair would be able to find her there, but apparently he'd underestimated the sheriff.

The snow made visibility difficult and Dalton felt the spin and slide of the tires on the slick road beneath them. The wind howled and buffeted the truck and he silently cursed the conditions that kept him from going as fast as he wanted to go.

Let her be okay. Don't let anything happen to her. Dalton's brain said the words over and over again, his heart pounding so loud in his ears he wondered if Trent could hear it.

Trent braced himself with a hand on the dash as the back of the truck spun out. Dalton quickly corrected the spin, the panic inside him nearly unbearable. But it wasn't the panic of nearly losing control of the vehicle, it was the sheer terror that had loosened itself inside him for Janette and Sammy.

"You going to kill us before we get there?" Trent finally said with a touch of dry humor.

"I'm trying not to." Dalton eased up on the gas, knowing that if they wrecked there was no way they could be any help at all.

His cell rang. He picked up the phone and checked the I.D. Zack, finally. "Zack, I need you to meet me at the cabin immediately."

"What's going on?" Zack asked.

"You know that woman Sheriff Sinclair was looking for? Janette Black?"

"What about her?"

He didn't bother trying to fill in Zack on the tape and details. "I've got her at the cabin and I think she's in big trouble." As Dalton spoke those words aloud, his heart squeezed so tight in his chest he momentarily felt light-headed. "Hurry, Zack."

Zack hung up and Dalton tossed the phone aside again, hoping and praying that there was a logical explanation for Janette not answering his calls, hoping and praying that she and Sammy were just fine and Brandon Sinclair was nowhere in the area.

The snow was both a blessing and a curse. As Janette ran from the cabin, she was glad that the heavy snowfall would make it more difficult for Sinclair to see her.

The curse was that it hadn't taken long for her feet to become chunks of ice, causing her to stumble more than once as she ran blindly into the night.

Sammy had awakened and fussed against her, and she tried to soothe him as she ran, afraid that if he began to wail Sinclair would hear and would be able to pinpoint her exact location.

Her breaths came in painful pants, the cold air stabbing her lungs with each intake of air. Her bare hands ached, as did her face where the icy flakes of snow clung to her lashes, her lips and her cheeks.

Somehow in the space of a dozen footsteps she'd become disoriented. She was no longer sure she was going in the right direction to find help and with each step she took she grew more exhausted.

Eventually the cold disappeared and instead she became numb, feeling nothing but the screaming in her head. And that scream intensified when she turned and saw the beam of a high-powered flashlight just behind her.

He was coming! A sob ripped from her throat as she stumbled forward. The snow and the darkness of the night couldn't hide her if his high beam fell on her.

The flashlight swiped from side to side, and she knew at the moment he didn't see her, didn't know that she was so close.

Exhaustion pulled at her, but she forced herself to

move on. She wasn't so worried about her own safety, but for Sammy's. She had to keep him safe from the man who had fathered him.

She pushed herself forward, putting one numb foot in front of the other in an effort to escape. She could hear him now, the swish of his pant legs as his thighs rubbed together, and her heart pounded so hard, so fast, she wondered if she were having a heart attack.

At least if she died she knew Dalton would somehow, someway get Sammy. Even if Brandon Sinclair plucked Sammy from her dead arms, she was confident it would only be a temporary thing. Because she trusted Dalton. Because she knew he'd fight for her son if she couldn't fight for him herself.

Cold.

She was so cold. It was becoming more difficult to put one foot in front of the other. She just wanted to lie down and sleep and dream of Dalton and what might have been.

She knew that was the cold talking and so she pushed herself forward. Half-blinded by the snow, she nearly crashed into the small shed. All she could think about was getting out of the snow before her legs stopped moving altogether.

Sammy had become an unbearable weight in her arms and no matter how close she held him to her chest, she knew he must be feeling the sting of the cold.

Without conscious thought, she opened the shed door and went inside, then shoved the door shut behind her. Without the aid of a light she couldn't see what the shed contained. All she knew was the blessing of being out of the howling wind and the icy air. She'd take a minute and catch her breath, warm herself just a bit before leaving the structure and continuing to run.

It wasn't until she heard Sinclair roar her name from just outside the shed that she realized what she'd done. She'd run herself into a dead end, a blind alley. The only way out was back through the door she'd entered and on the other side of that door was death.

Chapter 14

The mind was a strange thing. In the flash of a moment
it could process enough impressions and instincts to
make a man sick. Dalton was definitely sick as his brain
not only worked to wrap around the grim possibility that
Sheriff Sinclair had found Janette, but also highlighted
every mistake he'd made as her bodyguard.

And he'd made plenty.

"I shouldn't have left her out there all alone." He
spoke one of his biggest mistakes aloud.

"You did what you thought was right at the moment,"
Trent replied, once again bracing himself as Dalton
turned into the West property and nearly took out a
wooden post as the truck spun out. "Don't second-guess
yourself. That can make a man crazy."

Dalton's heart beat so fast it hurt. The snow had
stopped falling and a sliver of moonlight sliced

through the clouds, faintly illuminating the wintry landscape.

He flew past his dad's place, his brain screaming a litany of pleas. Let her be okay. Please let her be safe. Over and over the words played in his mind. It was as if, if he thought it often enough, that would make it so.

His hands ached from his fierce grip on the steering wheel, but that pain was nothing compared to the one that pierced his heart as he thought of Janette and little Sammy being in danger.

He raced by Tanner's house, skidded around Clay's half-built place and toward the grove of evergreen trees that surrounded the little cabin. He turned through the small lane and pulled up in front. Horror swept through him as he saw that the old wooden front door had been crashed in. He was out of the truck, gun drawn, in a frantic heartbeat.

Trent was right behind him and together the two men approached the silent cabin. Dalton stepped through the doorway and crouched with his gun held in both hands in front of him.

There was nobody in the living room. "Clear," he called out, and Trent stepped inside. As Dalton moved toward the kitchen his biggest fear was that he'd find only Janette's body somewhere in the cabin. The smashed front door seemed to cry that he and Trent were too late.

Emotion pressed thick in Dalton's chest and he drew a steadying breath as he entered the kitchen. Nothing. No body, no signs of any struggle, nothing. "Clear," he called to Trent, who followed at his heels.

Trent checked the bathroom, then stepped back into

the kitchen and both men looked at the bedroom door. It was closed, and a fear like he'd never known clawed at his insides.

Dalton moved to the door. His hand trembled, dread welling inside him as he reached for the knob. He flung open the door and the first thing he saw was the open window.

Relief shot through him as he easily realized the scenario. Sinclair had somehow found the cabin. He'd come in through the front door and Janette had escaped through the window. But the relief was short-lived as he realized it was possible he'd find her body in the snow.

"She's outside."

Together the two men hurried back to the front door. When they stepped outside the wind nearly stole Dalton's breath away. It cut sharp and deep, and frantic need welled up inside him. Even if Sinclair hadn't found her, the elements would be as deadly as the determined lawman.

They hurried around to the back of the cabin. Dalton stopped at his truck only long enough to retrieve a flashlight. Trent looked at Dalton. "Which way would she have run?"

Dalton stared out at the wide expanse of pasture that surrounded them. Janette was smart. She wouldn't have just taken off running without a plan of some kind.

She would have headed toward Tanner's house. Confirmation of his thoughts lay on the ground in faint footprints. However, it wasn't dainty small feet that had left the prints. It was big boot prints that filled his heart with a new sense of terror.

If he'd had any doubt of what had happened here tonight, those large footprints froze them away and also froze a part of his heart.

"Janette," he yelled, but the howl of the wind competed with his voice.

He and Trent trudged through the snow, following the barely discernible footprints as Dalton swept the flashlight in front of them. Dalton felt as if they were moving in slow motion as they systematically searched the area looking for Janette…or her body.

As they walked, the mistakes Dalton had made roared through his head. He should have gotten his family involved, but he'd been so busy isolating himself, so worried about giving any part of himself away, that he'd made what he hoped wouldn't prove to be a fatal mistake.

"Dalton!"

Dalton turned at the sound of his name and saw Zack running toward them. "What's going on?" he asked when he caught up to Dalton and Trent.

"Brandon Sinclair is trying to kill Janette," Dalton said. "He raped her, and now he's trying to kill her. We have proof." He could see that Zack was confused, but he couldn't take the time to go through everything. "I'll explain later. Right now we need to find Janette."

Find Janette.

Find Janette.

The words pounded in Dalton's head as it began to snow once again. He was relatively certain she was out here without a coat and possibly without shoes. She wouldn't have taken time to bundle up before escaping out the window.

If they didn't find her soon the icy cold and snow would do the job for Sinclair. Unless the sheriff had already found her. Unless it was already too late.

The gunshot exploded the night and the sound ripped through Dalton's heart. *Too late,* his brain screamed. *You're too late to save her.*

"It came from over there." Zack pointed to the right and they all took off running.

The cold air sliced at his lungs as he raced toward the direction where they thought the shot had come. The flashlight beam bobbed as he ran and fear made him feel as if he were dealing with an out-of-body experience.

As the flashlight beam fell on the old storage shed, Dalton's blood ran cold. Brandon Sinclair stood in front of the shed, and when he saw the beam of light he whirled around to face them. He had his gun drawn and wore a fierce look of determination.

"Sheriff West, I'm glad you're here," Sinclair said, ignoring both Dalton and Trent. "I have my suspect holed up in this shed. I need her out of there and placed in my custody."

Dalton started forward, but Zack grabbed his arm to hold him in check. "We heard a gunshot," Zack said.

"I fired a warning shot to let her know I meant business."

"Looks to me like you fired that warning shot right through the door," Zack observed.

"Look, I don't want any trouble here. I just want to get my prisoner into custody and get her back to Sandstone," Brandon said.

"You lying son of a bitch," Dalton exploded. This time it was Trent who grabbed hold of him as he tried to lunge forward. "If you've hurt them I'll kill you." He tried to escape Trent's firm grasp. He needed to get inside that shed.

Why didn't Janette come out? Was it possible that the single shot Brandon had fired through the door had found her and she was now lying bleeding—or worse—on the other side of the door?

"I suggest you get your brother under control, Sheriff," Sinclair said.

Zack narrowed his eyes. "I suggest you put your gun away and let me figure out just what the hell is going on here."

"I told you what's going on," Sinclair exclaimed, impatience obvious in his voice. "I just want to get my prisoner and go home." He must have seen something in Zack's eyes that made him holster his gun.

"I'm afraid that isn't going to be possible," Trent spoke for the first time. He looked at Zack. "I'm Trent Cummings, special prosecutor, and I want you to place Sheriff Brandon Sinclair under arrest."

"For what?" Brandon's hand moved down toward his gun.

"Don't do it," Zack warned as both he and Trent advanced on Sinclair.

"Rape. You're under arrest for the rape and attempted murder of Janette Black," Trent said as Zack plucked the gun from Sinclair's holster then cuffed him.

Dalton could stand it no longer. He raced for the shed door and tried to push it open, but it refused to budge. "Janette, it's me. Open the door."

The silence that greeted him was deafening. A sob ripped from him as he shoved and pushed against the door, hoping…praying that it wasn't her dead body blocking the way.

Trent helped, putting his shoulder against the door next to Dalton and together they managed to get the door open. "Janette!" Dalton cried, his flashlight frantically scanning the area.

He found her crouched behind an old love seat, her knife held tightly in one hand. "Is he gone?" she asked, her blue lips trembling uncontrollably.

The relief that crashed through Dalton nearly brought him to his knees. "It's over, honey. He can't ever hurt you again." Dalton helped her to her feet, noting that her eyes were huge in her deathly pale face. He hurriedly took off his coat and wrapped it around her slender shoulders as she cuddled Sammy tightly against her chest.

As they stepped out of the shed he gripped her closer to him as she saw Sinclair. "Whatever she's told you, it's a lie," he yelled and twisted his shoulders as if trying to escape from his handcuffs. "I'll admit we had sex, but she wanted it. She begged me for it."

Dalton tightened his arm around Janette's shoulders. "That's funny. The night you pulled Janette over for a speeding ticket, she had a tape recorder running. We've got that entire night's events on tape. You're going to prison."

Sinclair looked stunned.

Janette raised her trembling chin and smiled. "Gotcha," she said.

The night seemed to last forever. Dalton wanted Janette and Sammy to be taken to the hospital, but she refused, insisting that all she needed to recover from her ordeal was warmth.

They left the cabin and drove into town, where Sinclair was locked in the jail. The rest of them went to Dalton's apartment, where Janette was questioned by both Zack and Trent.

As the night progressed, she felt Dalton distancing himself. He grew quiet, adding nothing to the conversation, and his green eyes seemed to stare at everything in the room except her.

Her worst fear had been realized. Brandon Sinclair had found her, but she'd survived. Sammy had survived. And now Janette's future stood directly in front of her.

It was almost four when the talk was finally finished. She promised Trent that no matter where she and Nana settled, she'd give him their address so he could let her know when Sinclair would go to trial.

She would be the prosecutor's star witness, and that fact held a certain poetic justice that sent a sense of peace through her.

After Trent and Zack left, she fell into Dalton's bed, exhausted by the trauma of the night. Sammy slept peacefully next to her and she fought the impulse to pull him close against her, to assure herself that they both truly had survived.

As she'd hidden in the shed, she'd believed she wouldn't leave it alive. She had thought she'd never see Sammy take his first step, say his first real word. She'd believed she would never hear Nana's voice or see Dalton's handsome face again.

Sleep, when it finally came, drifted over her like a soft, warm blanket and held no nightmares. She awakened to the sun shining through the window and a sense of peace she'd never known before.

The man who had forever changed her life would now face Lady Justice and have his freedom taken away for a very long time. She no longer had to be afraid. She would not live her life looking over her shoulder.

She frowned as she stared at the window. The cast of the sun shining through the window made her realize it was late morning. Why hadn't Sammy awakened her?

She turned over and found the bed empty. Panic sliced through her for a split second, but it quickly ebbed. She wasn't sure exactly where Sammy was, but she knew he was safe, because they were in Dalton's apartment and Dalton wouldn't let anything happen to them.

Getting out of bed she tried to shove away the aching sadness that found her heart, the sadness of knowing that today she would tell Dalton a final goodbye.

After a quick stop in the bathroom to brush her teeth and wash her face, she belted her robe around her waist and went in search of the two men in her life.

She found them in the kitchen, and for a moment she stood just outside the door and peeked in. Dalton sat at the table with Sammy on his lap. He was trying to feed Sammy rice cereal, but it looked as if Dalton was wearing more than Sammy was eating.

A smile didn't make it to her lips, but it squeezed her heart as she watched the man she loved interact with her precious baby.

"Come on, buddy. We can do this," Dalton said. "Don't you want to grow up to be big and strong?" He held a spoonful of the cereal and Sammy laughed and waved his hand, striking the spoon and sending the cereal to the front of Dalton's shirt.

"Why don't I just lay you against my chest and let you graze off my clothes?" Dalton muttered.

"Problems?" Janette asked as she stepped into the room.

"If he makes this big of a mess with cereal I can't wait to see him with a bowl of spaghetti," he said.

Again an internal fist squeezed Janette's heart. They both knew he wouldn't be around to watch Sammy eat spaghetti. He wouldn't be around to see that Sammy grew big and strong.

"Coffee's made," he said, as if he sensed the awkward moment between them.

"Thanks." She moved to the counter and poured herself a cup. "Usually when he gets to the point that he's knocking it out of the spoon instead of eating it, I figure he's finished." She sat at the table.

"That works for me," he agreed easily. He stood with Sammy in his arms and carried the little boy over to the sink. "I'm not sure who needs to be hosed down first, you or me," he said to Sammy, who grinned and released a string of gibberish.

When he had Sammy clean she held out her hands and he placed the baby on her lap, then sat once again at the table across from her.

"You look well-rested. I figured you could use a little extra sleep this morning, so when I heard Sammy start to fuss I got him."

"I appreciate it." She took a sip of her coffee as he stared at a point just over her head.

A new silence descended and she guessed it was the awkward silence of the end of a relationship when there was nothing more to say. She finished her coffee, then carried her cup to the sink. "I'm going to go take a shower and pack up my things."

"I'll hang out with Sammy so you can get showered," he offered.

As he took her son from her, she wanted to say something to break the somber mood between them, but she didn't. She simply went into the bedroom to take her shower and pack her belongings in preparation for going to the motel to meet Nana.

It was as she stood beneath the hot spray of the shower that she recognized that she couldn't leave here without telling Dalton how she felt about him. If she kept her feelings inside, she'd always wonder what might have been different if she'd spoken them aloud.

As she thought of baring her heart, a touch of fear fluttered inside her stomach, and that seemed ridiculous given what she'd just gone through the night before.

She'd faced a man whose sole desire was to see her dead, yet her heart beat just as wildly as she thought of facing Dalton and telling him how she felt.

As she packed her suitcase she found herself revisiting each and every moment of the time she had spent with Dalton. Who knew that when she'd walked out of that bus station so alone, so afraid, that she'd walk into the arms of a man whom she'd want to hold her for the rest of her life?

And he didn't want a wife. He had no desire for a family. She knew she could do nothing to change that, that her words of love would probably fall on deaf ears. But that didn't mean she didn't intend to speak them, because she refused to live the rest of her life with regrets.

When she pulled her suitcase into the living room,

Sammy was propped up in the corner of the sofa and Dalton was playing peekaboo with him.

It amazed her that this big strong man had a soft center he displayed with Sammy. He was meant to be a father. He was meant to be *Sammy's* father. But, no matter how much she wanted it, no matter how much she needed it, she couldn't make him be something he didn't want to be.

He caught sight of her and stood. "It's still early," he said. "I thought maybe you'd like to go to the café in town and have lunch."

"Actually, I have something I'd like to say to you before you take me to the motel." She felt the swell of emotion in her chest as she gazed into his beautiful green eyes.

"Is something wrong?" He sank back to the sofa and patted the cushion next to him.

She remained standing, afraid that if she sat beside him, she'd fall to pieces. She searched her mind, struggling to find the right place to begin. "I don't know how I would have survived without you, Dalton."

He frowned and his eyes darkened. "You would have probably been just fine on your own. I spent most of the night kicking myself for all the mistakes I made."

"Mistakes? What are you talking about?"

"I almost got you killed last night because I didn't want to allow anyone else in my life. I should have had somebody at the cabin with you every minute that you were there."

"I have to accept part of the responsibility for the decision you made," she countered. "I made you swear that you wouldn't tell anyone I was there."

"But he could have killed you because I didn't do my job."

For the first time that day, she realized the deep torment he felt and hope blossomed in her heart. Surely a man who didn't care wouldn't be so tortured. Surely a man who didn't love her wouldn't care as deeply as what she saw shining from his eyes.

With a new courage she walked over to the sofa and sank down beside him. "You saved my life, Dalton. Without you I would have been out in the snowstorm alone and afraid. Without you I would have never had the courage to face Brandon Sinclair."

He smiled then, a soft smile that pierced straight through to her heart. "I have a feeling you would have been just fine on your own. You're an amazing woman, Janette Black."

"You're an amazing man. In fact, you're so amazing I've fallen in love with you." Her breath caught in her throat as the words hung in the air between them.

He stared at her, and she wasn't sure if he was stunned or horrified by her words. He got up from the sofa as if goosed by an invisible hand and stepped back from where she sat.

"Janette, I appreciate the idea that you think you're in love with me, but I'm sure once you get away from here, once you get away from me, you'll realize it's not really love."

She would have been able to deal with him telling her he didn't love her. She would have accepted him explaining that he didn't feel the same way about her. But his attempt to negate her feelings altogether shot an edge of anger through her.

"Don't try to tell me what I feel and what I don't feel," she exclaimed as she got up from the sofa.

Dalton swiped a hand through his hair and frowned at her. "Look, you've just come off a roller coaster of traumatic events. We've been cooped up together, and emotions got out of control." He cast his gaze away from her but not before she saw something in his eyes that encouraged her.

She stepped closer to him. "Dalton, I don't know a lot of things, but I know that I'm in love with you, and there have been times in the last couple of days that I believed that you were falling in love with me and with my son."

He looked at her then, his expression dark and unfathomable. "I'm sorry if I gave you that impression. I thought I'd been clear about the fact that I'm not interested in any long-term relationship or in having a family."

Even though she'd suspected their relationship would end this way, it didn't stop the hot press of tears that burned at her eyes. How was it possible that his eyes told her one thing and his mouth said another?

It didn't matter. Now that she'd bared her soul, all she wanted to do was escape. She walked over to where Sammy was sitting on the sofa and picked him up, cradling him close to her breaking heart. "I'd like to go to the motel now."

There was no point in spending another minute with him. She needed to get away, to cry, to mourn, to once again find some way to heal herself and move on.

He didn't argue with her. Instead he got her coat and silently they prepared to leave. She felt numb. She hadn't realized how much she'd hoped that he would take her in his arms, confess that he loved her, too, until that hope had been stolen away.

She should have known better, she thought bitterly as she got into his truck. He was an educated man who enjoyed listening to jazz and reading thick tomes. Why would he want to bind himself to an uneducated woman with a baby?

She gasped when she saw the infant car seat in the back seat of his big cab. The fact that he'd thought of Sammy's safety only broke her heart again.

The drive to the motel was silent except for Sammy's cooing talk. She kept her gaze averted out the passenger window, afraid that if she looked at Dalton she'd cry.

She'd endured a rape and being chased out in the snow by a man who wanted to kill her, and she'd survived. And she would survive Dalton West's rejection, as well. But it was going to take time.

Dalton pulled up in front of the motel office and parked, then turned to look at her. His eyes radiated a deep pain. "You'll be all right?"

"Of course we will," she replied, her voice sounding clipped, brittle to her own ears. "Nana will be here around three and we'll figure out where we go from here."

"If you ever need anything…"

"We'll be fine," she quickly interjected. "You've done more than enough for us already." She opened the truck door and took Sammy out of the car seat as Dalton got out of the vehicle.

He grabbed her suitcase from the back and carried it to the front door of the motel office as she followed just behind him. She'd known telling him goodbye would be difficult, she just hadn't imagined it would be this difficult.

"I can get it from here," she said.

He nodded and set the suitcase down. "Here's the key to the room." He told her the number. "I guess this is goodbye."

"Before I tell you goodbye, I just want to say one more thing." She searched his stern features, remembering how they had softened into something beautiful as they'd made love, how they'd transformed with laughter as he'd interacted with Sammy.

She drew a deep breath and consciously willed away the tears that threatened. "Even though you don't love us, I hope you'll eventually open yourself up to loving some woman. You'd make a wonderful husband, Dalton, and you'd be an awesome father." The tears she'd tried to hold in now splashed onto her cheeks. "I don't know what made you decide to live your life alone, but you're cheating some woman from finding happiness with you, and you're cheating yourself, as well."

She didn't wait for him to answer. She grabbed the handle on the suitcase, turned and hurried away, eager to get into a room where she could cry in private.

Minutes later, she sat on the edge of one of the two double beds in the room and tried to keep the tears from flowing. She was afraid that if she started to cry she wouldn't be able to stop, and she didn't want Nana to arrive and see the depths of her despair.

Besides, she had a future to plan, a life to live. She knew eventually her heart wouldn't hurt so much, but at the moment it ached with unrelenting sadness.

One man had raped her and the other had thrown away her love. Both had left indelible scars on her soul, but it was Dalton's kindness, his passion and laughter that would linger in her thoughts for a very long time to come.

She stretched out across the bed, grabbed one of the pillows and cried into it, not wanting her sobs to disturb her sleeping son.

Later she would figure out where her life went from here, but for now she'd give herself time to mourn what might have been.

Chapter 15

Dalton opened his apartment door, stepped inside and drew in a deep, weary breath. She was gone. All trace of her and Sammy were gone except the faint scent of honeysuckle that lingered in the air.

The silence felt odd, but he knew eventually it would feel familiar and safe. He shrugged out of his coat and hung it in the closet, then eased down in his chair and stared around the room.

The painter he'd hired hadn't even begun the job yet. The walls didn't really need to be painted, but Dalton wouldn't cancel the job. Maybe the smell of fresh paint would remove the last trace of her scent from the apartment.

He leaned back in the chair and closed his eyes, fighting against the emotion that pressed tight in his chest. He'd done the right thing. He knew how these things worked. He'd learned the hard way by his experience with Mary. He didn't believe in repeating past mistakes.

Janette would move on, build a life and realize that what she'd really felt for him was nothing more than gratitude. However, he wasn't confused about his feelings for her. He loved her. His feelings for Janette were far deeper, far more profound than anything he'd felt for Mary.

A solitary life. That's what he'd believed he wanted, but now he realized how selfish he'd become. He'd guarded himself from not only women and dating, but also from his family and life.

For the first time he thought about all the reasons he'd distanced himself from his family, and for the first time he realized the answer.

His brothers had all found love. They'd found the special women with whom they would spend the rest of their lives and build happy families. He'd been glad for their happiness, but their happiness had pointed out the utter emptiness of his own life.

He needed to go into the office. He needed to do something, anything to get away from his own thoughts. He'd have one more cup of coffee then head to the West Protective Services office and spend the rest of the day there taking care of boring paperwork.

As he entered the kitchen and headed for the coffee-pot his gaze fell on the bowl in the sink. It was half-full of rice cereal, and the sight of it convulsed his heart so hard, so unexpectedly, it brought tears to his eyes.

Janette wasn't the only one he'd fallen in love with. Sammy had stolen his heart the first time he'd grinned at Dalton and cooed.

"I did the right thing," Dalton said aloud, but his voice lacked conviction. He just didn't understand how doing the right thing could feel so terribly wrong.

"You look peaked." Nana stared at Janette closely as she stepped into the motel room. "You aren't getting sick, are you?"

"No, I'm not getting sick," Janette replied. Definitely heartsick, but that didn't count. She gave her grandmother a fierce hug. Nana dropped her small overnight bag on the floor and beelined to Sammy, who had awakened and had somehow found his own toes with his hands.

"Look at you!" Nana picked him up and nuzzled his neck. "You look like you've grown a foot." She settled on the bed with Sammy in her arms. "So, where are we going from here?"

Janette sat on the opposite bed and frowned thoughtfully. "I don't know. It's a decision I didn't want to make without your input."

"I'll be honest, if I had my way we'd go back to Sandstone and get a new trailer. I've got my friends there, but I know that isn't what you want, so whatever you decide is fine with me." Nana's smile was filled with love and her expression was soft as she gazed first at Janette, then at Sammy. "I just want you and this little boy to be happy. That's all I really care about."

At the moment happiness seemed a distant state that no bus ride could ever take her to, but she didn't tell that to Nana.

"We don't have to make a decision right this minute," Nana said. "What I want to hear right now is how you and this Dalton of yours got Brandon Sinclair arrested."

This Dalton of yours. How she wished it were so. For the next thirty minutes she related all that had happened to Nana.

She'd just finished her story when a knock sounded. Janette jumped off the bed and opened the door to see Dalton. She'd left something behind, that was the first thought that jumped into her head at the sight of him. He was here to deliver whatever item she'd forgotten to pack.

"We need to talk," he said without preamble. He started to step inside but she held the door to keep him out.

"I'm all talked out," she replied.

"Janette, please. It's important." His body vibrated with tension and a fierce intensity radiated from his eyes.

Janette looked over her shoulder at Nana seated on the bed holding Sammy, then back at Dalton. "We can't talk in here."

"In my truck, then."

She hesitated, wondering if she could handle any more from him. "Okay, I'll be out in just a minute." She closed the door and turned to face her grandmother. "It's Dalton. He says he needs to talk to me. It's probably about the case." She grabbed her coat and pulled it on. "I should be back in just a few minutes."

Nana stared at her for a long moment. "Follow your heart, honey," she said as if she knew everything that had happened between Janette and Dalton.

Janette slipped out of the door and headed for his truck, all the while telling herself that she'd followed her heart and it had led her into pain.

She opened the passenger truck door and slid inside. "What's up?" she asked.

For what seemed like an eternity he stared directly

ahead, as if she wasn't seated next to him and waiting for him to speak.

What was he thinking? Why was he here?

"A year ago I was on assignment in Tulsa guarding a woman who'd been the victim of domestic abuse." He didn't look at her but continued to stare out the front window. "We both got caught up in each other, started making plans for our future together. When the assignment was over I came back here to Cotter Creek, certain that within a short period of time Mary and I would begin to build a life together. But before that happened, she realized that she'd mistaken gratitude for love, had gotten caught up in the fantasy we'd spun. It was a fantasy that had nothing to do with reality."

His words stunned her, and her heart swelled with grief for him, for the dreams of happiness he'd obviously had for himself, dreams that had never come to fruition.

He turned and looked at her then, and his eyes were as dark, as mysterious as a primal forest. "My feelings for you have made me realize Mary was right. Not only did she not love me, but I wasn't really in love with her. I'm in love with you, Janette, but I can't go through it again. I don't want to bind myself to you heart and soul only to find out a month or two from now that what you feel for me really isn't love after all."

"Dalton, there are many things in my life at the moment that I'm uncertain about, but my love for you isn't one of them." She reached out and placed her hand on his forearm, needing to touch him.

"I don't love you because you gave me shelter from a snowstorm, and I don't love you because you saved me from Brandon Sinclair. I love you because when you look at me, I feel strong and beautiful. I love the sound of your laughter and that little wrinkle you get in your forehead when you frown."

Tears filled her eyes as she continued. "I love your strength but I also love your weaknesses. Oh, Dalton, don't you see? I'm a woman who has been able to separate my feelings about Sinclair and what he did to me and love the result of that horrible act. I'm certainly able to know the difference between my gratefulness to you and my love for you."

His eyes began to sparkle with a light that warmed her heart. "What weaknesses?"

She laughed, because she saw her future shining from his eyes. "Hopefully we'll have many years together for me to point out each and every one of them."

He leaned toward her and traced his finger down the side of her face, all trace of humor gone. "Stay, Janette. Stay in Cotter Creek with me. Let me be more than just a temporary bodyguard in your life. Let me be the man who stands beside you and Sammy for the rest of your life."

"Yes," she whispered. "I want that."

"And I want it, too." He dropped his hand from her face. "And now we need to get out of this truck so I can really hold you in my arms and kiss you hard enough, love you enough that you never doubt how much I love you."

"Dalton West, you take my breath away," she said as she opened the truck door. They met in front of the truck and he grabbed her in an embrace that left no room for doubts, no question that her future would be one filled with laughter and love.

Epilogue

"How soon can we get out of here?" Dalton leaned over and whispered in Janette's ear.

Here was a tent on the West property where Meredith West and Chase McCall had just exchanged their wedding vows. It had been a beautiful ceremony and the late March weather had cooperated with a day of sunshine and blue skies.

The band was playing and people not only danced on the wooden dance floor, but also helped themselves to the banquet that had been prepared for the big event.

"Why are you in such a big hurry, Mr. West?" she asked lightly. "It's a beautiful day and Nana is babysitting."

"That's exactly my point, Mrs. West." His eyes glittered. "We could be spending this entire afternoon in bed."

Mrs. West. She and Dalton had married in a quiet

ceremony at city hall two weeks ago, and she still thrilled at the words that identified her as his wife.

"Nana is keeping Sammy overnight so there's plenty of time for us," she replied with a grin.

At that moment Red West stepped up in front of them. "I make it a habit despite my arthritis to dance with every one of my daughters-in-law, and I haven't had the pleasure of dancing with you yet." He held out a hand to her.

Janette smiled warmly. "I'd be delighted." She took his hand in hers and together they walked toward the dance floor.

"I understand congratulations are in order," Red said as they began to move to the slow music.

A burst of pride filled Janette. "Yes. It was a long time coming, but I finally got my GED."

"And Dalton tells me you've already signed up for college classes for this summer."

"I have. I'm really excited about it. I hope to get a teaching degree and I'd love to teach first or second grade."

"You'll do well." Red smiled down at her and Janette felt his affection radiating from his pale-blue eyes.

Over the past two months, Dalton's family had embraced her with warmth. Nana had gotten settled into a brand-new trailer on the lot where her old one had burned down, and Janette and Dalton were house-hunting, as the apartment was too small for a family.

The biggest news over the past two months had been the eight women who had contacted Trent to tell him that they, too, had been raped by Brandon Sinclair. Much to Janette's surprise, she had found herself something of a local hero.

"I'm a happy man today," Red said, and she followed his gaze to the area where the family was congregated together. "Tanner has his Anna and their new little baby. Zack is happy with Katie. Clay and Libby and little Gracie are building a wonderful life together. Savannah was the best thing that ever happened to Joshua, and Meredith has finally married the man who makes her happy.

"Then there's you." Once again he smiled. "You and that little boy put a smile on my son's face and a lightness to his step. All my kids have found love, and I expect their mama is smiling down from heaven."

Janette looked up at the old man. "And she must be proud of you for raising her children to be wonderful adults."

"I expect she is," he agreed as the music ended.

As he led her off the dance floor Dalton stood, his eyes gleaming with wicked delight. "She's a keeper, son," Red said as they reached him.

"I know, Dad. Believe me, I know." As Red left, Dalton leaned down to Janette. "Now can we get out of here? All this wedding stuff has made me want to spend alone time with my wife."

"I'll race you to the truck," she said and whirled around and began to run.

She heard his burst of laughter just behind her and she slowed to let him catch her as love swelled inside her. The storm had passed and spring had come, and it had brought with it all her heart desired

* * * * *

LADY KILLER

BY
KATHLEEN CREIGHTON

Kathleen Creighton has roots deep in the California soil but has relocated to South Carolina. As a child, she enjoyed listening to old timers' tales and her fascination with the past only deepened as she grew older. Today, she says she is interested in everything – art, music, gardening, zoology, anthropology and history, but people are at the top of her list. She also has a lifelong passion for writing and now combines her two loves in romance novels.

For Tom and Deb, Bob and Melodie
whose acceptance and love enrich my life
beyond measure.

Prologue

In a house on the shores of a small lake somewhere in South Carolina...

"**P**ounding—that's always the first thing. Someone—my father—is banging on the door. Banging...pounding...with his fists, feet, I don't know. Trying to break it down."

"And...where are *you?*"

"I'm in a bedroom, I think. I don't remember which one. I have the little ones with me. It's my job to look after them when my father is having one of his...spells. I have to keep them out of his way. Keep them safe. I've taken them into the bedroom, and I've locked the door, except...I don't trust the lock, so I've wedged a chair

under the handle, like my mom showed me. Only…now
I'm afraid…terrified even that won't be enough. I can
hear the wood splintering…breaking. I know it will
only take a few more blows and he'll be through. My
mother is screaming…crying. I hold on to the little
ones…I have my arms around them, and they're all
trembling. The twins, the little girls, are sobbing and
crying, 'Mama, Mama…' but the boys just cry quietly.

"I hear sirens…more sirens, getting louder and
louder, until it seems they're coming right into the room,
and there's lots of people shouting…and all of a sudden
the pounding stops. There's a moment…several minutes…when all I hear is the little ones whimpering…and
then there's a loud bang, so loud we—the children and
I—all jump. We hold each other tighter, and there's
another bang, and we flinch again, and then there's just
confusion…voices shouting…footsteps running…glass
breaking…the little ones crying…and I think I might be
crying, too.…"

He discovered he *was* crying, but he also knew it was
all right. *He* was all right. Sam, his wife, was holding
him tightly, cradling his head against her breasts, and her
hands were gentle as they wiped the tears from his face.

"I'm going to find them, Sam. My brothers and sisters.
I have to find them."

Samantha felt warm moisture seep between her lashes.
"Of course, you do." She lifted her head and took her
husband's face between her hands and smiled fiercely at
him through her tears. "We'll find them together, Pearse,"
she whispered. "We'll find them. I promise you we will."

Chapter 1

The black SUV was parked just off the main road on the rocky dirt track that ran around the back side of Brooke's twenty-five acres. Not far enough off the road to be hidden by the live oaks that grew thickly there, so she couldn't help but see it as she slowed for her driveway a hundred yards farther on. She didn't need to see the license plate to know who the SUV belonged to, and the knowledge sent a shock wave of fury through her. There could be only one reason for that car being parked where it was.

Duncan was spying on her.

The cold, clutching feeling in her stomach was one she'd come to know well in the months since Duncan had filed for custody of Daniel. Although the divorce

had been no picnic, she'd never been afraid, not *then*.
Only relieved. But that had been before she'd had to
consider the unthinkable: the possibility that she could
lose Daniel.

I can't lose Daniel. Duncan Grant is not *taking my son.*

She wouldn't have thought such a thing could happen,
never in a million years. She was a good mother. She
owned her own ranch—twenty-five acres' worth, tiny by
Texas standards, but at least it was paid for—and thanks
to the untimely death of her parents in a freeway pileup
two years ago, she was also independently well-off. But
this was still a good ol' boy's county, and Duncan being
a deputy sheriff, he had powerful allies. And now, thanks
to that idiot at the feed store who'd lost her order, Duncan
might actually have that ammunition he'd been looking
for in his battle to win custody of their son.

Because of the delay at the feed store, she was late
getting home. Daniel would have been home alone for
at least an hour, and although Brooke knew he was an
exceptionally responsible child and quite capable of
taking care of himself for that period of time, she feared
a judge would consider only the fact that he was nine
years old and disregard any mitigating circumstances.

Damn Duncan, anyway. How could he have managed
to show up unannounced on the one day it mattered? He
wasn't due to have Daniel until next weekend. How had
he known? Unless—her stomach clenched again—
unless one of his buddies had happened to see her truck
in town and had reported it to him. It was the kind of
thing Duncan would do, set his network of good ol' boys
to spying on her for him.

Then she thought, Oh, Brooke, you're being paranoid.

But the thought came creeping back: why else would he be here, lurking on the back lane?

All that rocketed through her mind in a matter of seconds while she closed the distance between the lane and her mailbox, and her heart was tripping along faster than it ought to and the coldness was sitting in her belly as she turned into her driveway. The coldness spread all through her as she drove past the live oaks that surrounded her house and the accompanying assortment of outbuildings and animal enclosures that qualified the property as a ranch.

Where in the world is Hilda? And Daniel?

Normally, the Great Pyrenees—Duncan had given the huge dog, then only an adorable fur ball, to Daniel on his fifth birthday—would come bounding out to meet her, giddy with joy at her return, with Daniel not far behind. But the lane remained empty, and there was still no sign of either child or shaggy white-and-fawn dog as Brooke circled the house and drove across the yard to the barn and the feed storage shed next to it. The place seemed deserted.

That is, until she turned off the motor and opened the door. Then the noise hit her. Hilda's frantic barking. And something else. Something that made the hair prickle on the back of her neck: the unmistakable scream of an angry cougar.

Whispering—whimpering— "OhGodohGodohGod, please, God…no…" under her breath, Brooke tumbled out of the pickup and raced through the open middle of the barn. Out the back and down the lane between the

animal pens she ran, not even aware of her feet touching
the ground. The cougar's screaming and Hilda's barking
grew louder as she ran, filling her head, filling her with
a fear so terrible, she couldn't think, couldn't feel, could
barely even see.

What she did see, as if through the wrong end of a tele-
scope, was Hilda, lunging frantically at the gate to the
wire-enclosed compound far down at the end of the lane
and barking with frustration at her inability to get past
the high chain-link barricade. Brooke felt a momentary
surge of relief, followed by an even more desperate fear.

Lady—thank God! She's not loose, after all! But—
oh, God—where is Daniel? Oh, my God—Daniel!

Her son was nowhere in sight, but for Hilda to be so
upset, he had to be here. Which could only mean one
thing. He was *inside* the cougar's compound.

But why? Although she and Daniel had raised the
cougar together from a tiny kitten, the boy knew very
well Lady wasn't a pet, that she was a wild predator and
could never be trusted. Daniel would never go into her
cage. Not alone. He just *wouldn't*.

But he had. She could hear him now, his voice qua-
vering and breathless one moment, firm and command-
ing the next. *And he sounds so very, very young*.

Shouting, sobbing "No—no, Lady—*back*. Lady—
back!"

Sobbing herself now, Brooke reached the cougar's enclosure, and gripping the wire with both hands, she stared
in disbelief at the scene beyond the fence. Daniel, with
his back to her, *her child,* holding a rake aloft like a battle
sword and a folded saddle blanket over his other arm like

a shield, facing down a full-grown mountain lion. And the lion, teeth bared, screaming and snarling in fury as she backed slowly toward the door to her holding cage, pausing now to swipe at the air with her claws.

"Daniel!" His name felt ripped from her throat by forces outside herself.

He didn't turn, but she heard his breathless "I'm okay, Mom."

At that moment the cougar, for whatever reason—perhaps returned to sanity from whatever terrible place she'd been by the voice of the only mother she'd ever known?—gave one last huffing growl, turned and sprang through the door and into her cage. Daniel scrambled after her to throw the bar across the door. By that time Brooke had opened the gate to the compound and was there to catch him when he turned, sobbing, into her arms.

But he'd only let himself stay there a moment, of course, being all too mindful of the fact that he was the man in their household now. For the space of a couple of deep, shuddering breaths, he gripped her tightly, arms wrapped around her waist, and allowed her to smooth his sweat-soaked hair with her own shaking hands. Then he let go, stepped back and wiped his face with a quick swipe of a forearm, leaving a smear of mud across one hot red cheek.

"She didn't mean to, Mom. I know she didn't mean to." His words came rapidly, choked and breathless with his efforts to hold the tears at bay.

"Daniel, honey, what—" She reached for him, but he took another step back, eluding her, and shook his head with a heartbreaking desperation.

"She didn't mean to hurt him. I know she didn't."

"Honey, hurt *who?* What are you—"

"It's Dad." He grew still, with a calm that was some-how more frightening than the tears. He drew a deep breath and brushed once more at his damp cheeks. "I think he's dead, Mom." His eyes moved, looking past her.

Biting back another question, Brooke instead jerked herself around to follow his gaze and saw what she hadn't before, when her entire focus had been on her son and the cougar. Saw what looked like a pile of tumbled rags lying a little farther along the base of the chain-link fence.

She stared at it, shock numbing her mind, paralyzing her body, so that for a moment she didn't register what she was seeing. Then she couldn't believe what she was seeing. Couldn't let herself believe. The unthinkable.

Not rags, but clothing. A man's clothing—jeans and a tan-colored shirt. With blood on them. Scuffed cowboy boots turned at an odd angle. And a brown Stetson, the kind the sheriff's deputies wore. She knew that Stetson. She knew those boots.

She didn't know how long she stood there, unable to move, unable to think. Then Daniel moved, started toward the body—for that's what it undeniably was—on the ground, and she reached out and grabbed hold of his arm and pulled him back. "No, no, honey. Don't—" Her voice broke.

"But what if he needs help? What if he's—"

Brooke just shook her head. She simply couldn't make any more words come out of her mouth.

Then, from far off in the distance, she heard sirens.

Daniel heard them, too, and caught a quick breath,

his face seeming to brighten with hope. "I called nine-one-one. I bet that's them. Maybe it's the paramedics. They'll help him, won't they, Mom?"

Hearing the anguish in her son's voice, seeing the entreaty in his dark blue eyes, Brooke felt a measure of calm come to take the place of the shock that had kept her frozen and numb. She took her son by his shoulders—small shoulders, a child's shoulders, too small to bear such a burden—and held him tightly and with a terrible urgency so that he had to look at her. "Daniel, quick, before they get here, tell me what happened. How did this happen? How did he—"

"I don't know, Mom." His eyes grew bright, almost glassy, whether with shock or more tears, Brooke didn't know. "I got home from school and you weren't here, so I came in the house and got an ice-cream sandwich out of the freezer, because I was hungry. And then I heard Hilda barking. And she kept barking and barking. And I thought maybe something was wrong, and you weren't here, so I went out to see, and I brought the cell phone, like you told me."

The sirens were louder now, coming along the road, almost to the driveway. She gave Daniel's shoulders another shake. "Yes, yes, and…"

"And I saw Dad lying there, inside Lady's pen. I don't know how he got in there, Mom, I swear. I didn't leave the gate unlocked."

"Never mind that now. And Lady?"

"She was there, too, sort of crouched down beside… him. She had blood on her—you know, on her paws and stuff. When she saw me, she started snarling and screaming. I never saw her like that before, Mom. I didn't know what to do, so I called nine-one-one. Then I thought maybe he was—maybe Dad was…you know, still alive. So that's when I got the rake and started making her get away from him. She didn't try to attack me or anything, Mom, I swear. It was like she was just really upset. I know she didn't mean to hurt Dad. She wouldn't."

The last words were shouted above the noise of the sirens, which had risen to a deafening crescendo before dying away to a series of wails as the emergency vehicles—several, by the sound of them—pulled one after another into the yard.

Brooke gripped Daniel's shoulders harder. "Listen, don't say anything. I'll handle this. Let me handle it, okay?"

Daniel sniffed and nodded, but his eyes were filled with fear, probably the same fear that was in Brooke's heart. He put both their fears into words, in a very small voice. "They aren't going to kill her, are they? You won't let them kill her." They both knew what happened to animals who turned on their human keepers.

She shook her head and clamped her teeth together, tightening her jaws as she turned to face the fire department paramedics who were just coming through the barn, coming at a rapid jog-trot.

"In here! He's in here."

She opened the gate and held it as the EMTs—a young man she didn't know and a woman she knew from church, a heavyset Hispanic girl named Rosie—brushed past her. As she watched them kneel beside the body and immediately check for a pulse, Brooke reached for

Daniel and pulled him against her, held him snug against her front, with her arms crisscrossing his chest. She could feel him trembling and realized she was, too.

Then time seemed to slow, and it seemed a very long time passed while she watched the two EMTs bending over the body of the man she'd once loved, once shared a bed with, still shared a child with...watched them calmly and methodically going about their business, all of them knowing it was pointless but going through with it, anyway. That strange and dreamlike feeling persisted until she heard heavy footsteps and half-turned and took a step back to make room for the sheriff's deputies who were just arriving, and her heart sank when she saw one of them was Duncan's partner, Lonnie Doyle.

Of course, it would be Lonnie. This was going to hit him hard.

"Dunk? Ah, no—ah, jeez! Ah, hell—"

Lonnie had barreled past her and gotten close enough to what was lying on the ground being worked on by the EMTs to see who it was, and that whatever the medics were doing, it wasn't going to be enough. She'd unconsciously braced herself but winced anyway when he jerked to a halt, then whirled on her, his fleshy face red with rage.

"What the hell did you *do?* How did this happen? It was that damned cat, wasn't it? That cat killed him—killed my partner!" His hand was at his waist, gripping the handle of his weapon. "Hell, I'm gonna take care of this right now! Right here!"

"No—it wasn't—" Brooke began in a desperate gasp as Daniel uttered a wounded cry and tore himself away from her, hurled himself at the cougar's cage and spread-eagled himself across the door.

"It wasn't Lady's fault! It was mine. I did something to make her mad. She didn't mean—"

"No—it was an accident. Just an accident. That's all." Breathless with fear, Brooke planted herself between her son and the man bent on exacting his own version of frontier justice. Though what she hoped to accomplish by doing so, she didn't know. As tall as she was, every bit as tall as Lonnie, she was no match for the man and knew it. He was bullnecked, broad-shouldered and strong as an ox; even Duncan, half a head taller and in good shape himself, had always said he didn't have a prayer of beating Lonnie Doyle in a fair fight. Plus, the man was armed. And in a rage.

"What are you doing, man?" Al Hernandez, the other deputy, jerked at Lonnie's arm and half spun him around.

Lonnie shook off Al's hand. "What I shoulda done years ago. What I told Dunk he shoulda done. Shoulda drowned that cat the day he brought it home. I told him he was crazy. And lookit what's happened. Now I'm gonna kill that thing. I'm gonna shoot it right here and now!"

Al touched Lonnie's arm again. "Come on, man—"

"Not without a warrant, you're not." Brooke spoke loudly and calmly, and both men jerked their heads to look at her the way they might if the cougar itself had spoken. "This animal belongs to me," she went on, trying to keep her voice from quivering. "She is not an imminent threat to anybody now. You don't know what happened, or how it happened. You have no cause to shoot her, and if you try, you'll have to do it through me."

She saw Lonnie's small blue eyes glitter with a dangerous light, saw his jaw jut forward in a way she'd seen it do before, and wondered if she'd gone too far. She felt Daniel creep out from behind her to stand at her side. She felt his arm slip around her waist and wished, for his sake, she could stop shaking. She braced herself as Lonnie took a threatening step toward her.

But then Rosie came walking up, peeling off her gloves and shaking her head as she joined the two deputies. She spoke to them in a voice too low for Brooke to hear over the pounding in her head, and the two men turned and walked back to where the second EMT was packing up his gear. But not before Lonnie stabbed a finger at Brooke and said in a voice hoarse with fury, "This ain't over, Brooke. Count on it."

Rosie paused, looking uncertain, then came over to Brooke and reached out to lay a hand on her shoulder. "Brooke, Daniel—I'm so sorry. We did everything we could."

"I know you did. It's okay." Brooke felt her head nodding up and down, like a mechanical toy.

"Is there anything I can do? You want me to call Pastor Farley?"

"Yes, thank you. I'd appreciate that," Brooke murmured, although at that moment she didn't want to see or talk to anyone. All she wanted was to be alone with her son in her house, where she could fix him hot dogs for dinner and pretend the past thirty minutes or so hadn't happened. That it had all been a dream—a nightmare. She wanted desperately for it to all be a dream, a mistake, for there to be some sort of magic pill she could take to make it all go away.

Except she knew that wouldn't happen. And that the nightmare was just beginning.

Numbly, she watched the EMTs pack up their gear and make their way back through the barn to their parked vehicle. Al was speaking into the radio on his shoulder, calling for a forensics team, and Lonnie went loping off to the department SUV and returned carrying a roll of yellow plastic tape. Brooke had been the wife of a law enforcement officer for seven years; she knew what it all meant.

Her ex-husband, Daniel's father, was dead. This was a crime scene now.

Al finished talking into his radio and came over to where she and Daniel were standing, Daniel with his arm around her waist, still, his body rigid and straight as a post. Brooke, with her arm protectively around his shoulders, was the only one who'd know he was shaking, too. Al hauled in a breath and took on a cop's authoritative stance, with his thumbs hooked in his belt and his chest out.

"I'm gonna have to ask you to go on to the house now, if you wouldn't mind. We're gonna need to ask you some questions, but for right now, I need for you to move out of the way so we can do our job here, which is findin' out exactly what happened. You understand? We're gonna find out what happened to your husband."

My ex-husband! Brooke thought but only nodded.

Beside her, Daniel was shaking his head violently. "No—uh-uh, I'm not leaving. If we do, you'll shoot

Lady. And it wasn't her fault, what happened to Dad. I know it wasn't."

The deputy's stern cop face softened. He gave a little cough and said, "Now, son, nobody's gonna shoot your cat. I'm not gonna let that happen."

Daniel drew himself up and squared his shoulders. "You better promise." Brooke felt so proud, she almost smiled.

Al Hernandez did smile. "Yeah, son, I promise. There'll be an au—" he threw Brooke a look of apology, coughed again and said "—an investigation, and then a judge is gonna decide what to do about your cougar. Until that all happens, nobody's gonna touch her. Okay?"

Daniel didn't reply, and Brooke felt the resistance in his rigid body. The distrust. Though she understood just how he felt, she tightened her hold on his shoulders, and they left the compound together.

On the way to the house, she remembered the groceries still sitting in the truck. Daniel helped her carry them into the house and put them away, but when she asked him what he wanted for supper, he told her he wasn't hungry. Again, she knew how he felt but poured him a glass of orange juice, anyway, and as an afterthought, poured one for herself, too.

She pulled out a chair, and Daniel hitched himself sideways onto another, and they sat facing each other across the kitchen table, not looking directly at each other. Daniel took a cautious sip of his orange juice, then said, "I have homework."

Brooke took a sip of her juice and said, "What kind?"

"Math," said Daniel. "And social studies."

"I don't think you need to worry about that right now," Brooke told him, and he nodded and didn't ask why. That was the thing about Daniel; he understood so much without being told. Maybe too much for a child his age. Seen too much, too. Things no child of any age should have to see.

Brooke folded her hands together on the table in front of her and stared at them, marveling at how calm she felt. She wondered when it was going to hit her, the fact that Duncan was dead, killed by an animal she'd hand-raised from a kitten. And that he'd been found in a bloody mess by his nine-year-old son. She wondered when it was going to hit Daniel. She took a breath and looked at him and felt an awful twisting pain just below her heart.

"We have to talk," she said. "About what we're going to say when they ask us questions." Daniel continued to stare at his glass of orange juice. "Honey, I need you to tell me exactly what happened."

He drew a put-upon breath. "I already did. It was just like I said." He closed his eyes and went on in a singsong voice. "I got home, and I came in the house, and I got myself an ice-cream sandwich, and I heard Hilda barking, so I went out to see what was wrong, and I took the cell phone, because you told me I should always take it when I go out to the animals in case I need to call for help. And I saw…what I told you."

Forcing herself not to look at the fine blue veins in his eyelids or the bright spots of pink in his otherwise pale cheeks, Brooke persisted. "Honey, I'm sorry. They're going to ask you these things. Did you, um, look at your dad? Did you see any…" But she couldn't bring herself to ask him about the wounds. She didn't want to know about the wounds. Instead, choosing her words carefully, she said, "Daniel, did you see Lady bite your dad?"

He shook his head violently, and she saw him press his lips together hard for a moment before he answered, "No! I told you. She was just crouched down beside him, and she sort of…sniffed him, and then she pushed at him with her head—like this." He demonstrated. "Then she saw me, and she jumped back and started snarling and making that screaming noise and batting her paws at me. It was like—" He stopped, and the pink in his cheeks deepened.

"What, honey? It's okay. You can tell me."

He looked up at her at last, almost defiantly. "It was like she didn't want me to come in there, okay? Like she was trying to make me stay away. I know it sounds weird, but it was like she was trying to protect me. Like she didn't want me to see—"

"Oh, Daniel." Brooke wanted to smile at him, but the ache in her throat and in her whole face made it impossible. She could think of another reason for the cougar's behavior, of course, one more in keeping with the nature of a predator. She was probably trying to protect her "kill." *Sweetheart, don't you see that?*

But she didn't say it. So what if her son had found his own way of coping with the awfulness of what had happened? She'd let him keep whatever comfort he could for as long as he could.

"I knew you wouldn't believe me. That's why I didn't tell you," Daniel said as he scooted back his chair and carried his juice glass to the sink.

He was heading out of the kitchen, probably going to his room, but at that moment there was a knock on the kitchen door—the back door, the one they and nearly everyone who came to visit always used. Brooke could see Al Hernandez standing on the porch steps, looking off across the yard, where the CSI van and the medical examiner's wagon had joined the two sheriff's department SUVs. *Thank God,* she thought. That meant Lonnie would be out overseeing the processing of the crime scene and the…victim, and she was relieved not to have to deal with his anger and hostility. This was going to be difficult enough without that, she was sure.

When she went to let the deputy in, she saw that he had Hilda with him, on a makeshift rope leash. The dog was panting and grinning, interrupting herself frequently to lick her chops, a sure sign she was agitated. She'd been sitting quietly at Al's side, but when Brooke opened the screen door, she bounded past her, into the house, and Brooke could hear the scrabbling of toenails on the linoleum as she streaked across the kitchen, making, no doubt, for her favorite refuge, Daniel's room. She heard Daniel talking to the big dog in quiet tones as she nodded at the deputy and said, "Come on in, Al."

"Sorry about that," Al said, with a nod of his head in the general direction Hilda had taken. "I'd appreciate it if you could keep her in here until we're…uh, everything's done out here. She's been raising quite a ruckus."

"I can imagine," Brooke said, with a small huff of laughter—the nervous kind—and she wished she hadn't done it and made a note to herself not to do it again. She took a quick breath and added, "It's fine. I should have thought to bring her when I came in." She gestured toward the chair Daniel had been sitting in. "Have a seat. Can I get you anything?"

"No, ma'am. I am gonna need to talk to the boy, though. Is he—"

"I'm right here," Daniel said, coming into the kitchen. To Brooke, he said, "I put Hilda in my room, Mom. She's pretty upset."

"Daniel—" She held out her arm to bring him close, but he evaded her and instead pulled out another chair and sat down.

"I know. You want to ask me questions about what happened to my dad."

Brooke felt an unexpected urge to cry and clamped a hand over her mouth to stop it. Al Hernandez said, "That's right, son. I need you to tell me everything you can about what happened out there. Can you do that?"

Daniel said, "Sure," and went on to tell his story again, without the smarty-pants tone he'd used with Brooke, while Al jotted notes in a notebook he'd taken out of his uniform pocket.

"So, that's the first you knew anything was wrong?" Al asked when he'd finished. "When you heard the dog barking?" Daniel nodded. "And you didn't see anybody around the place? Hear anybody? Any cars?" Daniel shook his head. "And your dad—he didn't come here, to the house?"

Daniel shook his head again, rapidly this time, and began to fidget in his chair. "No, I didn't see him. I haven't seen him for a while, actually. Next weekend's his weekend to have me. I don't usually see him otherwise." His face was very pale, so that the freckles across his nose and the tops of his cheeks stood out like sprinkles of sand.

Al must have noticed it, too, because his eyes and voice were kind as he said, "Okay, son, that's fine. I think that's all. You did fine."

"So," said Daniel, "can I go now?"

"Sure, go on. Take care of your dog." The deputy waited until Daniel had disappeared down the hall and they heard the thump of the closing door. Then he leveled a look that was considerably less kind at Brooke and said, "Okay, now I'll ask you the same thing. Tell me exactly what you saw and did. Your son said you were gone when this happened?"

She cleared her throat and nodded. "Yes, that's right. I'd gone to town for feed and groceries, and I was late getting back because—" she gave that nervous laugh she'd promised herself she wouldn't "—well, I guess you don't want to know all that."

Al just looked at her and waited for her to go on. She told herself she had no reason to be nervous, but she was. So nervous her mouth felt like dust. She clasped her hands together in front of her on the tabletop and tried to make them look relaxed. Natural.

"Um…anyway, when I got home, the first thing I saw was Duncan's SUV parked on that back road, the one that goes around the property. I thought—" She paused, but Al just nodded and didn't interrupt. "I thought it was strange, him being there, but I came on to the house, and then I thought it was strange that Hilda—that's the dog—and Daniel didn't come running out to meet me, like they usually do. It wasn't until I turned off the motor and was getting out of the truck that I heard the noise."

"What did you hear, exactly?"

"I heard Hilda barking, and then I heard Lady—the cougar—scream. And that's when I ran." Her voice had begun to shake. She fought to control it while the deputy waited patiently, staring down at the notes he'd made.

She wished she could get up and get a glass of water. She wished she could run to her bedroom and crawl under the covers and pull a pillow over her head.

After a moment, she drew a quivering breath and went on. She described everything that had happened, and when she was finished, she was surprised to discover she'd been crying. For some reason, that embarrassed her, and she tried to wipe the tears away surreptitiously while Al was still looking down, writing in his notebook. She waited for him to ask more questions, and when he didn't, she cleared her throat again and said, "Al, can I ask you something?"

He glanced up, frowning.

"What did he—I mean, how did he look? You know, were the wounds…" She touched her lips with her fingertips, and more tears rolled down her cheeks. This time she didn't try to wipe them away. "I just really need to know. Did Lady kill him?"

"Ma'am, I can't make that kind of judgment. That's up to the ME." He paused, then seemed to relent. "I will tell you there's some blood on Dunk's clothes, and some—not a lot—on the ground. We'll just have to wait for the autopsy to determine how he died. Now, if you don't mind, I have just a few more questions…"

He asked her about the compound, the gate, how it was locked up and who had a key. He asked her how she thought Duncan might have gotten into the pen with the cougar, and why.

"That's what I can't imagine," Brooke said in a whisper. "Duncan was deathly afraid of that cat, although he'd never have admitted it. He always wanted to get rid of it. When I told him I wanted to start a refuge for big cats—you know, like, animals people take as pets, then can't take care of when they get big and dangerous—he thought I was nuts. He even insisted on buying a tranquilizer gun, just in case, because he said he knew I'd never be able to shoot her, if it came to that." Her voice broke, and as she paused to control it, a thought occurred to her. "I wonder why he didn't— Duncan, I mean. Didn't he have his gun?"

Al gave her an unreadable look. "It wasn't on him, no, ma'am. We found it in his vehicle."

He tucked his notebook and pencil back in his pocket and rose. "I guess that's all—for now. We'll be in touch once the medical examiner's done." He thanked her, nodded a farewell and left the way he'd come, through the back door.

Brooke sat where he'd left her, with one hand covering her mouth and her eyes closed, listening to the sounds of vehicles coming and going outside in the yard, and the distant mutter of men's voices. She didn't want to listen to the voices rumbling around inside her own head, but they kept intruding, anyway.

Something isn't right about this. I can feel it. Something's not right. It doesn't make sense.

Either Daniel wasn't telling her the whole story, or…or what? She didn't know. Only that something was wrong.

After a while—she didn't know how long—she realized the noises outside had stopped. That all the official vehicles had gone. Finally. The sun had gone down. It was past time to feed the animals. Only her ingrained sense of responsibility made her get up and go outside and throw some hay to the two horses, six goats and two alpacas, and close and bar the chicken-house door. She didn't go down to the far end of the corrals, where Lady's compound was. The cougar was in her holding cage and would be all right where she was until tomorrow.

Back in the house, she went to check on Daniel and Hilda and found both in Daniel's bed, sound asleep on top of the covers. Daniel had one arm thrown across the dog's body, and Hilda had her muzzle resting on the boy's chest. She went to her own room and got a comforter and spread it over the softly snoring pair. Then, after a moment, she lifted the edge of the comforter and lay down, stretching herself out beside her son. With her arm across his body and her face nestled in his damp hair, breathing the salty, small-boy smell of him, she fell asleep.

In the morning, she was in the kitchen, making blueberry pancakes—Daniel's favorite breakfast—when the knock came. Not on the kitchen door, the one everyone always used, but on the front door. Her hands shook slightly as she wiped them on a dish towel and went down the hall and through the living room to answer it.

Sheriff Clayton Carter stood on her front porch. He was wearing his brown Stetson, and his arms were folded across the front of his unbuttoned Western-style jacket. He didn't smile or remove his hat when Brooke opened the door, and she didn't smile and say that it was a nice surprise to see him and ask if he would care to come in for coffee.

"Ma'am, would you step out here please?" the sheriff said.

Moving as if in a dream, Brooke did, and two uniformed deputies she didn't know came up the steps behind the sheriff, and one of them took her arm and turned her around.

"Brooke Fallon Grant," the sheriff said, "I'm placing you under arrest for the murder of Duncan Grant. You have the right to remain silent...."

Then Brooke's head filled with the sound of high winds, and for some time she didn't hear anything else. Not until she was in the sheriff's car and being driven out of the yard, and she looked back and saw Daniel being restrained by one of the uniformed deputies. She heard his shrill and stricken cry.

"Mom! *Mama*..."

Chapter 2

The last thing Holt Kincaid had expected to encounter when he drove into Colton, Texas, was a traffic jam. According to the information he'd gotten off the Internet, the population still hadn't topped seven thousand, probably due to the fact that the town was just outside reasonable commuting distance from both Austin and San Antonio, and its residents hadn't yet figured out how to capitalize on its Hill Country charm and local history to bring in the tourist trade. From what Holt could see, the town's two main industries appeared to be peaches and rocks, and while there was still an apparently endless supply of the latter—in spite of the fact that nearly all the buildings on the main drag were constructed out of them—the season for the former was pretty much over. And it didn't seem likely the excess of vehicular traffic was due to rush hour, either, since it was mid-morning and, anyway, in his experience in towns like this, what passed for "rush hour" usually coincided with the start and end of the school day.

Also, it didn't seem likely that local traffic, no matter how heavy, could account for the high number of vans and panel trucks he was seeing, with satellite antennas sprouting out of their tops and news-station logos painted on their sides.

During his slow progress through the center of town, Holt was able to discern that the excitement seemed to be centered around the elaborate and somewhat oversized Gothic-style, stone—of course—courthouse, which was located a block off the highway, down the main cross street. A crowd had gathered on the grassy square in front of the courthouse, everyone sort of milling around in the shade of several big oak trees, the way people do when they're bored to death but expecting something exciting to happen any minute.

The sense of anticipation—almost euphoria—with which he'd entered the town, certain he was almost at the end of what had been a long and often frustrating quest, was replaced now by a sense of caution, developed over his long years of experience as a private investigator with a specialty in finding people. While it didn't seem likely this unexpected gathering of news media could have anything to do with his reason for being here in the town of Colton, he figured it wouldn't hurt to know exactly what he was getting into the middle of.

A few blocks past the courthouse, the traffic thinned out considerably, and Holt pulled off onto a side street and found a parking spot across from a diner, the inauspicious kind frequented by locals rather than passing-through motorists looking for a familiar franchise.

On his way into the diner, he dropped a quarter into a box dispensing the local newspaper, which he folded in half and tucked under his arm as he made his way past empty booths to take a seat at the counter—also empty, except for a waitress taking her mid-morning coffee break. Holt had an idea the usual denizens of the place could probably be found among the crowd down at the courthouse.

As he was taking his seat on one of the cracked red vinyl and chrome stools, the waitress wiped her mouth with a paper napkin, slid off her stool and swept, with a flourish, around the end of the counter to present herself behind the section he'd just occupied.

"Hi," she chirped. "My name is Shirley, and I'll be your server today. How may I help you?" And then she gave a throaty chortle to show she was just putting him on, and said in what Holt imagined was her natural Texas twang, "What can I get for ya, hon?"

Shirley was a heavyset woman in her forties, probably, with Day-Glo red curls piled on top of her head and laugh lines radiating from the corners of her vivid blue eyes. She had a nice smile, so Holt smiled back and said, "Coffee, for starters." He tilted his head toward the glass case behind the counter. "And maybe a piece of that pie there. Is that peach?"

"Sure is," Shirley said, beaming. "Local, too. And the season's 'bout over, so you hit it just right. Can I put a scoop of ice cream on that for ya?"

"No thanks—got to watch my waistline." He patted himself in that general area, and Shirley gave him a severe look and what could only be described as a snort.

"Oh, sure, like you need to worry. Mister, you turn sideways, you'd just 'bout disappear." While she was saying this, she was efficiently dishing up a slice of pie and placing it in front of him, with a fork and a spoon beside it.

Holt waited until a mug of steaming coffee had joined the pie, then picked up the fork and said, "Where is everybody?"

Shirley made that same inelegant noise as she leaned against the stainless-steel counter behind her and folded her arms across her ample bosom. "Down at the courthouse, probably. Along with just about ever'body else in this town. It's where I'd be, too, if I wasn't stuck holdin' down the fort here."

Holt dug into the pie, which was delicious, maybe the best fresh peach pie he'd ever eaten. "I saw the media trucks as I was coming through. What's all the excitement about?"

Shirley tipped her head toward his left arm. "Well, you could read all about it in that paper you got propping up your elbow there. One of our local deputy sheriffs got killed a couple days ago—by a mountain lion, it looked like. And then they went and arrested his wife— ex-wife, I should say—for murder. Biggest thing to happen around here in a while, I'll tell you. The whole state of Texas seems to have caught it now, too— because it was a cop that got killed, I guess. Or the lion angle, maybe. Anyway, it sure is a shame. They had a kid, too, a little boy. I guess he's been staying with the preacher at their church."

Holt didn't hear anything more. While the waitress had been talking, he'd unfolded the newspaper and spread it out next to his pie plate. There was the headline, pretty much the way she'd summed it up: Local Deputy Killed By Lion, Ex-wife Arrested, and under that a was photo of the deputy in his dress uniform, complete with Stetson. Holt had started skimming the article and had got as far as the name of the woman who'd been arrested and charged with murdering her ex-husband, Duncan Grant. The name jumped out at him, and it was about like having a rattlesnake coil up and strike right at his chest. *Brooke Fallon Grant.* Shirley's voice faded into a soft roar, and hot coffee slopped out of the mug and burned his hand.

"Oh—my goodness. Here let me…" Shirley was there with a towel, mopping up. "Hope ya didn't burn yourself. Coffee's pretty hot. Just made a fresh pot…"

He frowned distractedly at her, then relinquished the coffee mug, and she whisked it away and brought him a new one while he tried to absorb the words printed on the newspaper page in front of him.

Mrs. Grant was arrested at her home Thursday morning after an autopsy revealed the presence of large amounts of a tranquilizer in the victim's body. According to sources at the medical examiner's office, the drug had evidently been administered by a tranquilizer dart gun, the type used to subdue large animals.

Deputy Grant's body was discovered by his young son Wednesday afternoon in an animal

*enclosure on his ex-wife's ranch. The enclosure had
been used to house a mountain lion allegedly
hand-raised by Mrs. Grant. The animal was found
in close proximity to Deputy Grant's body and was
assumed to have killed him. However, in light of the
new evidence revealed by the autopsy, it is not
clear now what part the animal might have played
in the deputy's death.*

*According to information received by this reporter,
Mr. and Mrs. Grant had recently been involved in
a dispute over custody of the couple's nine-year-old
son.*

*Arraignment and bail hearing are set to take
place Friday afternoon at the courthouse in Colton.
A hearing to determine the fate of the mountain
lion has not been scheduled, pending further investigation. As the county lacks facilities to house the
animal, the mountain lion remains in its compound on Mrs. Grant's ranch.*

*In the absence of any known relatives, the couple's
son is being cared for by the pastor of Mrs. Grant's
church pending the outcome of Friday's hearing.*

"Yeah, it sure is a shame." Shirley was shaking her
head. "I used to see Duncan in here now and again. All
the deputies like to come in for the pie, you know. I
didn't know him all that well, though—I was a few
years ahead of him in school. Never met his wife... I
don't know, though...seems like a pretty heartless thing
to do, doesn't it? I mean, raise a cougar from a cub—
or whatever you call a baby one—and then try and blame
it for killing somebody? And letting your little boy find

his daddy's body? Hard to imagine a mother doing something like that."

"Sounds like the paper's got her pretty much tried and convicted," Holt said dryly as he slid off the stool and reached for his wallet.

Shirley made that sound again. "Yeah, well, this is kind of a small town, and the local law is real...visible, if you know what I mean. So...you're not plannin' on stayin' around to see how it comes out?"

"Actually, I might stay around for a bit." He laid some bills down on the counter and picked up the paper and tucked it under his arm. "S'pose you could recommend a nice, quiet motel for me? Or have all these media people got everything booked?"

"Seriously." She gave him a wry smile as she scooped up the bills with one hand and the dishes with the other. "They've been pouring into town all day. I'd say you'd probably have to go a ways to find a room."

"Yeah, I figured. Thanks, anyway. Great coffee, by the way. And the best peach pie I ever ate." Holt gave her his nicest smile and turned to go.

"Wait."

With one hand on the door, Holt turned. Shirley was gazing at him in a speculative way and chewing her lip.

"Okay, look, I don't know why, but you strike me as a nice guy. There's a motel just west of here, just off the main drag. It's called the Cactus Country Inn—it's not a chain or a Best Western, or anything, but it's nice. My brother and his wife manage it. They usually keep the room next to their apartment empty, on account of the walls are kinda thin, if you know what I mean. But if you tell 'em I sent you, they'll probably let you have it. Just don't throw any wild parties, though, okay?"

"I think I can promise that," Holt said.

An hour or so later, he sat on the edge of one of two neatly made-up twin-size beds in a fairly decent room— he couldn't remember if he'd ever been in a motel room that had twin-size beds before—in the Cactus Country Inn. He punched a number on his cell phone speed dial and while he listened to it ring, imagined it ringing in a room far away, in South Carolina, on the shores of a small lake. It rang four times before a machine picked up.

"Hello. You've reached Sam and Cory's place. We're both away from home right now. Leave us a message, and we'll get back to you.…"

He disconnected and sat for a moment with the phone in his hand, thinking. Then he pulled the laptop that lay open on the bed closer to him, found the page he was looking for, scrolled down the list of phone numbers on it until he came to the one he wanted. Dialed it.

Several minutes and several different numbers later, he'd learned several things. One, his employer was on assignment in the Sudan, and there was no way in hell to reach him. Two, his employer's wife was also on assignment; only God—and the CIA—knew where.

Three, he was on his own.

Holt Kincaid didn't often feel frustrated, but he did now. Here he'd finally managed to get a line on one of his client's missing twin sisters, and there wasn't anybody he could break the news to.

News that wasn't good.

And he was very much afraid that if he waited for the clients to return from their various assignments, it might be too late. So, he hesitated for another second, maybe, then scrolled on down to the bottom of the list of phone numbers on his computer screen, to the first one listed under the heading In Case of Emergency. He was pretty sure Sam and Cory would agree that finding the subject of their years-long search about to be locked up for murder would qualify as an emergency.

He punched the number into his cell phone and hit the call button.

Tony Whitehall was sitting on his mother's patio, watching his numerous nieces and nephews engaged in mayhem disguised as a game of touch football. The game was probably more fraught with violence than it might have been, due to the fact that it was being played on hard bare dirt, since his mother, being more than half Apache and a native not only of America but the great desert Southwest, had better sense than to try to get a lawn to grow on it. His mother did like flowers, though, which she grew in pots near her front doorsteps, where she could water them with a plastic gallon jug. The rest of her land-scaping consisted mostly of native plants—junipers and ocotillos and barrel cactus and tamarisks for windbreaks and some stubborn cottonwoods and willows along the creek bed, where for two months or so in the spring a trickle of water actually flowed.

For shade, there was the colorful striped fabric of the umbrellas and awnings, which mostly covered the patio that Tony was enjoying, along with a cold beer, when his cell phone rang. That surprised him, first, because cell phone service out here in the wilds of Arizona wasn't all that reliable, and second, because most of the people who had his private cell number were already here.

He fumbled around and managed to get the phone out of his pocket and opened up and the right button pushed before the thing went to voice mail. "Yeah," he said, then remembered to add, "Uh...Tony Whitehall."

Then he had to stick a finger in his ear to hear the person on the other end, because a gaggle of his sisters were at that moment gathered around their mother on the other side of the patio and were exhorting her loudly and passionately about losing some weight. This was an argument they were bound to lose, since Rosetta White-hall was quite content with herself just as she was and was countering her daughters' concerns as she always did by pointing out certain facts: "The women in my family have always been big, and we've always been happy, and we make our men happy, too!"

At the moment, Tony was just happy to have his sisters' attention focused for a few minutes on some-thing else besides him and his persistent state of bache-lorhood. The poking and prying and teasing and nagging was something he'd been putting up with since he'd reached the age of puberty, but lately it had begun to grate on his nerves.

The voice in his ear was still an unintelligible mumble, so he said, "Hold on, I can't hear you," and got up and walked across the patio and made his way around the corner of the house, where he'd be out of vocal range of both the football game and the sisters. "Yeah…okay. So who did you say this is?"

"Sorry. My name is Holt Kincaid. I'm a private investigator. I'm working for a friend of yours—Cory Pearson—tracking down his brothers and sisters, who got separated from him when he was a kid."

"Oh yeah…yeah, I knew about that. Found his brothers already, I heard. Fantastic. That's great. So why are you—"

"Cory gave me your name and number, told me to call you if anything came up while he was on assignment and I couldn't reach either him or Sam—his wife. So…they're both on assignment, and…something's come up. So, I'm calling."

"Wow. So…what? You find the baby sisters?"

"Well, yeah, one of them, but—"

"Hey, no kidding? That's *great*, man!"

"Yeah, well, maybe not. There's…a problem."

"Oh, yeah? What kind of problem?"

"It's a little complicated to explain over the phone, and this is a terrible connection, anyway. How fast can you get to Colton, Texas?"

Gazing off across the dirt yard to where the football game was still in noisy progress, Tony could hear that the voices of his sisters around the corner on the patio had died to a frustrated mutter. Which meant they'd be turning their attention back to him the minute he showed his face again.

"Colton—whereabouts in Texas is that?"

"Uh…roughly southwest of Austin and northeast of nowhere. Hill Country."

"Okay, how's about tonight? Say around dinnertime."

"What? Where in hell are you?"

"At the moment I'm in Arizona, at my mom's. It's her birthday. Talk about northeast of nowhere. Otherwise I'd be there sooner."

"Are you crazy? That's gotta be eight or nine hundred miles."

"What? You think I'm gonna drive it? Across West Texas? Now, that would be crazy. Hey, do me a favor, okay? Check and see if this town you're in has a general-aviation airfield. Failing that, any kind of level airstrip… piece of road—hell, even a cow pasture without too many rocks."

"I can tell you right now, *that's* not gonna happen," the voice on the other end of the phone said dryly. "But I'll look into the airfield and get back to you."

"Cool. I'm on my way."

Tony disconnected the phone and stuck it back in his pocket, then took a breath and summoned the courage to go and break the news to his mother that he was going to be leaving her birthday party a little sooner than expected.

Brooke's lawyer was an old-school Texan, a grand-fatherly sort named Sam Houston Henderson, from her father's old law firm in Austin. He drove her home after the bail hearing and left her surrounded by a welcoming committee consisting of Daniel; Pastor Steven Farley and his wife, Myra; Rocky and Isabel Miranda, her neighbors from across the road who'd been looking after the animals in her absence; and of course, Hilda, who almost knocked them all flat in her exuberant joy at having the missing members of her "flock" all together and back under her protection again. Brooke was glad to be back, too, of course, but her relief was tempered by what the lawyer had told her in the car on the way home.

"Now, Brooke, honey, you know just because the judge granted you bail doesn't mean you're out of the woods on this thing. You got bail because you've got sole responsibility for your boy and your animals, and because pretty much everything you own is tied up in your place and in that trust your daddy set up for you. So it's not likely you'd be goin' anywhere. And it's also not likely you'd be a further danger to society, so there just wasn't any justification in keepin' you locked up. But that is a deputy sheriff and a local boy you're accused of killin', so we've got one hell of an uphill fight ahead of us. You know that, don't you?"

"What about Lady?" Brooke had asked.

"Lady—oh, yeah, the cougar. Well, now…"

"Lonnie Doyle is going to do his best to have her put down."

"I'm gonna be honest with you, Brooke. It's gonna be tough to argue that lion isn't a dangerous animal. She did maul your husband—"

"Ex-husband."

"—and she did draw blood, whether that was what killed him or not. But for now I don't want you to worry about that. We've got some time before they get around to a hearing about the cat, and right now you need to get yourself rested up so we can figure out how to fight this battle we're in. Okay? Now, you go on and enjoy being with your boy, and have a quiet weekend, and I'll talk to you next week."

"Yes, sir," Brooke had murmured, and now she stood safe in her own home, surrounded by the warmth and love of her son, her dog and her good friends the Farleys and the Mirandas.

"It's gonna be okay, Mom," Daniel whispered as he let her hug him longer than usual.

"I know. Of course, it is." But as she watched Sam Houston Henderson's taillights turn the corner at the end of the lane, inside she felt nothing but cold and hollow and scared to death.

"Must be nice, having your own plane," Holt said to his passenger as they sped back to town on the two-lane FM road that connected it to its surprisingly busy airfield. He'd discovered airfields of the kind that served the town of Colton were pretty common in Texas, which made sense, seeing as how airplanes were probably the most practical means of bridging the enormous distances between anyplace and anyplace else in that part of the country.

"Yeah," Tony said, "the kinds of places my job takes me, sometimes it's about the only way to get there." He looked over at Holt. "Matter of fact, it was your client's wife—Sam—she's the one that taught me to fly."

"That right?"

"We had an…adventure, the three of us, a few years back. In the Philippines. Kind of got me hooked on vintage planes, I guess. She was flying a World War II Gooney Bird at the time. Mine's a little later vintage than that, though—1979 Piper Cherokee. I've got her equipped for long-range flying—extra fuel tanks and all that. Places I go, refueling can be a problem."

Holt glanced at the man taking up what seemed like more than his share of space in the car. From what little chance he'd had to take the man's measure, Holt couldn't in any way, shape or form call him overweight, so it must be something to do with charisma, he decided, that made Tony Whitehall seem larger than life. "So, you're a photographer?"

"Photojournalist," Tony corrected, but with a forgiving grin.

That was another thing Holt had noticed right away, the easygoing but straightforward manner that made a person both like and trust the man instinctively. He was beginning to see why Cory Pearson had put him at the top of his list of people to go to in an emergency.

"Well, you're gonna fit right in, in Colton," he said dryly. "The place is a zoo. Crawling with news media."

"Yeah?" Tony shifted around to look at him. "This wouldn't have anything to do with the 'problem' you mentioned, would it?"

"It would." Holt stared at the road ahead and thought about where to begin. Finally, he said, "You said you knew we found the boys, right? Cory's two brothers. Last summer. Found Wade—the oldest—first. He was a cop up in Portland. And since the two boys had been adopted by the same couple, he put us right in touch with Matt, down in LA."

"Right, and now you say you found the girls?" Tony prompted, but not in an impatient way.

"*One* of the girls." Holt let out a breath. "I thought it was gonna be a cakewalk once I found out they'd been adopted together, too. But turns out the parents were both killed a couple of years ago in a car wreck, along with their biological son—he was quite a bit older than the twins. I found out that this one—Brooke—had married and moved here to Colton. Married a cop, actually. Deputy sheriff. But there wasn't a thing about the other twin—Brenna. Nothing from high school on. She just disappears at that point. So, anyway, I come here to Colton to get a line on Brooke. Scope out the lay of the land, you know? Like I did when I found Wade. Wanted to see how things were, get an idea who this person was before I went to Cory with it. So we'd know the best way to spring the news, you know?"

"I hear you," Tony said, nodding. "You don't just walk up to a stranger and say, 'Hi, there. I'm the brother you didn't know you had.'"

"Right. And it's an even safer bet the twins wouldn't have any idea about having three older brothers, since they were practically just babies when they all got separated. So anyway, I get to Colton, and I find the town in an uproar because one of their deputy sheriffs has just been killed. Originally, it was supposed to have been a mountain lion that killed him—"

"Oh, wow—I saw something about that. It was on CNN just the other night. The cougar was the guy's ex-wife's pet, right? And their little boy found his dad's body. Supposedly an accident, I thought. I didn't get a chance to see the news today—it was my mom's birthday, and the festivities started pretty early. So now—oh, man, don't tell me. *This* is the missing twin? The dead guy's wife?"

"Ex-wife. And it's not an accident anymore. Seems they found something in the autopsy that puts a whole new light on things. In any event, they've arrested my client's baby sister for murder. First degree, premeditated. And in Texas, don't forget, they still have the death penalty. And use it."

Tony uttered a word his mother wouldn't have approved of.

"My sentiments exactly," Holt said.

"So what's the plan?" Tony asked Holt over a club sandwich at a local diner not far from the Cactus Country Inn, where they were staying. A club sandwich was pretty much Tony's standard order when he was in an unfamiliar eatery, since it was pretty hard to ruin one, but watching Holt chomp into his big, thick, juicy burger, he was beginning to regret his choice. "Somehow I don't think me being a photographer is going to get me an in with this lady just now."

The PI nodded as he chewed, then swallowed and said, "Yeah, I know. We're going to have to come up with something—" He broke off, and Tony watched him in amusement as he coughed and tried not to make it too obvious what he was thinking. Something along the lines of, *This guy looks like a bouncer in a mob hangout, and I'm supposed to get him close to a woman who right now is not likely to be trusting anybody short of Dr. Phil?* But it didn't bother him. He was used to it.

"How 'bout the lion?" he said, taking pity on the guy. "I can make it about the cat."

Holt raised his eyebrows over his burger as he prepared to take another bite. "Hmm. Maybe."

"No, seriously. I've done some wildlife pieces before. The reintroduction of wolves into Yellowstone, poaching elephant ivory…stuff like that. Plus—" he grinned around the sandwich he was biting into "—I have a thing for mountain lions."

Holt's eyes narrowed. "A…*thing.*"

Tony thought, *Me and my big mouth.* He didn't know what it was that had made him mention to this stranger something so personal he hadn't even told his best friends, Cory and Sam, about it. But it had been the reason the CNN piece had caught his attention in the first place— the bit about the lion. Now he had to find some way to explain without giving up more personal information than he wanted to. "It's an Indian thing. It's my spirit animal. Or so my mama says." He gave a self-deprecating half shrug.

"No kidding? 'My brother, the lion'—that kind of thing?"

"A little more than that. Hey, it's complicated, and to tell you the truth, I'm not sure my mama's people— they're Apache—were totally into that, anyway. I think she just told me that spirit messenger stuff when I was a little kid to make me get over being scared."

"Of the bogeyman, you mean."

"Something like that." And that was as far as Tony was willing to go on the subject. "Anyway, let's just say

I can make a pretty good case for why she ought to let
me do a piece on her cougar."

"Sounds good to me," Holt said as he polished off the
last bite of his burger and reached for his coffee. "Let's
hope it's good enough."

Chapter 3

Tony hadn't expected to be welcomed by Brooke
Fallon Grant, accused murderer, with open arms. On the
other hand, he hadn't exactly been prepared to find a
shaggy tan-and-white dog the approximate size of a
Shetland pony and a little blond kid armed with a rake—
a *rake?*—blocking the driveway to her house.

He halted the rented sedan he'd borrowed from Holt
in the middle of the tree-shaded lane and ran the window
down. He stuck his head out, smiled winningly and
called, "Hey, there. I'm looking for Brooke Grant. Would
that be your mom?"

"Maybe." The boy was holding the rake with both
hands, crossways in front of him, not smiling back.
"But she's not here."

Tony got out of the car and stood with one elbow leaning on the top of the open door. The kid took a step backward, then held his ground. The dog looked alert but wasn't growling, which Tony took as a positive sign. "Well, now," he said, still smiling, "I see there's a pickup truck parked up there by the house, and you look pretty young to be the driver. Are you sure your mom's not home?"

"Okay, she is, but she doesn't want to see anybody." The boy let go of the rake with one hand and reached into the pocket of his jeans. "If you don't leave, I'm calling nine-one-one on my cell. I have it right here, see?" He produced the object and pointed it at Tony like a pistol.

Tony put his hands in the air. "Hey, okay, son. I'm not here to bother anybody. Look, is it okay if I give you my card?" Not waiting for an answer, which he was pretty sure he wouldn't like, he took out the card he'd put in his shirt pocket for just such an eventuality. He showed it to the kid, then leaned over the open door and placed it on the hood of the car.

Looking as menacing as it's possible for a skinny kid with silky blond hair to look, the boy sidled close enough to snatch up the card, then retreated to his comfort zone and gave it a good look. "It says here you're a photojournalist." He gave Tony a sideways look of suspicion and hostility. "That's like a reporter, right? My mom for *sure* doesn't want to talk to any reporters." He began to thumb the cell phone.

Tony said, "No—wait," and stepped around the door. The dog advanced a step, tail held low and not wagging. Tony hastily returned to his previous position behind the door. "Um, see…it's *like* a reporter, yeah, but I'm not here about your mom, or your…uh, anything like that. Look, what I'm interested in, actually, is your lion."

"Lady?" The boy looked surprised, then uncertain and, consequently, very young. And when he lifted his chin, the combination of vulnerability and defiance made something quiver in the general vicinity of Tony's heart. "She didn't do what they said she did. But they want to put her down, anyway."

"Who does?"

"The sheriffs. Lonnie Doyle, mostly—he's my dad's partner. He says Lady's a killer and she should be put down. But she didn't hurt Dad, at least not on purpose. I know she didn't."

"Well, then," Tony said gently, "sounds like all the more reason to get her story out there, doesn't it? Look here—my Web site address is on that card. Why don't you go ask your mom if you can look me up on the Internet? I'll wait right here while you do it. How's that?"

The boy chewed his lip for a moment; then up came the chin again. "Okay, but you better not come any closer. Hilda, *watch him*," he said to the dog, then turned and headed back up the lane at a dead run.

The dog flopped down on her stomach with her paws in front of her in the attitude of the Sphinx and fixed him with her unblinking stare.

"Good dog," said Tony hopefully and settled down to wait.

"Mom, I think you should talk to him."

"Honey, he's a *photographer*."

"Uh-uh. A *photojournalist*."

"That means he's a reporter. Even worse."

"Uh-uh, I don't think so. He's won awards. It says so right there. And anyway, it's not you he wants to do a story about. It's Lady."

"Of course he'd *say* that. Honey, it's probably just a ploy."

"What's a *ploy*?"

"An angle—a gimmick. A way to get to us. Daniel—"

"I don't think so, Mom." He hitched himself halfway onto a chair and faced her across the kitchen table, his face flushed and earnest. "I don't know why, but I don't think he's lying. He's...I don't know how to explain it—"

"He *looks* nice, is that it?" *Oh, sweetheart, if only it were that easy to tell.*

Her son's expression was impossible to describe. "No. He doesn't. That's what's so weird. He looks really tough and mean, but—" He huffed in a breath, leaned his chin on one hand and pressed his lips together in concentration. Then he said, "It's like...in the movies when there's somebody that always plays the bad guy, and then suddenly he's in a movie, and he's the *good* guy for a change. And he still *looks* like the bad guy, but you just know he's not. Like when Arnold Swarzenegger was really bad in *The Terminator*, but then he was really really good in *Terminator 2*. Like that."

Brooke hesitated, running her thumb over the smooth surface of the small brown card in her hand. What if it was true? What if this man—Daniel's "good guy" Terminator—could help save Lady's life? *And maybe mine, too?*

Daniel slid off the chair with a long-suffering sigh. "Well, can we at *least* check him out on the Internet?"

Brooke gave an exhalation of her own and capitulated. "Sure," she said, handing him the card. "Why not?"

"Your card neglected to mention that one of those awards was a Pulitzer."

Tony jerked out of a heat-and-boredom-induced doze, closed his mouth and focused on the woman standing on the other side of the open car door. His first thought was, *Wow.* His second, more coherent, thought was, *Okay, tall, slim and blond—I see where the kid gets it.* His third thought, as he scrubbed a hand over his face and struggled to extricate himself from the driver's seat, was *Oh man, I hope I wasn't snoring.*

Being as how Brooke Fallon Grant was his buddy Cory's sister and his buddy Cory was a pretty good-looking guy, he hadn't been expecting a troll. But the woman standing before him with her fingertips poked into the back pockets of her jeans, regarding him with a not-at-all-sure-I-should-be-doing-this look on her face…well, the only word that suited her was *lovely.*

Tony had a photographer's eye, of course, one that saw beyond the fatigue lines, no makeup, and hair that was limp and dull and in need of washing. What he saw was dark blue eyes like Cory's, eyes that told you they'd seen more than they wanted to of the world's sadness and suffering. And amazing bones, the kind that made him itch to reach for his camera. Which was too bad, because he was pretty sure the first time he aimed a lens in the lady's direction, she'd sic that monster dog on him.

At the very least. He'd forgotten for a moment that he might be looking at the face of a cold-blooded killer.

Though strangely, all his instincts were screaming, *No way!*

"Tony Whitehall," he said, holding out his hand and turning on every watt of charm he had in him. "Mrs. Grant, thanks for seeing me."

"Thank my son, Daniel." She offered him half a smile along with her hand, which was big-boned for a woman's hand and strong. "He's convinced you're a good guy."

But you're not, are you? "Really?" he said. "Wow, coulda fooled me." His eyes dropped—though not far—to the dog, now standing relaxed beside her mistress and panting lazily. "That's quite a pair of watchdogs you've got."

She glanced down as her hand came to rest on the dog's broad white head, and the camera shutter in Tony's mind clicked madly. "They're very protective of me. Both of them are."

I see what Daniel means, Brooke thought.

There was just something about the man. Something that had nothing to do with his looks, certainly, because he couldn't by any means be called handsome or even nice-looking. He had a hawkish nose and broad cheekbones and dark, mahogany-toned skin, but under it his face seemed to almost glow with a kind of inner warmth. The warmth was there, too, in his hazel eyes, which were odd—shocking, even—in such a dark face. And in his smile, which was wide and generous and revealed an intriguing dimple in one cheek. He was completely bald—she thought he probably shaved his head—

which, coupled with his powerful shoulders and chest, ought to have made him look like a thug but somehow only enhanced an indefinable but undeniable *presence*. He wasn't tall—probably only a little taller than she was—but he seemed larger-than-life, and, at the same time, rock-solid, down-to-earth, completely human.

What the man had, she realized, was charisma. Oodles of it. Not to mention charm, of course, with those eyes and that smile.

"That's good," he was saying. "Understandable."

Oh, yeah—and a voice that sounds the way fur feels...

She drew her defenses around herself and said, with stiff politeness, "So, Daniel tells me you're interested in our Lady."

The smile splashed warmth across his face. "Lady—that's her name? Your cougar?"

"Daniel named her. She had a brother named Tramp, but he died just two days after we got them."

"How *did* you come by a pair of cougar kittens, or lion cubs, or whatever they're called?" His eyes seemed to glow with interest.

Staring into them, she realized she'd moved without consciousness, gravitated closer to where he stood in the open doorway of his car. Whoever he was, she thought as she took two quick steps backward, good guy or bad, in his own way Tony Whitehall was dangerous.

She said sharply, "I haven't decided whether I want to tell you that yet. But if we're going to discuss it, you should probably come up to the house. It's too hot to stand here in the road."

She turned and walked away, back up the lane, and

behind her she heard him say, "Yeah—okay. Sure." And then the car door closed and the engine fired. A moment later, the sedan came prowling slowly past her.

She gave him points for having the good sense not to stop and offer her a ride.

The house was stone, like most Tony'd seen in the Hill Country so far—the older ones, anyway. It sat on a little rise and had a wide front porch that looked out toward the lane and the live oaks and the paved road below. But the real view, he saw when he'd parked beside the pickup truck and gotten out of his car, was in back of the house. From here he could see the barn, of newer vintage than the house and built of wood and metal; several other storage buildings, which might or might not have been garages; a couple of feed storage tanks and some animal pens. These were all off to one side, while directly in back of the house a wide meadow swept down to a creek bed, which was dry now, in September, like most of the Southwest watercourses he was familiar with, and studded with granite outcroppings and copses of still more live oaks. The meadow was dotted with oak trees—not live oaks, but the big, spreading kind—and bordered by a fence rampant with fading sunflowers. A couple of horses and an assortment of brown-and-white goats and some llama-looking creatures occupied the shade provided by the oak trees. Beyond all that, the rolling Texas hills stretched away to distant blue haze.

"Nice," he said to the view's owner as she came to join him. The dog, he noted, was still glued to her side, and the boy had come now to the back-porch door and was watching him intently, arms folded and feet planted firmly a little apart. *Like a sentry*, he thought.

"You should see it in the spring when the bluebonnets are in bloom." It was a pleasant remark, but her face and her eyes reflected no joy or pleasure.

As if, Tony thought, *all the light in her life had been snuffed out like a candle's flame.*

She turned and went up the steps to the back door, indicating with a slight movement of her head that he was to follow. Squelching the empathy for her that kept intruding on his objectivity, and with the dog padding silently at his heels, he did, pausing to wipe his feet on the mat outside the door the way his mama had taught him. He entered the kitchen, and the dog squeezed past him and went to assume her Sphinx posture on a rug near the door that led to the rest of the house, making it clear to him his admittance went only this far and no farther.

A wave of his hostess's hand indicated he should sit down at the kitchen table, so he did. He felt as if he'd been called to the principal's office, which had the effect of rendering him, for one of the few times in his life when in the presence of a beautiful woman, at a loss for something to say.

Since he didn't seem to be much good at talking to Brooke, he looked across the table at her son, who had hitched himself halfway onto a chair and was studying him solemnly, with his head propped on his hands. "You're Daniel, right?" Tony held out his hand. "Hi, I'm Tony."

"I know." Daniel ignored the hand and, without

actually pointing, indicated the laptop computer lying open but dormant on the table. "I Googled you."

"Ah." Tony shifted so he was facing the boy more directly, though he was intensely conscious of the kid's mother drilling holes in the back of his head with those dark blue eyes. "Then you know," he said earnestly, "that I've done photo essays of all kinds of animals. Wolves, elephants, gorillas…"

Daniel nodded. "You've been all kinds of places, in wars and disasters and stuff. So how come all of a sudden you want to do a story about one little mountain lion?"

Tony sat back in his chair, and all he could think was, *Wow.*

Behind him he heard, softly, "I'd like to know the answer to that, too."

He turned halfway around in his chair, ready to launch into the story he and Holt had concocted, which he now had no real faith was going to hold up under the scrutiny of these two. "Mrs. Grant—"

Her eyes squinched as if she'd felt a sharp pain. "Oh, please don't call me that. Brooke is fine."

"Okay…Brooke. Actually," he said, glad that this was at least partly true, "I've been interested in doing a story on exotic animal smuggling and illegal breeding for quite a while. Like, what happens to these animals after their owners decide they can't or don't want to take care of them anymore—"

"That's not—" Daniel began, but a gesture from his mother silenced his protest.

Tony glanced at him, then forged ahead into the part of his story that was somewhat less than truthful. "I was doing research—yeah, okay, I Googled—and the news story about what happened to your, uh, with your cougar came up. At that point it was supposed to have been a case of—" he threw the boy a look of apology "—an unprovoked attack by a wild cougar who'd been raised as a pet."

This time it was he who held up a hand to hold off Daniel's furious denial. "So, since I was in Arizona, visiting my mom at the time, and that's right next door by Texas standards, I decided to come and see if you'd let me use your lion as the focus of my story. I didn't know until I got here about…what's been going on."

He sat back, relieved that he could at least end on a note that *was* God's honest truth. "Look, I'm truly sorry. I know this is a bad time for you. But like I said to Daniel, if doing a story on your cougar can help keep her from being put down…"

"Will Lady be on Animal Planet or something like that?" Daniel's face was flushed and eager, though his eyes remained wary.

"Yeah, that's what I'm hoping for. Or National Geographic, maybe. I don't know at this point." He didn't add that if the story was big enough and went the wrong way, it could wind up on some of the crime shows and even on TruTV.

Daniel looked past him and said, "Mom?"

Tony turned to look at her, too, and they both waited for her to say something.

For a long moment she didn't and just stood there leaning against the kitchen sink, with her arms folded, gazing at her son the way he'd seen his own mother do

when she couldn't think up a good enough reason to tell
him no. Finally, she hitched in a breath—the decision
had been made—and Tony held his until she said,
"Daniel, why don't you go see if Lady's up for visitors?"
When Daniel seemed about to argue, she added in a
firmer tone, "We'll be out in a minute. I have some
questions I need to ask Mr. Whitehall first."

Daniel slid out of his chair and was out the door in
the shot-from-a-cannon manner of little boys everywhere, and the dog rose to her feet, then sat back down
and watched him go, clearly torn by this division in her
flock. Tony braced himself while Brooke turned her
intent gaze his way.

"Mr. Whitehall—"

"Please," he said, with a teasing parody of her own
wince, "call me Tony."

She didn't smile—okay, so evidently she wasn't
going to be affected by his charm—as she pulled out the
chair her son had just vacated. She sat in it, then once
again fixed him with that stare.

He looked back at her, trying to look guileless and
all too aware that he'd never been much good at guile,
anyway. The air around and between him and the
woman seemed to quiver with suspense, until he
couldn't take it anymore and finally had to break it.
"Well, okay, you said you had questions."

"Actually," she said, with a defensive little jerk of her
head, "I'm waiting for you. So go ahead—ask it. The
question I know you're dying to ask." When Tony just
looked at her in a lost kind of way, she gave an impatient wave of her hand. "Oh, come on. Of course, it's

why you're here. Did I or did I not kill my husband?" She closed her eyes briefly and corrected herself. "*Ex*-husband. That's what you really want to know. I can practically hear what's playing inside your head. Did she really shoot her husband with a tranquilizer gun, then put him in a cage with a mountain lion, frame the lion for the killing and arrange it so her nine-year-old son was the one to find his father's body and provide her with an alibi?"

"Jeez," Tony said under his breath, unexpectedly shaken.

She clasped her hands together in front of her and leaned toward him across the table. "Look, I don't know if I believe your story about Animal Planet and all that, but what you told Daniel is true. You *are* in a position to maybe save an animal we love from being destroyed. So, I'm willing to let you do your story—or whatever you call it when it's photographs—as long as you understand it's to be about the cougar and *only* that. Nothing else. Not one word or picture of me or Daniel—"

He sat back and let out a breath through pursed lips. "Ma'am, I don't think that's possible. It's your lion. You and your son raised him, you said. I can't very well leave you out."

She put a hand over her eyes. "Oh, *hell*. No. I suppose not." The eyes hit him again, fierce and bright. "You know what I mean. You are not to make this about what happened to Duncan. What they say I did. Understand?" She waited for his nod, then sat back, looking like she'd just run a race.

She wasn't ready to trust him.

He'd had some experience coaxing wary creatures into an acceptance of him and his cameras, and he realized that was how he'd begun to think of her—as someone who needed to be wooed. Not as he would a beautiful woman, but as if she were one of the shy, wild things he'd stalked and filmed in their natural habitat. That experience had taught him that the way to win such a creature's trust was not to press, not to move too fast, but to hold back and let her come to him.

So, instead of accepting her invitation…demand… challenge…and asking her the questions she'd obviously prepared the answers for, he pushed back from the table and asked softly instead, "Can I see her—your lion?"

"Oh," Brooke said, and he felt he'd won a small victory when she looked taken aback. "Okay. I guess so. Sure."

Okay, fine. She led him back down the steps and across the yard to the barn in a grumpy silence, more annoyed with herself than with him. *So I psych myself up to tell you my story, and now you don't want to hear it? Fine with me.*

So why this odd and completely contrary sense of disappointment?

Maybe because…I really do want to tell him. Maybe because I want so desperately for someone to believe me, and I thought maybe, just maybe, this man who isn't from around here and doesn't know Duncan or have any reason to be wary of the local law would listen and believe I'm telling the truth.

But he didn't seem to want to hear the story from her point of view, which was probably just as well. Her lawyer would have had a fit, anyway.

"Don't you want to get your camera or something?" she asked as they passed his sleek gray sedan, parked alongside her dusty pickup.

"Animals tend to be suspicious of cameras aimed at them," Tony explained, aiming that smile across at her as they walked. "I imagine they must look something like guns—a threat, anyway. I like to let animals—people, too, actually—get used to having me around before I start shooting, photographically speaking."

"I don't think Lady's ever seen a gun," Brooke said, then thought, *Not until a couple of days ago, when somebody shot Duncan with a tranquilizer gun, maybe right in front of her.*

And she wanted so badly to tell him that, to talk to someone about how awful and impossible it was that anyone could think she'd do such a thing.

"Animals seem to have an instinct about things like that," he said. "Somehow they know."

Brooke nodded. After a moment, because the need to talk to someone was just too strong to resist, she said, "Lady's mother was shot and killed, but she was just a blind kitten hidden away in her den at the time, so I don't think she'd have any trauma from that." She glanced over at Tony. "That's how we got her. It was a drought year, and a lot of animals—deer and antelope—had come down from the mountains, looking for food. So, naturally, the predators came, too. And there'd been reports of livestock being killed, and then a hiker was attacked, so the sheriff's department was called in. Duncan and Lonnie—that's his partner—were the ones to find the cougar, and after they shot her, that's when they found out she had cubs. Or kittens. I don't know which one is right, either."

She threw him a suggestion of a smile, one that only hinted, Tony thought, at what a real one would be like. *Glorious*.

"Anyway, they looked for the den, but it was the next day before they found it. By the time they brought them home to me, the babies were weak and dehydrated, and the weakest one—the male—we couldn't save it. We fed Lady with an eyedropper at first—Daniel and I did. Daniel was just a little guy then, but he really did help."

"So…your husband is the one who brought you the cougar?"

"Yeah." She gave a funny little laugh that acknowledged the irony in that, but didn't say the words. "We kept her in the house at first. When she got bigger, she followed Daniel around and wrestled with him like a puppy—or like he was her littermate. She'd stalk him and pounce on him and play fight with him, the way puppies and kittens do. It's the way predators train to catch and kill prey, you know. Duncan always worried she'd hurt Daniel, but she never did—beyond a few scratches and teeth marks and tears in his clothes."

With the dog padding quietly along between them, they went through the center aisle of the barn, between rows of horse stalls and out the other side, into a lane flanked by fenced enclosures. Some of these contained small shelters, which, Tony surmised, were for the goats he'd seen in the meadow pasture. Down at the far end of the lane, he could see a high chain-link fence, like the kind usually used to enclose tennis courts. Daniel was kneeling in the dirt beside the fence, his fingers laced in the wire fabric. Tony's heart began to beat faster when he saw the sleek and tawny shape looming close on the other side, but when he and Brooke and the dog got to the enclosure, the cat had vanished.

"She's shy with strangers," Daniel explained, squinting up at them, and now Tony saw the cat farther out in the compound, standing wary and alert in the shade of an oak tree.

For cougar habitat, the compound ranked among the best he'd seen, with not only trees and brush for cover, but rocky outcroppings for climbing and a piece of the dry streambed running through it. "Nice," he said, and Brooke nodded.

"I had it built when I knew Lady couldn't ever be returned to the wild. Of course, I knew that when she got bigger, she'd become a danger to the other animals."

"Not to mention the people," Tony said, glancing at her. She looked away, but not before he saw a flare of anger in her eyes.

"You may not believe this, but as rough as she was with Daniel when she was little, that's how gentle she is now that she's grown. And with me, too. She's so sweet natured… That's why I can't—" She broke off, shaking her head as she stared through the chain-link fence. After a moment she went on in a voice tight with strain. "Duncan never liked her. And she didn't like him, either. I think they were both afraid of each other. As if…I always wondered if somehow Lady knew he was the one who'd killed her mother. And Duncan…" She paused. "Far-fetched, I know."

"Maybe not," Tony said. "Maybe he had the scent of her mother on him when he first picked her up. Her blood."

Brooke drew a sharp, quivering breath. "Can you get her to come closer?" she asked Daniel.

He shook his head as Tony crouched down beside him. "She doesn't like strangers."

"That's okay," Tony said.

And then there was silence. His pulse pounded in his ears as he stared across the open space between the fence and the oak tree, and from its shelter, the cougar stared back at him. He could hear the hum of insects and the far-off whistle of a hawk...the sound of a car or a tractor starting up somewhere...but, above it all, the beating of his own heart.

And then the distance between him and the cougar seemed to shrink, and the animal's distinctive dark mask grew larger, her vivid yellow eyes glowing like fire.

He heard a soft gasp from close beside him, and an even softer "Sshh..." from somewhere above his head.

He couldn't take his eyes away from that mask... those eyes. And slowly, they came closer, and closer still, until they seemed to fill his entire world, his whole field of vision, the way they had once before, long, long ago.

Chapter 4

His father had been working cattle in the high country that summer—the high-altitude meadows of the Sierra Nevada. The cow camp had cabins for the hands, so his mother and the four youngest kids—the ones too young to have summer jobs—had joined him for a month toward the end of the roundup season. Branding time. Josie and Anita had been ten and twelve that year, and they liked to go watch the cowboys work the cattle, but Tony and Elena had been too young to be trusted to keep out of the way, so they had to stay in camp with Mama.

Or they were supposed to.

We're bored, Elena and I, and Mama is busy in the cookhouse, helping the cook make biscuits for dinner, so we decide to go find our own adventures. We'll stay well away from the meadow where the cowboys and the cattle and horses are, we tell each other, so we won't get into trouble.

We're walking along, and we come around a big pile of rocks, and there it is, right in front of us. A mountain lion. We freeze, all three of us, and the lion seems as surprised as we are.

I can't seem to breathe. Everything inside me has frozen solid. All I can see is the lion's face, with its black mask and big yellow eyes. It seems huge, taller than I am, and I can almost feel its breath on my face. Beside me, Elena whimpers.

"Don't move," I whisper without moving my lips. But I feel my sister's hand creep into mine.

I don't know how long we stand there, the three of us, staring into each other's eyes. Then, suddenly, the lion twists its body and bounds away over the rocks and is gone.

Elena gives a little gasp and looks at me. Her face is pale, and there is moisture on her cheeks. "Don't tell Mama," I say, and she shakes her head, quickly and hard. "We can't tell anyone—ever," I say as she wipes her cheeks with her hands. "If we do, they'll come with guns and shoot it. You have to promise."

She nods, sniffs and says, "She didn't hurt us."

But she takes my hand again as we walk back to the camp, and I feel a prickling on the back of my neck, as if yellow lion eyes are watching me all the way.

* * *

"Wow," Daniel said. "She's never done *that* before. Look, Mom. She's not even afraid."

Tony looked up at Brooke and shrugged. "Just got the knack, I guess," he said, making light of it because his chest felt peppery inside and his world still shivered around its edges with the vividness of the memory flashback.

He heard her take a shuddering breath. "Daniel, time for you to get started on your homework. You have some makeup work to do. Don't even think about arguing."

Daniel hurriedly closed his mouth, evidently having been ready to do more than think about it. He let his drooping shoulders and hanging head show how unfair he thought it was, and lumbered off in the loose, disjointed way of disappointed children everywhere. Tony vividly recalled employing the same drama tactics, to roughly the same effect.

"He sure does mind well," he remarked, and she made a dry sound that might have been a laugh.

"He's been on his best behavior since...all this happened." She said it without much expression in her voice but couldn't keep the shadows of everything she'd been through in the recent past from flashing across her face.

Couldn't keep it from Tony, anyway, because he had an eye trained to notice such subtleties. The tension in her facial muscles made his own ache.

Gently, not wanting to distress her more, he finally asked the question she'd already offered to answer. "What happened here?" When she didn't reply immediately, he said, "I promised I wouldn't write or photo-

graph anything about it, and I won't. But you're right—
I would like to know."

He'd meant to leave it there, but she finished for him
as if he hadn't. "Whether you're in the company of a
killer or not?"

She crouched down beside him and put her face close
to the wire and her fingers through it, and the cougar
licked her fingers and butted her head up against the
wire like a house cat wanting to be petted. Tony heard
a peculiar rumbling sound, almost a vibration felt in his
bones rather than heard, and with a small sense of
wonder, he realized the animal was purring.

With her eyes closed, Brooke fought to gain control
of her emotions, wondering why it seemed so tempting
to give in to them here, now, with this strangely charis-
matic and imposing man. She drew in a breath and began.

"I was late getting home from town...."

He listened intently, not interrupting, and when she
was through with her story, she stood up, and so did he.
She looked down at Lady, who, at some point during her
narrative had flopped down at the base of the fence and
was lying stretched out with her back to them, close
enough to touch through the wire. She seemed completely relaxed except for the tip of her tail, which
twitched now and then.

"She seems to have accepted you completely," she
said with a small laugh, because she was in suspense,
wanting to know how he was going to respond. Because
she needed so badly to be believed. "For her to turn her
back on you like this, it means she trusts you."

"What can I say?" he said, showing that incongruous

dimple. Then he cleared his throat, and his voice was abrupt, almost harsh. "Mind if I ask you some questions?"

She shrugged and spread her hands. Not saying the words, but thinking, *What does it matter?* Feeling gray and dismal and hopeless.

"I guess what I don't understand is how they think you could have done this when your—excuse me— when Duncan was already dead when you got here, and Daniel is your witness to that fact. What? Do they think he's lying to protect you?"

She threw him a look, feeling faint touches of warmth and light that were like the first rays of the rising sun on a frosty morning.

"No, actually." She tried to smile and couldn't even manage irony. Fear was a cold chill in her belly and a brassy taste in her throat when she swallowed. "They think I set it all up before I left, before Daniel got home from school. They say I asked Duncan to meet me here, somehow lured him into the compound, shot him with the tranq gun, let Lady out of her cage, *then* went to town to do my shopping. That I never meant for Daniel to be the one to find him, which only happened because the guy at the feed store had lost my order and I was late getting home."

He was frowning, his tawny eyes intent in a way that reminded her oddly of the cougar's eyes.

"So…do you have a tranq gun? The one you're sup- posed to have used?"

She hissed out a breath. "I do have a tranq gun. *Did.* And that's weird, because it's gone."

"Gone? What do you mean? Like—lost, stolen…"

"All I know is, it's missing. Duncan bought it for me when Lady got big. He was afraid she might attack Daniel—or me, I suppose. He kept it in the tack room, in the barn, so it would be handy in case…in case Lady ever went berserk, I guess." She wiped her eyes with the back of her hand and laughed thickly. "Ironic, huh?" She sniffed and, after a moment, went on. "Anyway, I told the police—uh, sheriff's department detectives, you know—where it was, and they said it wasn't there. They had a warrant and searched the whole place for it, and so far they haven't found it. Which, as far as they're concerned, only proves their theory, that I did it before I left for town, took the gun with me and disposed of it somewhere on the way."

"I don't know," Tony said in a slow and thoughtful way. "It all sounds pretty circumstantial."

"Yes. But don't forget, I also have motive. Duncan was contesting our custody agreement. He wanted full custody of Daniel. And this being a county in which the good-ol' boys system governs just about everything, he actually might have won." She struggled again with the smile. "And don't they always suspect the husband or wife first? Especially—" she drew a shivering breath "—when there's nobody else to suspect. I mean, who else *could* it be, right?"

She looked at him, and he looked back at her, not saying anything. She thought he looked shaken. *Because he thinks I'm a murderer? Or because he sees, as I do, how hopeless it is…*

"So," she said when the silence had stretched as far as it could, "do you still want to do your story when the odds are I really am a cold-blooded killer?" To her own ears her voice sounded as thin and brittle as she felt. As if the wrong word would shatter her into a million pieces. She watched him closely, waiting for it…

But he only said, "Okay if I come back tomorrow? Looks like Lady's okay with me, so I don't see why I can't start shooting." He wasn't smiling, but it seemed to her— she wasn't imagining it?—that his eyes were kind.

She let out the breath she didn't know she'd been holding. "Tomorrow's fine," she said, not smiling, either. But once again she felt it—that faint touch of warmth.

"I don't think she did it," Tony said to Holt at the diner that evening. He had just put in his order for the deluxe Black Angus cheeseburger and was trying not to think about all the stuff his sisters had just been preaching to him about bad fats and red meat and cholesterol. He shook his head and reached for his beer. "But I'm not sure I'm gonna be able to stay objective on the subject."

Holt leaned back against the booth's red plastic upholstery and draped one long arm along the top edge of it and gave him a narrow-eyed gaze that reminded Tony of Clint Eastwood—minus the stump of cigar. "Why's that?"

Tony shrugged. "Well, shoot, man, she's my best friend's baby sister. Of course, I *want* her to be innocent."

It was enough of a reason to give Holt, but in his heart he knew it wasn't the only one.

He didn't know why, but he couldn't get the lady out of his mind. Images kept flashing through his head like snapshots in a slide show: a work-worn hand resting on the head of a huge, shaggy fawn-and-white dog; laugh lines at the corners of smoky blue eyes filled with tears; a head with spiky blond hair shooting every which way out of a haphazard ponytail, leaning against one side of a chain-link fence, with a mountain lion's head butting against it from the other; a pair of long, slim legs in blue jeans just inches away from his shoulder, folding up to lower a long, slim body down next to him, so close he could feel the heat of it.

Okay, so he was aware of her as a woman. He liked women. Especially beautiful ones. But he'd never had one get into his head like this one had, not in so short a time.

He drank beer, paused, then frowned and said, "The thing is, it doesn't look like she could be. I mean, it all points to her being the only one who could have done it. Circumstantial, sure, but add to that a good motive and the fact that she's the ex-spouse—I mean, hell, *I'd* have arrested her."

"But you don't think she did it."

"No, I don't. Call it a gut feeling, I guess." At least he hoped it was his gut he was feeling, and not some other part of his anatomy, the one known to be considerably less reliable in its judgments.

"Well, okay then," said Holt, and then they both leaned back to allow the waitress—a buxom, fortyish woman with shocking red hair—to deliver their dinner plates.

"Thanks, Shirley—looks great," Holt told her with a wink and a smile, and she smiled back at him, gave her fanny a little wiggle, said, "Eat up, hon. You need some meat on your bones," as she winked at Tony and sashayed off.

"Okay, so let's go from there." Holt picked up a bottle of steak sauce and studied his plate for a moment before applying generous amounts to his burger and passing the bottle on to Tony. "Let's assume she didn't do it. So…who did?" He picked up his burger, bit into it, looked at Tony and raised his eyebrows as he chewed.

Tony gave a bark of laughter without much amusement in it.

Holt leaned toward him, and Tony thought again of Clint Eastwood. "No, look here. It's a matter of logic. If she didn't do it, someone else did. So, we have to think who could have done the things she's supposed to have done. Take it one thing at a time." He held up a finger. "One, the victim was inside the cougar's cage. How did he get there? You said Brooke told you her ex was afraid of the lion. So, would he go in there by himself? Not likely. Not willingly, anyway. Which means somebody either had to put him in there after he was tranqed, or somehow enticed him in while he was still mobile."

"He was a big man, from what I understand," Tony said, beginning to get into it now himself. "And there were no drag marks, at least that I could see or anyone mentioned. Brooke couldn't have put him in the cage herself, I don't think."

"So," said Holt, with a shrug, after another bite and chew, "either it was somebody bigger than the victim, strong enough to carry him, or somebody he trusted enough to go into the cougar's pen with. That's not likely to be an ex-wife he's in a custody battle with, seems to me." He held up a hand. "Actually, that should have been point number two. Number one, what was he doing at his ex's ranch in the first place? His vehicle was there, parked on a dirt road that ran around the back of Brooke's property. A road that passes pretty close by where the cougar's pen is. I've been doing some scouting of my own," he explained when Tony started to ask how he knew that. "So, that's a big question. Why was he there? If he was there to see Brooke, wouldn't he just go up the driveway to the house? We have to assume he met someone there—the person who killed him, right? Who would he go there to meet? And why?"

"You have to think they—whoever the other party or parties were—they were up to no good," Tony said, chewing thoughtfully. "Otherwise, like you say, why not go on up to the house?"

"Right. Then there's the matter of the weapon."

"The tranquilizer gun." Tony nodded. "Which Brooke says was kept in the tack room in the barn, a room that wasn't locked. And now it's missing."

"Okay," said Holt, leaning back with beer bottle in hand. "Who knew about the gun? For starters, the man who bought it—Duncan Grant."

Tony was frowning. "Let's get this straight. Duncan Grant comes to his ex-wife's ranch when she's not home, parks where he won't be seen, meets some person or persons unknown, most likely male, gets the tranquilizer gun from the tack room—or tells his partners where it is and they take it—and somehow he winds up shot with it and left inside a cougar's compound to die. Then whoever the unknown killer is, he takes the gun and drives away, leaving a nine-year-old boy to discover his father's body, and the lion and the ex to take the blame."

Holt nodded. "That about sums it up."

Tony pushed his plate away with about a third of his burger still on it, having pretty much lost his appetite. "And it explains the dog," he said.

"The dog?"

"Yeah. Brooke's got a giant dog—some kind of sheepdog, I think. Very protective. I don't think she'd have allowed a stranger onto the place, but if it was Duncan and somebody he trusted—"

"Like a friend."

"Right," Tony said.

Then both he and Holt went silent as the diner's door whooshed open and a group of men wearing brown Stetsons and tan shirts came in together, bantering and laughing in the confident, swaggering manner of men who know they own their little corner of the universe.

Tony watched them until they'd settled into a big corner booth near the front of the diner, then turned back to Holt. He felt chilled. "And Duncan's friends are probably mostly gonna be…"

"Cops," said Holt.

Brooke was finishing up the morning chores when she heard a car drive up to the house. She didn't realize until she saw that it wasn't Tony Whitehall's sedan how much she'd been looking forward to his coming.

But it was a sheriff's department SUV. She stood in the big barn doorway and watched it come up the lane and stop beside her pickup, and she felt afraid. It was a cold, sick, queasy kind of fear, a fear that she hadn't felt in a very long time and had hoped she'd forgotten.

I'm afraid, because I know something bad is about to happen to me, and I know that I am powerless to do anything to stop it, and that there's no one I can turn to for help. I feel dirty and small, and I'm trembling inside, but I know I have to be strong....

The SUV's door opened and Lonnie Doyle got out. Hilda didn't go trotting out, with her tail wagging, to meet him, although she knew him well from all the times he'd been there with Duncan. Instead, she sat at Brooke's feet, close to her side, trembling a little, as if she, too, was afraid.

"Hey, Brooke," Lonnie said, sauntering toward her, wearing a big smile, as if he'd never made threats against her and her pet cougar, as if he had the right to still call himself her friend just because he was Duncan's. As if he had every right to be there, on her place, which of course, he did, she reminded herself, because he was The Law.

"Lonnie," said Brooke, without a nod or smile.

"Just thought I'd stop by, see how you're doin'." He had the grace to at least *look* a little awkward, although he didn't take off his hat to be polite. Probably, she thought, because it was a big part of what gave him his authority. His power.

"I'm doing okay." Her hand had come to rest on Hilda's silky head, and that gave her a small measure of comfort.

"How's Daniel?"

"He's fine. In school right now."

"Good…good…" His small eyes gazed past her, through the barn and off toward where the animal pens were. Where Lady was. Where Duncan had died. She saw his jaw clench.

Before he could say anything, she asked in a flat voice, "What do you want, Lonnie?"

His eyes flicked at her, then away, and he shifted his stance and folded his arms in a way he maybe meant to be ingratiating but somehow just felt intimidating instead. "Uh, look, Brooke, about the other day. If I came on too strong…" He coughed, and Brooke thought, *My God, is he trying to* apologize? Then he seemed to draw himself together, and the intimidation was back—definitely—as he went on. "Look, Dunk was my best friend—my partner. What that cat did to him. Hell, I would have shot him—"

"Her," Brooke corrected softly, but he didn't seem to hear.

"—if Al hadn't stopped me. I'm glad he did, because I wouldn't want to do that to the boy. To Danny. I'm sorry if I upset him. But, Brooke, you need to understand, that cat is a killer. For your own sake, and the safety of your boy, you need to let that animal go. Let animal control take it and put it down." When she would have protested, he held up a finger, like a teacher lecturing a class of small, unruly children, and moved closer to her, hemming her in. "Look, all you need to do is read the paper, watch TV. There was that case in Florida where two cheetahs turned on their keeper, tore her up good. And then the guy in Las Vegas. What was his name? Anyway, you got no business keeping a dangerous animal like that on your place when you've got a kid to think about."

"Thank you for your concern," Brooke said coldly. "If that's what you came to tell me, you've told me. So, if you don't mind, I really do have work to do."

"Look, I'm just trying to look out for you and Danny. Dunk was my best friend. It's the least I can do."

She felt a dangerous impulse to laugh. But he was standing too close to her, making her feel claustrophobic and, although she couldn't have explained why, *afraid.* It suddenly seemed important to placate him, and that impulse, too, brought back memories she wished she could forget.

She drew a steadying breath. "Lonnie, that's kind of you. But I don't need any help. Really. I've been getting along fine on my own for two years. Daniel and I will be just…fine."

Something glittered in his little blue eyes and quivered around the corners of his mouth, and Brooke thought about what Mr. Henderson had told her, and of all the evidence and suspicion against her, and for a moment she actually thought she might throw up. She felt clammy and cold, and there was a humming in her ears. She couldn't breathe.

Then the spell broke, and instead of humming, she heard the growl of a car making its way up the lane. She felt warm again, and not afraid.

"Who the hell is that?" Lonnie asked, as if he had a right to know. He was scowling, watching the gray sedan pull around and park on the other side of Brooke's pickup.

Brooke drew a breath that quivered with relief and a strange, unanticipated gladness. "Oh," she said in an offhand way, "it's just a reporter. He's doing a story about Lady." She folded her arms and smiled, enjoying the way Lonnie jerked back in surprise. "He's with *National Geographic,* I think. Or Animal Planet—one of those."

His lips curled in a sneer. "Yeah? Well, if you think that's gonna save that cat, think again. He's a killer, and I can guarantee you the judge is gonna see it that way, too, so you tell your Animal Planet big shot he's got until the hearing next week to get his story, because after that the cat is history. Count on it."

He stabbed a finger at her for emphasis as he turned and started for his vehicle, then abruptly turned back, smiling in a way that didn't even try to be friendly. "Oh—forgot to tell you. Just thought you'd like to know, we haven't found the tranq gun yet. Still looking for it, though."

Why did that sound like a threat? Brooke thought as she watched him stride away, barely acknowledging Tony as he passed him by.

She saw Tony pause for a moment to look back at Lonnie, wondering at his rudeness, maybe. When he came on, loaded down with his cameras and bags, he caught her eye, and she saw his tough, bulldog face break into its oddly sweet smile. Once again, that peculiar warmth came over her, along with reassurance, an overwhelming sense that she was safe, now. Because he was here.

Tony felt the animosity as he and the other man passed each other, a wave of something so tangible he could almost see it, smell it, like the smoke from a particularly nasty cigar.

He turned to watch the deputy get into his official sheriff's department vehicle, then continued on, frowning. But when he saw Brooke's face, and that she looked pale and scared, there was something about that and the look in her eyes that affected him in unfamiliar ways. He considered himself a nonviolent person, one much more inclined to make love than war, but he felt a sudden surprising urge to inflict great bodily harm on the individual who had put that fear in this woman's eyes.

He summoned the most reassuring smile he could muster and felt a strange lifting beneath his heart when she smiled back, even though her smile didn't reach as far as her eyes. "What's wrong? What's a deputy sheriff doing here?" he asked her, aware that his own bravado was equivalent to that of a nine-year-old's, secure in the knowledge that the school-yard bully had already departed the field of battle.

She shook her head, made a gesture, making light of it all. "Oh, that's just Lonnie." She took a breath. "Duncan's partner."

"Ah," said Tony. He glanced down at the dog, who was in her usual position beside Brooke, but panting lazily and gazing after the departing SUV, evidently not in the least concerned about Tony's presence there. He was remembering what Holt had said about Duncan's friends most likely being other cops. "He's...a friend, then?"

She gave a high, humorless laugh. "Not mine."

He could see her struggling with it, not sure whether she could trust him, afraid to say too much. But, of course, she already had told him a lot, much more than she probably realized. He was good at reading faces.

"Gotcha," he said, turning as if to walk on toward the barn's wide, open entrance, as if he didn't need her to say another word. Which, in the contrary way of people—women especially, in his experience—gave her permission to say what was on her mind.

"They grew up together, Lonnie and Duncan," she said as she came to walk beside him. "I swear, as long as I knew Duncan Grant, wherever he was, I could count on Lonnie not being far away. They played high school football together. Just generally raised hell together. Then they both joined the sheriff's department and went off to learn to be cops together, which kind of surprised everyone, I think. Most people around here probably thought they'd wind up in the same jail cell—together."

"Stands to reason he'd take his buddy's death hard," said Tony. "Sounds like they must have been really close."

She tilted her head in a thoughtful way. "Close? Yeah, they were…I guess. But the funny thing is, they didn't always get along. Most of the time, in fact. Those two probably had more bare-knuckle brawls than any two best buddies in the state of Texas, which is saying a lot. I guess maybe they were more like brothers who didn't see eye to eye most of the time."

Cain and Abel were brothers, too, Tony thought. But he said, "What about you?"

"I never did care much for him," she said in a diffident way, watching the ground in front of her. Then she threw him a look and a wry smile. "Can't stand the man, if you want to know the truth. And I'm sure the feeling is mutual. Lonnie being single, I imagine he didn't much like losing his good ol' drinkin' and hell-raisin' buddy— not that I noticed Duncan's lifestyle or priorities changed much after we got married. Or even after Daniel was born, for that matter." She went back to looking at the ground, forehead furrowed. "That's why I can't under- stand—"

"What?" he prompted when she paused, but she shook her head.

"Nothing. Really." She gave a soft, embarrassed laugh. "I can't imagine why I'm even tellin' you all this. Particu- larly after I said you couldn't do one little bit of your story about me or Daniel. I still do mean that, by the way." She gave him the last in a warning tone, but with a new light- ness in her attitude that made it seem almost like banter.

He looked over at her as they strolled, unhurried, down the lane between animal pens, with the dog trotting on ahead of them. Brooke had her fingertips tucked in the pockets of her jeans and her face lifted to the warm September sun. Her straight, layered, sun-streaked hair was twisted up in an artless style and fastened to the back of her head with a wide metal clip, leaving pieces sticking out and waving around her head in a way that was whimsical but oddly attractive. The camera shutter in his mind went *click*.

"No story," he said. "Just interested. What don't you understand?"

Again, she hesitated, then let out a surrendering breath. "Why Duncan even wanted custody of Daniel. I don't think Lonnie understood it, either. I would think Daniel would just have gotten in his way."

"What about Daniel? How does he feel about it?"

"The custody battle?" Her face was suddenly a study in anger...bitterness...pain. "He doesn't want to live with his dad, that's for sure." She threw him a look and quickly added, "Oh, don't get me wrong. Daniel loves his father. *Loved.*" She closed her eyes briefly, and he saw her throat struggle with a swallow. "But—" and her voice had gone harsh and soft "—he'll *never* forget what that man did to me."

Tony didn't want to ask, but of course he had to. "What did he do?"

They'd reached the cougar's high wire enclosure. Brooke halted and, with a jerky, angry gesture, lifted her hair away from her forehead to show him the white scar running into her scalp. She turned to him and tried, without success, to smile. "That's just the one that shows."

Chapter 5

Brooke wasn't prepared for the emotions that flashed across Tony Whitehall's rugged face. What she saw there made her feel validated, and at the same time, oddly, *scared*.

"He hit you?" He asked it very softly, not looking at her now. *Carefully* not looking at her, she thought, and squinting slightly, as if the sight of her might hurt his eyes.

Shaken, she tried to backpedal. Tried to laugh, make it sound like less than it was. "Damn. I guess that just gives me more of a motive to kill him, doesn't it?"

"It would have," Tony said, and to her relief, his voice sounded more like his normal voice. He was looking at her again, too, and the warmth was back in his eyes. "But you divorced him instead. Seems strange you didn't kill him back then, when you had good reason to…"

She felt shaky, trembly inside. Wrapping her arms around herself, trying without success to stop the feeling, she looked across the compound to where Lady was lying in the shade of an oak tree, ignoring them. "I guess it's a fairly common practice among cops."

"No excuse."

"No, but I have a feeling his dad was the same way. So maybe he didn't know how else to be."

He threw her a look, angry now. "What are you doing? Apologizing for him? He beat you. The woman he's supposed to love and protect. How can any man justify that? How can any woman put up with it? My mother would have killed my dad in a heartbeat if he'd ever laid a hand on her in anger. Guaranteed."

Brooke had no answer for that. After a moment she said flatly, "I guess you were lucky, weren't you?" And she walked away, once more feeling alone.

Tony watched her go, with the big dog trotting along beside her. He was wondering if there was some way he could take back what he'd said. Make it up to her, at least. Cut his tongue out, maybe?

Then he felt a moment's intense and familiar longing, thinking of his dad's rough, gnarled cowboy's hands, hands that had been hard as iron but never any other way but gentle when they'd touched his children or his wife. When he was home, how the kids—the little ones—used to love to climb all over him, messing up his hair, tugging his mustache, taking off his cowboy hat and putting it on their own heads.… And Mama, standing a little way off, just smiling in a quiet way. Like she was proud of him, Tony thought, even though he'd never brought home much money, for sure not enough for the eleven kids he'd given her to raise. Eleven kids that had somehow all gone to college, which he knew was mostly thanks to Mama, but still, it was his dad he missed with an ache that never seemed to get smaller, even though it had been fifteen years since the heart attack that killed him.

"You're a jerk, you know that?" he told himself out loud.

But he was watching the cougar now and thinking about the job, and the fact that if he was going to be able to get any decent shots of the animal, he was pretty much going to have to go inside the compound with it. Again, he flashed back to that day when he'd come face-to-face with a wild mountain lion, and the pact he and Elena had made afterward. He could see the tear tracks on her face and could hear her whisper, "She didn't hurt us."

He looked at the gate in the high chain-link fence, which was fastened with a chain but not locked. He looked at the lion, still lying on her side out there in the shade of the oak tree, gazing off into the distance. Maybe sleeping?

Are you dreaming, Lady? Dreaming about the days when this land belonged to you, and there was no one to contest your mastery of all your surveyed?

Ignoring him, anyway.

Scolding himself for his cowardice—and telling himself he could always beat a hasty retreat if the cat made a move toward him—Tony closed his eyes briefly, then unhooked the chain. It made what seemed like a hellishly loud noise.

Out in the compound, the cougar turned her head to watch him but didn't get up.

"Nice kitty, kitty. Nice Lady…" he said on an exhaled breath as he slowly opened the gate and slipped into the lion's den.

"You know what I was thinking?" Tony said to Holt after he'd told him about it that evening at the diner. "That it felt wrong, that animal having a fence around it. You know what I mean? The buffalo, the wolf, the lion and the grizzly bear—we've crowded them off their land, stolen it from them. Like the white man stole it from the Indians—my people."

Holt's eyes had crinkled up at the corners, but he swallowed the bite of steak he was working on before he said, with exaggerated seriousness, "Your people? How much Native American are you?"

Tony shrugged. "Okay, my mama's about three-quarters Apache—maybe half, I don't know—so that makes me less than half, but still. Doesn't change what happened—to the natives or to the animals."

"No," Holt said agreeably. "So, the cat didn't attack you, I gather?"

"Didn't bat an eye. I was busy getting out all my equipment, and she just lay there, twitching her tail once in a while. Mind you, I didn't try to go and pet her, or anything. But she pretty much ignored me the whole time I was in the pen with her. Even rolled over on her back and put her paws in the air and squirmed around—just like a big kitty cat, you know?" He paused to shake his head and let out a breath, remembering the sense of awe he'd felt. "It was…pretty amazing." He picked up his fork and pointed it at Holt. "And if you ask me, it makes it pretty hard to believe that animal attacked somebody. Not without some serious provocation."

Holt pushed his plate aside and sat back. His eyes had that Clint Eastwood glitter. "You said that deputy—Lonnie Doyle—made some threats?"

"Sure sounded like it. I was getting my equipment out of the car at the time, so I didn't hear everything he said, but he seems to have a real hate for that cat. And no great love for Brooke, either." He paused, giving himself time to control his voice before he added, "She's afraid of him, I know that."

"And he and Duncan Grant were best friends…." He left it dangling.

Tony sat and looked at him for a long moment, not saying anything. Then he shook his head…made a jerky gesture of rejection. "Nah. I mean, fistfights is one thing, but to shoot a guy with a tranquilizer gun and leave him to die in a lion's cage? I can't see it. What possible reason would the guy have to kill his best friend?"

"It happens," Holt said. He leaned forward again, arms folded on the tabletop. "And when it does, it's usually over one of two things. A woman or money."

"Well, it's not a woman," Tony said. "Not this woman, anyway."

"So," said Holt, picking up his beer, "that leaves money."

*   *   *

Brooke had stopped what she was doing—raking old bedding straw out of the horses' stalls—to watch Daniel and Tony down in the pasture. As always, Daniel was surrounded by a motley herd of animals—horses, goats and alpacas. Tony stood close by and was obviously trying to ignore the goats nibbling at his pockets and shirtsleeves, looking for treats. Hilda was off down by the creek, nosing around, looking to scare up a squirrel or a rabbit to chase. A warm September breeze was blowing, bringing with it the smell of autumn and the sound of voices.

Daniel's husky alto, first. "Yeah, but that's just the way alpacas chew, see? They're really tame, too—come on, you can pet 'em, if you want to…feel how soft their wool is…"

And Tony, his warm laughter soft as the alpacas' wool on her ears. "You sure do know a lot about animals."

Daniel, with a self-conscious shrug. "Yeah. I'm going to be a veterinarian. It takes lots of college, though. Almost as much as a real doctor. And I have to take a lot of math, which doesn't make me very happy…"

"Hey, vets *are* real doctors. Especially nowdays."

"I meant *people* doctors. *You* know. Actually, it's harder to be a vet, 'cause animals can't tell you what's wrong with them. So you have to be twice as smart to figure it out."

"True. But I think you're going to make one helluva vet—oh, shoot. Sorry about that."

"That's okay. My mom says hell sometimes. Worse stuff than that, too. I already know I'm not s'posed to say it, you know, because I'm a kid…."

Brooke let go of a bubble of laughter, and when she

put a hand up to stifle it, she was surprised to discover some moisture on her face as well. She brushed it away hastily, but it was harder to dispatch the ache of yearning that had come over her suddenly. A yearning she couldn't put a name to, but that whispered, softly as the breeze, *Oh, if only…if only…*

Down in the pasture, Tony took off the Arizona Diamondbacks cap he'd put on to protect his scalp and wiped his head with his sleeve as he squinted at the lowering Texas sun.

"Speaking of math…" he said, and Daniel groaned. "Don't say it. I know…I have homework."

Knowing how much he'd hate it, Tony resisted an urge to tousle the boy's thick blond hair and instead laid his hand on one sturdy shoulder. "Just keep your eye on the prize. Keep telling yourself it's what it takes to be a vet someday. You'll get through it."

"Yeah, but…I wish…" He didn't finish his sentence, but walked with his head down, in his dejected slouch, as they made their way slowly up the slope.

Feeling helpless, Tony gave the kid's shoulder a squeeze. While he was racking his brain for something to say to cheer him up, Daniel kicked at a clump of dried horse apples and said fervently, "I wish you didn't always have to go."

Oh, hell. He hadn't expected that. It was like getting slugged in the stomach when he wasn't prepared for it; it took his breath away.

"Hey," he said softly. And then, after a little cough that was supposed to mask how moved he was, he added, "I'll be back tomorrow."

"I know...."

"And," he added, as inspiration struck, "you can always call me, you know. Anytime."

Daniel's head came up, and smoke-blue eyes—his mother's eyes—shone bright in his flushed face. "Really?"

"Sure," Tony said, rubbing at the persistent peppery itch in his nose. "Uh...let's see. Okay, I know. My cell phone number's on that card I gave your mom. Still have it?"

"Yeah—I think. Yes." He was nodding eagerly, making the standing-up strands of his hair bob. "Mom has it. I'll ask her."

"Well, then, there you go. Call me whenever you feel like it."

Tony hauled in a breath and was grinning in the goofy, relieved way of a man who'd managed to come through a scary moment unscathed. He gave the kid's shoulder one final squeeze and watched him shoot off in the direction of the house at a pace that was only a memory for anybody past twenty. He was feeling pretty good about the way he'd handled things with the boy, until he looked up, and there was Brooke looking back at him. And there *he* was, feeling like he'd been socked in the stomach again.

She was standing in the doorway to one of the horse stalls, one hand leaning on the half-open bottom section of the Dutch door, the other holding a propped-up pitchfork. Her face was pink and sweaty, and wisps of her hair clung to her forehead and cheeks like wet feathers. She ducked her head to wipe her face on the arm braced on the door, and when she looked back at him, her expression was…vulnerable, he thought, so vulnerable it made his heart sore. And at the same time, the lift to her chin seemed defiant—even angry.

"Don't make promises you can't keep," she said in a hard, clipped voice.

"I don't think I did," Tony said carefully as he angled across the pasture to join her. "But, hey, look, I'm sorry if I was out of line."

She made an impatient gesture and looked down at her feet, clad in clumpy knee-high boots. "It's not that." She took a breath and shot him a fierce, bright look, one he'd seen on his own mother's face and knew very well: Mama Bear protecting her cub. "He's very vulnerable right now. He just lost his dad." She paused, and to the fierceness was added an intriguing layer of something he could only think must be embarrassment. "He's… For some reason, he's developing an attachment to you. But you're only here for a couple of days. What is he supposed to do when you're gone?"

To his astonishment and dismay, the words "I'm not going anywhere" popped into his head and almost—*almost*—came out of his mouth. Thank God he stopped himself in time. What was he thinking? She was right. He was only here for a couple more days. He'd probably already got enough cougar photos to fill an article for *National Geographic*, and enough video for a couple of Animal Planet shows as well. He couldn't tell her his real reason for hanging around, of course.

Which is to somehow get her cleared of murder

charges and reunite her with her long-lost brothers, after which my job here will be done and I'll be long gone.

Right?

"Gotcha," he said, and then added, frowning earnestly, "I understand. I hear what you're saying." He said some other basically meaningless stuff—he wasn't sure what—but he hoped he'd assured the mama bear that he wasn't planning to inflict emotional harm on her cub.

He was pretty sure he said "Good-bye" and "See you tomorrow" in there somewhere, too, and a short time later found himself sitting behind the wheel of his rental car. He sat there staring through the windshield and listening to his heart thump faster than it should while images flashed through his mind: A grubby little boy's hand gently stroking soft, thick alpaca wool...bright little boy's eyes gazing eagerly up at him. Sweat-damp feathers of blond hair sticking to a lovely woman's forehead and cheekbones—bones that would still be lovely when they were ninety. Nothing new there—he had a photographer's mind. What was making his pulse rate climb and his sweat grow clammy were the images that were drawn from pure fantasy: his hands stroking those feathers of hair back from that lovely woman's face...his lips kissing her sweat-damp brow...and then her cheeks...her mouth....

He huffed out an explosive breath, along with some blasphemy his mama definitely wouldn't have approved of, started up the car and drove—too fast—down the lane and onto the FM road that would take him back to town and sanity. He hoped.

It wasn't until he'd calmed down some and his pulse had resumed a more normal rhythm that he thought to check his rearview mirror. That was when he saw the sheriff's patrol car behind him.

His heart gave a guilty kick, the way it probably did for most people when they looked up and saw a law-enforcement vehicle in their mirror. He swore out loud and tried to think whether he'd disobeyed any traffic laws while in his state of lapsed consciousness, all the while making sure to hold steady just under the speed limit. After a while, though, when the lights on top of the SUV didn't start flashing, it occurred to him to wonder why a deputy sheriff would be following him at all, because in his—admittedly limited—law-enforcement experience, the sheriff's department seldom bothered to police traffic-law violators.

And this guy seemed to be sticking to him like glue.

Well, that's weird, he thought. He tried to see who was behind the wheel of the SUV, but the windshield showed him only a reflection of the sky, a dusky slate splashed with clouds and just beginning to reveal the amber and gold tints of impending sunset. For reasons he couldn't quite explain, his heart rate had kicked into high again.

The SUV followed him when he made the turn onto the main highway. At the first stoplight heading into town, where the highway widened into four lanes, it pulled up beside him on the left, crowding him just a little more than it needed to. The window rolled slowly down, and a fleshy face wearing aviator sunglasses and topped with a brown Stetson swiveled toward him. For a long, long minute, those dark, blank shades stared at him. Just stared.

Then...the light turned green, the window rode up and the SUV pulled away.

After another sharp exhalation and some more blasphemy, Tony drove on, too.

"I hate to admit it, but it spooked me," he said to Holt a little while later, as they waited for their dinners—they were both having the barbecue tonight, which was on special and which Shirley had assured them was the best in town, if not in all of West Texas. "It sure as hell *felt* like a threat—or a warning, maybe. The only thing I can't figure out is *why*."

"The fact that you've been spending quite a bit of time with a woman suspected of killing one of their own might have something to do with it," Holt said mildly.

Tony frowned. "I wish I could have gotten a better look at the guy. I *think* it was the one I ran into at Brooke's place yesterday—Lonnie Doyle—you know? The dead cop's partner and supposed best friend. Hard to tell for sure, between the hat and the shades. He'd be my first choice for—"

"Speak of the devil," Holt said, without moving his lips.

Three deputies, including Lonnie Doyle, had just come into the diner, not really swaggering, not exactly talking, but somehow taking up more than their fair allotment of oxygen and space, it seemed to Tony. He and Holt watched silently and without seeming to as the three took their usual corner booth, and even without looking directly, it was impossible to miss the glances the lawmen aimed their way.

Shirley went over to the deputies, carrying three mugs and a pot of coffee, and Tony and Holt picked up their own coffee mugs and exchanged looks of silent warning. Tony felt a curious crawling sensation on the back of his neck and wondered if it was the same primitive reflex that made a wolf's hackles rise.

A moment later, Shirley came out of the kitchen, carrying two platters of barbecue, and at the same time, Lonnie Doyle slid out of the corner booth and began to stroll, unhurried, past the row of booths lining the outside wall of the diner, timing it so that he arrived at Tony and Holt's booth about the same time their dinner did. He stood there, with one hand on the back of the booth near Tony's shoulder and the other on his belt, heavy with the cops' usual gear, including weapon, and his barrel chest puffed out. He'd positioned himself so he was blocking Shirley's path, leaving her standing there with the two heavy platters in her hand, and looking uncertain and maybe a little scared.

Tony didn't often lose his temper, but he could feel it rising like the mercury on a blistering hot Arizona day.

"Know what, Shirl? I think my friends here have decided they'd like those ribs to go," Lonnie drawled, staring down at Tony, with his lips curled to one side in a bad imitation of an Elvis Presley sneer.

Tony opened his mouth to give that the reply he thought it deserved, but before he could get a word out, Holt kicked him under the table and said to the waitress, quietly and with a reassuring smile, "Thanks, darlin'. And, if it's not too much trouble, would you mind throwing in a couple pieces of that apple pie?"

Shirley turned without a word and went back to the kitchen.

Lonnie slapped the back of the booth in a business-concluded kind of way. Then, as if it was only an afterthought, he turned back to say in a soft undertone only they would hear, "You might want to watch who you get friendly with, you hear? In this town we don't take kindly to folks who kill cops. And that goes for critters, too." Then he tipped his hat in a parody of politeness and went sauntering back to his buddies, calling good-natured greetings and friendly insults to a couple of other diners on the way.

Too mad to say a coherent word, Tony stared narrow-eyed, across the table at Holt, who locked his gaze with his in a silent warning as he picked up his coffee and drank. A moment later, Shirley came hurrying up, with two plastic bags containing to-go boxes and an assortment of napkins and plastic utensils.

"Guys, I'm really sorry," she muttered under her breath. "I don't want any trouble with those guys, you know?"

"Neither do we," Holt said. "Don't worry about it—not your fault."

As Tony reached for his wallet, Shirley made a quick, furtive gesture of refusal. "That's okay. You can pay me tomorrow—next time you're in. And," she added as an angry flush rose to her cheeks, "the pie's on the house."

Outside, in the cool September evening, Tony clamped his Diamondbacks' cap on his head and let out a string of cusswords he didn't use but once in a blue moon, concluding with, "What the hell was that?"

"Looks like we've struck somebody's nerve," Holt said, sounding almost cheerful.

"Yeah, well, it reminds me of one of those movies—you know, about the poor out-of-towner who wanders into some small town ruled by a corrupt all-powerful sheriff...."

They'd come in Holt's new rental car. While he unlocked it and put his dinner in the backseat, Tony went around to the passenger side and did the same. When they were both settled in the front seats, Holt sat for a moment without starting the engine. Then he looked over at Tony and said, "Might be time we make another try at getting in touch with Cory or Sam. Maybe they've got some connections with the feds...."

Tony nodded grimly. "Sam does, for sure."

"I think," said Holt as he turned the ignition key, "we're going to need some outside help on this one."

It wasn't often Tony was awakened by a ringing cell phone. It happened so seldom, in fact, that it took him awhile to figure out what it was. He opened his eyes and discovered it was still dark—relatively, which didn't mean much in a motel room with the curtains drawn.

In the twin bed next to his, Holt was stirring. "Is that yours or mine?" came the sleep-husky voice.

Tony swore. "Mine, I think." He groped for the offending instrument on the nightstand, at the same time trying to get a look at the alarm clock, which was turned just enough so he couldn't see the lighted numbers. He found the phone, thumbed it on and croaked a raspy "H'lo?"

"Tony?"

He sat up, if not wide awake, at least adrenaline-charged. "*Daniel?*"

"You said I could call you, right?" The voice was a whisper, but hoarse with urgency. "I mean…if I needed you, or something…"

"Yeah, yeah…so what's—is something wrong? What time is it, anyway?"

"Not that early. Almost time for the school bus. But I'm not going. Tony, um…can you come over? Right now?"

"Now?" He threw the covers back and got his feet on the floor. His heart rate had kicked into high gear, and there was a cold knot forming in his belly. "What's goin' on, son? Is your mom—"

"No—she doesn't know I'm calling. But I didn't know what else to do. They're taking Lady. I think they're gonna kill her."

"What do you mean, kill her? They can't, not without a court order. There hasn't even been a hearing yet." He glanced at Holt, who was up and heading for the bathroom.

"Yeah, but Lonnie and a bunch of other deputies—some of 'em I don't even know—they're here right now, and they have a pickup with a big cage—it's from animal control, or something—and they said they're taking Lady and they're holding her until the hearing. But I think they're going to do something to her. I know they want to kill her because they think she killed my dad after…you know. My mom—"

"Yeah. I know. Okay, listen. You sit tight, you hear me? I'll be right there. You think you and your mom can hold 'em off until I get there?"

He heard a sharp exhalation. Sheer relief. "Yeah. But hurry, okay?"

The line went dead before Tony could reply.

He was pulling on his pants when Holt came out of the bathroom. The guy was already fully dressed except for his shoes.

"Sounds like Deputy Doyle is making a move," Holt said as he sat down on the edge of the bed, took a holstered handgun out of his overnighter and calmly began checking it over.

"Uh…yeah," said Tony. "Do you think it's a good idea to take on the entire sheriff's department? I don't see how we're going to be able to do my buddy's sister much good if we're sitting in jail."

Holt glanced at him, eyes glittering in the dim light. "This is just in case. I believe in being prepared."

"Yeah, okay," said Tony, "but here's the thing. Way I see it, the only person who can stop those deputies is a higher authority. Since we don't know how deep into the department this—whatever it is—goes, or how high, that means a judge. The only person a judge is going to listen to, especially this early in the morning, is a lawyer— Brooke's lawyer, in particular. She told me his name is Henderson, and he's in Austin. That's all I know."

"Should be enough." Holt rose, tucked the handgun back in its holster and buckled the holster around his waist so the gun nestled snugly in the small of his back. "I'll see what I can do," he said as he shrugged into his jacket. "Meanwhile, see what you can do to stall 'em. Be careful, though—I think those guys are dangerous."

He paused to shoot Tony a look. "Any idea what you're going to do out there?"

"Me?" Tony let out a breath and reached for his cap and car keys. "I'm gonna try not to think of Custer's Last Stand."

"Wait—didn't the Indians win that one?"

"Yeah," said Tony grimly, "but it was Custer who was outnumbered."

Chapter 6

"What the hell's the kid doing? How long does it take to find a damn rope?"

"I told you to let me go," Brooke said tightly. "He doesn't know where it is." She had her arms folded across herself to keep her inner shakes from leaking into her voice. Anger or fear? She couldn't be sure. All she did know was that somehow Lonnie's nervous fidgeting made him seem bigger than he was. And definitely more dangerous.

Lonnie gave her a look, that arrogant sneer, which was one of the reasons she disliked him so much. In this case it said louder than words, "I don't trust you out of my sight, lady, not after you killed my best buddy in cold blood."

She didn't know whether he'd have actually voiced the sentiment out loud, because at that moment she saw Daniel emerge from the barn and start toward them, head down, dragging his feet. Her relief was short-lived when she saw what he had slung over one shoulder: not the rope Lonnie'd sent him for, but Lady's old collar and the leash they'd used to take her out around the ranch before she'd gotten too big for both the leash and the house.

"Oh, honey," she said when he came shuffling up in the boneless way that meant he really didn't want to be there at all. "That's way too small for her now. You know that."

He shot her a look she couldn't read, but before he could say a word, Lonnie snatched the leash and collar out of his hands and snarled, "What the hell's the matter with you? I told you to bring a *rope*, not a damn dog leash."

Fear and adrenaline shot through Brooke's body, and she braced herself to step between her child and whatever violence Lonnie might have in mind. But Daniel wasn't about to be intimidated. Sadly, she knew that in his young life, her son had had to deal with a lot worse than a puffed-up bully like Lonnie Doyle.

In spite of her fear, she couldn't help but feel a glow of pride as she watched Daniel step up to the deputy without flinching, face flushed with anger. "What good's a rope gonna do? Don't you know anything? You can't rope a cougar, she's not a *calf,* you know."

Lonnie's face darkened. "You back-talkin' me, boy? You watch your mouth. You understand me?" He moved closer to Daniel, and with her heart pounding, now Brooke *did* step in front of her son.

And the other deputy, Al Hernandez, was there, laying a restraining hand on Lonnie's arm. "Hey, man, what're you doing? The kid's right. No way we're getting a rope on that cat. What we need is a tranq gun."

Lonnie's eyes shifted quickly from Daniel and Brooke to Al and back again in a way that reminded her of something, she couldn't think what, not then.

"I used to have one," she said evenly, ignoring Lonnie. "Unfortunately, somebody took it."

Lonnie swore explosively. "Well, great—that's just great." He shook off Al's hand and went stomping off to confer with the other two deputies, who were lounging against their patrol vehicle, arms and ankles crossed, dark shades on and hats tilted against the rising Texas sun. With a look of what almost seemed like apology, Al went to join them.

As soon as the men were out of earshot, Brooke felt Daniel tugging at her shirtsleeve. She turned on him, saying in a furious whisper, "What were you *thinking?* Are you trying—"

"Mom—Mom—no, wait." He was making frantic shushing gestures, darting sideways looks toward the knot of deputies. "We have to stall for time. That's what I was trying to do. We have to stall them, Mom."

"Daniel? What do you mean, stall? Why? What did you do?"

Flushed and breathless, he put his hand in his pocket and pulled it out just far enough so she could see the shine of metal. His cell phone.

She sucked in a breath and cast the same nervous glance toward the gathering of deputies. "You called

someone? *Who?*" For the life of her, she couldn't think
of anyone who could help her. Nobody who could stand
up to Lonnie and his buddies, anyway.

"Tony," Daniel said, biting his lips to contain his excitement. "He's coming. He said to sit tight, and he'll
be right here."

She didn't know whether to laugh or cry. The idea of
Tony facing down four armed bullies with badges was
ludicrous. She hadn't known him long, but one thing
she'd come to understand in that brief time was that in
spite of his tough-guy appearance, Tony Whitehall was
a very gentle man. But the hope in her son's eyes made
her heart ache, and suddenly she was angry—angry
with the circumstances, and with Tony, for inciting a fatherless boy to futile hero worship.

"Honey—" her voice shook, and she fought to control
it "—Tony's a photographer. What's he going to do
against four deputies?"

"I don't know." Daniel folded his arms, and his chin
had a stubborn tilt that reminded her—with a surprising
pang—of his father. "But he'll help us. I know he will."

"Oh, Daniel…"

At that moment, Lonnie came swaggering back to
them, thumbs hooked in his belt, hat tipped back. His
bullying stance. He planted himself in front of Brooke
but looked down at Daniel as he spoke. *Probably to
make himself feel even bigger*, Brooke thought.

"Okay, here's what's gonna happen. You two tell me
that lion's such a big pussycat, so what you're gonna do
is you're gonna go in there and get that cat into its cage.
You understand me?"

"We won't do it!" Daniel yelled before Brooke could reach for him and get a hand over his mouth to shut him up.

Lonnie gave a snort of laughter and looked at his buddies, who were all suddenly looking at the ground, the trees, anywhere but at Lonnie, Brooke or Daniel. "Well, okay, let me tell you what's gonna happen if you don't. If you don't get that cat into that cage, we're gonna shoot it. How's that?"

Daniel gave a gasp of pure outrage. "You can't!"

Lonnie leaned over until his face was on a level with Daniel's, showing his teeth in a mirthless smile. "You wanna bet? The lion attacked. We had no choice but to shoot it, to save your lives."

"That's a lie," said Daniel in a trembling voice, and Brooke pulled him against her side. His body was hot and sweaty; she wondered how she could feel so cold.

"The word of four officers of the law says otherwise," Lonnie said with a shrug, rocking back on his heels. Again, he looked at the other deputies, and in his self-confident smile and their obvious discomfiture, Brooke suddenly saw the truth.

Daniel's right—they're going to kill Lady. No matter what happens, regardless of what Daniel and I do, they're going to shoot her down and claim it was to save us from being attacked.

It's always the same. Something terrible, something awful is going to happen to me. And I can't do anything to stop it.

I—a woman—am powerless.

"Well, looks like I got here just in time."

Brooke gave a violent start as Daniel jerked away from her with a glad cry. "Tony!"

She clamped a hand over her mouth, smothering a small whimpering sound that might have been relief or fear. Somewhere inside her were ringing bells and joyful songs to equal anything of Daniel's, and that in itself was a fearful thing. But drowning out the unexpected gladness she felt at the sight of the man strolling toward them, laden down with his usual array of cameras and bags, was the doubt…the fear. The question, what can he possibly do against four armed deputy sheriffs?

Lonnie had moved to intercept him, one hand held up like a cop stopping traffic. "Hey—where do you think you're going? You got no business here."

"This is going to make a helluva story on tonight's news," Tony said, ignoring him, and although he had several cameras draped over his shoulders and around his neck, he was looking down at the small object he held in one hand. A cell phone. And as he was rapidly stabbing buttons on it with his thumb, he glanced up to add a gleeful, "Terrific follow-up to the story about the killer cat. News flash—Deputies Shoot Pet Cougar in Cold Blood!"

"Hey! You ain't bringing those cameras in here." Lonnie's face was flushed dark with anger. "You hear me? You take one more step and I'm gonna take 'em offa you myself."

Tony smiled. It was his sweet, face-transforming smile, and Brooke, watching, felt something crack and shift inside her. It felt oddly like ice melting.

"Hey," Tony said in his easygoing way, "you're

welcome to 'em. You should probably know, though, that if you damage anything, I'll be filing a lawsuit against the department, the town and the whole damn county the minute the courthouse opens up this morning. And see—" he squinted his eyes and shrugged his broad shoulders "—the thing is, it won't matter, anyway, because I just sent a video of that interesting threat you made to Mrs. Grant and her son here, to my editor's computer." He held up the cell phone and gazed at it with apparent awe. "Amazing what you can do with a cell phone nowadays."

"Cool…" said Daniel on a gleeful exhalation.

Brooke sucked in a breath as Lonnie made a growling sound and took a threatening step toward Tony.

Once again, Al Hernandez interceded. "Come on, man. Don't make it worse," he said to Lonnie as he stepped between the two men. He held up a placating hand to Tony. "Look, all we want to do is take the cougar into custody until the hearing. That's all, okay? Just like we'd do if there was a dog that bit somebody. It's a matter of public safety. The only reason we didn't do it before now is because we didn't have the facilities to hold a dangerous animal like that lion."

"And now you do?" Tony looked and sounded like an interested news reporter. "Mind telling me what arrangements have been made, then, for the animal's safety?"

Lonnie snorted and turned away, his face a study in fury and frustration. Al was staring nervously at the cell phone in Tony's hand. "Ah…well, we, uh…"

"Yeah," Tony said softly, "that's what I thought."

At that moment, the cell phone in his hand began to

play the opening notes of "The William Tell Overture." A smile broke over his tough-guy features, and to Brooke, it seemed like the sun breaking free of clouds. He thumbed the phone on and said, "Whitehall." He listened, and his expression grew somber. "Yes, sir, he certainly is." He held the phone out to Lonnie. "Deputy Doyle? It's for you."

Lonnie took the phone and held it about the way he would have if it had been full of live killer bees. He lifted it to his ear, and there was at least an attempt at bravado, with his deep and abrupt, "Yeah. This is Deputy Sheriff Lonnie Doyle—whom I speakin' to?" Then, looking like he'd been whacked upside the head with a shovel, he spoke in a considerably higher and thinner tone as he pivoted, turning his back on his fascinated audience. "Yessir. Uh…no, sir. No, sir. Yessir, I do understand…."

Brooke felt something warm and solid come to fill the empty space next to her and realized it was Tony. Realized, too, that she still had one hand clamped hard across her mouth. She took it away and looked at him and gave a shivery laugh. "Who—"

"Sshh…" he said, with a slight warning shake of his head, not looking at her but somehow managing to make her feel cloaked in warmth and safety just by being there.

Swallowing her questions and holding inside herself a new sense of wonder, she watched Lonnie take the phone away from his ear. When he turned, his teeth were bared, his face a mask of rage. He looked as though he would have liked to hurl the offending cell phone at the three of them, but once again, it was Al Hernandez who interceded, taking the object from him and handing it back to Tony.

"This ain't over," Lonnie growled, stabbing a finger at Tony, then Brooke. "You hear me? We ain't done, not by a long shot." He stomped over to his sheriff's department SUV, climbed in and slammed the door.

Al threw Brooke a wary glance and went after his partner, getting in on the passenger side. As the SUV bounced back down the lane and through the barn's open breezeway, the other two deputies got into the pickup truck with the cage in the back and followed.

As the sound of the two vehicles faded and a mild morning breeze swirled their dust into eddies, Brooke turned silently and blindly against Tony's broad chest.

He didn't know which surprised him the most: the fact that she'd done it, or that it felt so natural when she did. His arms went around her, and her head came to rest on his shoulder, and her body seemed to fit against his as if they were two broken halves put back together again.

She was trembling in waves, the way someone did when they were crying and trying not to, trying at least not to let anyone else know. He wanted to stroke and comfort her, but the cell phone in his hand was getting in the way. Then somehow it wasn't, as Daniel happily relieved him of it without being asked. And that was another source of wonder to Tony—the fact that not even Daniel seemed to find it odd that a strange man had his arms around his mother.

"Hey," Daniel said, "this isn't a iPhone. It doesn't even have a camera."

Tony let go a gusty breath of laughter. "Okay...busted."

Daniel let out a squawk. "You mean you—"

"Yeah. Sorry. I lied."

Brooke lifted her head to gaze at him with drenched and incredulous eyes. "Dear God—that was a *bluff?*"

"Yeah…" At least, he thought he said something like that. His vision was filled with her eyes, swimming with tears, like sunlight on water, thick lashes clumped together and her mouth all blurred and soft. His senses were overwhelmed with the sweet warmth of her breath and the clean scent of her skin, and the vibrant and graceful curves of her body, nestled against his. It was all he could do not lift his hands to cradle her face and bring it softly…sweetly…gently to his.

Then she was laughing, the back of her hand pressed to her mouth, and he came to himself and reared back with mock outrage. "I'm a professional photojournalist. You think I'd sink so low as to have a camera in my *phone?*"

Her laughter became something that sounded more like a whimper. "Remind me never to play poker with you," she said as she turned to lace her fingers through the fabric of the chain-link fence and rest her forehead on her arm.

"I'm a lousy poker player, actually," Tony said softly, and it took all the will he had not to move close behind her and lay his hands over hers and bury his face in her hair. "A lousy liar, too—normally. I don't know what got into me."

"Well, you did one helluva a job when it counted," she said on a rueful little coda of laughter.

And Daniel crowed, "See? I told you she cusses sometimes."

"Daniel," his mother said in a careful tone, the one mothers everywhere used as their first warning, "don't you think you should go and let Hilda out?"

Tony snapped his fingers. "That's who's missing."

"Yeah," Daniel said, and his face grew dark with anger, "Lonnie made us lock her in the house. He said he'd *shoot* her if she got in his way."

"She's…very protective of us," Brooke said in a low voice as Daniel went running off to the house. "And she really doesn't like Lonnie."

"Interesting," Tony murmured, and he moved up beside her to search the apparently empty compound with narrowed eyes. "Where is she?"

"Hiding. Over there in those rocks. I've never seen her do that before. She senses…" She turned her head to look at him over one braced arm. "Thank you for what you did this morning. You saved Lady's life. I'm sure of it. But—" the muscles in her face flinched, and she finished in a whisper, "—this won't be the end of it. I've never seen Lonnie so mad. He's going to be back."

"He sure does have a hate on for that cougar." He managed to keep his tone light while oily coils of anger were writhing in his belly.

"Oh," Brooke said as she turned, "I'm sure he blames her for Duncan's death."

They walked slowly back toward the house, side by side. "Seems to me," Tony said, "it would make more sense for him to blame you. Since you've been charged with killing him."

"Yeah…" Her forehead furrowed with the little water-mark frown as she studied the ground in front of her.

"Doesn't make much sense, does it?" She gave her head a little shake and looked up at him. "You know what else doesn't make sense? How you managed to get hold of a judge and still get over here so fast. It couldn't have been fifteen, maybe twenty minutes after Daniel called you."

"Oh," Tony said. And then he added, "Well," to buy himself time, while nasty little bubbles of guilt burned in his chest like the aftereffects of a bad meal. "I didn't actually get hold of the judge. That would have been your lawyer—what's his name? Mr. Henderson?—he called him."

"Okay…" Brooke said slowly. "But then, you had to call him, didn't you? And you'd have to look up his number, and it couldn't have been easy to reach him, since it was before office hours in the morning…right?"

Memories of childhood flooded him, of being grilled by his mother or sisters after being caught in some misbehavior, and then worse, of being caught in the lies he told to try and save himself. The fact that the desire he'd felt for this woman still sang through his body made the memories weirdly discomfiting. He ran a hand over his scalp and tried to smile. "Actually…I had help. I've been staying with a friend…in town and, uh…"

"Oh," she said. "I'm sorry—I didn't realize—"

Warmth flooded his chest as he saw her cheeks turn pink with embarrassment and understood the conclusion she'd jumped to. "A guy," he said gently. "His name is Holt Kincaid." And then it was his turn to feel the heat of embarrassment as her eyes widened with new understanding. "No—wait," he added, laughing. "It's not *that* kind of friend. No—he's just… He had business in town, and we ran into each other, and with all the media in town for your, uh— Anyway, there weren't any motel rooms to be had, so we've been sharing. That's all. It's not what…" His words dried up under her steady blue gaze.

"Well," she said, with a wry little smile as she faced forward again, "it would have explained a few things."

A gust of surprised laughter escaped him. "Like what?"

There was a pause, but she didn't look at him. Then she hitched in a breath and said, "Like why someone like you isn't married."

He wanted her to look at him again. He wanted her eyes and mouth facing him across a chasm of inches, not feet. He wanted to be having this peculiar conversation with her in a place with soft light and soft places to sit and soft sweet music playing. But she walked beside him and lifted her face to the morning sun, and he had to content himself with watching it caress her skin and cast golden lights into her hair and with imagining his fingers and lips there instead.

He managed to make a small, nonspecific sound, and before he could think of actual words to follow it with, she said, "So…this Holt is the one who called my lawyer?"

"Uh…yeah," he said, "that's right."

"So…is Holt a reporter, too?" She said it warily, defensively, like someone bracing for a disappointment.

And he, so eager not to give it to her, naturally bungled it completely. "Holt? No, no—not a reporter. Nothing like that."

"What does he do?"

"He's, uh…" For a horrible moment, his mind went blank. And then he said the first thing that came into it— from where he didn't know, "He's a traveling salesman."

She nodded and was silent while he mentally closed his eyes and berated himself for an idiot. Then she threw him that wry little smile and said, "Yeah, I can see why you'd be terrible at poker."

He was saved from having to answer that by the 120 or so pounds of canine joy that came hurtling across the yard just then to launch itself upon them from what seemed like every direction at once. There followed an interlude of complete chaos—Hilda barking and whining, wriggling and leaping; Daniel and Brooke both laughing and scolding and yelling, "Hilda! Stop that!" and "Hilda, get *down!* What's the matter with you?"

Tony wasn't spared the dog's attentions, either. Seemingly carried away by her own exuberance, Hilda gave his face an enthusiastic licking, then appeared to realize she might have overstepped her boundaries and, for a moment, seemed to hesitate, almost in apology. But when he gave her a reassuring hug and ruffled her fur, she responded with renewed fervor, her delight seemingly boundless. Tony hadn't had a dog since he'd left home to go off to college, and the lump all this canine affection brought to his throat took him by surprise.

"I guess she's decided she likes me," he said when the pandemonium had subsided enough to allow speech.

"She's a Great Pyrenees—they're herding dogs, you know," Daniel informed him. "She thinks you're part of her flock now."

"Yeah?" Tony couldn't seem to keep the goofy grin from sprawling across his face. Why did that seem like the greatest accolade he'd received since his Pulitzer?

"Hey, Mom," Daniel yelled. "We didn't have breakfast.

Can we have blueberry pancakes? Tony—did you have breakfast yet? Mom—can Tony eat breakfast with us?"

What could he say?

What could she say? Brooke watched her son go off with the big, tough-looking photojournalist in tow, like a little jaunty tugboat pulling a beat-up barge; and again, she didn't know whether to laugh at the sight or cry.

Why do I trust this man? How can I trust him? He lied about this...Holt Kincaid guy. And he's right. He's a terrible liar. But why? Why would he lie?

And she had such a lousy track record, trusting men.

"My mom makes the best blueberry pancakes in the whole world." Daniel drew a forefinger across his plate to scoop up the last of the whipped topping mixed with blueberry juice and popped it in his mouth, then aimed a look of wide-eyed innocence at Tony. "Don't you think?"

"Daniel," Brooke breathed.

And Tony said obligingly, "Absolutely. The best."

"My mom's a really good cook," said Daniel, slyly avoiding Tony's eyes.

Brooke rolled her eyes. "Oh, brother. Come on, kiddo. Crisis time is over. This isn't a holiday, so if you're finished stuffing yourself, go get yourself ready for school."

"Aw, Mom…"

"Daniel…"

"But I'm not missing anything important, Mom, I don't have any tests or anything. Honest. I can miss one day. Mrs. Hackley won't care. I know she won't."

Brooke leaned against the sink, arms folded, pancake

turner in one hand, and regarded her son. *My protector.* Because she knew that was what was on his mind. He was afraid to go off and leave her alone. Afraid Lonnie might come back. The thought of Daniel facing down Lonnie made her go cold all over. "Daniel," she said softly, "I'll be all right. He's not going to come back. Not today."

Her son stared at her, holding her gaze with his eyes fierce and dark, and she wondered if he was remembering, as she was, all the times she'd held him or sat beside his bed and soothed him with those words. *Oh, Daniel, I hope not....*

"I can stay," Tony said. Brooke jerked and looked at him, and so did Daniel. Tony shrugged and shifted half around in his chair so he was facing her, although it was to Daniel he spoke when he added, "Just in case your mom needs help. How would that be?"

Daniel considered for a moment, then nodded judiciously. "Okay. I guess that would work." He slipped off his chair and crossed the kitchen at a mature and dignified walk. Until he reached the doorway. Then he took off like a shot.

Brooke gave a little squeak of laughter, closed her eyes and put her hand over her mouth. She waited until she heard Daniel's bedroom door slam, then looked at Tony and said, "Thank you."

"No problem." His eyes had a warm glow. *Like honey*, she thought. Not lion eyes, not this time. "He's worried about you," he said softly, tilting his head in the direction Daniel had gone.

"He's always been like that." She sighed and turned

to drop the pancake turner in the sink. "He's very protective of me. I think he gets it from his father."

Behind her, Tony made a sound, incredulous and disbelieving. "How is that? The man was protective of you, so much so that he bought you a giant dog and a tranquilizer gun, and then he *beat* you?"

She stood still, eyes closed, gripping the edge of the sink, fighting for control. Then she turned and said carefully, "It's not that unusual, actually. Or contradictory. It's probably two sides of the same coin." Tony shook his head and looked away, squinting as if the sight of her had become painful.

She went to sit in the chair Daniel had left vacant and leaned toward him, hands clasped on the tabletop. "I know you don't understand." *Oh, and I want you to. Why is that, I wonder?* "But the fact that Duncan was protective of me was one of the things that attracted me to him in the first place. I *needed* that."

"Protective is one thing. Abusive is another." Tony's eyes were hard and glittery, and his face had a set, bunched look that reminded her of a pit bull.

"Yes," Brooke said gently. "But sometimes they go together. It was all part of him thinking of me as his possession, I suppose, but at the time, I loved the attention, and the way he fussed over me. I was—" She sat back abruptly and cleared her throat. "You probably don't want to hear this."

"Yeah, I do." It was a low growl, and that reminded her of a pit bull, too.

"Okay, then." She lifted her head and faced him defiantly. "I hadn't ever had that kind of attention—not from a man. My father was…indifferent, I guess, is the closest I can come to it. You see…I was adopted. There were two of us. I have a sister, a twin. Fraternal, although we're nothing at all alike. My parents had a natural son—Cody. He was about ten years older than my sister and me."

She paused, and Tony said, "Was?"

She nodded. Having tested herself and having felt nothing, she was glad to know the walls she'd built around that part of her life were still holding fast. "Yes. He died in the same car accident that killed my parents. I don't think my dad ever wanted to adopt in the first place. He was happy with his only son. But he agreed to it to make my mom happy, because she wanted a little girl. He was never cruel to us or anything like that. He was just…distant. I don't think he could help it, really, but at the time I thought there was something wrong with me, that it was my fault he didn't love me. Or my sister. So I didn't have a lot of confidence when it came to boys, you know?"

Oh, God, do I sound pitiful? I don't want to! I'm not!

She wanted to tell him that. Tell him she wasn't that needy creature anymore, that she didn't need anyone protecting her, that she was capable of protecting herself. Why, she didn't know, but it suddenly seemed so important that he know—and maybe even more important that *she* know—she wasn't that person and wasn't making the same mistake all over again.

Oh, God, I'm not…am I? Am I drawn to this man because he makes me feel safe?

There were things she wanted to say to him…ask

him. But he sat so silently, his big body still as stone, looking at her with eyes that weren't soft any longer but burning like fire. Lion's eyes again. A strange shivering awareness poured through her body, rolling over her just beneath her skin, raising goose bumps and tightening her breasts until her nipples hurt. It was scary and at the same time exciting, and she didn't know how long it might have lasted or how it might have ended, because Daniel came dashing back into the kitchen, with his backpack slung over his shoulder, and just like that the spell was broken.

"Mom, you have to take me to school, because I missed the bus," said Daniel, stating the obvious.

Tony shoved back his chair and stood up. "I left in kind of a hurry this morning. I'm going to need to go pick up some stuff at the motel, so I can drop him at school, if you want."

"Cool," said Daniel. Then, remembering, he added, "Mom? Are you gonna be okay?"

"I'll be fine," she assured him, and Tony added his assurances that he'd be right back.

Brooke stood on the back porch steps, hugging herself, and watched her son get into a car with a man she'd known all of a few days. And again, she asked herself, *Why do I trust this man?*

And then, Do *I trust this man?*

Something was bothering her, an uneasiness that hadn't been there before. *What is it? Something's not right. But I can't think what it is!*

She gave Hilda's head an absentminded pat and went back into the kitchen. And it was while she was clearing away the last of breakfast from the table, and replaying that strangely intense conversation with Tony in her mind, that it came to her.

He didn't ask.

All her life, whenever anyone learned she was adopted, and that she had a twin sister, they always, *always* asked questions, showed curiosity. At the very least, interest.

Tony was a naturally curious person, in addition to being a journalist. He asked questions about everything. Was curious about everything. Interested in everything.

But he hadn't asked a single question when she'd told him she was adopted. That she had a twin. He hadn't shown any sign of curiosity or interest in knowing more about it.

How odd, she thought. It's almost as if he already knew.

Chapter 7

Walking into the motel room he'd been sharing with Holt for the past several days, Tony experienced what he thought of as a reverse epiphany—not a burst of light and knowledge, but an enveloping shroud of shadowy self-doubt.

What was he thinking? Just because his belly was full of the best blueberry pancakes he'd ever eaten in his life, his ego pumped up with the hero worship of a fatherless boy, and his libido in a state of itchy alert brought on by the unexpected embrace of the most beautiful woman he'd met in a long, long time, that was no excuse for completely losing his functioning mind.

"What are we doing?" he said to Holt, who was bent over his laptop, peering intently at the screen. "Why are we trusting this woman? Okay, I know we decided to proceed on the assumption she did not kill her ex. But what if we're wrong and all the evidence that says she did is right?"

Holt glanced up at him and said mildly, "Afraid you're losing your perspective?"

Tony snorted. "Like I ever had any. I told you at the beginning, she's my best friend's long-lost baby sister, I *want* her to be innocent. Then there's the fact that I've never seen a more beautiful woman in my life. And I'm a photographer, man—I mean, I've seen some beautiful woman, you know?"

Holt's smile was sardonic. "Come on."

"That's right, I forgot. You've never seen her." He picked up the camera he'd been doing most of his shooting with and popped out the flash card. From the front pocket of his accessory case, he took a card reader, inserted the card and handed the whole thing to Holt. "Here—that thing's got a USB port, right? Plug this in. Maybe you'll see what I'm dealing with."

Holt took the card reader with a shrug and plugged it into his laptop, and a few moments later both men watched in silence—a silence that bordered on reverence—as a slide show of images flashed across the computer screen. Presently, Holt cleared his throat and said, "Okay. Just because she's…"

"Gorgeous…"

"Okay, that works—gorgeous, yeah. That doesn't make her an evil person."

"What? I never said that."

"Then why," Holt said blandly, "are you holding it against her?"

"What? I'm not. That's just…"

Holt ejected the card and reader and handed it back to him. "Look, you've been out there every day for the past…what? Three days? Spending time with the lady. You haven't had these doubts about her before, so… what's up? What's changed?"

"Nothing," said Tony, with all the conviction of a kid standing in front of a broken window with a slingshot in his pocket.

Holt gave him a narrow look, then grinned. "Ah—I see. Getting a little too close for comfort, are we? Looking for a reason to bail out while you still can?"

"No! What are you talking about? Nothing of the kind, man. She's my buddy's baby sister, she's in a jam, and I'm trying to help her out—that's all. End of story." He paused, then added, with an uncomfortable shrug, "Anything else would be creepy."

"Yeah, yeah…" Holt was on his feet, shrugging into a leather jacket. "Having been a commitment-phobe all my life, believe me, I know one when I see one. Anyway—beside the point. It's not just a matter of taking Brooke Grant on faith. We know there's something off about those deputies, Doyle in particular. If this were a court of law and we were the jury, we'd have all kinds of grounds for reasonable doubt. You ask me, I think the kid's got reason to be worried, and I think it's a good idea you plan on staying out there with them for the time being."

"You know something I don't?" Tony asked, going still inside.

Holt nodded, looking grim as he pocketed his wallet

and tucked his weapon into its holster in the small of his back. "Finally got hold of Sam. She contacted a friend in DEA. Seems they, in cooperation with ICE, have been looking at our local sheriff's department for a while now." He reached for the doorknob, then turned. "I'm heading into Austin now to talk with the agents. I don't know what, if anything, this has to do with the murder of Duncan Grant, but you watch your back, understand?" He went out, muttering under his breath.

"You betcha," Tony said to the closing door. He wasn't absolutely certain, but what it sounded like the detective had said there at the last was, "Just what I need…get my clients' best friend killed…"

He hauled in a breath to quiet his accelerating pulse and began to pack.

Driving back to Brooke's, he tried to direct his thoughts toward the ramifications of a whole sheriff's department engaged in corruption and illegal activities of various kinds, and what that might mean as far as Brooke's and Daniel's—and his own—personal safety was concerned. But, like a badly trained horse, his mind kept wanting to go somewhere else.

Commitment-phobe? Me?

Ridiculous, he told himself. *This woman is my best friend's baby sister, and she's in trouble. Taking advantage of her would be unforgivable.*

And his mind whispered in Brooke's voice, *It would have explained…why someone like you isn't married.*

Look, he told himself, *I have perfectly good reasons for avoiding permanence in relationships, number one being a job that takes me to the far corners of the earth most of the time.*

And his mind replied, You grew up mostly without a dad for the same reason, didn't you?

Yes, he told himself, through mentally clenched teeth, *but that doesn't make me a commitment-phobe. I intend to settle down someday...at the right time...with the right person. I* will.

Lost in the dismal swamp of his thoughts, he almost missed the turnoff to Brooke's driveway. Did miss it, in fact, and had to back up a few yards to make the turn. As he was doing that, he noticed a man working with a horse in the pasture across the road. The man was wearing jeans and a blue work shirt and a straw cowboy hat, and looked Hispanic. Being the son of a cowboy, and with some considerable experience with horses himself, Tony paused to watch the man in action. He was admiring the trainer's skill and patience when the fellow looked up and noticed he had an audience. Tony nodded and waved. The horse trainer quickly ducked his head to hide his face and turned away. Coiling his rope to make a short lead, he led the mare at a brisk trot back toward the barn and corrals, which were just visible on the other side of a stand of live oaks.

Huh, Tony thought as he turned into Brooke's lane. *Friendly fellow.*

Brooke came out to meet him when he parked in what had become his usual spot, beside her pickup truck. She looked flushed and eager, as if she'd been waiting for him. Watching for him.

Inside his chest he felt a little tremor of gladness at the thought. Gladness...and some unease.

"Everything okay?" he asked her.

She nodded. "Daniel…?"

"Made it to school just fine."

Then, for a moment, there was silence while they looked at each other, and there was a new awkwardness, which hadn't been there the other times he'd come, loaded down with his cameras, to spend the day taking pictures of the cougar. This was no longer about the cougar, and they both knew it. Somewhere, somehow, when he wasn't paying attention, a line had been crossed. Just what kind of line and what it meant, he didn't know.

"Uh, hey," he said, clutching at something to fill the awkward moment, "I was just watching your neighbor over there across the road. Has some nice horses."

"Oh, yeah, that's Rocky." She poked the tips of her fingers into the back pockets of her jeans and hitched one shoulder. "The Mirandas—they're great. They help me out sometimes—a lot, actually."

"Huh," said Tony. "Must be me, then. He practically ran off when I waved."

She smiled and made a little gesture as if to hide it—a kind of shyness he'd glimpsed in her a time or two before. "Oh, that was probably one of their, um, cousins."

"Cousins?"

"Yeah. Rocky and Isabel have a lot of, uh, cousins. They come and work for them sometimes…you know?" He stared at her blankly, and she gave him a sideways look of exasperation. "Oh, for heaven's sake. *Illegals,* Tony. He probably thought you were INS, or ICE—

whatever they call themselves now. Poor guy—he's probably packing to leave as we speak. Well, I'll call Isabel…tell her you're harmless."

Are you harmless, Tony? Why is it I doubt you when you're out of my sight, and the minute I see you, I'm right back there, trusting you again?

Now, when I've got no business trusting anyone, much less a man who looks like a gang enforcer.

Feeling awkward suddenly, needing something to do with her hands, she opened the backseat passenger-side door and peered in. On the other side of the car, Tony was gathering up various camera and equipment bags, leaving a small duffel bag on the seat. "Do you want this, too?" she asked, picking it up.

"Yeah—here. Give me that." He took the duffel bag from her, then held it, hefted it and looked at her in a way that made her wonder suddenly if he felt as awkward about this as she did. The idea made her want to smile, with a strange shivery excitement that made her think of her twelve-year-old self passing notes to Tommy Hanson in English class.

"I hope you don't mind," he said. "I thought it would be best if I stayed…you know, for a while. If you don't have a spare room, I can sleep on the couch."

"Oh. Well, are you sure? That's… Thank you." The shivery feeling expanded inside her, and her heart began to beat faster. She folded her arms across her chest and laughed a little as she turned to walk beside him. "You don't have to sleep on the couch, though. I've got a spare room, if you don't mind the mess." Glancing down at the duffel bag, she said, "Is that all you've got? No suitcase?"

He gave a wry puff of laughter. "Nope—that's it. I came kind of on the spur of the moment."

"Well then…" She paused to look over at him. "You must be about out of clean clothes. If you have any laundry, I'd be glad to—"

Having preceded her up the back porch steps, he opened the door for her, even though he was the one loaded down with bags. And smiled down at her as she came up the steps after him. "Okay, I wouldn't mind the use of your washing machine, but I'm capable of doing my own laundry."

"But I don't mind, really—" She was facing him on the top step, crowded close to him while he held the door for her to slip through. She should have felt claustrophobic, being so close to such a big man, one she barely knew. But his eyes had that mellow honey glow, and the distance between them seemed…not too narrow, but too wide.

"Brooke," he said softly, in a voice that reminded her of the mountain lion's purr, and her vision grew shimmery around the edges. "We're letting the flies in."

"Oh." Unnerved, she moved past him, onto the screened porch. He followed her, letting the door slam shut, and she watched the way the muscles bunched in his arms and back as he lifted the duffel bag onto the washing machine. She hoped he hadn't noticed her schoolgirlish lapse, prayed that that revealing moment at the top of the steps had somehow slipped past him.

He turned back to her, shifting the bags hanging by their straps from various parts of his body. "I do *not* expect you to wash my clothes." And he was smiling that incongruously sweet, heart-melting smile. "See, I was raised by a mom, along with seven sisters, not one of whom believed they were put on this earth to wait on a man."

She let go a laugh, which emerged sounding light and casual; only she would know it was rooted in desperation. "Wow, tell me again why it is you aren't married?"

"Funny," he said as his smile slipped awry. "My sisters keep asking me the same thing."

What is it with everybody lately? Tony thought as he followed Brooke down the hallway to what really was more of a "spare" than a "guest" room, being cluttered with all the usual things there was simply no other place for—sewing machine and ironing board and books and a boy's outgrown toys. Suddenly everyone he knew seemed to be interested in his marital status. And, frankly, it was beginning to irritate him. Holt calling him a commitment-phobe…his sisters pointing out to him the fact that he was the last unmarried holdout in the family… What should it matter to them, anyhow? It wasn't as if his mom was desperate for grandkids—she had so many now, he didn't know how she kept track of them all. A couple of his oldest brothers and sisters even had grandkids, for God's sake!

He'd chosen a career that wasn't conducive to hearth, home and rug rats, that was all. What was he supposed to do? Give up his livelihood? Find a new one? The hell with *that!*

He dumped his cameras on the double bed that occupied a good bit of the available space in the small room and stood for a moment, frowning at nothing as a memory came crowding into his mind. A memory from a few years back, a time when he'd come close to losing everything—including his best friends and his own life.

Cory…and he's had more beer than he usually drinks, and he's leaning in toward me, across the table in a restaurant in the Philippines, and I can hear him saying, "…I'm thinking maybe it's time to be settling down, cut down on the travel, have some kids before I'm too old to enjoy 'em."

And me, nodding my head like I know all the answers and saying, "You've got the old nesting urge. Happens. Hasn't happened to me yet, but I've heard about it."

And he thought about Sam, and how she had thought she couldn't have her career and Cory both, and had almost lost everything by waiting too long. And now look at the two of them—happily married and both still off to the far corners, doing their thing.…

No kids yet, though. Kids make all the difference. Kids need their parents around while they're growing up. Both of 'em, preferably.

He still had a few things to bring in from the car—his computer, mainly. He went down the hall and through the kitchen, and was struck by how quiet it seemed—and how empty—without Brooke. It had been all of five minutes since she'd left him in the spare room and had gone out to take care of some chore or other. And already he missed her.

And what the hell was *that?*

He went outside, telling himself he was just going to get his laptop, that he wasn't going to go looking for Brooke, who had her own business to attend to, after all, and didn't need him tagging along, getting in her way. He'd gotten as far as unlocking the trunk when he looked up and saw three people walking up the lane. One of them was the horse trainer he'd been watching earlier, and he was accompanied by a Hispanic couple, who Tony assumed must be the nice neighbors, Rocky and Isabel.

Intrigued, especially after what Brooke had told him about the nature of the neighbors' "cousins," Tony looped the strap of his laptop carrier over his shoulder, closed the trunk and waited.

The trio had reached the yard when Hilda came bounding out of the barn to greet them, with her whole body wagging, along with her tail. Obviously, the neighbors were on her favorites list. Brooke followed a moment later, and she and the woman—pretty, and shorter and plumper than Brooke but probably about the same age—exchanged hugs. The woman's husband spoke to Brooke, gesturing from time to time toward his "cousin," who stood by with his hat in his hands, looking exceedingly uneasy. Tony had already started to amble toward them, in what he hoped was a non-threatening manner, when Brooke's head jerked toward him, and the look on her face made him quicken his step and his pulse kick into high gear.

"What is it?" he asked in a low voice as he moved close beside her. "Something wrong?"

She opened her mouth, but before she could say anything, Tony said, "Hi, I'm Tony," nodded at the woman and leaned forward to offer his hand, first to her husband, then to his cousin. The cousin hesitated, then shook his hand, bobbed his head and mumbled something in Spanish, while Brooke made hurried introductions.

"Rocky and Isabel—my neighbors. This is Tony. He's, uh…"

"You are her friend," Rocky said. "We have seen you here. That is why when my cousin told me what he saw, I told him he should tell you."

Tony nodded but didn't prompt him. His senses felt honed, razor sharp, and he had in his mind an image of a cougar watching a fawn…eyes like lasers, body gone still and taut, only the tip of her tail twitching….

Beside him he felt a tremor run through Brooke, like a fine electrical current. He wanted to put his arm around her and nestle her against his side. Wanted to so badly, he folded his arms to keep himself from doing it.

"Tell him," Brooke said in a rasping voice.

Rocky nodded and glanced at his cousin, who looked at the ground. "The day Duncan—Mr. Grant—was killed, my cousin, he was working there—" he made a sweeping gesture with his arm "—with the horses. He saw a sheriff's car—one of the four-wheel-drive ones—drive out of the lane over there, the one nobody uses."

"Where Duncan's car was found." Brooke's voice was barely audible. She cleared her throat, and Rocky went on.

"*Sí*—yes. And that was also a sheriff's SUV. But that is not the one that drove away."

"You're saying," said Tony slowly, "there were *two* sheriff's vehicles here that day?" His heart knocked hard against his breastbone.

Rocky nodded. "*Sí*—yes. That's right. And one drove away. My cousin didn't say anything at first, because he didn't want any trouble with the police, you know?" He glanced at his cousin, who continued to stare steadfastly at the ground. "And when he told me, I didn't want to say anything, because I was afraid for *her*." He tipped his head toward Brooke, but he spoke to Tony, in a low and intense voice. "She was alone, you know? I didn't know what they might do. But now that you are here..." It was his wife he looked at now, and she stepped up beside him and he slipped his arm around her waist.

"You can do something," said Isabel fervently, and her dark eyes glistened with appeal. "Maybe?"

It was late that evening before Tony managed to pass the news along to Holt. He'd been leaving messages on the detective's voice mail all day, and finally got a call back around ten, while he was in his room, folding his freshly washed underwear.

"Sorry—I've been in conference with members of various federal law-enforcement agencies all day. What's up?"

Tony told him. "As far as I'm concerned," he concluded, "this cinches it. One of Grant's fellow deputies killed him. Most likely Lonnie."

"Only one problem. A little thing called motive."

Tony let out an explosive breath. "I was hoping you'd come up with something on your end."

"Wish I could say I had. The feds are investigating the Colton County Sheriff's Department, along with several others in reasonable proximity to the border, on suspicion of trafficking in drugs and illegals. All they'll tell me is it's an ongoing investigation, and they don't want anybody coming in and messing up their case until they're ready to make their move. They did say both Duncan Grant and Lonnie Doyle are—or in Grant's case, were—quote, 'persons of interest.'"

"Okay, so...a falling-out between partners in crime? That doesn't seem much of a stretch, given these two were always going at each other anyway."

"True. But why do it like that—with a tranquilizer gun and a mountain lion? At the guy's ex-wife's place? *That's* what doesn't make any sense."

"And now Lonnie Doyle wants the lion dead. That doesn't make sense, either. It's not like she's an eyewitness, not one that could testify against him, anyway."

On the other end of the line, there was a soft hissing sound—an exhalation. "The key to this whole thing," Holt said, "is that cat."

After that conversation with Holt, Tony felt too wired to even think about sleep. The house was silent, and in the stillness, those words keep playing over and over in his head: *the key is that cat.*

He opened his door and stepped out into the hallway. Brooke's door, across and a little way down from his, was closed. Daniel's was open a couple of inches—for the light, Tony imagined, remembering how he'd liked to leave his door open when he was a kid, because there was just enough light from the one left burning on the front porch to dilute the darkness in his room to shadowy grays. Here the light was from the kitchen— Brooke had left one on above the stove. He moved through the kitchen and onto the back porch, treading lightly and opening and closing doors without sound.

Standing on the porch and looking out, he discovered the yard and the landscape beyond bathed in the pewter glow of a rising full moon. He paused there for a moment to appreciate the subtle variations of blue and silver and gray, wishing he'd thought to bring a camera with him, unwilling to make the trip back to his room lest he wake someone, knowing he didn't really have the equipment with him to capture the magical quality of the light, anyway.

Opening the screen door—with only one squeak, though it seemed incredibly loud in the stillness of the night—he went outside and down the steps. And a magnificent beast with a silvery-white coat that seemed to lift and float around her like feathers came romping toward him from the direction of the barn.

"Hey, Hilda," he whispered, offering his hand. "How you doin', girl?"

The dog accepted his hug with a lick and a grin and went dancing back toward the barn, clearly delighted with the night, the moon and his company. Tony didn't know whether he'd intended to go that way, but with the dog as his flagship, her tail floating behind her like a banner in a light wind, how could he not follow?

He went through the deeply shadowed barn, and when he stepped out into the moonlit lane that led down between the animal pens to the cougar's enclosure, he wondered if it had been more than restlessness and the cougar's haunting…more even than moonlight and the dog's guidance…that had brought him to that place.

He'd never thought of himself as a mystical soul, and no doubt the influence of the moonlight had something to do with it, but he found himself thinking of things like... *fate*. And whether there really might be something to the notion that some people...some souls...were simply destined to find each other, no matter the time or place or the odds against it.

Inside the cougar's compound, blurred by the silvery netting of the chain-link fence, he could see the dark and slender form turn when she heard the dog come bounding up...turn, then stand, waiting, alert and still, with one hand resting on the head of the magnificent animal beside her.

His breath stopped; his heartbeat surged. He yearned... grieved...mourned for his cameras, the way only another photographer might understand.

It was, simply, the most breathtakingly beautiful thing he'd ever seen. The stuff of legend and fantasy, woman and lion, motionless in the moonlight, frozen in time and space. They stared at him and he stared back, while memory returned him to that moment on the trail in the High Sierras when he'd come face-to-face with a beast that could have killed him with one swipe of her paw. He'd been afraid then, of course, because he was old enough to know he should be afraid. But mostly what he'd felt was a profound sense of wonder. Of *awe*.

Now, gazing at the woman and the lion in the moon-light, his grown-up self felt the same wonder, the same awe...and the deepest fear, a kind of fear he'd never known before.

He felt stripped and vulnerable, naked and afraid. Because he knew...he *knew* in the depths of his being that his heart wasn't his anymore. That somehow, when he wasn't paying attention, he'd given it away. And in doing so, had given to another human being—to this woman—the power to hurt him as he'd never been hurt before.

All of this—the changing of his life forever—took place in the space of a moment, a few dozen heartbeats, no more. Then the cougar turned on herself in the fluid, boneless way of all felines and went streaking across the compound like a trick of the light, toward the rocky outcropping, flowed up and over it like quicksilver, and was gone.

Brooke came on, and he knew her eyes were locked with his, even though her expression was undecipherable to him, its subtle nuances lost to the moonlight shadows. He waited for her in silence, fingers of one hand woven through the chain-link fabric, those of the other through the silky fur of the dog panting happily beside him. And he understood now why Brooke so often did the same. He waited while she opened the gate and stepped through, then closed it carefully behind her and clicked the padlock into place.

She turned to him, and he would have spoken then. He drew breath to break the silence. And she reached up and touched his face...laid her hand along the side of his face while she looked into his eyes. He saw the moon reflected in the blackness of her eyes just for a moment. Then she swayed upward, just enough, and kissed him.

Chapter 8

The kiss was light and soft and sweet. He held his breath and closed his eyes because it seemed not quite real, except for the heavy thumping of his heart.

A great stillness came over him. Later, when he thought about it—when he could think again—it seemed to him like the stillness he felt when waiting for an elusive subject to move into the perfect spot, waiting for the exact moment when he would finally capture it. His body was still…but inside, every nerve and sinew and sense vibrated with energy and excitement and that sense of awe and wonder that never seemed to diminish no matter how many times he experienced that moment.

But this was different, of course, and it ended just when he felt his hands begin to lift of their own accord, and he knew he was about to touch her—her arms, first, then…who knows?—against all good sense and his better judgment. It ended when she rocked back on her heels—although she let her hand linger a while longer on his face before it slid down to rest on his chest—and he let his breath go, carefully. She went on gazing at him then, with her head tilted slightly, and her hair, loose, for once, in a carefree fall of subtly curving layers, seemed to lift and float around her face like feathers.

"Are you absolutely sure you're not gay?" Her voice was a rusty sound, and he responded with a feeble noise, which he, with his manly self-image, would not accept—could not possibly believe—was a whimper.

"Positive," he managed, more croak than voice, and tried to laugh.

"Hmm…well." Her hand moved slightly on his chest, drifting more than stroking, and where it paused again, he felt the heat of his body soak through his shirt and merge with hers. "Just so you know—" she hitched in a breath "—I only act like a brazen hussy during the full moon, so you'd better take advantage of the opportunity while you can." And he heard a new note in her voice, one he had no trouble recognizing, though she'd tried her best to hide it under a camouflage of sultry laughter.

"And…that's the problem," he said gently, on firmer ground now that he understood how vulnerable, how uncertain she was. "I would be."

"Oh." Her hand stilled…curled on his chest, and from only that contact, he felt the fine tremors coursing through her. "I see—you'd be taking advantage of me in my present desperate circumstances." Her chin came up, and her hair slithered back over her shoulders. He could see her lips curve in a smile that even the metallic colors of moonlight couldn't rob of softness and warmth. "Tony," she said in a husky whisper, "you are a very sweet man."

He gave a spurt of laughter. "Oh, thanks—just what every manly man wants to he—"

"Stop." Her fingertips, laid warm against his lips, caught the last word. "You have no idea how appealing that quality is to me."

"And you…have no idea how appealing you are…to me." He felt her arms, the skin cool but warming rapidly under his palms, and wondered when his body had given itself permission to touch her.

"Then why…"

"Don't I want to kiss you? Because I know if I do, I won't want to stop." And why do my hands insist on slipping up to your shoulders? *And…is this your neck I feel, so warm and vibrant, your pulse racing like a wild thing against my palms?*

"Well, darlin'—" and the pure Texas in her voice made him smile "—nobody's askin' you to."

"Brooke…" His heartbeat was thunder, not fast but slow.…

"Hush up." She swayed toward him. "Let's just cross that bridge when we come to it, okay? For now, why don't you try it, and if neither one of us wants to stop, we'll just keep on doin' it—how's that?"

I am *a brazen hussy*, she thought. When did this happen?

She didn't care. All she wanted—and she wanted it

with a desperation that astounded her—was for him to kiss her again. *Not again—I kissed him the first time. That doesn't count. Tony...kiss me...please...because if you don't, I think I will die of embarrassment, and if it's possible to die of wanting, I will do that, too.*

And then he *was* kissing her, and his hand cradled her head like a newborn babe. She gave a whimper of thankfulness; and her arms went around his big, solid body; and it felt to her like a bulwark, a bastion of safety in the chaos her world had become.

The kiss was sweet and gentle, as she'd expected his kiss would be. What she hadn't expected was that it would be—she was no expert on kissing, but the word *skilled* came to mind. Thorough...sensitive...not over-bearing, and yet...utterly devastating. Something shattered inside her, leaving her groundless and trembling. She lost her place in the world; now she clung to him as she would hold on to a tree in a hurricane.

Panic seized her. Her mind cried out to him to stop.

And he did. Gently easing his mouth away from hers with soft caresses, which lingered on her lips like something so delicious...so heavenly that she licked her lips to keep the taste of him with her just a little longer, already knowing she was addicted. Already wanting more.

"Hmm," she murmured, eyes closed, swaying a little. "See, I knew you'd be a good kisser." She heard the slur in her words and knew she sounded drunk...or besotted. And didn't care.

He laughed, and the fact that it sounded shaken rather than smug endeared him to her even more. His arms enveloped her, and she felt small and cared for—a novelty for her, being five-ten in her socks. She tilted her head back so she could look at him, marveling at the rugged landscape of his face in the moonlight, marveling that a man with such a face could be so incredibly tender. And it came to her then, in that moment, that his face was actually...beautiful.

"Why did you stop?" she asked in a whisper.

He tipped his head to look at her, bringing his mouth close to hers again. "I thought you wanted me to."

"I did." She swallowed. Audibly. "Just for a minute. I was...I couldn't—"

"Yeah," he whispered, "me, too."

"I'm okay now, though, I think. Can we do it again?"

"Are you sure?"

"Yes...please..."

This time they broke from the kiss, both of them, breathless and shaky. Tony cradled Brooke's head against his rapidly thumping heart and stared bleakly over her head at the colorless landscape beyond the chain-link fence and wondered how he could have let himself come to this in so short a time.

She trusts me. Daniel trusts me. Hell, even the dog trusts me. And I've lied to them all. She doesn't know who I really am or why I'm really here. She doesn't even know who she really is. How am I going to tell her?

Oh, God...I have to tell her, now.

"Brooke—" he began, at the same moment she said, "Tony—"

He paused, and they both said together, "There's something I have to tell you—" They both stopped again, laughing in a rueful, pain-filled way.

"Me, first," she said in a thickened voice, pulling back and gazing earnestly at him. The back of one hand was pressed against her nose, and above it her eyes were dark and still, like deep forest ponds, reflecting only the moonlight. It was only because he was holding her that he felt her shiver.

"Okay," he said, "but only if we find a warmer spot first. You're cold." But it was he who felt cold—on the outside where her body had nestled, and inside, deep in the pit of his stomach, where the fear was.

She shook her head but turned in his embrace and slipped an arm around his waist as they began to walk together back toward the barn. "Not cold. Nervous, maybe." She glanced at him, then quickly away, making him realize what an understatement that was.

He wanted to say something to take away her fear, but his own was so deep, he didn't trust himself to utter a sound. He couldn't ask her what she might have to confess, to be nervous about—how could he, when uppermost in his mind was that she was about to tell him she'd killed her husband, after all, and that he'd been wrong about her all along? So he walked beside her in the moonlight, her arm around him and his around her. It occurred to him that they must look like lovers, but while her body felt warm and vital against him, the cold he felt inside was the sick and clammy chill of dread.

In the barn, they sat on a bale of hay in a patch of moonlight framed by the big open door, side by side, like children on a bench. Brooke shifted, turning to half face him as she took one of his hands in both of hers. Her shoulders lifted as she took a breath.

"Brooke," he burst out, unable to stand it anymore, "I can understand if it was self-defense—"

"What?" She blinked and shook her head sharply, as if coming out of a daze. Then clapped a hand to her forehead. "Oh—oh, God. You thought—oh, stupid me." She stared at him for a moment, then smiled crookedly and said, with that Texas twang he was beginning to find so unexpectedly endearing, "Tony, you poor thing. You're sittin' there thinkin' you're about to find out you've just been kissin' a cold-blooded killer, aren't you?"

"Well," he said in a garbled imitation of a frog.

"No, it's my fault, and I'm sorry. I should have thought." She faced forward again and didn't reclaim his hand, bracing hers on the edge of the bale instead as she rocked herself slightly. She gave a faint laugh. "Funny thing is, I never even thought about…that. Can you believe that? I actually forgot for maybe a minute." Her voice took on an edge, and she threw him a quick, intense look over her shoulder. "The answer to the question that's eatin' you up inside is, no, I did not kill my husband. *Ex*-husband," she amended wearily, closing her eyes. "You can believe that or not…but it's true."

Tony cleared his throat and found his voice was functional again, and that the cold place in his belly was fading. "I do believe you. I have been believing you. That's why I'm here."

"But you've had doubts." She looked at him over her shoulder again, sadly this time. "Otherwise, you wouldn't have thought I was about to confess."

He tried to smile. "I can't argue with the logic of that,

so I'm not even going to try. But since we both know you're not a murderer, what is this *thing* you feel you have to tell me?"

She looked at him for a long time, her eyes lingering, not on his eyes, but on his mouth…his shoulders, his chest. The stark hunger…yearning…he saw on her face nearly stopped his heart, then quickened it again. She turned away quickly, but not before he saw her lips quiver…saw her press them tightly together to stop it.

In a voice so low he had to lean closer to hear it, she said, "I want you to know…it felt so good, you holding me. Felt *too* good, you kissing me, me kissing you—I didn't want it to end. But…I thought, before I let this go any further, you should know exactly who you'd be kissing." She gave him that over-the-shoulder look again, and now it reminded him of one of the wild things he'd stalked with his cameras, watching him as he approached her comfort zone, wary and uncertain, not quite sure whether to be afraid. "There are an awful lot of things you don't know about me."

I probably know more about you than you can begin to imagine…things you don't even know yourself, Tony thought. But aloud he said indulgently, with all the confidence in the world, thinking no matter what she had to tell him, it couldn't possibly rival the bombshell he was about to drop on her, "It's all right. You *can* tell me, Brooke."

She nodded. Said, "I know. All right." Cleared her throat, sat up straight, looked him in the eye and said, "I was molested."

He couldn't have been more stunned if she'd hauled

off and slugged him. He stared at her blankly. The words she'd spoken had no meaning; they rang in his ears like the discordant clang of a broken bell.

She rushed on, filling his silence with more of those incomprehensible words. "Abused. Sexually. Raped... actually. When I was a child. By my brother—*adopted* brother."

He was—had always been—a man who respected, even revered, women. The very idea that a man could mistreat or terrorize a woman—any woman, of any age—was simply appalling to him. But *this* woman... and a *child*... He wanted to cover his ears like a child himself. Wanted to tell her to stop. He could feel the edges of his world curling in on him, shimmering... turning dark. And still the words came.

"He was older—ten years older. It started when I was fourteen—that's when my sister ran away. He'd been doing it to her since we were about...eleven, I think. Maybe even before that. I think I knew, but I didn't want to, you know? So I didn't tell anybody. Then my sister ran away, and that's when he...he turned to me."

Why didn't you tell someone? His mind, finally functioning again, shrieked the question, but he couldn't bring himself to ask it. It seemed too much like an accusation. Like blame. And that was the last thing she needed, he realized. She'd been blaming herself far too long already.

He didn't ask it, but she answered as if he had. "I didn't tell my parents, because I knew they wouldn't believe me. I'm sure that's why my sister didn't tell anyone, either. He—Clay—was their *son*. Their *real* son, you know?" There were tears on her cheeks now. He wondered if she even knew. "He would have denied it or else blamed us. I know he would have. My parents were very religious—the hellfire and damnation kind of religious. I was sure they'd disown me if they knew. My father would have, anyway. I think I told you, he never wanted to adopt us to begin with. I think he just went along with it because he knew Mom wanted a little girl so bad, and she couldn't—well, I told you about that." She cleared her throat, paused and then went on.

"So…finally, I ran away, too. In a way. I was seventeen when I met Duncan, and he was so strong, so protective…and I thought, Here's somebody who'll take me away from here, and Clay can't ever touch me again. So, I…"

"You married him." He heard the harshness in his voice but couldn't seem to make it softer. "Did he—your husband—did he know?"

She nodded and brushed absently at her cheek. Her voice became a whisper. "I told him on our honeymoon. He'd figured out I wasn't…you know…so I had to tell him. At first he seemed okay with it—sweet, even. Angry, but not at me. I thought. But then, when I got pregnant, he started acting so jealous, possessive, like he didn't trust me. He actually doubted Daniel was his child. And that's…when he started…"

"Hitting you."

"Yes."

"My God." He discovered he was shaking. Shaking with a rage that demanded violence, a primitive rage

that wanted to smash, break, kill. He shook because
what was required of him instead was tenderness.
"Brooke…" He wanted to hold her, wrap her in his arms
and stroke her hair and kiss away her tears. But in his
fractured state, he was afraid to touch her. "You do
know none of it was your fault?"

She nodded…drew a long, shuddering sniff. "In *here*
I do—" she touched her temple "—in my grown-up
head, I do." Then her chest. "But in here…I don't know.
Sometimes there's this person in here, inside me, this
little girl, and she feels…ashamed and dirty and scared—"
Her voice broke, and a huge shudder ran through her as
she gathered herself to flee.

He didn't think, wasn't aware of moving, but somehow he had her wrapped in his arms, with her face
pressed against his heart. He murmured things…
soothing things…sounds without words, and she began
to sob like a heartbroken child. She fought it, though,
her body rigid, hands clutching at his shirt, gathering
fistfuls of it, as if she wanted to rend something—anything. And he held her and stroked her hair and shielded
her face from the chill and the light with his hand, as if
she were a small, terrified orphan creature he'd found.
And he let her cry.

He held her until she grew quiet, and when he felt her
stir and resist his embrace, he let her go.

She pulled away and straightened a little, fingers
plucking at the sopping wet front of his shirt. "Boy," she
said groggily, "do I know how to kill a moment, or
what?"

He looked at her, smiling a little, too overcome with

tenderness for her even to laugh. "There will be other moments."

"Yeah, but…" She cleared her throat, sat up straight and wiped her cheeks with both hands, not looking at him now. "Here I was, all set to seduce you into carrying me off to bed and making love to me all night. Guess *that's* not gonna happen."

Laughter rose to his throat in a painful lump. He thought, *God, what am I going to do about this? If I hurt this woman, I deserve all the hellfire and brimstone You can muster.*

"Not tonight, anyway," he said gently as he stood and held out his hand to help her up. He smiled. "Although I am going to carry you off to bed."

Her eyes widened above the hand she'd pressed to her still-streaming nose. "You are not! Big as I am, you'd have to be crazy. Probably cripple you for life."

He slipped an arm around her waist, laughing. "That was a figure of speech. Although," he added wryly as they walked slowly together, in step, back toward the house, "I have to tell you, it doesn't do much for my machismo that you don't think I could."

She swiveled her head toward him, and when he looked at her, he saw that her eyes were dark and grave, and that she wasn't smiling. "Honestly, Tony?" she whispered. "I believe you could do just about anything you set your mind to."

He couldn't answer her. And again, fear and guilt were a painful tangle inside him. *Dear Lord…what am I gonna do?*

Like a proper gentleman, he walked her to her

bedroom door and kissed her. And although her fingers lingered on his chest and he felt the tug of her longing as if it were something tangible—a rope, a lasso around his heart—he said good-night and left her there.

"Sleep well…" he whispered as he touched his lips to her forehead, knowing he would not.

Brooke woke to sticky eyelids and a dry mouth and the feeling that she'd spent the past several hours at the bottom of a deep, dark well. Climbing out of it seemed not worth the effort—until she heard noises from beyond her bedroom walls and remembered. *I remember…moonlight, and Lady…and Tony. Tony… and me being a brazen hussy. Tony kissing me. Me… talking. Me…crying. Tony…*

A profusion of emotions, many of them in conflict with one another, nibbled furiously at her: shame and longing…fear and delight. Shameless longing…

She threw back the covers and rose, only to discover she felt as wobbly as if she'd been in bed a week with the flu. *What is this?* she thought. *Am I sick? I'm never sick.*

The noises she'd heard had become voices—Tony's and Daniel's—and they were coming from the kitchen. Curiosity overcame both physical and emotional weakness, and she pulled on jeans and a T-shirt, raked her fingers through her hair and tottered across the hallway to the bathroom. When she emerged a few minutes later, she felt marginally better, but also keenly aware that she'd overslept. It had to be nearly time for the school bus, and Daniel—

These worries carried her as far as the kitchen doorway. There she halted, transfixed, as if caught in some paralyzing force field. She stood absolutely still, bathed in warmth and light, and knowledge sifted into her consciousness like sunbeams. *Love. That's what this is. I love this man.*

The tableau in the kitchen consisted of two people and one dog, all three, for the moment, unaware of her presence. Tony—he was standing in front of the stove, and he was wearing an apron. An apron! Where he'd found it, she couldn't imagine; even *she* never wore an apron. Daniel—he was at the table, busily assembling his lunch while keeping up a revealing commentary on the personality quirks of his various teachers. Hilda—she sat at attention between the two but had eyes only for Tony, for reasons that became evident when he flipped her a slice of what appeared to be…

"Hey—Mom! Tony made French toast. With cinnamon. We had it with applesauce, 'cause it's healthier for you than syrup, and it was really *good*, Mom. Hey—is it okay if I take the last piece of chicken for my lunch? And we're out of bananas, but that's okay, because Tony said he's going to town, today, anyway and he can get some more, so I'm taking grapes instead."

Her son's words fell on her ears and rolled away like raindrops on feathers. Encased in her shaft of enlightenment and towed by the tractor beam of Tony's gaze, Brooke floated into the kitchen. She murmured absent replies to Daniel's questions and didn't think to scold Hilda, who knew very well she wasn't supposed to eat people food or beg for treats from the table or stove, and had, in fact, already slunk off to her corner, looking guilty as sin. Tony smiled at her, and she smiled back.

"Hope you don't mind," he said, hefting a pancake turner in one hand, a griddle in the other. "We thought we'd let you sleep in this morning."

"No—of course, I don't mind." She said it with a gasp as she grabbed hold of the back of a chair and held on to it, fully aware it was all that was keeping her from drifting on into his arms for a good-morning kiss. Which would be the natural way for a woman to greet her man the morning after they'd made love. Which they hadn't, of course. But they would…soon. That knowledge— that certainty—made her voice husky when she added, "That's…nice of you. You didn't have to do that. But thanks."

"No problem. Happy to do it. I told you—the sisters. I don't want you to have to wait on me."

And she got lost in his eyes and his sweet, sweet smile….

Blessedly oblivious to adult undercurrents, Daniel chattered on as he stuffed his lunch bag into his backpack, slung it over his shoulders and shrugged it into place. He brushed her cheek with a kiss, bumped knuckles with Tony, and went charging out the door, with Hilda on his heels. And silence crept into the kitchen, heavy with awareness and charged with tension, like a spring storm cell.

Tension sang in the clanging Tony made as he put down the pancake turner and griddle, rumbled in the grating sound of the chair as Brooke pushed it aside.

Then she was across the kitchen, and his arms reached for her, and when her body collided with his, Brooke felt as if all the forces of a storm were breaking loose inside her. The fury and power, the excitement and wonder of it filled her mind and took over her body, leaving no room for fear or questions or doubt. No room for thought. She only knew when his mouth found hers...at last.

She tasted of toothpaste, he discovered, and for some reason, he found that endearing. A moment or two later—or it could have been longer; he'd rapidly lost the ability to track time—he discovered she wasn't wearing a bra under her T-shirt. *That* he found not so much endearing as—not surprisingly—sexy as hell. Accepting the inferred invitation, he slipped his hands under her shirt and brought them up along her rib cage to cradle the sides of her breasts in his palms. And her gasp tore her mouth from his, and she buried her face in the curve of his neck and shoulder.

"Hey..." He whispered it with his lips close to her neck, just below her ear. "I thought you said you only turn into a brazen hussy during the full moon."

"Moon's still full out there somewhere," she mumbled from the depths of her hiding place.

He wanted to laugh, but her hands were busy behind him, untying the apron's strings...tugging his undershirt free of his waistband, and then the feel of her hands on his skin drove every hint of mirth from his mind.

Then he did laugh, not because anything was funny, but because the emotions raging inside him needed some kind of safety valve, and for a grown man, laughter seemed infinitely preferable to tears. It was soft laughter, low and breathy, but it shook him to his core.

"Brooke, honey," he said feebly, "I think it's time I carried you off to bed now."

"If you insist," she murmured, smiling at him, and her eyes, peeking from under her lashes, had a pixieish glint.

He did. He swept her up in his arms and was amazed at how light she seemed. Or rather, how strong and powerful *he* felt.

He was amazed that this woman could make him feel things he'd never felt before, when he'd known...well, quite a few women in his life. Every one had been special to him in her way, but *this* woman...*Brooke*... She was his birthday and Christmas, the most wonderful Christmas of his life, with an endless supply of packages, each one to be slowly unwrapped and savored, each one revealing something new and exciting and wonderful. Somehow he knew that with this woman, he'd still be finding new packages to open when they were both ninety.

The realization stunned him and tempered his passion with a tenderness and care he was sure he'd never felt before.

And didn't want to look at too closely—not then.

He carried her to his room—the spare room—not hers, and wasn't sure why. Some primitive instinct, maybe, that made him want to bring her into *his* place— a kind of *claiming*. And that, too, was something he'd never felt before. And didn't want to look at closely.

He looked instead into her eyes and lost himself there.

"I hope you don't think—" she began, and he dipped his head and silenced her with a kiss.

"I don't," he whispered. *This isn't a time for thinking, love. If I let myself think—*

He couldn't let himself think.

He wanted her. Wanted her as he'd never wanted a woman before. Wanted her with the finest nerve endings in his skin and the deepest marrow in his bones. But it was a strange kind of wanting, because he wanted not to *take* something from her, but to *give* it. He wanted to give her pleasure and joy. He wanted to give her happiness. And hope. He wanted to give her all the good things in the universe, tied up with flowers and ribbons, and watch her face while she opened them. He wondered whether he would be able to give her all those things...and then knew, beyond any doubt, that he was the only one who could.

All that was in his eyes when he looked at her, in his mouth when he kissed her, in his hands when he touched her. It was in the unhurried way he removed her clothes and smiled at her shyness and at her whispered, "Guess I'm not such a brazen hussy after all..."

It was in the way he gave himself over to her so she could undress him at her own pace, even though her explorations—sometimes shy, sometimes brazen—made his muscles knot and his jaw creak with their demands on his self-control.

Her skin tasted to him like ice cream melting in the sun, and smelled of old roses. When she tasted his, it felt like the most exquisite torture and the greatest pleasure he'd ever known.

He groaned—could not help it—and she whispered, "Are you going to have your way with me now?"

"I think—" and he could barely form the words "—you've got it backwards. You…are having your way with *me*."

She tilted her head, and her expression was poignant, eager and sweet. "May I?"

"Yes, love…oh, yes. Whatever you wish."

And so she straddled him and gave to him the gifts he'd wanted for her: pleasure and joy and happiness and hope. And he watched her face while she gave to him, and knew he'd never be the same again.

Sometime later, when the earth had righted itself and resumed its normal spin, and she'd become reoriented to her place in it; when they lay together in the tumble they'd made of the double bed, talking in sleepy murmurs of the wonders and coincidences of fate, Brooke remembered.

"You were going to tell me something," she whispered. "Last night…before I…ruined the moment." And her ear, pressed against his chest, felt his heartbeat quicken.

"Hmm…can't remember now. Must not've been that important." His voice was a lazy growl, and his hand never faltered in its silken slide up and down her naked back.

But just the same, she knew he lied.

Chapter 9

"I have to tell her." Tony stared bleakly into his coffee cup, having refused Holt's offer to buy him lunch at the diner. It had been hours since the French toast he'd had for breakfast, but it—or guilt—still lay heavy in his stomach. "This changes everything."

"Yeah, it does." Holt stabbed at a chunk of the meat loaf special. "You couldn't have waited until all this was over to sleep with her?"

Anger lanced through Tony, driven, no doubt, by more guilt. "Look," he snapped, "it's not like I planned it, okay? Hell, do I look like the kind of guy who'd move in on his best friend's sister, particularly at a time when she's in dire straits?"

"I don't know what kind of guy you are, frankly," Holt said. "I just met you myself, remember?"

"Yeah, well…I'm not. Trust me." He shifted and added darkly, "Okay, maybe you shouldn't. *She* trusts me, and I'm not exactly being straight with her, am I?" He let out a breath. "That's why I have to tell her. Now."

Holt picked up his napkin and wiped his mouth with it, then reached for his wallet. "Hold off on that, if you can. Just a little bit longer. At least until Cory and Sam get here."

"No kidding—they're on their way?" Tony picked up the check. Even the coffee had turned sour in his stomach. "Where'd you find Cory? Sam track him down?"

Holt nodded. "He's been somewhere in Africa—the Sudan, I think. Covering the latest uprising, I guess. Anyway, he just got airlifted out a couple days ago by the 'independent security contractors' along with the entire U.S. embassy staff and their families. I talked to him this morning. They should be here tomorrow some-time." He raised his eyebrows at Tony as he slid out of the booth. "What? I figured that was *good* news."

"Brooke told me some things. About…herself. Uh… jeez…" The last word was mostly breath. Holt looked another question at him, and he shook his head. "Personal stuff. About what happened to her when she was a kid, growing up. Her sister, too. The reason she got married so young. The reason her sister ran away from home." He paused, and even thinking of talking about it left a bitter taste in his mouth. "Hell, Kincaid, do I need to spell it out?"

"Her father?" Holt's voice was soft and dangerous.

"Brother. He was a good ten years older than the

twins. An adult, anyway. And they were just kids when…it happened."

They left the diner, with Holt muttering under his breath what sounded like swearing and blasphemy.

Tony nodded his agreement with the sentiments. "Anyway, Cory probably needs to know, and I guess I'm gonna have to be the one to tell him." He paused, then added bleakly, "He already blames himself for what happened to his family—the kids getting split up. This is going to just about kill him."

Brooke had never been so late with her morning chores. It was nearly noon when she turned the chickens out of their house, and they clucked petulantly at her as they stalked past her and through the door. Several of the hens were already on their nests—sulking, she was sure. She cooed apologies to them while she replenished their feeder with scratch and made a point to clean and fill their water bowls with fresh water. She gave the goats, alpacas and horses a little extra measure of grain, and gave the horses a good brushing before she turned them out to pasture.

She went to say good morning to Lady, but the cougar stayed on her rocky battlement and refused to come close to the fence. "Are you mad at me, too, my Lady girl?"

The cougar's head was low and her shoulders tensed—her stalking stance—as she stared intently past Brooke, toward the lane and the barn and beyond. A chill went down Brooke's spine. Clearly, something had upset her.

She thought of the SUV that Rocky and Isabel's "cousin" had seen driving out of the back road, and the look on Lonnie's face when he'd said, "This ain't over." And she walked back to the house, feeling small and exposed and vulnerable, like a rabbit in an open field, sensing the hawk circling high overhead.

She found Rocky and Isabel just coming down the back porch steps.

"We were looking for you," Isabel said, and she looked anxiously at her husband.

They exchanged a brief glance, and Rocky said, "We were worried. Ever since my cousin told us he saw the SUV again. This morning he sees this SUV drive past your driveway, going very slowly. It drives down to the back road and turns in, then backs up and turns around and drives past your house again. He says it did this three times, that he saw. He says he thinks it was the same one he saw the day Duncan was killed."

Brooke felt her body go still, while inside, her heart pounded hard and fast, and in her mind, a little girl's voice whimpered, *Tony, where are you? Come back! I need you....*

Then the voice was gone, and the stillness was inside her, too. She said quietly, "Where is your cousin now?"

Again, Rocky and his wife exchanged glances. He cleared his throat and shifted nervously. "He is gone. He left this morning—after he sees—*saw*—the SUV. He is afraid because—" Another anxious glance at Isabel.

Isabel stepped forward and said angrily, "He's afraid because he knows the sheriffs are crooked. They are bad men, Brooke. I'm sorry, but Duncan was, too. They take money, from the…from people like our cousin, and then they tell them they must get more money or they will kill them and send them back to their families in Mexico in little pieces."

"How does your cousin know this?" The voice came from the vast stillness inside Brooke.

"He had a friend—Ernesto. They came over the border together. The sheriffs stopped them, but they didn't make them go back or put them in jail. Instead, they took their money and told them they must get more from their families or friends here in the United States. Ernesto told them he had nobody here, and they took him away that night. My cousin never saw him again. My cousin managed to get away, and he came here, to us. So you see why he is afraid."

Brooke nodded. She folded her arms across her body and rubbed at her upper arms to try to warm herself, but she felt cold clear through, anyway, in spite of the September sunshine. She said, with a calm that amazed her, "Whoever was in the SUV your cousin saw…I don't think he was after your cousin—or me. It's Lady he wants."

"The lion? But why?" said Isabel.

"He wants to kill her," said Brooke. And in her mind was the image of Lady crouched on her rock pile, a clear and easy target. "I don't know why. Maybe because he believes she killed Duncan, in spite of what the medical examiner says. Maybe he's just crazy. But if I don't do something, he's going to kill her." She looked pleadingly into her neighbors' eyes. "Will you help me? Please?"

* * *

Tony drove back to Brooke's place on autopilot. His mind was lost in a swamp of confusion, where dark shadows and deep waters held unknown perils, and anxiety lurked like the indefinable fears and bad dreams of children.

He hadn't known such anxiety since he *was* a child, and he realized he was feeling it now for the same reason he'd felt it then: because he was vulnerable. Overnight, it seemed, he'd come to care for someone in a way that up to now had been reserved for blood kin: mother, father, sisters and brothers. This woman and her son—Brooke and Daniel—had somehow become his responsibility and concern, and their well-being and happiness vital to his own. The realization made him feel warm and excited and happy in a way he couldn't recall ever feeling before, but at the same time it made his heart tremble and his stomach fill with a cold, hard knot of fear.

The first thing he saw when he drove into the yard was that Brooke's pickup truck wasn't parked where it usually was. The second was that Hilda hadn't come bounding out to meet him. The formless fear inside him coalesced and grew and threatened to become panic.

He got out of his car and slammed the door, leaving the groceries he'd bought sitting on the backseat. He called her name. And that was when he heard it—the sound that sent a chill shooting down his spine: the squall of an angry cougar.

He ran, and each footfall on the hard Texas soil jarred his head and his chest like hammer blows. She's okay.

She's okay, he told himself, without rhyme or reason for either the fear or the futile attempt at reassurance. A hundred what-ifs tried to crowd into his mind all at once and only created a nightmarish chaos in his imagination.

From inside the barn, from the point where he had a clear view down the lane to the cougar's compound, Tony could see Brooke's pickup, and that it was backed up close to the gate in the chain-link fence. And what looked like the lion's holding cage was sitting in the back of the pickup. And Brooke's neighbors, Rocky and Isabel, were standing beside the pickup, their attention focused completely on what was happening inside the compound. He saw no one else, no big fawn-and-white dog, no sign of a sheriff's SUV or deputy in or out of uniform.

With his worst fear unrealized—that Lonnie had come back for Lady and that Brooke was involved in a deadly face-off with an armed and dangerous deputy—and his heart more or less free to resume its normal function, he now felt it swan dive into his shoes. *Oh, Brooke...what in the world are you thinking?*

Having already halted his headlong dash, faced with the improbable scene before him, Tony forced himself to proceed now at a less panic-stricken pace. He strolled down the lane, with his thumbs hooked in his pockets, showing no sign, he hoped, of the fact that his whole body was vibrating with adrenaline.

"Hello," he called when he was within a few yards of the pickup, and two heads jerked toward him in tandem, eyes widening with alarm. He nodded in a friendly way meant to calm the couple and said, "What's going on?"

Isabel looked at her husband, and Rocky gave a shrug. "She is trying to catch the puma. She says she is going to set it free."

"Jeez…" Tony whispered.

Isabel gave him a crooked smile and said, "Yes, I have been praying, too."

Beyond her shoulder, Tony could see Brooke out in the cougar's compound. She was standing with her back to him in the middle of the open area between the fence and the rocky knoll, facing the cougar, who was crouched on top of the rock pile. And even from where he stood, he could see that the lion's ears lay flattened against her head and her tail was twitching furiously.

Having been acquainted with quite a few domestic felines in his lifetime, Tony knew a very scared or angry—and in this case, dangerous—cat when he saw one.

He opened the gate and slipped inside the compound, closing the gate carefully behind him. "Brooke, honey," he said, marveling at how calm his voice sounded, "what are you doing?"

She turned her head to look at him, and for a moment his heart stopped. *Don't turn your back on her, sweetheart—please don't turn around.*

Her face was streaked with dirt—dust mixed with moisture that was either sweat or tears—and her voice shook. "I don't know what's wrong with her. I've never seen her act like this before."

"She's scared," Tony said, and the lion screamed and cringed back against the rocks as he started across the compound to where Brooke was. *And that makes two of us. I'm six years old again, and that cat is looming over me, just the way I remember. And my sister's hand is trembling in mine....*

Then he was beside Brooke, and it was her hand he held tightly. "Don't move and don't make a sound," he whispered, without moving his mouth—or was that a memory, too?

She looked at him with tear-filled eyes and whispered, "Lady's not a killer. She would never attack me."

"She's a cougar, sweetheart. And right now she's operating on instinct. If you turn your back on her and retreat, she just might."

Letting go of her hand, he slipped his arm around her waist and began to walk her slowly backward. Out on the rock pile, the cat let out one more squall, then did that doubling-back-on herself maneuver, flowed like liquid amber over the rocks and, in a blink, was gone.

When they were safe on the other side of the fence, Brooke turned silently into his arms, buried her face against his chest and gathered his shirt in fisted handfuls. Rocky and Isabel were nowhere to be seen. Tony wrapped his arms around her and let his cheek rest on her sweat-damp hair, but he was in no way ready to let her off the hook for scaring him to death.

"Brooke...honey... What were you thinking?" He gave an incredulous spurt of laughter. "You were going to turn her *loose?* Lady's not feral—she'd never survive in the wild. You know that."

She pulled away from him, brushing furiously at her cheeks. "Of course, I know that. It's just better than...at least she'd have a fighting chance. Here—" she swept her arm in an arc that took in the whole compound "—she's trapped. A sitting duck. Fish in a barrel. I just don't want to come out one of these mornings and find her shot dead. Or worse, have Daniel find her."

"You mean Lonnie." He got his arm around her waist again and began walking her back toward the barn.

She nodded and sniffed, then threw him a look along her shoulder. "You heard what he said. He said he'd be back, and he won't wait for a judge's order, either. I know him. And when Rocky told me about his cousin—"

"What about his cousin?" Tony prompted when she paused as if she'd said too much.

She hissed out a breath. "He said he saw a sheriff's SUV again. He said it drove by the house several times. Slowly. I know it was Lonnie—probably trying to see if I was home or not. I think when he saw your car, he must have decided not to risk it. But that's not all." She paused again to look at him, and her eyes were dark with anguish. "Tony, Isabel said some of the deputies are involved in some kind of extortion ring. Involving the illegals, you know? A lot of them come through here, because it's right on the way from the border to the big cities, like Dallas and Fort Worth, but off the interstate, where most of the patrols are. These deputies, if they catch them, they make them pay money so they won't get sent back or put in jail, and if they can't come up with the money…" A shudder ran through her, and she threw him a bleak look. "Isabel says they kill them, Tony. She said Duncan was in on it, too. Do you think…could that have anything to do with why he died?"

"I don't know," he said, and it was the truth. He was

frowning, thinking he needed to get this information to Holt as soon as he possibly could, although he still couldn't imagine why, if Duncan Grant had had a falling out with his partners in crime, they hadn't just shot him and dumped the body somewhere out in the vastness of West Texas. He was also thinking he needed to tell Brooke everything, and wondering if this was the right time.

He'd about decided it was never going to be the right time, and this was probably as good as it was going to get, when Brooke suddenly gasped and said, "Oh God—Hilda. I hope she hasn't broken the door down," and took off running for the house.

Giving his heart time to settle back into a normal rhythm, Tony followed at a more sedate pace. He was crossing the yard when Hilda came galloping out to give him a lick and collect the fur-ruffling hug that was her due, then loped off to the pasture to see how the rest of her flock was faring. And he went on to where Brooke was waiting for him on the porch steps, drawn now by the tractor beam of her eyes.

"We shut her up so she wouldn't scare Lady away," she said, and the quick-time thumping of her heart and the hitch in her breathing made the words jump in an unrhythmic pattern. She pressed a closed fist against her chest and tried not to let her feelings show.

This *wanting* was new to her. Even without going further into her sexual past than her marriage—*no, I'm not about to go there!*—she'd never *wanted*, not like this. It wasn't that she hadn't sometimes enjoyed herself with Duncan, although not nearly as often as she'd pretended to. She'd even initiated the lovemaking once in a while, because she'd known it made Duncan happy when she did. But every time, when she'd known it was going to happen, there had been that moment of fear. That little clenching in her stomach, that flash of thought she tried not to notice because it seemed shameful and unnatural, and she dared not let Duncan or even herself know it was there. Just that teensy little, there-and-then-gone-again *no!*

But with Tony, she *wanted*. Wanted *him,* with a hunger that astounded her. Astounded, because it didn't embarrass her at all, but only made her want to smile.

Watching him bend down to ruffle Hilda's neck fur, seeing his hands, so dark against the dog's white-and-fawn coat, she hungered for those hands, wanted them touching her body again the way he'd touched her this morning. Was it only this morning? *It seems like forever ago. And how can I be so hungry for him already?*

Watching him straighten and come on across the yard, seeing his mouth curve in that honey-sweet smile, she wanted his mouth kissing her, kissing her everywhere, wanted it the way a starving person wants, smelling the delicious aroma of food. Juices pooled in her mouth, so that she had to swallow and lick her lips, and her lips burned in spite of the moisture she'd put there.

Watching him reach the bottom of the steps and pause to look up at her, seeing his eyes glow golden at the sight of her, she felt her body grow heavy and hot, and pulses jump in places still tender from their earlier union with his body.

She knew he was watching her, seeing her eyes grow slumberous and her smile seductive, seeing the way her nipples beaded in sharp outline beneath her shirt, and she didn't feel even a flash of fear or self-consciousness, not even a faint echo in her mind of *no!*

He'd come to the step below hers and, without a word, reached out and hooked an arm around her waist, pulled her to him and lifted his face for her kiss.

But she didn't kiss him, not right away. She took his face between her two hands and gazed down at him, stroked the broad planes of his cheekbones with her thumbs and marveled at how beautiful he was, and that just looking at him could make her feel so...*happy.*

What did I do to deserve this? Especially now, when I have no right at all to be happy.

"Are you going to kiss me, or what?" Tony said.

She gave a faint whimper of a laugh. "I was afraid it might be too soon."

"Hey, I'm a guy—when it comes to sex, we have short...mmm..."

It was all the encouragement she needed. She let herself sink into his kiss and felt her body grow weightless and her mind go floating off into a pale pink haze. *Yes...this is love. I...adore...this...man.*

She was barely aware when he came up to her step, then tangoed her backward through the door and onto the porch...then into the kitchen. There he paused to look into her eyes and whisper, "Your place or mine?"

"Mine..." She murmured it without opening her eyes, and they were moving again, and she couldn't have cared less where they wound up as long as it was together.

They undressed each other standing up this time, not in a frantic hurry, but not too slowly, either. When they were both naked, Brooke placed her palms on Tony's chest and watched her fingers fan on his smooth mahogany skin, and she shivered, not with cold, but with a surfeit of feelings.

"So beautiful," she whispered, lost in the miracle of him.

He lowered his forehead to hers. "What is, love?"

"You…your skin…your body. You are."

"Me?" He gave a little gulp of laughter. "Man, that's a first. I mean, I am many things, some of which I'm even proud to admit to, but *beautiful?*" He shook his head in a dazed kind of way and, holding her waist with his hands, took a small step back from her so he could rake her body with his eyes. *"You,* on the other hand—"

"Hush." She shuddered and slipped between his arms, brought her arms around him and stopped his words with her mouth. Then laid her head on his shoulder. "As long as I am to you," she said huskily, and tears seeped between her lashes. "That's all that matters."

She felt a ripple pass through his strong, solid body, and his fingers glide through her hair with the delicacy of a harpist coaxing beauty from the strings of his instrument. His lips moved against her temple. "You are…more so than you can possibly imagine. And…I'd like to make love with you now. If you're ready." He cupped her head between his hands and tipped her face so he could look into her eyes. "Are you ready, sweetheart? Do you want me? Do you want me to love you now?"

Oh, yes...if only you would. Could you love me, Tony? Not just my body, but...me?

She drew a shaken breath and whispered, "Yes... please."

And as he had given the reins to her this morning, now she gave them, and herself, over to him. To his skilled kisses and artist's hands that made every nerve in her body shiver with delight...and to his tenderness that made her ache inside with longing. He took her to places she'd never known existed, gave her glimpses of joys she'd never imagined, lifted her to heights of ecstasy that terrified her, then gave her release that seemed to go on forever. And afterward, she wept and couldn't tell him why.

She couldn't tell him she was crying because it had ended too soon, and she was afraid she'd never feel anything so wonderful again. And because she was in love with him. Loved him desperately, irrevocably, with all her heart and soul, and had no idea whether he might...if he could ever...love her back.

I think I love this woman.

It slipped into his mind while his guard was down, while he lay relaxed and spent, with her head gently rising and falling with the movement of his chest and her tears cooling on his skin. And once it was there, it seemed pointless to try and deny it. It didn't even seem as frightening as he'd always thought it would be. In fact, acknowledging it was an almost giddy relief, like finding unexpected rapport with someone he'd been dreading to meet.

The fact that she'd cried didn't surprise him. It wasn't the first time a woman had cried in his arms after making love. What did surprise him was the way *he* felt, which was not like crying, of course—because he didn't do that sort of thing, at least not very often—but rather so full of feelings he didn't know what to do with that his chest hurt. For a moment he wondered if telling her how he felt would help, but decided it would probably only make things worse. After all, she had enough on her emotional plate right now, the last thing she needed was to have to deal with the burden of some stranger falling in love with her.

Then he thought about what she'd said about him being beautiful, and the fact that she'd seemed utterly sincere when she'd said it. That she could think such a thing about someone—he had no illusions about this—as flat-out ugly as he was just about took his breath away.

Of course, she was beautiful to him—okay, obviously, she was beautiful to anybody who wasn't completely blind—but beautiful to him in ways that couldn't be captured on film or a digital memory chip. Was it possible she saw something similar when she looked at him?

Could she? What the hell does it mean?

A strange shimmering sensation had begun to dance beneath his skin, raising goose bumps just about every-where, when Brooke stirred and lifted her head to say groggily, "What time izzit?"

He lifted his arm and peered at his watch. "Hmm… 'bout three. Why?" Then, before she could answer, he thought, *Daniel!* and went rigid. "Oh, hell. I forgot. What time does—"

"About three-thirty." She stretched languidly and kissed his chest. "Don't worry. Plenty of time. We could even take a shower." She looked up at him from under her lashes, and her smile was impish.

"Brazen hussy," he growled, giving her bottom a gentle pat. "Tempting…but you're forgetting something." He shifted her off to one side and sat up, then turned to look at her and smiled. He couldn't help it, given the way she looked lying naked on her side, propped on one elbow, with her head slightly tilted and her hair feathered across one flushed and tanned cheek, lips still swollen from his kisses… The camera in his mind went *click*.

He said gently, "There's a cougar cage sitting in the back of your pickup, remember? Are you sure you want to try and explain that to Daniel?" She lay back with a groan and put an arm over her face. He laid his hand on her flat stomach and stroked downward, chuckling when she gasped and squirmed. "Come on, sweetheart—upsy-daisy. Let's do this. If the three of you managed to get that thing up there, I think you and I can probably get it down. Especially since we have gravity on our side."

He leaned over and kissed her, then gathered up his clothes and left her. And deep in his heart, he was grateful for the distraction that had made it possible for him to avoid answering the question that had popped into his mind just before she asked him the time.

It turned out not to be too difficult a job, with the help of the ramp and roller bars she used to transport cages full of goats and alpacas in and out of her truck.

"When you're a woman alone, you learn to find ways of doing things that don't rely on brute strength,"

Brooke told him after they'd wrestled the cougar's cage back through the compound gate. She dusted her hands and paused to catch her breath. "Of course," she added, smiling at him, "I never say no to brute strength when it's offered."

"Just out of curiosity," Tony said when they were back on the outside of the compound and Brooke was locking the gate in the chain-link fence. "Where were you going to take her? Do you have any idea how big a wild mountain lion's range is?"

"I do, actually." As she so often did, she laced her fingers through the chain-link and gazed beyond it, to where the cougar now lay relaxed in the shade of the oak tree, seemingly without a care in the world. He saw Brooke's eyes squint a little and knew it wasn't from the brightness of the sun. "The truth is, I didn't know exactly where I was going to take her." Her voice roughened. "Just knew I had to try and save her from Lonnie. Somehow."

She threw him a look, and the wistful longing in it kicked at his heart. "It was my big dream. I wanted to turn this place into a refuge for big cats. We're crowding them off the planet, you know. I have the room. The part you see here, the house, barn, pens and pasture—that's only about five acres. I have another twenty over there." She made a sweep with her arm. "That's all mine. I could do it—thanks to my parents' will, I have the money—but I don't suppose it's possible now. Not after this. Especially if I go to—" She swallowed convulsively, and it hit him suddenly—not a little kick, but a wallop that took his breath away—what she was facing and how terrified she must be.

He said gruffly, before he could stop himself, "Look, don't give up. And don't do anything stupid, okay? Holt and I—please, just give us a little more time."

"Holt." She turned to look at him, still holding on to the chain-link fence with one hand. "That would be…"

"The guy I've been sharing a room with—yeah. He's—"

"Obviously not a traveling salesman." She said it with a hint of a smile on her lips, but no humor at all in her eyes.

Tony felt a sickening dropping sensation in his stomach. He knew it was finally here—the moment he'd been dreading, the moment he'd known would have to come. And he knew it was going to be worse than he'd imagined, even before she said the words, in a voice that chilled him to his core.

"So, who is he, Tony? And while we're at it, who are *you?* And why are you really here?"

Chapter 10

The amazing thing, Brooke thought, was that she felt nothing. Except for a strange quivering in her stomach, she was numb. She remembered she'd experienced much the same sensation the day they'd come to arrest her for murder, so she understood that this was some kind of shock, and that it would wear off eventually, and when it did, the pain would bury her. She could only hope she'd be alone when it happened.

In the meantime, in the calm and unreal world she lived in now, she watched Tony's face, and it seemed to flicker and shimmer like the images on an old-time movie screen.

"I'm exactly who I told you I am," he said in a voice that seemed unnaturally calm. Then he paused, and his eyes flared golden for an instant before he closed them. "As for why I'm here…"

"Who's Holt?"

He let the breath out with a hissing sound. "A private investigator."

"A private investigator." The shivering inside her was spreading through her body, and she wrapped her arms across herself in a futile effort to contain it. "So, who's he investigating? Me?"

"Not exactly…"

"Who hired him? Was it you?"

"No! Brooke, listen to—" He reached for her, and she threw up her arms to fend him off and stepped back, violently cringed away from him.

"So, *what* then? Let me guess. He hired you to come out here and spy on me, right? Who put him up to it, the sheriff? The state's attorney?" Now her voice had begun to shake. The shell was cracking. She gathered its remnants around her as best she could and whispered desperately, "You better tell me, Tony. Right now. *Who*, dammit?"

"It's nothing like that. It's got nothing to do with Duncan, or what happened here the day he was killed. It's—" He ran his hand over his scalp, something she'd never seen him do before, and his face contorted with what looked like pain. "Look, it's complicated. Can we go someplace—"

"No. I want you to tell me *now*."

"Brooke—"

"*Now*, Tony."

He reached for her again but pulled his hand back

before it touched her and jammed it into his pocket instead. He frowned, then cleared his throat, as if in preparation for a profoundly important declaration. "Okay. You know you were adopted, right?" He grimaced, as if in pain. "Of course, you do. Okay. So...what do you know about your birth parents?"

"Only that they're both dead. What's that got to do—"

"Hold on. I told you it's complicated. What about siblings? What do you know about them?"

"I told you. I have a twin sister."

"Well—" he whooshed out a breath...dragged in another...gave a small laugh "—actually, you have more than that. You also have a brother."

He watched the blood drain from her face. She seemed to sway, and she put out a hand to grope for the support of the chain-link fence as she whispered, "I have...a brother?"

"Three...actually." He tried to smile. Air seemed in short supply suddenly, and gulping it didn't help much. "The way I understand it is, you were all separated when you were children, after your parents died. You and your sister were the youngest, just toddlers at the time. So you probably don't remember at all. But your oldest brother, Cory—well, a couple of years ago, he hired Holt Kincaid to find you—the four of you. He finally located your brothers early last summer. He'd just found out where you were and was coming into town to see...uh, to talk to you, when...all this happened. He got here the day of your bail hearing."

He stared at her and she stared back, not saying anything. Her eyes were like chunks of obsidian.

He threw up his hands. "Well, jeez, Brooke, what was he supposed to do? He didn't know you from Adam. For all he knew, his client's baby sister was a cold-blooded murderer! Both your brother and his wife were un-reachable at the time—another long story—so he called me, since I happen to be a good friend of both Cory and Sam's, and…so, here I am."

"Spying on me."

"Ah, hell, it wasn't—"

"It's just like I said, isn't it? This Holt person hired you to check me out. You gave us that lion story so we'd let you get close to us. You lied to me, Tony. You lied to Daniel. That whole thing about saving Lady— we *trusted* you. *I* trusted you." She made a wide sweep with her arm, one that took in the dog, who was napping, oblivious, in the shade of the pickup truck. "Even Hilda trusted you. I gave you my—" And now the gesture she made was small, a brief touching of herself in the general area of her heart.

Then she wrapped her arms around herself again and looked away. She was crying, tears welling up and pouring from her eyes in a way that was all the more devastating by being utterly silent. To Tony, watching in helpless anguish, it was as if her very soul was bleeding.

"Brooke," he whispered, "it wasn't like that. We— Holt and I—we just wanted to help you. Lord knows, I never meant—" *To fall in love with you.*

There—he'd said it. Only in his mind, but still. He'd admitted it, what he'd known for a while. Now, finally, when it was too late. *I love this woman. I love her child, too. And I've screwed things up badly and probably lost both of them.*

"Why couldn't you just have told me? Once you knew I wasn't—before I—before we…" The look she gave him, the hurt and accusation in those shimmering indigo eyes, tore at his heart. "Or," she whispered, "is that why you didn't tell me. You still think I'm a murderer?"

"God, no! Brooke, you know I don't."

"But that's just it—I *don't* know. I don't know *you*. I thought I did, but now… How can I ever know whether you're lying to me or not? How can I ever trust you?"

"I didn't lie." His voice felt like crushed rock in his throat. "Not about the important stuff. Brooke, I—"

"No." She held up both hands, a wall between them. "I want you to leave. I want you gone."

"Brooke—"

"Now. Before Daniel gets home. I don't want him to see you."

Something inside him shut down. A kind of fatalistic calm descended. "All right. Okay," he said. And walked away.

Halfway through the barn, he met Daniel, still wearing his backpack from school. When he saw Tony, the boy's face lit up with a smile was like an arrow in his heart.

"Hey—Tony. Where's—" And Daniel, too young to have gotten so good at reading catastrophe in adult faces, halted, and the smile vanished. "What's wrong? Where are you going?"

Tony wanted to rush on by without explanation. Pain was writhing and coiling all through him, and the last thing he wanted to do was break another heart. Then he thought, *You jerk—you brought this on yourself. You owe this kid. Be a man, for God's sake.*

So he paused, put a hand on the boy's shoulder and took a deep breath. "I have to go." He put up a hand to stop Daniel's stricken *"No!"*

"Son, I'm sorry. I haven't exactly told you and your mom the truth. She—well, I guess I've kind of screwed things up. So…I have to go now. I'm sorry."

This time walking away was like ripping himself in half and leaving the torn and bloody remnants behind.

"Mom! What did you *do?*"

Brooke straightened, brushing at her cheeks, and turned to face her son. He'd halted a few yards away, breathing hard, his face flushed and furious.

"Why is Tony leaving? What did you say to him?"

She gave a high, meaningless laugh. "It's not so much what I said…"

"Then what? I don't understand."

She put her hand over her mouth and nose, sniffed, wiped, then stuck her hand in her pocket and cleared her throat. "Daniel, um…Tony didn't really come here to do a story on Lady. He came—" she cleared her throat again and caught a quick breath "—to spy on us. On me."

He recoiled as if she'd slapped him. "I don't believe you. Tony wouldn't do that." And then, as uncertainty crept in, he added, "Why would he?"

Tears were welling up again. She shook her head. "It's a long story, Daniel. I can't—" But he was waiting, glaring at her, and his face had a mulish look she knew well. She brushed at her cheeks and said, "He was hired...by someone. Someone who wanted to know if I was—if I killed your dad. He was hired to come here and find out."

Daniel gave an impatient shrug. "So, he found out you didn't, right? So, what's the problem?"

"Honey, he lied to us. He's not who he pretended to be."

"He is, too!" He lifted his arms and let them fall with an angry slap. "So what if he didn't tell the truth? He was helping us. He's gonna save Lady, too. Tony's a good guy, Mom."

"Oh, Daniel. You don't know—"

"Yes, I do. He *is* a good guy. It's like I told you before. You just *know*." He turned around and started to run back toward the barn.

"Daniel! Where are you going? Daniel—"

"He can't leave. We need him. We have to stop him, Mom."

"Daniel, we can't—"

"Well, I can! I'm not...going to...let him leave. Tony...Tony, wait!"

Brooke stood still and watched him go, one arm wrapped across her waist, the other hand clamped over her mouth to hold back sobs. She watched him until he'd disappeared inside the barn. And as silence descended, she heard a faint voice, Tony's voice, somewhere inside her head.

You also have a brother. Three...

Oh, God—what if it were true?

It was too much, finally. Simply too much, on top of

everything else that had happened to her recently. She gave a desperate, laughing sob…then another, and another. Hilda woke with a start and came trotting over to see what the noise was, and Brooke sank to the ground and wrapped her arms around the dog's neck and buried her face in her thick fawn-and-white ruff.

Oh, God…Tony…

I have brothers?

I…have…brothers.

Tony was dumping his camera gear and duffel bag into the trunk of his car when Daniel came dashing up, face flushed and streaked with tears. Tony hadn't thought he could possibly feel any worse than he already did, but he'd been wrong.

"Is it true?" Tony went on loading camera bags into the trunk. Daniel slipped off his backpack and let it fall to the ground with a crunch. "Is it true what Mom said? That you lied to us?"

"About a couple things. Not the important stuff." Tony was beginning to feel a bit abused and sorry for himself, if the truth were told. After all, what had he done that was so bad, except try and help her? That was all he'd wanted to do, damn it. *Help.*

He slammed the trunk lid and turned to face the boy. "I should have told you guys the truth about why I was here, once I got to know you and…well…" He took a breath and gritted his teeth. Forced the words out. "Your mom's right to be mad at me. I'm hoping she'll change her mind. If she doesn't—"

"No! I don't want you to go, Tony."

"If she doesn't…I want you to know I meant what I said. I am going to do everything I can to save your cougar, okay? I wasn't lying about that. And what I said about you being able to call me anytime—I wasn't lying about that, either. You have my cell number, right? If you need me, or if you just want to talk, you call me. Okay?"

Daniel didn't answer, just stared at him with eyes full of accusation, betrayal, disappointment and grief. When Tony couldn't stand to look at those eyes any longer, he turned, got into his car, started it up and drove away.

He didn't want to admit how upset he was, or that his vision was a bit blurred, which might have been why he didn't notice the sheriff's SUV parked on the dirt lane, the one that marked the boundary of Brooke's property.

Brooke had dried her tears and was trying to tell herself she'd been foolish for shedding them in the first place.

After all, what did she have to cry about? How long had she known Tony? A week? Less? So he'd lied. Not exactly an unprecedented event in her history with men. She'd been an idiot to throw herself at him. What had she expected him to do? Turn her down? And how would *that* have felt?

No, she concluded, *you have no right to be hurt, and you have nobody to blame but yourself.*

This, too, will pass.

And so, she hoped, would the awful ache in her heart.

In the meantime, there were chores to be done… animals to be fed. And now that the commotion had died down and Hilda had gone back to her shady spot beside the pickup and Brooke was alone, Lady had come to the fence to say hello.

"Oh...you sweet, beautiful lady, you," she whispered, putting her fingers through the wire for the cougar to sniff, then lick. "I don't know what I'll do if they take you away... How could anyone want to destroy something so beautiful?"

Lady's reply was a rasping purr as she butted her head against the wire, asking to be petted.

In the next moment—less than a moment—the cougar gave a scream of fury and recoiled away from the fence and Brooke, one paw raised in defense and fangs bared in a fearsome snarl.

Brooke was on her feet, cold with shock and vibrating with adrenaline. "Lady? What's the matter, girl?"

Then she heard Hilda growl. She jerked around, just in time to see Lonnie step out from behind the pickup truck. He'd come, she realized, not from the direction of the barn and the front yard, but across the strip of live oaks, cactus and rocks that separated her animal pens from the back road.

"Told you I'd be back," he said, smiling.

"Lonnie—"

But his smile vanished, as quickly and suddenly as Lady's transformation from house cat to killer, became something evil and menacing as his eyes jerked and his stare arrowed beyond her.

"Mom!"

Her heart lurched, felt wrenched from her body. She screamed, "Daniel, go back! Call—"

But Lonnie was too fast for both of them. In one long

stride, he lunged past her, caught Daniel's arm and wrenched the cell phone from his hands. "Oh, no, you don't, Danny boy. Mama's boyfriend and her high-powered lawyers ain't gonna save that cat. Not this time."

He hurled the cell phone as far as he could into the cactus and live oaks.

When his cell phone shrilled at him from the sedan's center console, Tony thought for sure it was Daniel. He was smiling as he picked it up, thumbed it on and said, "Hey, D—"

"Tony—glad I caught you." Holt's voice, not Daniel's. "Thought I better warn you. Just got a call from Shirley—from the diner? She overheard a bunch of the deputies talking a while ago, this afternoon. Lonnie wasn't with 'em, and they were talking about how they were worried about him. Said he'd gone off the deep end over 'that damn cat.' That he was going to screw things up—not quite the words they used—for everybody. And they were thinking it might be time for them all to get out while they still could."

Tony swore, and Holt rushed right on over it. "I've contacted the feds. Told 'em they might want to haul this bunch in while they still can, otherwise they're gonna be gone, in the wind. They're on their way. So's Cory. But I think Lonnie might be coming to a boil as we speak, and I'm afraid he's gonna blow before they get here. You need to—"

Tony swore again and hit the brakes. Holt yelled, "What was that? Where in the hell are you? Are you in the *car?* Holy mother—tell me she's with you, at least. Tell me you didn't leave her and the kid out there alone."

"She kicked me out," Tony growled as he made a jerky three-point turn in the middle of the highway. "I told her everything, and she threw me out."

Now it was Holt who was swearing with everything he had. "I don't care if she just peppered your butt with buckshot. Get yourself back there—*now*. If that crazy deputy comes after her lion, you know what she'll do, don't you?"

Tony did know, and he was so cold and scared, he could hardly drive. "On my way," he said and dropped the phone onto the seat beside him.

But not before he'd heard Holt on the other end, muttering something that sounded like, "Gonna get my client's baby sister killed!"

"Why, Lonnie? Please…just tell us why."

Brooke stood facing the deputy and tried not to look at the gun in his hand. She had one arm across Daniel's chest holding him tightly against her, and with the other hand kept a death-grip on Hilda's collar, both for the same reason: to keep them from lunging at Lonnie and probably getting themselves shot. All three—she, Daniel and the dog—were shaking.

"Lady didn't kill Duncan. The tranquilizer dart did. The ME said so. Why do you want to kill her?" It was the only thing she could think of to do, the only hope she had. If she could just talk him down…reason with him…

"It was that cat's fault! It shouldna happened."

Lonnie's eyes darted crazily, in that brilliant, unnatural way she'd noticed before, and for the first time, it occurred to Brooke to wonder about drugs. Then his face seemed to crumple. "It wasn't supposed to happen like that!"

Brooke felt herself go still inside. "Lonnie, what are you talking about?"

His eyes darted back to her, and to her horror, she realized they were swimming with tears. "I told Dunk it was a crazy idea. I told him. But he wouldn't listen to me. He wouldn't listen…."

"What idea? Lonnie, what did you do?"

"It wasn't my fault!" He swiped at the tears on his cheeks with the back of his hand, the one holding the gun, then gestured with it toward the cougar's compound. "It was that damn cat…."

Drugs, Brooke thought. *Either that, or dead drunk.* For one moment she wondered if she could reach him in time to knock the gun out of his hand, but, of course, it was an insane idea. He'd still be able to overpower her, and what then? What would happen to Daniel and Hilda—and Lady—then?

"See, Dunk had this idea, how he was gonna show you were an unfit mother because of havin' a dangerous animal on your place. So he could get custody of the kid, right? So he was gonna make it look like the cat got out of its cage and killed a bunch of your livestock, and that would prove it was a danger to the kid."

"My God…" Brooke felt numb, couldn't believe what she was hearing. There was no sound from Daniel, either.

Lonnie went on. "Nobody was supposed to get hurt! Okay? He had it all planned. He knew you had a tranq gun, so if anything went wrong, you know? That's why he wanted me to meet him here, so I could be his backup. But then the damn stupid cat wouldn't come near the gate!"

"She was afraid of Duncan," Brooke said softly, but Lonnie didn't seem to hear her.

"So then Dunk, he decides to go in the cage and chase the cat over here. He had a key to the gate. But he thought she'd be afraid of the gun, so he gave it to me and told me to cover him. We'd left our service weapons in the vehicles—couldn't shoot the cat with department issue weapons, figured that would raise up too many questions, kind of defeat the whole purpose, you know? So anyway—" he gestured again with the gun "—Dunk gets about halfway out there, out in the middle of the pen, and the cat's up there on those rocks, there, and she starts screamin', making that god-awful sound. And Dunk just stops in his tracks. Like he was frozen."

"Dad was afraid of Lady," Daniel said, and Brooke marveled at how calm, how grown-up he sounded.

"Yeah, well...he shoulda been." Lonnie sniffed loudly and wiped his nose with the back of his gun hand. "The cat was starin' down at him, like she was gonna jump him, and he started backin' up, and next thing I know, he's runnin' back toward the gate, and the cat's runnin' after him, and Dunk's yellin' at me, 'Shoot it! Shoot it, dammit!'"

Lonnie was pacing up and down now, back and forth in front of the fence.

"Only I can't shoot, because Dunk's in my line of fire, see? Then—it all happened so fast. One minute Dunk's zigzaggin', so I figure I've got a clear shot, and the next minute he's lookin' at me, and he's got a damn dart stickin' out of his neck. And he's yellin' at me, why'd I shoot him instead of the cat? And I'm yellin' at him why'd he zig back into the line of fire, and…the next minute his knees are bucklin' up, and he's down on the ground, kind of flopping and flailing his arms around. And before I could do a thing, that cat was right on top of him, and she grabs ahold of his shoulder. Like this." He demonstrated, clutching himself at the bend of his neck and shoulder. "I got the tranq gun up, but before I could get off another shot, the cat takes off back up into those rocks. So, I went over to see about Dunk, see how bad the cat got him, and…he's just lyin' there, starin' up at the sky, and he's not breathin'!"

"So you…you just *left* him there?" Brooke had never felt such rage. She could feel Daniel's body shaking with sobs. Tears were running down her cheeks, too, but she barely knew it.

Lonnie's face contorted with anguish. "No! 'Course I didn't. I—he was bleedin'—you know, from where the cat bit him. And then the blood quit comin', and I knew his heart had stopped, so I started CPR, you know? But it wasn't any use. I could see that, and I figured you were gonna be comin' home any minute, so I took the tranq gun and got the hell outa there. Well, hell, Brooke, I couldn't leave it behind, could I? Not with my prints all over it."

"So you left Duncan there for Daniel to find. And for

me to get blamed for killing him. My God, Lonnie, how could you? He was your *friend*."

He waved his arms wildly, crying again. "Well, hell, how do you think *I* feel? He was like my brother, had been since we were in first grade. It wouldna happened if that freakin' cat hadn't come after him like she done. What was I s'posed to do, Brooke? You tell me. What was I gonna do?"

Chapter 11

Brooke never knew what she might have answered. She never got the chance.

In the next instant she saw Lonnie's face change, his eyes snap into focus and harden as they looked past her. "I know what I'm gonna do now," he said, and she saw his chest expand as he drew breath. The gun came up, held steady in the lawman's two-handed grip.

She jerked herself around to look where he did, shot through with adrenaline. And there, on the other side of the fence, only a few yards from where they stood, was Lady. She had come silently, stealthy as only a panther on the hunt could be. Her head was low, her shoulders hunched, and her golden eyes burned with a predator's stare…focused…intent…and aimed straight at Lonnie.

It all happened at once: Daniel jerking away from her, free of her grasp, his cry piercing her soul; his name, her son's name, ripping through her throat, tearing her throat like a lion's claws; Hilda's snarl as she lunged, breaking Brooke's grip on her collar; the clang of a heavy body hitting the chain-link gate; the deafening sound of a gunshot only a few feet away.

Then, in silent slow motion: Lady streaking off across the compound; Hilda staggering a few broken steps before crumpling in a heap of fawn-and-white fur; Daniel on his hands and knees, sobbing, scrambling through the dirt to reach her side; Lonnie lurching drunkenly, slowly bringing the gun around, searching for a target. And from out of nowhere, a big, powerful body hurtling through the air, hitting Lonnie with a flying tackle that knocked him flat on the ground.

Tony never knew how he managed to cover the distance between the barn and the cougar's fence so quickly. He'd never been a great one for speed—more the offensive lineman type than running back. But in the end, even what was surely a personal best for him wasn't enough.

Through a reddish haze, images jerking and shifting as he ran, he saw the drama unfold. Saw the man bring his arms up, and the gun clutched in both of his hands. Saw Brooke turn, and first Daniel, then Hilda throw themselves at the gunman. Then he heard the shot, and all thought stopped.

As he launched himself through the air, he heard a guttural sound, a bellow of rage he'd never imagined could come from his throat. He was a primitive being, governed by instinct and adrenalin. This man was his enemy, threatening everything he loved. He wanted to *kill.*

His body collided with that of his enemy with a force that knocked the breath from his lungs and carried them both to the ground, but he felt no pain whatsoever, only triumph, and a kind of primal *pleasure.* He felt his enemy struggling beneath him, and his flesh was in his hands, and he was pounding, squeezing—

"Tony—no—*please!* Tony!"

It was the only sound that could have reached him through the roaring rage filling his head. Brooke's voice. He stopped, breathing hard, and his hands went slack. He felt her hands on his shoulders and turned his dazed eyes to her.

"Tony, Hilda's been shot. Daniel needs us. Please, Tony…"

"Okay. Yeah." He shifted his weight off Lonnie, who lay quietly now, except for the sobs that were shaking his whole body. Keeping one hand planted between the deputy's shoulder blades, Tony grabbed first one of Lonnie's wrists, then the other, and brought them together behind his back.

"Get his cuffs," he said between gulps of air, and Brooke's strong hands were there, unhooking the deputy's handcuffs from his belt. He took them from her and clipped them onto Lonnie's wrists, and as he stood up, then looked down at the man on the ground, he thought he understood the primitive urges that had motivated his distant ancestors to take the scalps of their vanquished enemies.

"Tony." Brooke was tugging at his arm. He looked at her and saw that she was crying. "He shot Hilda. I need your cell phone. He threw Daniel's somewhere. I don't know where...."

"Help's already on the way."

And he was bending over Daniel, who was kneeling beside the dog's body. The boy had taken off his shirt and had it wadded up and was holding it pressed to her side. His hands, the shirt, and the dog's fur were wet with shiny red blood.

Daniel turned his face up to him, and it was tear streaked but calm. He spoke rapidly, breathlessly. "The bullet missed her heart. She's alive, and she's still bleeding. But it might have punctured a lung, 'cause she's having trouble breathing—see? We have to get her to the hospital *right now*."

Tony dropped to one knee and got his arms under the dog's body. "Okay, son, keep pressing on the wound, okay? I'm gonna lift her now...." He managed to get to his feet with his burden and threw Brooke a look as she stood hovering, eager to help. "I swear, she weighs more than you do," he muttered, and she gave a helpless whimper of laughter and clamped a hand over her mouth.

"We'll take my car," he gasped as he and Daniel began making their way toward the barn, shuffling awkwardly sideways with their shared burden. He nodded at Brooke. "You drive—keys are in it."

She nodded and ran.

Behind them now, Tony could hear Lonnie squirming and struggling on the ground, grunting with his efforts to free himself from the handcuffs. Tony discovered he no longer gave a damn.

It seemed to take forever to get to the barn. Then through it. When they reached the far side, they met Brooke, who had turned Tony's rental car around and was backing it up to the barn doors.

Once again, she was amazed at how calm she felt. As if, she thought, all the terrible things she'd seen and heard in the past half hour or so had been neatly packaged up and placed in cold storage to await processing. Right now she was focused totally on the task at hand: getting Tony, Daniel and Hilda into the backseat of the sedan.

Which was why she didn't quite grasp what was happening, at first, when a whole fleet of vehicles came roaring and bumping up the lane and into her yard, raising a cloud of dust. They seemed to be everywhere around her, and the setting sun turned the dust into golden fog, from which came slamming doors and shouting voices and the stutter and shuffle of running footsteps.

"He's back there," Tony yelled, jerking his head toward the barn. "He might be running, but I don't think he'll get far."

Then men were jogging by her as she sat behind the wheel of the car, men wearing dark clothing and carrying weapons, and as they passed, she saw they all had large letters stenciled on the back of their jackets.

"Feds," Tony said from the backseat. "They'll take care of things here. Come on—let's go. I assume you know the quickest way to the nearest vet."

Brooke nodded and began to maneuver the car

through the maze of parked vehicles. But when they reached the lane, another car was on the way in, blocking their way.

"Wait," Tony said. "Stop."

The other car, a sedan very much like the one they were in, cleared the lane, then pulled over and stopped. Both front doors opened and two men got out. The man on the driver's side was tall and thin and wore jeans and a gray, western-style jacket and sunglasses. His hair was brown, streaked with silver and longer than the current fashion. The second man was tall, too, though not as thin as the driver, and was wearing faded black cargo pants and a khaki-colored long-sleeved Henley shirt. His hair was darker brown, cut shorter, but also showed flecks of silver. He was wearing sunglasses, too, and he took them off as he walked toward her. And although there were tears in his eyes, he smiled.

She heard a small whimpering sound, realized it was coming from herself and clamped a hand over her mouth. She'd begun to shake.

Oh, God—I know those eyes. Those are my eyes... Daniel's eyes. Oh, God—it's true, what Tony said....

The man was bending down, looking at her through her open car window. He gave a self-conscious laugh but didn't acknowledge or apologize for his tears as he said huskily, "Hello, Brooke... You don't know me, but I'm your brother Cory."

She nodded and let go a sob...a laugh...both mixed together.

"The other guy is Holt," said Tony from the backseat.

"And I hate like hell to spoil the family reunion, but, uh…we've got a wounded hero here.…"

And Daniel, kneeling on the floor, with his hands pressing the bloody shirt against the dog's side, added his breathless, "Yeah, Mom, can we go—please?"

Holt reached around Cory to open Brooke's door. "I'll drive. Mr. Pearson, if you'll ride shotgun…"

Cory nodded, and she felt his hand on her elbow as he helped her out of the car. He opened the back door and she slid onto the seat beside Tony.

"Tell us where to go—we'll get you there," he said softly, bending down to look into her eyes.

He has such kind eyes. Daniel's eyes. She nodded, and he straightened up and slammed the door. A moment later he was climbing into the front seat and Holt put the car in gear and they were off.

"Left at the road," she called and felt something stir against her thigh. She looked down and saw Hilda trying to lick her hand. Tenderly, she lifted the great shaggy head onto her thigh and burrowed her fingers deep into the dog's white neck ruff. Her vision blurred.

"She's so protective of us," she whispered.

"Yeah," said Daniel. "She saved Lady's life. I didn't even know she *liked* Lady."

Brooke gave a teary spurt of laughter, and Tony said gruffly, "It was your life she was trying to save, son, and if you ever do such a dumb thing again, your mom ought to skin you alive."

She turned her head to look at him, and the tears in her eyes spilled over and ran down her cheeks. "Tony,

I'm so sorry. This was my fault." Her voice was a very small squeak.

He shook his head and started to say something, to protest, tell her none of it was in any way, shape or form her fault, that he was the rotter who'd bungled things from the beginning. But she plunged on.

"I was stupid. Childish. I shouldn't have told you... what I told you. He was—he came from the back road. Right after you left. I think he was just waiting for you to leave. If I hadn't—" She jerked her attention back to the road ahead. "Oh—right at the stop sign." She drew a shaking breath. "If I hadn't made you leave—"

"He would have come for the lion sooner or later," Holt said as he made the turn on screeching tires. "And chances are it would have ended up worse than it did."

Tony got his arm around Brooke's shoulders and drew her against him. "The only thing I can't figure," he said as she laid her head down on his shoulder and he kissed the top of her head, "is *why.*"

Brooke's head popped up, and she looked at him with eyes wide and dark. "Oh—that's right! You weren't there. You didn't hear him. It was Lonnie. He killed Duncan. But it was an accident. He never meant—"

"It was my fault." Daniel's voice was soft and husky. His head was bowed, but Tony caught the silvery flash of a tear as it fell. "The whole reason Dad got killed is because of me. 'Cause he wanted me to live with him, and I told him I didn't want to, and I was gonna tell the judge that, too. So he tried to make it so I'd *have* to go and live with him, no matter what. And that's why he's dead."

For a few seconds, there was absolute silence in the car. Brooke had her eyes closed and her hand clamped over her mouth. Tony was thinking how wrong the kid was on so many different levels, and trying to figure out how to say it in a way the child would believe. Then Cory shifted around, reached over the back of the seat and laid his hand on Daniel's head.

"Son, believe me, I know how you feel. I spent most of my life feeling certain the terrible things that had happened to people I loved were my fault." He spoke to the boy, but his eyes were on Brooke, and she opened hers and looked back at him. The two pairs of eyes, so much alike, clung to each other with such intensity, it seemed an almost *touchable* bond connected the two of them. Watching, Tony felt an ache in his throat and a knot in his chest roughly the size of a baseball.

Cory went on, speaking in a voice that was vibrant with emotion, firm yet quiet. The kind of voice that can banish a child's nightmares. "It's taken me most of my life to realize that it's the mistakes and bad choices adults make that cause terrible things to happen to children, and that most of the time there's not a darn thing the children can do about it. Except survive. Be strong." He paused to smile at his sister, a smile of such sadness and regret, it was hard to look at, but one filled at the same time with such love and joy, Tony couldn't look away. "I'm telling you this now because I didn't have anyone to tell it to me when I was your age and in your shoes. If I had, maybe I'd have been able to come looking for you a lot sooner. I might have found you years ago."

"But then, if you had," said Brooke, smiling at her brother, giving him the same heartbreakingly radiant smile, "I wouldn't have Daniel." She turned the smile on Tony and whispered, "Or you."

Tony saw Cory's eyebrows shoot up, and he gave his best friend a shrug and a shaken laugh. "Yeah," he growled as he drew his woman's head back down into its nest just over his heart, and then he closed his eyes.

And into his mind came the image of a cougar's tawny face, with its black mask and glowing yellow eyes…the image of his own childhood nightmares. He thought then about what his Apache grandmother had told him of spirit messengers, and wondered whether there might be something to that stuff, after all.

"Uh…guys? Brooke?" Holt's gravelly voice came from the front seat. "Am I supposed to be turning anytime soon?"

It was late, long past midnight, when they got back to Brooke's place. They'd left Hilda behind in the veterinary hospital, sedated and resting comfortably after the long surgery to repair damage to her lungs—Daniel had been correct in his diagnosis, to his great satisfaction—and also to her ribs and some other stuff, the names of which Tony wasn't sure about. Holt and Cory had dropped Tony, Brooke and a sleeping Daniel off at the back porch steps and had taken Holt's rental car back to town, to the Cactus Country Inn.

The waning moon was high and bright in a cloudless Texas sky, and it lighted their way up the steps of the dark house—they'd left it in a hurry and before sundown. Brooke held the door while Tony carried Daniel into the kitchen, then slipped past him and down the hall to pull back the covers so Tony could lay him gently down on the bed. Together, they slipped off his shoes and jeans and the jacket Cory had given him to wear when the evening grew cool, since Daniel's shirt was now somewhere in a biohazard trash can at the vet's. Brooke folded the covers over the sleeping child and leaned down to kiss him while Tony let his fingers linger in the boy's soft, silky hair. Then they both tiptoed silently out of the room.

Brooke pulled the door closed. And they stood in the hallway and faced each other in the darkness, close but not touching. They both drew breath and spoke.

"Brooke…"

"Tony…"

He felt her fingers on his lips, and she whispered, "I'm sorry. For what I said to you."

He caught her hand and held it. "No apology necessary." His whisper was much deeper and gruffer than hers.

"Can you stay?"

"As long as you want me."

He heard her breath catch. "Do you mean that?"

"I do," he said, fully aware that it was a vow.

He could feel her shaking, so he drew her close to him and held her, wrapped in his arms. Her arms came around him, and her head came to rest in its special place. He laid his cheek against her hair and drew a deep breath, breathing in the smell of her that had already become familiar to him. "I was thinking… about that dream of yours. About the big cats? Since it looks like you're going to be able to do that now, after all…it seems to me like you might need a partner."

"I will," she said, fully aware that it was a vow. She could hear his heart thumping against her ear, like a drum deep inside his big chest. "Absolutely."

They stood there like that for a long time, as close as two people could be, neither of them wanting to separate from the other, neither of them wanting the moment to end.

After a while, Tony cleared his throat and said, "I want you to know, you've made my mother and a whole bunch of sisters very, very happy."

She gave a soft laugh. "Yeah, well…Daniel, too." She tipped her head to look at him, and a tiny hint of uncertainty crept into her voice. "And you?"

"Happy doesn't begin to describe it." He managed to get that much out before words failed him completely.

After that, it seemed easier just to show her.

The next morning, Brooke was making blueberry pancakes when the knock came—on the front door, not the back porch door, which everyone always used. She left Daniel and Tony laughing over something or other and went to answer it, wiping her hands on a dish towel.

Sheriff Clayton Carter stood on her front porch, wearing the same Western-style jacket he'd had on the day he'd come to arrest her for murder. His brown Stetson hat was in his hands.

"Why, Sheriff," Brooke said, holding the screen door

open and smiling at him, "what a nice surprise. Would you care to come in for coffee and blueberry pancakes?"

The sheriff gestured with his hat and didn't smile back. He cleared his throat and tried to look her in the eyes, but his frowning gaze kept sliding past her. "No, ma'am— thank you for askin', but I can't stay. Just wanted to tell you personally, the charges against you are bein' dropped. And, uh…wanted to extend the department's sincere apologies to you and your boy there." He tried again to make eye contact, and this time managed to hold on long enough to add, "I'm sorry as I can be about your husband, ma'am, and I hope you can find it in your heart to… uh—" He waved the hat once more, then put it back on his head. "Well, that's all. Just wanted to let you know," he said as he turned to go down the steps.

"That's nice of you, Sheriff. I do appreciate you stoppin' by," Brooke said, and there was nothing in the world that could take away her smile—not today, maybe not ever again. "Are you sure you won't come in for coffee?"

With a wave of his hand, the sheriff went on down the steps. "Thanks. I 'preciate the offer, I really do, but I've got to get back to the barn. Got feds swarming all over the place…."

Brooke closed the door gently and went back to the kitchen. And was greeted there by two smiles, both so different, both so unbelievably sweet…and two pairs of eyes, one deep and dark like hers, like his uncle's, the other warm and golden, like sunshine…both of them lighting up at the sight of her.

Two faces glowing with love…for *her*. Two men—
her men. The two people she loved more than anyone
on earth, more than she'd thought it was possible to love.

As she joined them, she was laughing, laughing with
a happiness that went all the way deep down inside of
her, all the way into her heart and soul.

Epilogue

"I never thought it would happen," Cory said to Holt over steak and eggs at the diner. "Not to Tony. He's always been… Well, let's just say, he's somewhat of a lady's man. I didn't think he'd ever find…"

"The *one?*" Holt lifted one eyebrow. "Who's to say there's a *one* for everybody? Maybe some people just don't have *one* to find."

"Like…you, for instance?" Cory's eyes narrowed thoughtfully as he picked up his coffee cup. "What's your story, Holt? I sense there is one—probably a helluva one, too."

Holt smiled sardonically but was saved from answering as Shirley arrived, brandishing a pot of fresh coffee.

"Sure is somethin', about Lonnie and them," she said as she topped off their cups.

"Well, we owe you, darlin'," Holt said, lifting his cup in a little salute. "I don't think we could have gotten there in time if you hadn't told us what you heard."

"Yeah, well…" She took in a breath that strained the buttons on her blouse. "I'm just so glad they're okay— her and the little boy. Too bad about the dog, though."

"She's gonna make it. Thanks to you, darlin'."

Shirley gave him a smile with a wink and a wiggle as she moved off to the next table. Holt looked at Cory and found him smiling, too. "What?"

"Nothing—just that you're sounding more and more like a Texan. Time to move on, my friend. Which brings me to the question I've been dying to ask. What about my other sister? You said her name's Brenna, right? Where is she, and when can I meet her?"

Holt let out a breath and pushed his plate away. "That's…gonna be a problem."

"Why? What problem? You said the twins were adopted together, grew up in the same family. Surely they've stayed in touch."

"I wish that were true." Holt picked up his coffee and blew on it, stalling for time. But there was no way around it. It looked like he was going to have to be the one to break the bad news. "Mr. Pearson, I'm sorry to have to tell you, but Brenna ran away from home when she was just fourteen. Brooke hasn't seen or heard from her since." He spread his hands in utter defeat. "I have absolutely no clue where she is. Or even where to start looking."

* * * * *

0210/46b

 **INTRIGUE**

Coming next month

2-IN-1 ANTHOLOGY

THE COLONEL'S WIDOW? by Mallory Kane

Two years ago Air Force officer Rook faked his own death to protect his beloved wife Irina from terrorists. Now he's back and determined to regain her trust – and her love.

CAVANAUGH PRIDE by Marie Ferrarella

When Julianna is sent to help hunt a killer, detective Frank can't deny his attraction towards her. But will professional Julianna let passion come before the case?

SINGLE TITLE

SECOND CHANCE COWBOY
by BJ Daniels

Cowboy Hank is determined to find Arlene's missing daughter and soon they are both discovering that it's never too late to fall in love!

SINGLE TITLE

SENTINELS: JAGUAR NIGHT
by Doranna Durgin
Nocturne™

Shapeshifter Dolan needs to stop a deadly manuscript getting into the wrong hands. But wild loner Meghan has the book. Can he win her over to his cause and his heart?

On sale 5th March 2010

Available at WHSmith, Tesco, ASDA, Eason and all good bookshops.
For full Mills & Boon range including eBooks visit
www.millsandboon.co.uk

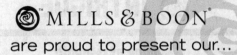

millsandboon.co.uk Community

Join Us!

The Community is the perfect place to meet and chat to kindred spirits who love books and reading as much as you do, but it's also the place to:

- **Get the inside scoop from authors about their latest books**
- **Learn how to write a romance book with advice from our editors**
- **Help us to continue publishing the best in women's fiction**
- **Share your thoughts on the books we publish**
- **Befriend other users**

Forums: Interact with each other as well as authors, editors and a whole host of other users worldwide.

Blogs: Every registered community member has their own blog to tell the world what they're up to and what's on their mind.

Book Challenge: We're aiming to read 5,000 books and have joined forces with The Reading Agency in our inaugural Book Challenge.

Profile Page: Showcase yourself and keep a record of your recent community activity.

Social Networking: We've added buttons at the end of every post to share via digg, Facebook, Google, Yahoo, technorati and de.licio.us.

www.millsandboon.co.uk

2 FREE BOOKS
AND A SURPRISE GIFT

We would like to take this opportunity to thank you for reading this Mills & Boon® book by offering you the chance to take TWO more specially selected books from the Intrigue series absolutely FREE! We're also making this offer to introduce you to the benefits of the Mills & Boon® Book Club™—

- **FREE home delivery**
- **FREE gifts and competitions**
- **FREE monthly Newsletter**
- **Exclusive Mills & Boon Book Club offers**
- **Books available before they're in the shops**

Accepting these FREE books and gift places you under no obligation to buy, you may cancel at any time, even after receiving your free books. Simply complete your details below and return the entire page to the address below. You don't even need a stamp!

YES Please send me 2 free Intrigue books and a surprise gift. I understand that unless you hear from me, I will receive 5 superb new stories every month, including two 2-in-1 books priced at £4.99 each and a single book priced at £3.19, postage and packing free. I am under no obligation to purchase any books and may cancel my subscription at any time. The free books and gift will be mine to keep in any case.

Ms/Mrs/Miss/Mr _____ Initials _____

Surname _____

Address _____

_____

_____ Postcode _____

Send this whole page to: Mills & Boon Book Club, Free Book Offer, FREEPOST NAT 10298, Richmond, TW9 1BR